MW01005687

NIGHTSHIFTED

NIGHTSHIFTED

CASSIE ALEXANDER

St. Martin's Paperbacks

This is a work of fiction. All of the characters, organizations, and events portrayed in this novel are either products of the author's imagination or are used fictitiously.

NIGHTSHIFTED

Copyright © 2012 by Erin Cashier.
Excerpt from *Moonshifted* copyright © 2012 by Erin Cashier.

All rights reserved.

For information address St. Martin's Press, 175 Fifth Avenue, New York, NY 10010.

ISBN: 978-0-312-55339-5

Printed in the United States of America

St. Martin's Paperbacks edition / June 2012

St. Martin's Paperbacks are published by St. Martin's Press, 175 Fifth Avenue, New York, NY 10010.

10 9 8 7 6 5 4 3 2 1

For anyone who ever got paid a little extra
to stay up very late.

ACKNOWLEDGMENTS

This book would not have been possible were it not for the efforts of many other people, only some of whom I'll get to recognize here. Firstly, my husband, Paul, for understanding completely what I'm trying to do; my agent, Michelle Brower, for believing in this crazy book; and my editor; Rose Hilliard, for buying it and her excellent input afterwards. I am forever in the debt of my alpha reader, Daniel Starr, who played an incalculable role in making me the writer I am today. I will always appreciate my beta readers, Tina Connelly, Anna Eley, Patrick Weekes, and Julia Reynolds, for letting me borrow their brains and time. I promise to return their brains soon. My parents for not always getting this, but being supportive anyway. My writing friends Rachel Swirsky, Blake Charlton, David Moles, and Barry Deutsch for getting it, and still being supportive, even though being on the publishing inside they knew everything that that would entail. Thanks to Matt Bellizzi for showing me how to shoot a gun, Vera Nazarian for help with Russian, and my girlfriends V, C, M, and J in real life, for listening and making me occasionally leave my house.

Any mistakes in this book are mine. No part of this book constitutes actual medical advice. Not all doctors are bad, just some of them can be annoying.

Last, but not in any way least, I want to thank the girls on my work weekend for keeping me out of trouble. Thanks for not letting me accidentally kill anyone. I appreciate that most of all.

CHAPTER ONE

"How can your liver be this good?" I stood outside Mr. November's room, watching him stir restlessly. Normal people couldn't get 20,000 micrograms of fentanyl and 80 milligrams of Versed an hour and live, much less still be attempting another slow-motion escape from their hospital bed.

But I knew Mr. November wasn't normal. From my assessment, when I'd seen his chipped yellow fangs around his titanium-tipped endotracheal tube, and from the way he was restrained in bed—six soft cuffs, two on each arm, one on each leg, a Posey vest wrapped around his chest and tied beneath the bedframe—and from the fact that he was here on Floor Y4 to begin with. No one here was normal, except for me. I was human and looked it: average brown hair, average blue eyes, average hips. My patients here? Let's just say "average" was not the first adjective you'd pick for them if you saw them on the streets. Or the twentieth.

Mr. November continued to squirm. I wondered which cheerful member of our daytime staff I'd be giving a report to come seven A.M. with him crawling out of bed behind me. I could almost feel them judging me now.

His IV pump beeped empty and his cuffed right hand made rabbit-punching jabs. Crap.

"Hey, you!" I shouted and leaned into his room to try to attract his glazed attention. "Stay still!" I commanded through the door. Sometimes with agitated patients the voice of nursing authority buys time. I dashed to the supply room, unlocked the narcotics drawer, grabbed a bag of fentanyl, and made it back to his room as he started to thrash his head from side to side.

"Stop that!" I hauled on my isolation gear as fast as I could. If he managed to knock his endotracheal—ET—tube loose, that'd be the end of his ventilator-assisted breathing, which'd be the end of him. I put my gloves on, snatched the bag, and rushed inside. When I silenced the pump alarm's beeping he visibly calmed.

"You have to stay still, sir. You've got pneumonia and you're in the hospital." I switched out the bags and reset the pump. I inhaled to say more, but I saw Meaty, my charge nurse, rise up like a moon behind the nursing station outside, holding one thick hand up in the shape of a phone. It was the international nursing gesture for, "Call the doctor?"

I nodded. "More sedation. Now. Please."

Mr. November's hands spasmed again. I didn't know if he was reaching for me with a purpose, if he just wanted to be free, or if he didn't understand what was happening—not unlikely, with all the meds he was getting—but I grabbed his nearest hand in both my own. "You've got to rest now, okay?" His grip tensed and so did I—most of the training videos I'd watched before starting this job had emphasized the "minimal patient contact" rule, for vastly good reasons—but then he relaxed, letting me go.

I stepped back from the bed, took off my gown and gloves, washed my hands, and went outside.

"You okay there, Edie?" Meaty asked as I returned to sit behind my desk, just outside Mr. November's door. I grunted a response and flipped open Mr. November's flow-sheet to hide behind. Meaty didn't check in on Gina or

Charles unless they called for help. But I was new here. Just when I was starting to feel like I knew how to be a nurse at my last job, only a year out of nursing school, my brother overdosed. On heroin. For the third time.

An unknown "friend" (read: dealer) had been kind enough to leave Jake on a curb and call 911, which'd brought him here. By the time I got to the emergency department they were on his second dose of Narcan. They'd put an IV line into his neck because he had too many tracks on his arms to find a vein. Only some cruel miracle had stopped him from getting infected this far. If he kept it up, I knew his luck wouldn't hold.

I wanted to touch him and I didn't want to touch him, because it didn't take being a nurse to know all the diseases he might have. And so, as I was finding some gloves to wear to hold his fucking dumbass junkie hand, a man came by and said, "Wouldn't you like to see your brother clean?"

I thought he was going to tell me about Jesus, and I was getting ready to tell him where to shove himself, when he offered me a job.

CHAPTER TWO

Before, when I'd worked in a nice private hospital, if someone had done something particularly boneheaded, or exhibited poor nursing judgment, they'd have been asked, "Hey, where do you think you work at, County Hospital?" or, "Looks like you did a County job to me."

But what if no one called 911 the next time around? Or Jake ignored a septic sore? Working at County seemed preferable to watching him die, knowing I could have done something to prevent it. I didn't understand what I was signing away exactly, only that they promised to keep him straight—and unlike all the rehab programs my mom had scrounged to send him to, it'd worked.

So now I really *was* at County. Only worse. Floor Y4 was for the daytime servants of vampires, sanctioned donors, werewolves, zombies, you name it—and purgatory for us, their staff. We were in the bowels of County, off the records and off the charts. I signed forty things in triplicate, got special badge access to the special elevator, and when I took the special ride down, I found myself in an ominous hallway where my badge opened just two doors. One led to our locker rooms and bathroom. The second went here to Y4, an eight-bed intensive care ward with an institutionalized appearance: exposed ducts, dim lights, and where everything could use a fresh coat of a lighter shade of paint.

Peeking over my flowsheet and into the room, I saw Mr. November at it again, this time kicking himself off the bottom bedrail. "Be still!" I scolded. Reminded anew, he relaxed. That's the hassle with Versed. It's an amnesiac. On the plus side, it helps patients forget the horror of having an ET tube sit in their lungs and a ventilator helping them breathe. On the downside, it means that every time you warn them they have Tubes in That They Should Not Pull On, that warning has a half-life of about thirty seconds before they forget and try pulling again.

"Meaty, any word?" I asked, as Mr. November switched gears and tried to reach his ET tube, one millimeter at a time.

Meaty gave a negating grunt. While Meaty was likely not Meaty's actual name, he or she was Y4's charge nurse, which meant they were the resident expert on all nursing-related chores, the general patient coordinator, and our physician liaison. With an androgynous face and an abdominal drape that almost reached the floor, Meaty brought scrubs from home to accommodate his or herself, the bathroom in the locker room wasn't sexed, and I hadn't had the balls yet, metaphorically, to ask.

Frustrating as it was, it wasn't Meaty's fault the doctor hadn't called back. They probably wouldn't ever call back, and Mr. November would be squirrelly all night.

"Damn." I flipped through the nursing chart to write another note on the restraint form, choosing "restless" and "continually pulling" for Mr. November's past hour of activities. Too bad there wasn't a form for my opinion on the state of things—I would have written "bleak" and "under-supported by other hospital staff." I hoped the call had woken the doctor up.

Even though he'd been here for a few days, Mr.

November's chart was mostly empty, except for his tox screen. The emergency department here surreptitiously checks people for various conditions—such as "porphyric hemophilia" (likely vampire-exposed), "leprosy" (likely zombies), "rabies" (likely were), and "sisters of junkies who were suckers" (me). Everything else, all of our plans, treatments, and patient response, was unofficial. But surely some actual records were kept somewhere, if only for accounting's sake. The drugs we used alone must cost a fortune. And even if my fellow nurses were getting paid just as poorly as I was, someone was footing our bill. The only thing in other charts that gave me any clues was the patient information page saying patients belonged to a health insurance group I'd never heard of before, the Consortium.

But not Mr. November—we didn't even have his real name. Hence being named for the month. He'd been found outside, dehydrated, with a kicking case of pneumonia, too run-down to move. He looked eighty. Thin white skin hung in empty folds around his sharp features, like ice melt off a glacier, so thin that lifting tape wrong would tear it. During my assessment I could smell the bad breath of a body going metabolically awry. He had a central line going into the femoral vein on his thigh, channeling in medications and, of course, blood.

Not because he'd bled out—but because technically he's almost a vampire. Not a full one, but a "vampire-exposed human," some real vampire's daytimer.

Despite all the legends about instantaneous infection, it usually takes repeated exposure to vampire blood for it to change you—assuming you weren't allergic and didn't just die instantly from anaphylactic shock.

Mr. November had been exposed to a lot of vampire blood at some time. His fanglike canine teeth, which I could see now as he tried to work his ET tube out with his tongue, meant he had to have come close to changing. I wondered why nobody had ever finished the job and wished they had; it would have saved me this night of work. Because now, even though he was probably three hundred and twelve, vampire blood having life-extending properties, he could still die on my watch. People who've been exposed live long, but they aren't full vampires, and they don't get to live forever. As if fighting this fact, Mr. November started leaning forward in bed again.

I went back in the chart to see what medications I could give him. He was maxed for now, but come four A.M. if Dr. Turnas hadn't called back, I planned to reintroduce him to my friends lorazepam and oxycodone in a big, big way.

Charles walked over from his side of the ward. His patients were asleep or quietly watching TV. "Need any help, new kid?"

I was fairly sure Charles knew my name by now, and just as sure that it wasn't worth letting it get to me. "Not unless you're hiding an extra bag of fentanyl," I said. He laughed. Charles was my height and older, with brown hair turning gray. I'd noticed that no matter how hectic the night felt to me, Charles never let it show. I was jealous of his ability to keep his act together, but I'd like him more if he didn't pretend I was twelve.

"You'll be fine, new kid," Charles said, but he wasn't looking at me. I followed his gaze to see Mr. November making plucking gestures with his right hand. I thought Mr. November was reaching for his IV despite the pillow I'd placed in his way, until all but one of his fingers curled inward, leaving only his pointer out. He started to move it deliberately. Spelling things. I groaned.

"Stay out," Charles advised. Mr. November didn't stop.

"He's trying to communicate," I said.

"Just because he's trying to doesn't mean he can."

Which was true. Most times patients would scribble off the page and onto themselves, if they had enough reach. But then again, a few could tell you if they were cold, or hot, if they wanted the lights on or the TV off. You'd be surprised what people can obsess on when they're doped up and have nothing else to do. Once a guy told me in Spanish that he wasn't getting enough *aire*. I did a blood gas to check, and he'd been right.

My patient, my call. I grabbed paper from the copier, a Sharpie, and a clipboard, and suited up to see.

Because working on Y4 is like being in a hybrid ward for biohazards, trauma, and psych, isolation gear carts sit outside each room. They're equipped with gowns, face masks, hair nets, and gloves, just like every other isolation cart you'd find in County, until you get to the CO_2-propelled tranquilizer rifles loaded with suxamethonium chloride darts in their top drawer. During training when I asked why we didn't have garlic and crosses, I was told that garlic doesn't work, and the Consortium doesn't allow vampire-specific discrimination.

I pulled my gloves on and gave Charles what I hoped was a sorry-for-ignoring-you shrug before walking in.

The same badge that granted access to the elevator and locker rooms triggers the light set over Mr. November's door, so Meaty will know where I am if there's a lockdown. Charles knows where I am too, and is unimpressed, leaning on the doorway behind me.

"Okay, sir. Do me proud." I removed both the restraints on Mr. November's right hand, positioned the pen in it, then braced the clipboard upright for him against the pillow. "Are you in pain?"

I couldn't imagine that he was, but he *was* still awake. He ignored my prompt, and began working on a laborious capital *A*.

"Do you need to have a bowel movement? Want the TV on? Lights off?" I ran through my routine, while he made three—no, four—*n*'s in a row. Typical intubated patient. I sighed. I glanced over my shoulder and saw Charles smirking.

I launched into my stock speech number three.

"It's two A.M. in the morning on Sunday, November twenty-ninth." And I'd been working straight through since Thanksgiving, courtesy of being the newest nurse and having a desperate need for holiday pay. "I know it's frustrating when you can't communicate, but you're in the hospital. We're taking good care of you." I reached out and patted his arm. "Save your strength and rest."

He finished another letter, a lowercase *a*. I took the clipboard from him.

"Annnna . . . Anna?" I sounded out aloud, and he nodded, tubes and all. A small triumph, potentially imaginary. "I'll see if we can contact her for you." The light of human connection—or whatever passed for it here—flashed in his eyes and his lips curved into a smile. If I didn't know he had fangs and was getting a rhino-killing dose of narcotics, he'd look like any other elderly patient. I took the pen from his hand and his eyes closed.

Then the Versed pump started beeping. I hit the alarm silence button, and looked imploringly out to Charles.

He rolled his eyes at me. *He* would have never gowned up to come into a patient's room and not brought in the medication they were almost sure to run out of next. "I'm on it."

"Thanks," I said, and gave him a winning smile hidden by my mask. I hit the alarm silence button a few more times and when Charles brought me the Versed, I hung it as quickly as possible before sneaking back out of the room.

"So, Meaty—" I held Mr. November's clipboard out over the nursing station desk like it was proof of something. "This guy—no word on him yet?"

Meaty shook a large hand in an indeterminate fashion. "Sorry, Edie. We sent his photo out to all the Thrones."

I looked at the clipboard and sighed. At least with

patients at my last job I could make assumptions. I used to know that when someone had too high a drug tolerance, or too low a pain tolerance, that maybe they'd been a user back in the day. Here at Y4—maybe they're a werewolf? Or weretiger. Or weremanatee. I snorted. Gina down the hall was a vet and an RN, in charge of the were-corrals in rooms one and two. I knew someone was in one now, because they were howling. Last night was the full moon. We kept track of that here.

Mr. November might be completely new to town, since the local vampire Thrones hadn't jumped to claim him. It'd take longer to figure out which Throne he belonged to the farther he was afield. Maybe vampires only put out missing vampire bulletins at night.

"He doing okay?" Meaty asked. I didn't know if Meaty thought I would hurt patients by my mere presence, or if I gave off a bad-nurse aura. It wasn't that I didn't appreciate the repeated check-ins, I just didn't like feeling like I must need them all the time.

"He's fine, I'm fine, everything's fine," I said, with just a touch of sarcasm. Meaty squinted at me, then went back to ordering morning labs on the computer.

The desk between Meaty and me had the telemetry monitor on it, a computer screen that showed all the vitals from all the occupied rooms, in coded colors. Heart rhythms were largest, in bright green, and when alarms sounded these were usually to blame. It was hard to keep lead stickers on squirming patients who were sometimes slick with sweat. So when an alarm sounded, I glanced over, wondering who'd flatlined momentarily while scratching themselves.

But none of the green waves changed, and the alarm went on. Mr. November's corner of the screen lit up. I leaned in closer, actually reading numbers. After the obligatory oh-shit second, Meaty looked up, and I saw Mr. November's oxygenation saturation go from an acceptable

92 percent, to a potentially emphysemic 85 percent, to an incompatible-with-life 40 percent.

"Wake him up!" Meaty yelled.

"On it!" I leaped and ran around the station to his room, racing inside without gear.

CHAPTER THREE

I stood there for a second, overwhelmed. I'd left his right hand unrestrained, and Mr. November'd pulled his ET tube out. Inadequate ventilation = certain death. The heart monitor over his bed warned of an atrial fib before its green line dove flat.

Charles blazed past me at a speed walk. He slammed the bed into CPR mode, and pointed at me. "Ambu bag, now!"

I swallowed and nodded and pulled it off the wall. It felt like it took me an hour to assemble the pieces, to shove the face mask and bag together, the one that was supposed to be breathing for Mr. November but wasn't until I finished the fucking job. I managed it, and shoved the bag over Mr. November's open mouth.

Which reflexively closed.

On my left thumb.

"Shit!"

I yanked my thumb out, catching it on his teeth, and put my fingers under his jaw for a better seal.

I hadn't even seen Gina come in, but there she was, with epinephrine from the crash cart. Charles was already performing CPR. Meaty began counting cycles.

"Fifty-nine—switch!"

I vaulted onto the bed to straddle Mr. November, pumping with my injured hand, trying to pretend he hadn't just bitten me, that a motherfucking daytimer had not just bitten me. What if the tests we had run were wrong? What if he was infected? What if it didn't take repeated exposure? My thoughts flowed in time with my CPR, and just like his ribs, they resisted at first, then relented with a sickening crunch.

"Epi!" Meaty announced. I saw Gina push it.

Mr. November bucked beneath me, dislodging the ambu bag, sending the titanium-tipped ET tube by his head clattering to the floor. He stared at me, hard.

"Save her!" he commanded—but he was only mouthing the words. He'd shredded his vocal chords when he extubated himself. "Save her!" he mouthed again, before collapsing beneath me, expiring.

I sat there on his chest in shock. And then—the movies sometimes got this part right at least—he went from what'd once been a living, breathing thing, to a dough, then a dust. He crumpled in on himself, leaving a dark soot-colored stain on the insides of my thighs. All of the rest of his tubes and restraints fell and landed where they would have been were he an anatomically correct ash sculpture, something stolen from Pompeii. I wasn't sure what to make of this, or what to do next—I sat there stunned, before dismounting with excessive care. Meaty, Charles, Gina—they were all staring at me, silent.

"Can't the Shadow-things fix this?" I asked, my voice rising. The Shadows were some mystical protection for our floor, or so I'd been led to believe in training. I hadn't seen them myself, but I'd write Santa Claus and clap my hands for fairies right now if I thought it would help.

"Nope," Charles answered, and my shoulders slumped. He pointed at the remnants of Mr. November's hand. "Wasn't he supposed to be restrained?"

I nodded and Charles shook his head. "Awwww, new kid."

"I'll need an incident report," Meaty said, dismissing

the whole situation with a head shake. "Gina, stay here and show her what to do for the coroner."

My mouth went dry. I'd killed a man. My mistake killed him. No—not a normal man, a daytimer, a vampire servant, and likely already alive way past his normal life span. But—he'd looked like a human, and he'd felt like a human, and he'd died, because of me.

A tall man I'd never seen before came up behind Meaty. His embroidered lab coat read DR. EMMANUEL TURNAS in red thread italics. "You rang?"

"More sedation. Please," Meaty said, without the hint of a smile.

"Don't breathe the dust. It's bad for you and it's flammable." Gina put my mask on me while I stood there, numb. She was my age or younger, I couldn't tell, and Latina with dark even skin and straight black hair. Stylish bangs went from short at her right temple down to chin length at her left cheek. She'd probably be pretty if I ever got to see her smile. I suspected she wouldn't start today.

"First code?"

I swallowed and nodded. "Down here, yeah. And ever. That too."

"I could tell." She stared me down and then her gaze softened with pity. "You know, the last nurse who did something like that here died. I liked her a lot too." I didn't even know how to respond as she went on. "So look at it that way—you lived, right?"

"Yeah. Right," I said, my voice flat. If I hadn't gotten cocky and undone his wrist, if I'd ignored him—if he'd just behaved!

Gina ducked under the bed and unfastened the empty Posey vest. "Did you learn something?"

"Don't kill people?" I mouthed off—sarcasm being my best defense against crying—and instantly regretted it.

She rose and frowned. "Will it make you a better nurse?"

I sure as hell hoped so. "Yes."

"Well, then. Good." She opened the drawers containing Mr. November's personal items. "It's a hospital, new—" I inhaled to complain, just as her eyes found my badge. "Edie. Sometimes accidents happen. He was agitated and undersedated." She pulled out a huge black overcoat. "If Dr. Turnas believed us every time we told him patients were crawling out of bed, or if God forbid he was here himself to see it—"

I blinked. "You mean this happens a lot?"

"About once a year." She shrugged. "No one believes night shift."

I wasn't sure how that was supposed to make me feel better, but this conversation would be shorter if I pretended it did. "Great, I guess." It was only then that I remembered my hand. It ached where Mr. November had bitten me. I snuck a look while Gina went through his coat pockets. I couldn't even see where he'd broken the skin, if he had. But a flat purple bruise was growing, tracking the passage where his teeth had been.

"Well, this is interesting," Gina said.

I looked up, quickly hiding my left hand behind my back. Gina held two small bottles with crude red nail polish crosses on their sides.

"Holy water?"

Gina spritzed the air and sniffed. "Unknown vintage, and who can say what it was cut with?" She handed them to me and I took them with my good hand. "Put them in the incinerator box."

The glass bottles clinked in my palm. They were repurposed cologne bottles—my mom used to sell Avon, I recognized the styles. "Why would a vampire have holy water?" I asked.

"Maybe he was unpopular?" She shrugged.

I could sympathize. I peeked at my hand and thought I saw the bruise on my bad hand beginning to spread. It might just be in my head, but— "Um, Gina?" I said, interrupting her search of his pants.

"Yeah?"

I held out my injured hand. "He bit me."

Gina squinted. She ran her gloved thumb over my naked skin, feeling for the telltale rough edge of torn skin. "That was dumb."

"I know." I watched her inspect my injury and wished she'd say something comforting.

"Looks like a bruise for now. Keep an eye on it." She released my hand. "You didn't get any of his blood on you, right? So you're probably not exposed."

Probably fine? Was that good enough? Not when matters of my potentially becoming a vampire were at stake. But I bit my tongue and nodded like that was good news as she left the room, leaving me alone with a corpse.

I finished the rest of my charting and waited for the coroner to arrive. When he got there, he was a dour-looking man in a dark suit. The only color on him was a tie tack, a bright green Christmas wreath over an American flag. Maybe he had one for every season—perhaps I'd missed the flag-waving Thanksgiving turkey by mere days. He wore a canister vacuum under one arm, and in one hand he carried a package of vacuum bags.

I followed him into the room wearing just a mask and gloves and collected Mr. November's belongings to follow his vacuum bags into the afterlife. Shoes, shirt, the pants that Gina dropped—and in the pocket of these, a lump. I reached in and found a silver pocket watch. On the back of it, in a florid script, was a golden letter A.

Nurses are natural kleptos. You don't want to be in a room without enough supplies, so every time you walk past the med-cart you pocket another saline flush. By the end of the shift you can look like a chipmunk if you're not careful. Some days it's hard to remember that the gum at the end of the grocery checkout aisle isn't there just for you.

From beside me, the coroner began. The vacuum cleaner's sound made me jump, and I had only a moment to decide what to do with the watch. I could announce that I had it, and then what—trust the coroner to turn it in? He'd probably trade it in for another tie tack. Mr. November's death was my mistake, and the burden of figuring out who to give the watch to belonged to me. Staring at Mr. November's pile of diminishing ashes, I put the watch in my scrubs pocket, next to the bottles of cologne.

I waited until the coroner finished, as Mr. November was swept away. He'd probably lived for hundreds of years, until he caught pneumonia and met me. It would be nice to pretend that the pneumonia was where things had gone wrong, but I knew the truth. I finished my charting with a sinking stomach, then put all the paperwork on the nurse station ledge.

I didn't have to stick around to give the report to day shift. There's no report to give when your patient's become dead.

CHAPTER FOUR

I never turn my cell phone off. Not even when I'm asleep, after working the night before. I tell myself it's because I want to be available if the County calls to offer extra shifts, but the real reason is that I'm afraid they'll call after I've gone home, to ask me some important question, to remind me of something I should have done that I forgot to do or chart. And/or fire me. On the phone. I know I can sound a little paranoid, but it felt plausible today.

My voice mail message says I work nights and sleep days. Everyone who knows me, knows this. And still, people who aren't employed at the Nursing Office feel compelled to call me before three P.M. Certain people feel compelled to call me repeatedly, until I pick up—namely, dicks.

I sent three calls to voice mail and then gave up and answered on the fourth.

"Hello?" I croaked.

"Edie—Edie, I need money."

And I already knew who it was. "No, Jake."

"Aw, come on, Edie . . ."

"I have these things called student loans." I blinked beneath my blindfold and rubbed it up onto my forehead. "Not to mention taxes. Lots of taxes."

My brother made an exasperated sound. He doesn't

know what I've done for him. At least it wasn't the floor calling me, to tell me to not come in ever again—

The events of last night came rushing back. Jake was asking me something but I didn't hear him—all my concentration was on my left hand and the bruise upon it. I'd killed a patient. My patient. A daytimer—but still my patient. Any chance of sleep evaporated like cool alcohol off warm skin.

"Edie? Are you listening?"

I yanked off my blindfold. Had the bruise changed shape? I couldn't remember. I leaned over my bed and rummaged through last night's scrubs to find a Sharpie. Mr. November's watch fell out, along with alcohol swabs and an empty bottle of heparin.

"Come on, Edie—" my brother continued, just as whiny as every other patient I've ever had who knows that they are "allergic" to anything less than oxycodone.

"I said no, Jake. No means no." I braced the phone against my shoulder and traced the margins of my bruise in Sharpie so I could see if it expanded later.

"Some help you are," he said with exasperation.

"I wish you knew," I muttered, as he hung up on me. Finished with my personal arts and crafts project, I dropped the phone and picked up the watch.

It looked old. The inlaid golden *A* remained clear, but any finer details on its silver case had been rubbed smooth by time. I found the latch with my thumbnail and swung it open.

A photo was inside the lid, old if it was legit. A family portrait in sepia: two men, a woman, and two children, a boy and a girl. I guessed one of the men could have been Mr. November, give or take a hundred years. The men had strangely shaped hats, and the women wore kerchiefs on their heads.

Which one was Anna? The woman or the child? I stroked my discolored thumb over their miniature faces.

The watch itself was ticking. It might be worth as much as a student loan payment if I sold it on eBay. Which . . . maybe I'd do eventually, if I couldn't figure out who it belonged to. It wasn't like I could call up *Antiques Road-show*—"Hi, I stole this off an elderly patient . . . where did it come from?" Who was I kidding, thinking I was Nancy Drew? I flipped the watch back and forth in my hands, its silver glinting in the light. I knew I didn't want closure. I wanted absolution.

An edge of the photo stuck out, rough against my thumb. I worked to pry the photo loose. It popped out and fluttered to land facedown on my floor—and the words "Reward if returned" stared up at me. I picked up the photo again.

A series of addresses were written in a tight script. All of them were crossed out except the last: "336 Glade St. Apt 12." With surprise, I realized I recognized the address. I'd driven my brother to that street once and pretended to not watch him score.

My cat, Minnie, jumped onto the windowsill. "What are the chances that it's the same place? In this city?" I asked her. She contemplated me with crossed blue eyes. "What are the chances that if I go there, they'll steal my car?"

"Meow."

"That's about what I thought." But it was still daylight, and there was always the train.

The train ride gave me just enough time to feel foolish. My coat was bulky but not worth stealing, my boots had steel toes, and my money was in my bra along with a credit card. I hoped my best "don't fuck with me" look would do the rest—that and Mr. November's bottles, which I carried in my pockets like guns in hip holsters, one to each side.

The train shuddered to a stop and I was the only one to exit. Outside the station the buildings were tall, and the snow had an oily sheen. I passed a few tenements, ignored a few offers, and waited until Seventh before turning onto Glade.

Glade has not been a glade since forever. Mr. November's address was a single shorter building, surrounded by giants on both sides. I rang the bell.

A woman who might have predated World War I appeared on the far side of the door. She squinted at me through a broken windowpane, a cigarette lolling from her mouth. "Yeah? What?"

I hadn't realized until that very moment that I didn't have much of a plan. Hopefully someone lived here who remembered him, and I could hand off the watch. I wouldn't assume a daytimer had relatives, but I'd take anyone, from that Anna person to an affectionate neighbor down the hall. Maybe the kids next door looked up to him.

Funny how much life you could wedge into someone else when you didn't know anything about them at all.

"I, um . . . That is, an older tenant here—his condition is grave." Which was understating the situation quite a bit. "Does he have a next of kin? Someone named Anna?" She squinted at the name.

"Not that I know of." Her eyes narrowed even further. "You from the hospital?"

I nodded, even though I didn't have anything on me to prove that I was from the hospital, other than a set of plastic gloves in my chest pocket. Nurses and chipmunks.

I held a limp glove up. "I need to get emergency contact information for him. If you could—" I suggested, hoping she'd fill in the rest.

"Yeah, yeah. I seen *House* before. If I don't let you in, you'll just break in later."

Metal creaked and clicked while she undid the locks. I pulled on the blue latex gloves.

"I appreciate your cooperation," I said.

"His rent's good through the fifteenth. Any longer than that, and I'll evict him. And tell him I won't store his stuff."

"Will do."

She took my measure again. "Hang on." She left me waiting in the doorway until she came back with three brown paper envelopes, addressed to this address. One said Andrei Tarkovsky, the other Novaya Zemlya, the third Trofim Lysenko, each with different handwriting.

"I know there's not three people living up there. But I'm not snoopy. That's why people like to pay me rent."

I suspected if there were three people living up there, and the lease had only room for one, she was the type who wouldn't let it slide. I put the envelopes into my pocket and she let me in.

"If you find some weird fungus, I don't wanna know." She paused and reconsidered. "Maybe *I* want to know, but don't tell the other tenants." I nodded, and she stepped away from the door. "That guy's on time with the rent, but there's something wrong about him, you know?"

I nodded again. After all, she was right.

As I walked up the slumping stairs, past apartment doors with loud children and louder TVs behind them, I supposed I should be grateful to *House M.D.* I'd only been able to watch it until I'd started nursing school and actually hung around a hospital. After that, the idea of a doctor doing lab draws and hanging IV bags was preposterous. They didn't even know how the pumps worked.

I reached Mr. November's apartment and knocked on the door. "Hello?" I tried the handle; it wasn't locked. Would a vampire ever bother to lock their door? Wouldn't they encourage Jehovah's Witnesses? Unlikely in this neighborhood, but a vampire could dream, right?

I reached inside the door and flipped on the light switch. The few working lights illuminated dirt created from the kind of privacy that only consistently on-time rent could guarantee. A low table crowded the entryway, surface cluttered with knickknacks. Cobwebs stretched out from these like lonely neurons seeking company, and I knew one thing Mr. November hadn't had—a dust allergy.

"Hello?" I repeated, making a right turn off the hallway. I found a small kitchen with an old refrigerator. I pulled the lever-action handle and peeked inside.

Unwise. Bags upon bags of cats in various states of decomposition were neatly stacked and labeled, like an honors bio class had recently vacated the room. My stomach didn't turn, but I was extremely grateful for my gloves as I slammed the door shut.

That . . . was a lot of cats for just one daytimer. And on Y4, I'd never seen a cat on a dinner tray.

"Hello?" I tried again. "Anna?"

I could leave now. No one would know I'd been here. It wasn't like some other vampire was going to go to the police and report me. "She just walked in and looked at my dead cat collection, Officer." I was, so far, still safe.

And it was still daylight, wasn't it? Y4 was underground to protect its patient population. So if there was another vampire here, they'd be asleep. Unless it was a daytimer with a two-cat-a-day habit.

"Hello?" I tried again. "I'm from the hospital—" I announced, walking farther in. There was an open closet in the hallway, taped shut around the edges of its sliding doors, with an empty sleeping bag upon its floor. That was a relief—unless it was his spare bedroom. I turned a corner, trying to be prepared for anything.

Of course, that didn't work. Because sometimes, nothing can prepare you.

CHAPTER FIVE

The bedroom, if that's what it was, was full of photographs. At first, they appeared undifferentiated, like multicolored static, but then they resolved to pictures of girls. Little girls. Their eyes. They were layered so they covered one another, leaving mostly eyes peering out. And their eyes, well—the look in them was clear terror. Some were being molested. Others bitten. Some both.

Bile rose in my throat, bitter and angry. I doubled over. I'd have put out a hand to steady myself, but I didn't want to touch them. They'd already been touched enough.

I swallowed hard a few times and took a deep breath. In a rush, I pulled the envelopes out of my pockets and tore them open. I didn't think I'd ever been so glad to have gloves on in my life as when I saw the contents inside, the same kind of photos as were on the walls. I let them fall to the ground and put my hands to my face in horror.

"Mr. November—how could you?"

The only place safe to look was the floor, until I realized there were rows of boxes on the far side of the room. I walked over to these, saw they were labeled with names in alphabetical order. Marion. Sascha. Veronica.

I steeled myself and opened a lid. Neat hanging files full of photographs dangled inside, tabbed with what seemed like improbable dates. Melinda 1976–1981. Melinda 1985–

2002. I checked at the beginning of these photos, and at the end of them. While the men, women, and backgrounds differed, the girl looked exactly the same. If the dates were right Melinda hadn't aged in twenty-six years.

"Oh, God," I whispered.

At the end of the file was a note. "Saved."

What did that mean? Was it true? I looked around the room. The terror in their eyes seemed plaintive now. Seeking.

Was Anna one of these girls? And if she was, where would she be?

The EMTs had found Mr. November lying out in the street in the middle of the night in another bad neighborhood. They estimated he'd been there for about two hours before anyone local had thought to call. They were amazed he still had his wallet and shoes. After being his nurse, I wasn't. He'd been a fighter. And there was something strange about vampires, even merely partial ones, that seemed to naturally bend human attention away.

But why would a daytimer care about little girls? I looked around the room. Why did I care? I could still leave right now, pretend I hadn't seen all this. But—I couldn't help myself. I didn't know what "saved" meant—but I thought maybe I knew why he was saving them. To get to her. Anna. Only he hadn't made it, this last time.

Because of me.

I knelt and dug through the other boxes, the ones not marked "Saved," and scattered the images around me on the floor until I found her.

Anna. The girl in his picture, the one I still had in my pocket. Almost a century of pictures, they started off as family portraits, the family of five, until the other members disappeared and they withered into pornographic acts. From sepia tones, to black-and-white postcards, to color Polaroids, and finally prints of digital stills.

I couldn't imagine how horrific it must be to have the

only record of someone you loved be photos of others degrading them—while you hoped and prayed that you could match a blanket to a wall, a wall to a place, a place to a person, until they were finally free.

"So where is she?" I asked the room at large. My coming here, Mr. November's death—this had to have a point. I needed it to. "He knew and you've seen her. Hell, you are her. Where is she?"

Their eyes silently stared, accusing, sad. This couldn't be the end.

"Dammit, Edie," I whispered, banging my fists on the carpet. My left hand's nerves stung. Tears sprang to my eyes and I blinked them back as I took off my glove. The bruise was far past the Sharpied outline, encompassing my whole thumb, flowing with dark streaks into my palm.

And then—there was an industrious rustling behind me, ripping and tearing. I froze with fear, my back to the wall, and stared down at the worn carpet, my hands curled into its thin pile, one growing bruise-black, the other one with knuckles corpse-white, until my sense of sharing the room ended.

The Filipino women I used to work with believed in ghosts. After working in Y4, I probably should too.

I sat up and turned around. A portion of the photographs had been ripped off the walls revealing mold underneath, dark and crusted, like deep scabs. Shredded images littered the floor showing little strips of flesh, the corners of stained mattresses, and bleak stares with darkness behind.

"I'm so sorry." I started backing out of the room, unwilling to turn my back on what was there, out of fear and shame. "I'm so, so sorry."

A cold wind went through the room, stirring the photos like fall leaves. And when it finished running through me and out the door behind, the fragments of photos on the floor resolved into the shape of an address number and a name.

I remembered a quote from my grandma—just being sorry never helped anyone. I dusted my hands off and reached for my phone.

Three cab companies and a credit card number later, I found someone who'd pick me up. They wanted me at the curb at 7:12 on the nose and if I wasn't there, they'd gladly keep my deposit. After I hopped in I gave the cabbie my next address—much different from the one I'd given his company on the phone.

"You gotta be kidding me."

"I'll triple your fare." It was do it now, or not at all.

I watched him weigh the extra money against his personal safety, divided by the time of night, and he must have gotten an answer he agreed with, because he went my way.

I stared out the window as the cab ignored stop signs, rolling through perpetually grimmer neighborhoods until he brought the car to a halt.

"You sure you want off here? I ain't coming back for you."

"If this is the right address." I peeled bills out of my bra and handed them over. So much for this month's student loan payment. The cab rushed off the moment I closed the door.

There weren't address numbers posted here, but I saw that the third floor on one building had metal sheets nailed up over all the windows. A homemade asylum, a pot farm, or a dark place to keep vampires in captivity—someone had something to hide. I pulled out a cologne bottle and headed for the door.

The air inside this new place had the smell of cat pee and vinegar—the pungent byproducts of cooking large-scale meth or personal-use heroin. Luckily, I was used to junkies. A hairless girl in the stairwell was picking at a nonexistent scab. I skirted her and mounted the stairs two at a time.

My hand began to throb as I walked down the third-floor hall. I took off my winter gloves and found the bruise covering my entire palm, and it ached, bad. Without thinking about why I knew to do it, I placed my hand on one door after another until I found one that was cold, and the pain stopped.

No landlady and no House here. I hit the door with my marked hand, hard. "Delivery!"

"What?"

"Delivery!"

There were sounds behind the door. Metal scraping against metal. Whispers. The door opened to reveal a narrow-faced man, and the smell of sex and blood washed out around him.

I knew I was in the right place. I just knew.

"What do you want?" he asked. I held up the cologne bottle and pressed the plunger, hard and fast. Nothing happened. He tried to slam the door shut and would've too, if my steel toe hadn't been in the way.

"Fuck this." I unscrewed the cap and sloshed the contents at him. He started shrieking. Mr. November had managed to get the good stuff.

"Jesus Christ!" He stumbled to his knees and started scratching at his face.

"Something like that." I shoved him out of my way with the door. "Anna?"

The room's devastation was almost complete. Two lightbulbs dangled from the ceiling on threadbare wires. Waterlogged wallpaper sagged down to the floor. A shiny black camera on a tripod occupied the center of the room, keeping its mechanical eye on a dirty mattress on the dirty floor, where a girl was chained like a bad dog. She looked about nine, but I knew there was no way to tell.

"Anna?" I repeated.

Her eyes flickered over my shoulder, which is why I ducked just in time.

All the sexy vampires on TV and all the weakened half ones I'd seen on Y4—nothing prepared me for the disgusting creature that hurled itself at me, arms out, lips stretched tight against a smile full of knives. I twisted away and ran to get my back against the wall. His breath washed over me as he passed by, with the scent of smoke and rotting apples. I held the open bottle of holy water out in one hand, and held the other up like a grenade, unscrewing its cap with my thumb.

"I just want the girl!" I shouted.

Was killing a vampire still murder? The man I'd first hit with the fluid was still writhing around the floor, his hands against his face—only now, dust was leaking through the gaps between his fingers.

"Get out!" the fresh attacker said with a heavy accent. His gaze flickered to the open bottle. His nose was flat, his nostrils mere slits, and the skin of his cheeks rippled upward to accommodate his wide swath of teeth.

"Hell, no." She'd invited me in. Or Mr. November had. I needed to be here. Stone-gray eyes regarded me and then looked at his dust-weeping friend. He squinted and sniffed the air deep, like an animal, then came to a decision.

"Fine." He reached into his pocket and found a lighter, lit it, and backed away from me and toward his accomplice.

What was it Gina had said? The dust was bad? It was—flammable? I dropped to one knee and braced.

What it was, was like gunpowder.

A flash of heat billowed out. I threw my arm up to protect my face. Not all of the first vampire was dust yet— the part that wasn't screamed until it couldn't anymore.

When I could see again, the second vampire had taken off, running down the hall. By then, what was left of the first one was debatable.

I looked to the girl. She watched the burning vampire, the light of his fire glittering in her eyes.

"Anna?" I asked again. She made no response for or against the name. "Look—" I began. I was pretty sure the apartment wouldn't go up in flames, but she couldn't stay chained here. I gestured with my free hand so she could watch me put the bottles back in my pocket. And then I reached out with my bruised hand, not for her, but for the pipe that she was chained to.

She lunged forward like a feral cat and bit my out-stretched hand. I felt her grind her teeth together, scissoring through my flesh, one fang hitting bone. I screamed and fell to my knees. She stood above me, my blood smeared across her face, teeth latched into the crotch of my hand.

CHAPTER SIX

I thought I might pass out from the pain. My vision was narrowing, and my breath came in gulps. My free hand found the full cologne bottle in my pocket—I could give her what I'd given them. Then I felt the photo I'd brought beside it. I had one choice, before she bit off my thumb.

"Stop!" I said, with the voice of nursing command, the voice that made it through even the densest skulls and thickest stupors.

"Anna!" I shouted, and I showed her the picture, the half-dollar-sized photo that may or may not have had her in it.

The chewing lessened. Slowly, almost regretfully, she unfastened her bite from my hand with a sickening pop.

"Thanks." I took a moment to breathe, and stumbled to stand up, to get farther from the temptation of the floor. I was riding adrenaline and endorphins now, and maybe narcotic vampire saliva too. I'd get through, but for how long? I looked at my mangled hand like it was someone else's, wound my scarf around it, and shoved it in my pocket. I needed to finish what I'd come to do.

The dwindling embers of the vampire behind us gave me enough light to work by. I popped the camera off its tripod, ejected its media, and tossed it onto the vampire's dying flame. It went up in bitter smoke, and I pocketed the camera before turning to reach for the ridiculously ancient plumbing. Anna'd been too short and light to pull down the pole she was chained to herself, but I was healthy and tall—I reached for it with my unharmed hand and hauled down with all my weight.

The pipe crumbled in my hands. Flakes of rust showered down and some foul, puslike substance oozed out from its upper end. Anna saw the free end appear and ran for it, unlooping her chains and running away at full speed. She leaped over the embers of the first vampire's corpse, off into the night.

Was that saving her? Did I rescue her, or set her loose? My pocket was heavy with the warm weight of my own blood. I fumbled for my cell phone, hit the history key, and redialed up a cab.

The same cabbie picked me up, despite his promise to the contrary. Funny how cash will do that to people.

"It was you or an ambulance," I explained as I got inside. I didn't think he could see the blood, as it was dark and my coat was black, but I would have bet all my remaining cash that he could smell it.

"This shit is why we do not come down here," he said. He started driving uptown. I slumped against the passenger side window.

"Take me to County."

"What?" He spared a glance at me. "I'm taking you to Providence General."

"No, take me to my hospital."

"County's a shithole," he said. I didn't have the strength to argue, and besides, he was right.

I dialed Jake next, my brother. He picked up on the third ring.

"I knew you'd come around, Sissy—"

"Jake—you gotta meet me at County."

There was a pause. I could almost hear him making up

excuses. "It's late." The truth was he'd lose his bed at the shelter for the night if he left.

"You can crash at my place for a few days." I flexed my bleeding hand, unwisely. Pain lanced up my arm and I hissed into the receiver. "I need someone to watch Minnie. Take a cab over, right now, I'll pay."

"You sure?" An unfamiliar worry tinged his voice.

"Yeah. Just hurry, okay?"

He'd already hung up.

I fought to stay awake as the cab flew along. We passed the exit for Providence, another freeway, up toward the nicer part of town. But my cabbie stayed the course, going south, until a blue HOSPITAL sign glowed outside the window, the cab's headlights making its silver right-turn arrow into a shining command.

He pulled into the emergency drop-off, and came around to open the door for me. "Glad you lived, kid."

"Me too." I staggered up, standing on the curb in the cold. I paid him, then he was gone.

Only the fact that I was already standing kept me up. There were other people outside this late, well-bundled smokers leaning on IV poles, security officers making a perimeter sweep. I was safe in the umbrella of the drop-off's light—safe from everything but my own stupidity. I could feel cold in my hand now, and I didn't know if it was from the outside or internal. The narcotic effects of vampire spit were definitely wearing off. I stared up at the oddly clear sky, watching the barely waning full moon sail overhead, when I heard a double honk.

"Sissy!" Jake hollered, from the window of a cab.

I walked over as he got out. His pupils were wide and as he gestured I noticed his hands were spastic. My flaky Jakey, coming to the rescue. I'd have gone off on him, only it seems we'd both made bad choices recently. And really, the fact that he'd had his phone on him *and* he'd answered my call while he was slightly high or trying to become so was impressively functional. Behind him, inside the car, the cabbie loudly demanded his fare.

"Ten thirty-five!"

"Sissy?" Jake asked. He was closer now; I hadn't seen him leave the cab—I'd been staring at the cab's fuzzy snake-eye dice instead—but now Jake was standing beside me. "Sissy, what happened?"

"Ten thirty-five!"

With my good hand, I turned over my keys and the cash I had left. Hopefully it was enough, I couldn't do math right now. "Watch my cat. You can eat all my food. Whatever you do, do not let Minnie out."

Jake nodded. After a second thought, or maybe a fourth, I handed him the small video camera. "Pawn this too."

He nodded again, and walked back to the cab. Before he got in, he turned toward me, eyes wide and bright. "Sissy—what happened?"

"Don't ask," I said, and turned toward County. There was a pause, then I heard the cab door open and close solidly behind me.

I didn't walk toward the emergency department's doors, though they automatically slid open as I passed. I went for the County's true doors, to the lobby that smelled like piss and diluted bleach in turns. I waved my badge at the guards and went into the depths of the hospital, up corridors and down stairwells, into an elevator that sank into the earth without seeming to move until it dinged and coughed me free. The final set of doors swung outward toward me, like welcoming arms, like one-way valves, like cilia moving mucus. Like mental impairment due to shock due to blood loss, I'd bet. I stumbled forward.

Meaty saw me first, as I held up my mutilated hand in response to his/her/its raised eyebrow.

"Room three. Now."

CHAPTER SEVEN

When they were done with my hand and had weaned me off the IV pain meds, Meaty pushed a bariatric cardiac chair into my room. In a world where night shift time served = time to eat = girth = experience, Meaty knew all about everything.

"You want to tell me about it?"

It was the first time anyone had asked, except for Charles trying to get me to bring visitors down. I'd balked at the thought of bringing Jake in; he'd be like a kid in a candy store with other people's meds, without supervision. Plus, how would we explain the howling?

But you didn't last long as a nurse if you told your charge nurse no. So I shared from the beginning, until the part that was known, me, here, with a messed-up hand. The scars across the back of my left hand were already tightening—thanks, hack from plastics—and I rubbed them with a grimace.

"You were under a compulsion," Meaty said.

"A what?"

Meaty settled down farther in the chair. "A compulsion. Vampires use them to order their servants around."

I sank back farther in my bed. "It didn't feel like that." What it felt like, was like every other bad decision I'd ever made. I'd had a lot of practice.

But was it bad? I'd saved that girl, Anna, right?

Meaty ignored me. "Most daytimers can't use compulsions, but maybe he was on the cusp."

I looked down at my hand again, and thought about going home soon, the mountain of cat litter that surely needed changing, and how my house would now smell like black tar and pot. "I don't think it was a compulsion. If I could go back in time, I'd probably do it again," I said, more to myself than him. "The saving the girl part, not the killing him on accident part," I amended.

Meaty rocked forward to leverage off the chair. My audience was over. "Compulsion, guilt, pick your poison." Meaty shrugged. "You make a better nurse than a patient. You're discharged, go home."

I barely had my legs out of the bed when Gina arrived with a patient belongings bag. She wandered around the room, gathering my things.

I pulled my jeans and boots on, but instead of wearing my sweatshirt, I wrapped another gown around my back, and put my bloodstained coat on top. I knew I was a sight, but Gina had the kindness not to say anything. Between my week's worth of bedhead, and the bloodstained sweatshirt in my bag, I knew I looked like every other patient released from emergency psych that A.M. But I left my room and tried to walk toward the hallway door with a little dignity regardless.

"Hey, new kid!" Charles called out, as my hand touched the button for the automatic door.

I turned around. "My name is Edie," I enunciated slowly.

He grinned. "I know. Welcome to Y4."

CHAPTER EIGHT

I tried calling Jake twice from the pay phone by the Charlie Brown Christmas tree that'd been erected in the lobby during my stay. It wasn't real, but someone had hung a pine-scented car deodorizer on it, in addition to the Christmas ornaments from 1973. I ran out of quarters, and my phone was out of juice, but a transit pass came free with discharge. So I bussed home, very conscious of the other bus patrons' stares. I walked from the bus stop up to my door, glad I hadn't had to make a transfer, and knocked on my own door before unlocking it.

"Jake?"

I looked around my short entryway. It smelled like smoke—not cigarette, but something more vinegary and foul.

"Minnie?"

Her plaintive meow came from underneath the couch. Which I realized I could see quite clearly, because for some reason, my dining room set was gone. I stared at the dimples the table legs had left in the thin carpeting.

"Jake? Jake!"

"Hang on!" There was stomping in the bedroom, behind the closed door. Jake's head peeked out furtively, like he thought it might be someone else to whom I'd given a key. Seeing me, he smiled. "Edie!"

"Who else would it be?"

"You're all right! I was worried!"

Worried didn't equal calling, apparently—my phone hadn't had a single message before its batteries ran out. Or picking up his phone when I'd called him earlier, that either.

My brother engulfed me in his arms. He smelled like flop sweat and his week-old bristles were rough against my cheek, but his hug was a throwback to an earlier Jake, one I hadn't seen in quite a while.

When he pulled back I caught his chin with my left hand. "How are you?" I asked, looking deep into his eyes for pupillary response.

"I'm— Stop that, Edie."

"I'm just wondering—"

"I'm not high. Promise. And it's not for lack of trying."

"Um, yay?" I dropped my bag and went over to my couch. "Where'd my table go?"

"I was performing an experiment."

"Which was?"

Jake began walking back and forth in my narrow living room. "For the past couple of weeks I've been having problems getting high."

"And this is bad why?"

"Edie—just listen, okay?"

Pacing, he looked like the older brother I remembered, the one who was nervous before a calculus test or wanted advice on asking a girl out to the prom.

"I've tried everything. And I mean everything. Lots of it. And I just *can't get high*. Not like I used to. I feel it for a bit, sure. But not for long enough to count."

"How's this tie into my table? And chairs?" I pointed at the place where they'd been.

"I needed to sell them to afford my final test."

"What?" I stood up. "You sold them?"

"I pawned them. With the camera. You can get them back still." He stopped at the outer parabola of his pacing arc and snorted. "They weren't worth much."

"Jake—you stole from me!"

"Pawned. Pawned. It's different."

"No it's not!"

Jake grabbed my arms. On his whip-thin frame, I could see the exit and insertion sites for all of his muscles, the keloids beginning on his antecubital spaces from too many needlesticks. "Edie, I did two grams of heroin. I'm still alive. That much heroin would have killed a horse."

And that's why I worked at Y4. I wasn't sure how the Shadows kept him clean, but when Jake treated his liver like a chemistry lab, I had no choice. If he'd really done as much heroin as he said he had—I shook myself free. "Or you bought shit drugs from a shit supplier and you've done too much long-term brain damage to know the difference."

"Oh, I'd know. I'd know," Jake said, mostly to himself.

"Jake, you stole from me." I crossed my arms.

"But I'm like Superman!"

"Superman doesn't shoot smack, Jake."

"Edie, you just don't get it—"

I sliced through the air with my newly scarred hand to cut off his protests. "What I get is that you stole from me."

"Pawned. You can get them back next paycheck. Nurses make a ton."

"Jake—" I pointed at my door with my left arm. My hand was shaking, either from disuse or anger.

"I'm going, I'm going. Let me get my things." He turned and ran down the hallway.

"At least you still have things!" I shouted at him.

"I left you the couch!" he shouted back.

"Only because you couldn't carry it yourself!"

He returned with a small backpack and my keys on a

chain. "Your cat's almost out of food. Your neighbor's kid is creepy. And you have shitty taste in music."

I snatched my keys from him. "Shut up."

"No one listens to Merle Haggard anymore."

"Get out, Jake."

He mimed a salute in midair. "See you around, Sissy."

I watched him walk out my door, and then followed to watch him leave from my doorway, his backpack on his back.

"Jake—Christmas?" I called after him.

"Yeah." He waved a hand without turning around.

It was cold out this morning, tonight'd be freezing for sure. I hoped he made it to the shelter in time. I watched him till he turned at the end of my apartment complex's parking lot, my healing hand throbbing in the cold.

First order of business was me and a long shower. I hadn't let anyone give me a bed bath during my internment—it was humiliating enough to be in Y4 for my recuperation, bed baths from coworkers would have made it intolerable. Where were easily intimidated nursing school students when you needed them?

After that I changed the sheets on my bed and crawled into it. A shower, clean sheets, and a bed without side rails? This was high cotton. I fell asleep without a second thought.

When I woke it was dark. Just before nine P.M. with winter outside making it seem later, between the early sunsets and the omnipresent clouds. I could still remember the nearly full moon from the emergency drop-off zone—I might not see another until April or May. I lay back in my dark room, pulled the sheets high, and tried not to think about anything.

It was hard. For the first time in a long while, I felt rested. I'd kept night shift hours in the hospital, the company of my own coworkers far preferable to those on other shifts. It'd been easier to distract myself with people to talk to and TV to watch, under the comforting dullness that Percocet pulled up every four hours. Here at home, without drugs or distractions, it was hard to forget that I'd done at least three stupid and potentially horrible things: I'd accidentally killed a patient, I'd intentionally killed a vampire, and I might have set a monster loose on the world. Minnie emerged from wherever she'd been hiding, to stroke her head along my outstretched hand.

"I'm glad he listened to me about that at least, Minnie." I knuckled the space between her ears. There was no way I was going to get any more sleep, not tonight.

I petted Minnie till she couldn't stand it any longer and she squirmed out of reach. Then I sat up in bed and stared into my open closet, my shoes and clothing illuminated by the parking lot's lamplight filtering in through my blinds. "I'm alive, I'm awake, and I'm not on call," I announced to myself. "I should go out."

CHAPTER NINE

Going out means different things to different people. For some, they like to go to a movie or dinner alone; for others, they go out to get lit and laid. For me, it meant dancing, with a side of laid, should a worthwhile opportunity present itself.

The ten pounds of weight night shift had put on me hadn't sized me out of my favorite skirt just yet. I pulled it on, then found a matching shirt that clung in all the right places. My hair was wavy, shoulder length, generically brown. My eyes were a complimentable blue, and I had a good smile. I knew when I went out that I wasn't the prettiest girl in the club—but I also knew I could hold my own in someplace with a few shadows where the cocktails were reasonably priced.

Not that I ever drank while I was out. Years spent living around an alcoholic father had seen to that—that, and it just wasn't safe to let your guard down. I still liked places that served drinks, though. Booze gave you a plausible deniability the next day that Frappuccinos did not.

On my way out, I tucked my ID into my hospital badge's holder, unclipped it from my lanyard, and pushed this into the back pocket of my skirt. I tossed on a coat, pulled on tights for the millimeter of warmth they'd afford me, and tugged on low snow-proof boots. Then I walk-jogged to the train near my house and gathered heat until my favorite downtown stop. The place I liked to go was a few blocks away from the station, and by the time I got there my calves were freezing, but the heat inside the club made the short misery worthwhile.

The bouncer knew me—we gave each other a cursory nod—and I got in without cover, one of the few perks of being a single girl. I checked my coat—not having a guy to watch it being points against singleness—and went for the dance floor.

Nyjara's "Forget This!" was playing, a bass-heavy techno-remix, and I could feel the pounding bass shake through my chest. The words of the song were appropriate, but even without them, the bass might have saved me. If you're close enough to the speakers and you do it right, dancing is like being high. The music can fill you and crowd out the knowledge that you've been a failure; the memories of all the times when you've let people down, the late nights and the later rent. It fills up all the spaces and doesn't leave room for anything but itself. I stood still for a moment at the edge of the dance floor until the refrain, and then I let the music drag me in.

Seven songs later, I was winded. My hair clung to the back of my neck, and I knew the little makeup I'd put on had already melted away. But I felt alive in a way I hadn't before I started dancing—and in a way I knew I wouldn't, when I eventually went home. For here and now, every time I'd swung my hips around and tossed my head into the air, I was chasing away my ghosts, and claiming possession of my body for myself. I strode over to the bar in sweaty triumph like a winning Thoroughbred.

My first water I gulped down. The second one I took with me to sit in the dark in a chair that someone had just left.

People-watching was fun. Not having to talk to people? Also fun. Nursing was all about talking. Here it was too loud to have a real conversation—I was alone, but not alone. Just the way I liked it.

Then a man sidled up to me. I pretended not to see him and the shadows were in his favor. He leaned in.

"You dance well," he shouted over the bass. He had a British accent, which was unusual in this town. It probably got him a lot of girls.

"Thanks," I answered. I glanced at him out of the corner of my eye. He had dark hair in chunky locks, and nearly black eyes. I didn't really have a type, so my parameters for one-night stands were pretty wide. I also knew I didn't want to be alone just yet. Whether that meant I spent more time dancing, or more time with him . . . "Do you?" I shouted back to him. "Dance?"

He smiled and rattled the ice of his nearly empty drink at me. "Only after a few more of these."

"Oh." I smiled back and shrugged. It was against my code of ethics to buy a guy a drink, as drinks cost money, and I now needed all the money I could get to rescue my table from hock. Water was free. I looked at his clothing— if the cut of his shirt was any indication, I couldn't afford to buy him anything he didn't already have.

"What are you drinking?" he asked. He put his hand out for my glass.

I pulled back a little. "Water."

"Can I get you more?" he asked, his hand still held out.

"No." I swatted his hand away gently.

His eyes went wider in surprise at the skin-on-skin contact. He laughed—at me, or at himself, I wasn't sure. He leaned closer, and the air from his words tickled against my ear. "Are you uninterested, or exceptionally vigilant?"

"A little of both."

"So you're saying you're not interested?" he asked, overly loud, even for the club.

"I'm saying I'm vigilant," I protested, unwilling to rise to his game. A song I particularly enjoyed came on, and my water was gone. "I'll be back," I told him, setting my empty glass down.

"And?" he pressed, making the word hold more than one question.

"You're saying you're not interested?" I mimicked him, and went back to the dance floor.

If I hadn't already danced to so many songs, I couldn't have done it. It's hard to go out cold when you know someone is watching you. But I'd already held the music in my bones once that night, and I still had demons to excise.

I ignored him completely when I danced. I knew he was there, even with my eyes closed, but I moved for myself, letting my arms flow out and then spin back in, touching myself as the music touched me.

I could go home alone tonight, with no music, and no distractions, and spend very many hours thinking about why I was who I was, and how many times I'd gotten into trouble just by virtue of being me.

Or—the song wound down, and so did I. I swayed to the final beats and then brought my head back up, brushing my hair out of my face. He was still there, still sitting beside my empty cup. I walked back to him, making sure my hips rolled like a ship in a storm. I stood in front of him, as tall as he was, at least while he was sitting on the bar stool. He was handsome, with strong cheekbones and well-made lips. I was close enough to kiss him. I gave it serious thought.

"I should warn you I'm dangerous. I recently killed a man." Daytimer, man, close enough.

His dark eyes narrowed in apparently serious thought. "Are you planning on killing again?"

"Not intentionally." I shrugged.

"How about you only kill me if you have to?" he

suggested, standing. He was definitely taller than me. Closer now, his aftershave smelled like vetiver.

"How about you take me home?" I said.

His lips quirked up, amused. They were kissable, I knew it. He took my hand, and pulled me toward the door.

CHAPTER TEN

We drove in his car back to my place in silence. The car smelled like his scent and leather and it handled the light snow with ease. He parked in front of my apartment without offering any comment on the fact that his car cost as much as the three cars parked beside it combined.

We didn't talk because I think we'd both done this sort of thing before. When you're quiet, you can envelop the other person in the fantasy of what you want them to be. Talking only gives them a chance to mess it up. I trotted up to my door and unlocked it and pretended that I was shivering just because of the cold.

There was only one hallway in my apartment. He walked past me and down it like he'd been there before and I found myself drawn along in his wake. When I reached my own room, it was like he was waiting for me there, like it was a lair, his place, not mine. He turned toward me and stared at me for half a second. This was my last chance to change my mind, to make him leave, I knew it.

But I never back down. If I ever gave fear a fighting chance, my life would be all but over. I smiled defiantly and he caught my head between his hands and pulled me close.

Kissing wasn't the word. It began as tasting, but then—biting. I stiffened for a moment, wondering if I'd been fool enough to invite a vampire home with me—but no. The

teeth that pulled at my lips were human. But the need behind them—he was as hungry as I was. I wondered what
he was running from, and then his hands were at my hips.

Teeth at my jaw, neck, and collarbone, while his hands,
cold from outside, ran up my back. I pressed into him,
away from their chill, as his fingers ran under my bra and
then forward, to cup my breasts. He walked me backward
into the wall and pinned me there, lifting my shirt on his
arms, pushing it up so that he could reach my nipples with
his teeth.

I gasped at his cold nose and cheek against my breast,
and then I reached forward to grab at his shirt, to claw it
up his back. He pulled back and yanked it off himself, as
I did the same, and then he reached for me. He picked me
up easily, tossed me onto my own bed, and knelt beside
me there.

He was above me, his pants still on, back arched, looking down at me. I felt like prey and I liked it. He wanted
me weak and helpless, and maybe for a second I wanted
those things too. Wordlessly, he grabbed my hands and
yanked them over my head, to pin both down with one
hand. He reached down and undid his belt buckle with
his other hand, then plunged his fingers under my skirt,
yanking my tights and panties down to find a ready home
within me. My hips arched and I fought against my con-
finement—at first, just testing boundaries, but then, fighting just to fight, to see if I could get loose, how tight he
would hold, how serious he was in keeping me still.

His one hand clenched around my wrists, while the
other made come-hither motions, deep inside of me. He
sped up as I writhed, pinned on his fingers, and I stopped
trying to escape.

I was full of him, but not full enough yet. I looked up
into his charcoal-dark eyes.

"Yes?" he asked, his lips drawn to the side in a soft
smirk.

"You can fuck me now."

He laughed. "Gladly."

He pushed my legs apart with his knees, pulled out his cock, and entered me all in one smooth movement. I curled forward and bit his shoulder when he hit the back of me, crying out in surprise at his length, then ground my hips against his in desire.

We made the quiet noises of fucking then, the moans, the sound of skin hitting skin, the buckle of his belt chiming with his thrusts.

When I remembered, I would fight him, pushing back with my arms against both his hands now trapping me down. I didn't want to find I could get free.

His cock found the back of me again and again, and I kept shuddering in delight, but—I just couldn't relax enough to come.

He rocked above me, olive skin slick with sweat against my paler hue. He was beautiful, goddammit, and the sex was hot, but my mind wasn't all there. No matter how much I fought him or gave in to him in turns, I couldn't fuck away my fears.

I thought about faking it, but that'd be a disservice to all womankind. So I fought against him harder, found his mouth with mine, biting him back till he was too distracted to stop himself. He thrust into me hard, harder, hardest, until he came with a gasping exhalation deep inside of me.

He lay above me for a moment, sweat dripping from his chest onto mine. Then he carefully rolled off me, to my side. I saw him inspecting me by the lamplight my blinds let in. Maybe he hadn't even really looked at me until now. I brought my hands down from above my head, my arms sore, and rested one hand on my cheek, the other on my chest.

"You should come too—" he said, and reached down my stomach toward the space between my legs.

"No, that's okay." I caught his hand with mine. "It's just one of those nights."

He brought my freshly scarred left hand up in his and inspected it by the lamplight outside. "What's this? Did I hurt you?"

It was Mr. November's mark upon me, Anna's bite, and my suture scars. Everything I'd tried to throw away from me tonight had followed me home. I shook my head. "It was an accident." I clasped my hand into a fist. He turned my hand toward him and kissed my closed fingers lightly before releasing them back to me.

He rocked up to sitting, and then to standing by the side of the bed. Everything he did was fluid—I wondered if he'd lied about not dancing, before.

"I've got to go."

I laughed, and made a show of covering a yawn. "Fine, Cinderella. I was just about to kick you out."

He paused from the labor of his belt buckle and looked at me again. "You know, you're the first girl who's said that that I think meant it. What's your name?"

I shook my head. "No names. You know where the door is. Forget the address on your way out."

"Ahhh. A tough girl, eh?"

"Quite," I said, and pointed down the hall.

He tilted his head like a curious dog. He'd been in power all night long, but me there on my own bed, naked in the lamplight—I was like a Greek goddess as an odalisque, while he scrambled to find his clothing on *my* floor. "All right, then. See you around, I hope."

His accent was still as lovely as he was. I did my best to keep my advantage, and gave him a languorous smile. "Perhaps." He tucked his shirt in and smiled mischievously at me before heading off down my hall. I waited till I heard his car engine rev before heading there after him, to lock my door. Then I went back to my room, where everything still smelled like sex and there was a layer of condensation on the window.

I lay down in my bed and inspected my hand by the lamplight. I hadn't banished everything for very long, but I fell asleep, fast and hard. Even nonorgasmic sex can be a pretty good exorcism too.

CHAPTER ELEVEN

In my dreams, I was on a boat. That was my first clue I was dreaming, since I had an epic fear of open water based on viewing both *Titanic* and *Shark Week*.

It was a clear night and the stars shone overhead. Two people stood on the top deck's edge, staring out at a black sea. They were facing backward, as if looking at their past.

As I concentrated, my perspective changed and they grew nearer. From here, wherever dream-here was, I realized they were just kids, dressed in that oddly formal way of children from long ago, like little adults. They stood near one another, bundled up against the cold, holding on to the railing—and the little girl I knew.

It was Anna, the vampire that'd bitten me. Blond wisps of hair peeked out from underneath her hat and I could almost imagine her mother's last kiss upon her brow. She appeared healthy but looked unhappy, staring out like she distrusted the ocean as much as I did.

"Don't worry. I'll protect you," the boy said, in a language I did not understand but instinctively knew the meaning of. He set one of his hands atop hers, and they held on to the railing together.

When I woke I knew there'd been more, but all I could remember was looking out at the horrible sea.

* * *

I slept in till four P.M. or so, and didn't have any more creepy dreams based on my dual fears of vampires and the ocean. I knew I had the next three days off, but I didn't know my schedule beyond that. My dining room set wasn't going to buy itself back. I was already pulled thin beforehand, and now courtesy of Jake and Jake's monkey, I was stretched drum tight. I called in to see if anything was open that night.

"Sure, I'll go to pediatric intensive care," I heard myself tell the Nursing Office on the phone. I hung up before I could say no.

I tried to put things in perspective on my way there. After all, pulling a shift in pedi ICU was better than being in Med-Surg with all the whining postknee ops, strapped into their continuous passive-motion machines. And Y4 had given me pediatric training—some sanctioned donors were children, though I hadn't met any of them yet—and so I was pediatric life-support certified. That didn't mean that I was comfortable around kids—rather, I was the opposite—but I figured I could keep two of them alive for the night.

Most importantly, I'd really, really loved my dining room set. I hoped this shift was worth it.

The pediatric wing was attached to County like an extended middle finger. It was newer than the rest of the buildings, and nicer too, although compared to Y4, anything with a view of a parking lot would be an upgrade.

The lights were already dimmed when I arrived, which muted the bright colors on the walls. Smiling yellow suns appeared menacing and gray above little villages where bowed farmer-people tended fields. A human-sized teddy bear occupied the wall in front of the nurse's station. I was sure in daylight he looked friendly, but right now he looked like he hoped the charge nurse was hiding a steak.

One of the things I was glad about on Y4 was that we

dressed out from the locker room's supply of green OR scrubs—that way I didn't have to wear dumb ones with smiling cartoon cats. The Pedi ICU's charge nurse's scrubs had winking Betty Boops holding out oversized bandages and lollipops. They looked sarcastic. I almost approved.

"I'm your float from the Nursing Office," I told her, and gave a short wave. She looked me up and down slowly, and her left eyebrow rose. I was wearing an old pair of OR scrubs brought from home, freshly washed, but not wrinkle-free, and my ponytail was of dubious quality. I could see her doing the math of letting me, a potential ingrate, nurse some of the children in her care. If you thought plain intensive care unit nurses were overprotective and judgmental—which I frequently did—you hadn't met a pediatrics intensive care nurse yet.

I tried to give off my best "I won't kill anyone tonight, honest" vibe, and waited for her to come to her assignment decision.

"You're in sixty-two and sixty-three. Call if you need help."

I walked away confident that I, as a float nurse, had been given the easiest assignment on the floor. I'd probably have two kids with broken legs, or a dehydrated baby. I found my set of rooms at the very end of the hall near the fire escape stairs.

The curtains were closed, and I could hear speaking in a foreign tongue. The charge nurse hadn't mentioned relatives. Pediatric patient parents were the worst, either hovering or incompetently neglectful. "Is that German?" I asked aloud.

"Night shift?" came the response. "Come help."

I sniffed the air. Closed curtains were rarely a good sign. It smelled sweet—

"Hello?" asked the outgoing nurse.

"Tying my shoe—sorry!" I lied, and ducked inside.

The patient was a boy who looked about twelve, with a

ventilator connected to a tracheotomy tube in his neck. His whole body was flaccid, and his head was tilted to one side. The nurse had a plastic tub full of water balanced on the bed, bathing him. She handed me a dry washcloth. "Glove up."

I sniffed the air again. "Strawberry?"

"Ensure. He gets 45 ccs an hour. But I didn't connect his peg tube right, and I pulled the covers up and—" she said, and I saw the problem. For some reason this kid had a tube from his stomach to the outside world, and she'd set the feeding pump on when the tube was disconnected. Instead of going into him, the Ensure'd spilled all over him, as pink as the painted walls above his bed. But why didn't the kid say anything?

"Shawn was in a motor vehicle accident four years ago. He's a C3 quad now."

"Ooooooh." C3 meant a neck fracture, high. "And now?"

"Recovering from autonomic dysreflexia. He's in the clear, we're just watching him one more day is all."

I nodded to head off any extra questions. She went through the rest of her report, while we finished the bath. All his monitors were on and all of the parameters were currently normal. I wrote things down at the appropriate times, and she seemed confident she was passing Shawn over to a competent nurse, one who hadn't gotten a patient killed on the last active shift she'd had.

There were family provisions stocked up on the shelf near the windows, Doritos, Diet Cokes. The German continued from a small CD player set up with speakers by the table at the head of the bed. It made everything we were doing sound more dramatic than it was, like I was about to Nurse in Space, or in a fairy-infested cave.

"And over there?" I gestured to my second patient, in a crib on the other side of the room.

"Downs syndrome and RSV."

"Ahhhhhh." What the hell was RSV? Some pedidisease.

In my mind, I scanned through lecture slides. Respiratory-
something-virus, my brain pulled up, relieved. I walked
over and peered into the crib. The baby was surrounded
by teddy bears that actually seemed cheerful. She had a
nasal canula taped to her cheeks and an extra tube, like a
ventilation duct in miniature, pointed in front of her nose,
with air hissing out, taped atop a teddy bear's arm. "No
lines?" I asked, after scanning nearby for IV poles.

"Nope. Just oxygen. You gotta watch her oxygen
saturation—when she sleeps too deep, or rolls away from
the blow-by," the nurse said, waggling the duct-taped teddy
bear pressed into service, "she drops."

Desats, I knew about. "Okay. Got it." I looked around
the room. Not bad so far. I almost felt as confident as I
sounded. "What's up with the German?"

She shrugged. "I think it's his grandfather, some phi-
losophy professor. He likes to listen to it before he goes to
sleep. Also"—and here she scratched at her own cleavage, in a way that indicated she was talking about my
own—"he's a bit of a perv. Hormones and all. His trach is
uncuffed so he can talk around it in whispers. He likes it
when you lean over a lot. I suggest you pin up."

"Heh. Thanks."

She smiled warmly at me, happy to be going home.
"Have a good shift."

A girl could hope.

CHAPTER TWELVE

The two pedi rooms faced each other, like the mirrored sides of a clamshell. Each room was lined with privacy curtains, but I knew if I closed these I'd just make the charge nurse nervous.

The sinks, monitors, and standard room items were at the perimeter of the rooms: ambu bags, pediatric-sized, suction pumps, and the oxygen pumps that were already in use, the baby with her nasal canula, and Shawn with his ventilated trach. Bed right, crib left, and in the far rear corner of each room was a small bathroom for guests. The back wall had two couches if parents were spending the night; thank God both were empty.

I assessed the baby first. Dry diaper, nothing doing. She had spiky dark hair like a troll doll and she was contentedly asleep. I wasn't going to change that.

I went over to Shawn's side and waved down at him. He regarded me with the sort of disdain only a preteen can muster. "I'm Edie, your nurse tonight."

He made a soft noise in response that I couldn't hear over the rising German. I leaned over. "Duh," I heard, more clearly.

I did my assessment under his bored gaze. "Do you need anything?" I asked at the end of it.

He cocked an eyebrow. "A blow job?"

"Nice try. You kiss your mother with that mouth?"

"Mom's dead. Same accident."

"Um. Sorry to hear that."

His eyes rolled. "Right."

After coming to this amazing détente, I felt sheepish. "Well, I'll be over here if you need anything." I backed out of his range of view, and did my charting.

Between the sliding glass doors that led into each room was a stretch of desk with a computer and . . . the Internet.

I sank into the chair and checked to see if the charge nurse could see me—not if I didn't lean out too far. The night was looking up! Two patients who ought to sleep all night long, and an Internet connection. How lucky was I? Pretty damn lucky, at least until someone needed a diaper change.

I started clicking away on the Web, reading local news, catching up on the things I'd missed while I'd been incapacitated. The murder rate didn't seem to have gone up, and if there was an uptick in the number of cats going missing, it hadn't been worth reporting on.

I got into a routine of clicking on a page, reading a paragraph, then glancing over my shoulder at both monitors. Half an hour passed idly by, and Shawn's German philosophy-loving grandfather stopped shouting. I heaved a sigh through pursed lips, and clicked onto the next page of celebrity gossip.

Two pages later, after reading about everyone who might possibly be pregnant any time this next century, the German began again.

"Shawn, get to sleep," I muttered. And then I turned around. Quadriplegic patients weren't known for their ability to hit the play button. I stood up and craned in his direction, looking for an adaptive stick that maybe he'd used with his teeth. The volume of the German voice increased.

I walked over. Shawn was completely asleep. There was

only the small hiss of his ventilator pushing air through his trach. I turned the CD player—well out of reach of anything that Shawn could use—off. Its green "on" light went dark. I glared at it for a moment.

A woman wearing pink Hello Kitty scrubs knocked on the glass door. "Mind an early break?"

"Not at all." I briefed her on both of my patients and took off for my one A.M. dinner.

I fished my badge for Y4 out of my back pocket as I walked back to the old building. As I neared the right elevator bank my stomach started to clench—what if it didn't work? What if I stood out there, waving my badge around like an idiot, and it never worked again? No one would believe that I'd ever worked with vampires. I'd be condemned to pick up float shifts in the rest of the hospital for all eternity, the Flying Dutchman of RNs. I closed my eyes, shoved my badge toward the reader, and listened for the click.

I didn't *hear* a click, but I did smell the sharp tang of fresh urine. I was home—or close enough. I opened my eyes, stepped forward into the elevator's waiting chamber, and tried not to breathe while the elevator hurtled down.

"Why," I asked myself upon exiting, gasping in fresh air, "must the elevators always smell like pee?"

Gina came out of the break room with a cracker in her mouth. She smiled at me around it, and I instantly felt relieved. "Hey, Edie—wait, you're not on tonight, are you?"

"I'm picking up in Pedi ICU." I shrugged with practiced nonchalance. "I've got a cat to feed, you know?"

"As your local vet nurse, I approve."

I grinned at her. "Speaking of—why is our elevator a litter box?"

"It's the weres, a territory thing. They can't help it. Even in human form, when they visit during the days."

I looked down at my shoes. I wore different ones on

the floor, I kept them in the locker room. But I hadn't considered the cooties I'd get on my real-life shoes, just by riding in the elevator *to* the locker room. "Ew."

"You'd think the Shadows'd stop them, but no." She shrugged. "I gotta get back." She waved and went around the corner.

The Shadows this, the Shadows that—I'd asked Charles about them once, when our breaks had overlapped. He said they spent most of their time in the emergency department. He claimed one had touched him once, but he wouldn't tell me more. They were a little like King Arthur, where the County equaled England, occasionally running in to rescue us, a threat to keep our assorted patient populations in line. Some help they'd been, though, back when I was accidentally killing someone.

I wanted to believe they were anthropomorphic, as I assumed I'd met one—the man who'd gotten me to sign the dotted line when I was first here with Jake. I hadn't seen him since. But Charles said "they" (complete with scare quotes) lurked in the corners by our entrance door, screening visitors, unseen. Since that made them sound like omnipotent dust bunnies, I preferred the version of them in my own imagination.

We did have ancillary staff, and not all of them were permanent Y4 employees. I felt sure the daytime social workers were, the nursing managers, and of course the doctors and all us RNs. But the respiratory therapists that came through and an occasional extra janitor usually seemed to pause in the doorway an extra second or two, both on their way out and on their way in. When you saw them above in County's normal hallways and waved, they were usually polite in return, but their faces had that look of "Who are you?" that never reached any satisfactory conclusion. Sometimes I waved at them for the fun of it.

I ducked into the break room and surveyed the food-for-all left out from prior shifts on the small table.

"Awwww, you miss us," Charles said from the door, peeking in.

I put on my best "hardly" face, borrowed from Shawn. "No. You guys just have the biggest refrigerator." But he was already gone. I pulled a Diet Coke out of the fridge that I'd been holding in reserve, grabbed my PB&J, and followed him to the floor.

"So who's here tonight?" I asked.

"Two motor vehicle accidents, one end-stage cancer, and one really advanced STD." He jerked his chin forward. "Go check out the corrals."

I did as I was told, walking around the nursing station toward rooms one and two. I waved to Meaty, who nodded without looking up. Turning the corner I found Gina with a large flowsheet spread out over two of our skinny desks.

"Whatcha working on?"

"The schedule." She fluttered a stack of pink time-off requests, and I felt my stomach drop again. Just because they hadn't deactivated my badge didn't mean they weren't going to shortly take it away.

"Am I back on soon?" I asked, glad my voice didn't break.

"What, you miss us?"

The flush that I denied Charles, I let rise now. "No. My cat. Bills," I stammered.

"Uh-huh." She chuckled. "You're on in two nights. And then I scheduled you straight through a week so you wouldn't have to burn out your paid time off on your sick leave."

Brillant! Not that I'd ever be able to afford a vacation, but I derived a certain satisfaction from accruing the hours. "Thanks, Gina, that's great."

"No problem."

There was a rustling and then a scratching sound behind steel door number one. "Who's on first?"

She pointed up to the closed-camera TV without looking.

I looked up and blinked twice. It isn't every day you see something that you've never seen before. The daytimers and vampires—they look like humans. And high-level zombies (the Haitian-magic kind, not the grungy movie undead) and most of the weres I'd seen, when they visited, all looked human too. No one came in shaped like a wolf, though sometimes once they were here they ended up that way. Those forms were all on my radar, from walking down the street, movies, the zoo or the Discovery Channel. But what was on the camera's circuit right now was something I was completely unprepared to believe existed.

A dragon.

It roiled around the steel-plated room, two sizes too small for it, overlapping its scaly self. It was a deep emerald green, like it was carved out of moving jade, and it didn't have any wings, but it had four legs, a tail, and a snout that was muzzled.

"Sweet Jesus Jones."

"Pretty awesome, right? They're freaking rare." Gina put her spreadsheet down. "I've only seen one twice before."

My jaw was still dropped. "What—how?"

"Weres can happen in all sorts of forms. He, as a human, was in town on business. He doesn't have any other members of his clan here for a safe house—they're mostly seen in Europe and Asia. He noticed some problems with his parts"—her hand swirled over her lap, indicating her nether regions—"so he came in."

"What's he sick with?"

"Syphilis. Would you believe it? We're treating him now, huge amounts of penicillin, and he'll be fine, but you can see why we didn't want him out spreading it on the streets."

I snorted, remembering a youth misspent reading fantasy novels. "Yeah, just think of the virgins."

Gina glared at me.

"You're serious?"

"Totally. He probably wouldn't get anyone pregnant in human form—the were dragons *are* pretty inbred. But he could totally transmit his disease, and he does have a genetic proclivity toward pretty young things. He's very charismatic too. I talked to him some before his form came on. Lovely British accent."

My heart skipped a beat. "Really?"

She nodded. "Why?"

I shook my head. The chances of me having recently slept with a charismatic dragon with an STD had just gone from absolute zero to something in the finite range. Compared to this, my angry Germanic mystery in pediatrics was boring.

Charles came around the corner. "Finding a virgin in this town must be pretty hard, charisma or no."

Gina shrugged. "It does happen, you know."

"Hell, finding a virgin in this hospital must be pretty hard," Charles continued. I gave a nervous laugh.

"Since seventy-six here," Meaty offered from around the bend.

The three of us looked from one to the other. Was that when Meaty had lost his/her/its virginity? Or the last time he/she/it had had sex? I shuddered. There were some things about your charge nurse that you didn't want to know.

After an awkward silence, Gina cleared her throat. "Anyhow, move along, there's nothing to see here. I've got scheduling to do."

I went and sat back at the station for the rest of my break, eating dinner there like we're not supposed to, and reviewing the charts of the patients that might be mine if they stuck around till I got back.

CHAPTER THIRTEEN

When I returned to pediatrics, the German was rising to a fever pitch.

"Did you turn that on?" I asked the Hello Kitty nurse who'd relieved me.

She raised an eyebrow. "I thought you'd put it on?"

I waved my hands. There was an effing *dragon* on Y4. Who cared about a broken CD player now? "I probably did and forgot. Did I miss anything?"

"Nothing, really. I charted your vitals and kept an eye on the fort." She packed up her things. "Oh, a diaper change on the little one. Weighed seventy-five grams."

Score! Only five more hours to avoid a diaper change for the rest of the night. It was hard to resist pumping my fist in the air in triumph.

"Thanks so much!" I said, and she waved through the glass door as she left.

I set up shop on the desk again, stethoscope, charts, pen, and notes just the way I liked, and then paced around the table to see where the CD player was set. I turned it off, flipped it over, and popped out the four double A's.

"There," I said, and set it back down.

I'd only taken three steps away when the German began again. I looked down at the batteries in my hand, and back at the CD player. The CD player's on light was shining a defiant green.

"You have got to be kidding me."

The only other thing on the table with the CD player was the telephone. And then it occurred to me—what the hell was he saying?

I picked up the phone and dialed the hospital translation hotline. I got their night message and waited on hold for an operator.

"Hello—I need a German translator, please."

"One moment!"

There was hold music while the German continued. Would they be able to hear it too? It wasn't just in my head, though, Hello Kitty had heard it—so had the P.M. shift nurse.

"Hello?"

"Hello—I have a German patient here, and I need to translate their questions. Can I put you on speaker phone?"

"Certainly."

The translator on the phone sounded much more perky than I felt. Maybe she was in a time zone where it was daylight outside. I hit the speaker button and set the headset down.

The German continued. It rose and fell in inflection, always with the same serious tone, but now that I listened to it, it sounded like a Bible story, preachy and full of hidden meaning.

"Is this some sort of prank?" the translator asked. "Or a test?"

"What are they saying?" I pressed.

"I think they're telling a story about Wayland the Smith."

"Really? What kind of story is that?"

"You're wasting my time—"

"Who else needs German translators this time of night?"

"I also speak Tagalog," she huffed, then hung up.

I looked down at the little CD player that could. Well, well, Wayland the Smith. At least that was a start.

I made sure to catch up on all of my charting before hopping online for my current goose chase. I sat down behind the desk, double-checked that the charge nurse couldn't possibly see me again, and did a search on Mr. Smith, Wayland the.

Through the County's loose firewall, I found a few pages. It was an olden-times story, mostly myths, about a smith capable of producing great jewelry and weapons. An evil king wanted Wayland to work for him alone, so he captured the smith, then hamstrung him to trap him on an island. In retaliation, Wayland took the king's sons, who'd come privately to him for their own work, and killed them and made their skulls into goblets and brooches from their teeth, sending these back to the king. In the end, he'd escaped captivity on wings he'd forged himself.

I could get the parallel between a mythical hamstrung Wayland and a quadriplegic Shawn; it was just a bit morbid, was all. I looked back at Shawn, the player's green light illuminating his face. Maybe the CD was full of charming German folktales to tell kids at hospitals. Kids love being threatened with ovens for liking candy. But if it provided him solace, who was I to question? After Mr. November's apartment, I was willing to believe in ghosts. I pulled the batteries from my pocket and set them back inside the machine. "Sorry about that, Grandfather."

I'd spent another lovely hour trying to reach the end of the Internet with an accompaniment of German when the phone on the baby's half of the room rang. I looked at the receiver in disbelief as it rang again. It had to be a wrong number. Surely the call wasn't for the eight-month-old. I walked across the room and picked up the phone.

"Hello?"

"Edie—it's Gina."

"Awww, so you guys miss me?" I teased.

"Edie, it got out."

"What did?"

"The dragon."

I looked around the room, with its cheerful pink paint and my peaceful sleeping patients. It seemed so safe. "Is this some sort of hazing? Because I'm new, I get it but—"

"It tore off its muzzle and melted a hole in the back wall."

Just then, the fire alarms went off. The red lights set into the hallway ceiling began flashing, and nurses up and down the hall began fire safety routines. I heard and felt the thunk of closing doors.

The intercom coughed to life above. "Fire on floor seven, building M."

"Oh shit," I whispered.

"I think his transformation kicked the syphilis up a notch," Gina continued. "He stopped responding to verbal commands an hour ago. If I had to guess—and remember, I was never a reptile expert—I'd say he's got syphilitic insanity. I gave him a lot of tranquilizers when he started getting restless. They should slow him down."

"Anything else?" I hid my conversation from the nurses in the hall by ducking behind the privacy curtains.

"He's coming up your stairwell," Gina went on. "He could just want to get outside the building and fly off, but I thought you should know. The Shadows are on it, regardless."

"Got it. Thanks."

"You're welcome." She paused, and I thought I could hear her swallow. "Good luck."

CHAPTER FOURTEEN

I closed the doors to my rooms, per fire safety protocols. Most fire alarms were drills. But hospital protocols weren't set up to take care of dragons. Fire-breathing dragons. Fire-breathing *insane* dragons.

And . . . syphilis? Really? Like Al Capone? I paced around from one room to the other. Sure, nurses were all trained on STDs. That hadn't stopped me from having unwise and unprotected sex with a British stranger two nights ago, though. Shit.

I looked from Shawn to the baby. Both of them were technically virgins. And both of them needed oxygen to survive. There were mobile tanks for times like these. I went out to the charge's desk.

"Shouldn't we move them down the hall?"

"It's probably burning popcorn on the Med-Surg wing," she said coolly.

"Are you sure?"

She sat straighter before responding to me. I could tell I was close to getting yelled at. Maybe afterward, one of the Betty Boops would offer me a lolly. "Just stay in there till it's over."

I walked back and looked like I was doing patient care for the baby, closing the curtains to give myself time to think. Where should I go? What should I do?

Surely the Shadows would take care of things, quickly. They would, right? Which actually was my second problem. If the dragon did come here—was coming right past here, according to Gina's implications—I couldn't react ahead of time. If the Shadows *were* coming, and they *were* going to fix things, they might not erase everyone's memory about how that float nurse panicked and covered herself and her patients in water before pushing them up the hall without O_2. If I panicked now over nothing I'd never get to work in PICU again, or any other floor, for that matter. Hospital gossip travels faster than stat drugs down an IV line. And really, where could you go to hide from a dragon, anyhow?

A fresh string of German startled me. I looked over and saw the small light on the CD player glowing yellow. I walked toward it and noticed that as I did so the temperature in the room shifted, becoming warmer. I paced back—cooler. Toward Shawn? Warmer. Downright hot. We didn't have radiant heaters overhead here to malfunction, and there were no air vents nearby jetting out warm air. The scent of burning plastic began to permeate the room. If the dragon were just in the stairwell, we'd be fine. If it wasn't, though—I ran to both sides of the room and hauled the curtains closed.

"Everything all right in there?" my charge yelled through the door. I barely heard her.

"Fine!" I shouted back. "Just have to clean him up is all!" How close was the dragon? I poured water into a plastic tub, then splashed it onto the floor. It went everywhere—and at the metal seams where the floor met the wall behind Shawn's bed, it hissed into steam.

"Fuck." I leaned over. "Shawn. Wake up. Shawn." I touched his shoulder, then realized my mistake, and began tapping at his cheek. "Shawn!" I hissed, whispering as loud as I could.

"Wha?" One eye blinked open.

"I've got to move you."

He closed his eye again. "Then move me already."

"No, not like that. Like off the bed."

Now both eyes opened. "Why?"

"I can't really explain it. But you and I and the baby—we've gotta get into the bathroom over there."

Confusion crowded his features together. "Is it a tornado?"

That was a more plausible reason than any other I had. "Yes. It's coming fast."

I grabbed the pediatric ambu bag off the wall, and assembled it, swallowing hard. Last time I'd done this . . . but this time would be different. It had to be. I put the bed on max inflate, and shoved a side rail down.

"I can't breathe for you while I move you," I said while popping the vent off his trach and replacing it with the ambu bag. "So I'm going to hyperventilate you now."

His eyes were large and frightened. The German rose around us as the temperature did, encouraging me to quicker action.

"Okay. On the count of three, here we go!"

I put the ambu bag down and leaned backward.

Shawn wasn't thin for his age. And he couldn't help me move him at all—he was the proverbial sack of potatoes. I hauled him out of bed like a rag doll, and lurched into a squat under his new weight.

"Come on!" I said as much to myself as to him. I staggered back till the curtain ended, and then went quickly toward the bathroom on the baby's side of the room, as far away from his wall as I could get, dragging him in a duck walk, my calves screaming in pain. When we got there I pulled him through the door, and dropped him on the ground, panting. I gave him two long puffs of air before hauling him until his legs were inside and I could close the door.

"I've gotta go get the baby now, okay?" I told him.

"I thought you were kidding," he whispered around his trach.

"I wish."

Two more puffs from the ambu bag, and then I went outside. The CD player's light was shining a furious red behind the curtain in Shawn's corner. I grabbed the baby and turned the oxygen and her monitor off, carrying her quickly into the bathroom, locking and closing the door behind me. We waited.

I alternated between breathing for Shawn and the baby, and all the while it was getting hotter.

There was a thump from outside the bathroom. I flinched, and Shawn's eyes went wide. The handle started to turn.

"Float nurse? Are you in here?" The locked handle shook. "You'd better be in here!"

"Shit." I heard a scraping at the outside of the lock. There was nothing in a hospital that couldn't be unlocked. Except for the were-corrals on Y4.

"I can't explain right now. Just go away!" I shouted, but I heard the jingle of keys. I reached up and held the handle.

"Look, lady—Enid! Esther! Whatever the hell your name is! Open up!"

I strained back but I couldn't reach Shawn's trach and hold on to the door. I let it go, and it opened forcefully, thudding into Shawn's immobile calf.

"What are you doing in here?" the charge nurse yelled through the crack in the door as she tried to force it wider.

I looked up at her. The Betty Boops on her scrubs were shuddering in rage. Pediatric nurse anger combined the best elements of maternal wrath and the worst elements of wronged woman. "I'm sorry." I knew she couldn't go away. If I were in her shoes, I knew I wouldn't.

The heat radiating in from behind her was tremendous,

like an oven heating to broil. She leaned down to shove
Shawn's leg out of the way of the door. "What the hell did
you do to the thermostat?"

"It's the fire—" I sputtered. "It's below us."

"Then why the hell didn't you have me wheel you out
of the room?"

"Popcorn, remember!" I shouted at her.

"Not the patients. You. I would have gladly wheeled you
out if I'd known you were going to do this. Do you know
what kind of incident reports I'll have to write now?" She
glared at me.

"That's the least of my concerns," I said, still alternat-
ing breaths for Shawn and the baby, taking the ambu bag
and squeezing it over the baby's face and attaching it to
Shawn's trach in turns. She was sweating, I was sweating,
Shawn was sweating. It was time to go for broke. "Look—
there's a fucking pissed-off dragon coming up the stairs.
We need to hide until the Shadows get here."

"You need to hide till security gets here—that's for
damn sure," she muttered. She took a step back, and I
knew she was going for the phone to call me in.

Then the room was filled with an unholy roar, like a
hundred cars crashing into one another at high speed, so
loud it hurt. The charge nurse's jaw dropped open and I
knew she'd heard and felt it too.

I reached down and yanked Shawn's legs up. "Get in
here." She did so without question, without turning around,
closed the door, and I heard her flip the lock.

The lights in the bathroom flickered and went out. We
sat there in the dark with only the sound of the ambu bag
exhaling sweet air into Shawn's trach, which I held with
one hand, and then at the baby, whom I trusted to remain
in the general vicinity. I prayed that this last door would
buy the Shadows enough time.

"What *is* that?" the charge hissed.

"I told you." How could I expect her to believe me? I'd never even seen a were in person because Gina was always the were-vet-RN.

"Not that. That." I felt her hand at my chest and looked down. My badge was glowing faintly, a warm gold. *Huh*.

"My penlight," I lied. I could see the fear on her face from its dull glow. Shawn's eyes were still wide, and the baby, not smart enough to be scared, reached out for my hand as I held the ambu bag above her face.

I couldn't let them down. I couldn't lose anyone else. I couldn't be that person again.

"Here—" I grabbed the charge nurse's hand and put the ambu bag into it.

"Why? Where are you—"

"Just stay here." The baby cooed. I stroked her soft hair with my free hand. "Keep everyone quiet."

I stood and tapped the door's handle, to see if it was hot. It was, but not so much that I couldn't grab it. I beat on the door to get the dragon's attention. "I'm coming out!"

I'd only been on Y4 for a month, and one week of that had been watching lame training videos, some of which had involved puppets. And not good Jim Henson puppets, but hand-up-the-ass puppets, especially the videos about weres. I was completely unprepared for this, but goddammit, there had to be something I could do.

"My name is Edie Spence! I'm a noncombatant! You can't hurt me! I'm coming out!" That much I remembered from training. I stepped swiftly out and closed the door behind me. I heard the charge nurse quickly relock the door.

I only had a second to take the room in. The dragon had slagged a hole into the room from the stairwell outside. It was still clawing its way through, using Shawn's bed frame for traction. The fire-alarm light above made everything strobe red, like a haunted house.

And then it saw me. Its sleek green head lunged out, whip-fast, teeth clashing in midair. I screamed and jumped backward, my back slamming against the bathroom door.

"I'm a noncombatant!" I shouted, as I made myself small. I tried holding my badge up again. "You're not allowed to hurt me!"

The dragon hadn't gotten the memo. Maybe there weren't noncombatants in Europe. It began scrabbling faster now, writhing its muscular body to snake inside.

I crawled around the perimeter of the room. Maybe I could draw its attention away, buy some time for the Shadows to hurry their mythical asses up.

It leveraged itself up by half a foot, scales scraping on the broken wall. I could see its round belly now, where an emberous glow was taking hold. It stretched its head out again, snapping at me, then went for the bathroom's door.

CHAPTER FIFTEEN

"Over here, you stupid thing!" I reached up against the back wall, unhooked a suction canister, and threw it at the beast. It hit the dragon's side. The suction pump was next—made of solid metal, it was bound to get its attention. "Over here!" I shouted again, and then threw the pump at it with all my might.

The dragon's head looped away and the pump thumped down into the shredded mattress. The dragon stretched forward like a cat and with one final lunge pulled itself free. It sat on its haunches on Shawn's demolished bed, shrieking its triumph. I fell to my knees under the onslaught of its roar—lion, velociraptor, Godzilla, all rolled into one. Its tail lashed in violent sweeps, knocking down spare IV poles, tearing curtains, and it sent Shawn's CD player skittering across the floor. I picked it up as the dragon lurched toward the bathroom.

"Hey!" I jumped up and waved my arms to get the dragon's attention. It ignored me completely. "Hey, damn you—hey!" I threw the CD player at the dragon. It sailed end over end, like an oversized pill. The dragon snapped it out of midair and gulped it down. "Stop this! You have got to stop!"

At long last, the fire sprinklers went on, pouring down rust-laden water. I sputtered and edged back toward the bathroom. "You have got to stop this now!" The dragon paused and sat back on its haunches. I waited, and it waited—maybe I was getting through! I took a step forward, repeating myself. "I'm Edie Spence. I'm an official noncombatant. You're not allowed to hurt me. You need to stop this." The dragon bowed its mighty head. My heart raced. Was this a victory?

The light that I could see so clearly in its belly was moving higher now, like rising mercury on a summer day. It pulled its head down to rest on its own chest and I saw the light inside its stomach rise up into its neck.

I should have recognized the expression. Lord knows I'd seen enough patients puke.

"Fuck." I cast my glowing badge up in front of my face, fully expecting my illuminated employee number to be the last thing I'd ever see.

And then the German began. I didn't know what Grandfather was saying, but he was pissed. The German rose in tone and intent, louder and louder in volume, until it became more frightening than the dragon's roar, even though it too was coming from inside the dragon. It became louder than any concert or club I'd ever been at, each syllable reverberating in my chest—I could feel it change the course of my beating heart.

The dragon opened its mouth as I heard one last Germanic battle cry.

By the light of its own belly, the dragon ruptured. It split at the seams—legs, stomach, spine—and chunks of hot dragon flesh flew outward, sizzling as they touched the water raining down. A large piece caught me in my chest and knocked me on my ass. I could hear dragon pieces land with wet smacks across the room, and a stench worse than from any rectal tube rose up. I was covered in dragon meat, green scales, pink bone, charred flesh—the room was slimed with it, the crib, the teddy bears, Shawn's bed, the bags of Doritos. I had to fight to keep myself from gagging.

In the middle of all the chaos and gore, the melted CD player's power light glowed a baleful low-battery yellow before finally winking out. I crawled through the muck over to it.

"What—how?" I picked it up and shook it. From my vantage point on the floor I could see people walking toward the rooms, past the curtains, outside.

And then the cavalry arrived.

They weren't dust bunnies after all.

Spots on the ground that were shaded by monitors, desks, and chunks of dragon meat started moving. Anywhere darkness pooled it gathered and grew, tendrils of black snaking along the ground. The Shadows—the protectors of the hospital, the ones I'd heard stories about but had never had occasion to see—were here at last.

A heat-popped soda can spun in small circles near my foot, like a firework going out—the Shadows covered this in passing, and it disappeared. A sheet of them formed where the curtains darkened the floor, and I saw them merging on the walls in between the light strobes. A group of them started pooling in *my* shadow, and I grabbed for my badge instinctively. They ignored me, washing around me and through-underneath-over the bathroom door, which opened without a turning of the handle or a loosing of the lock, and pulled out one shell-shocked charge nurse and my two respiratorily compromised patients. They appeared frozen in time and space, stiff like mannequins, hoisted into the middle of the room on a wave of black. The fire-alarm light stopped and the sprinklers ceased. I watched while all around me they washed over every surface, cleaning it, like demented fairies from a children's tale, where the price of clean dishes and fresh linen was blood. I didn't know what they did to the dragon's remains—did they incinerate it? Eat it? But the hole in the wall sealed up after their passage, and a reunited mattress emerged from underneath a separate slick of black.

They replaced Shawn and the baby in their respective beds, and surged the charge nurse out-through-between the closed glass doors back to the desk outside. I peeked at the clock, half expecting them to wind back time too. And then they were done, except for—

"Oh, no—" I backed away from the pool of them growing at my feet. But I was the last thing that needed to be cleaned. I gasped as they lapped up, colder than ice, crawling down inside my socks, rolling up against my skin beneath my scrubs, to pull themselves toward my scalp, submerging me completely in their dark.

In a second I was nowhere. I was no one. No—I was me, but I was suddenly aware of how inconsequential being me was. I didn't matter, nothing I would do would ever matter, I would eat, breathe, and shit just like everything else on this planet, but nothing would ever have a consequence. I was worthless, my small life utterly bereft of meaning, and when I died, I would die alone. I gasped like I'd been punched in the stomach, and then they began to let me go.

I caught the baby's crib to stay standing, and leaned against it, wishing I could undo . . . undo . . . everything, really. From the beginning. Just everything at all.

Then they receded like a tide of La Brea tar, holding just as many bones, leaving me with honest dark. I stood in the middle of my reconstituted room, with my two living patients, and a set of memories that were mine alone. I looked out through my now open curtains and the charge nurse down the hall waved cheerfully at me. I waved weakly back.

Then I slumped down into my chair, hidden by the computer desk, and put my head between my knees. The intercom clicked on above. "The fire drill is now over. Thank you for your participation."

You're welcome, I suppose, I thought. It was a long while before I sat upright again.

CHAPTER SIXTEEN

Everyone stuck around to hear my story in the locker room hallway that morning. I told it as quickly as I could, except for the part where the Shadows had submerged me, which I didn't share at all. Charles nodded knowingly, Gina hung on my every word, and Meaty was, well, Meaty.

"You did all right, all things considered," Meaty said.

I snorted. "I didn't want to die roasted to death in a bathroom, all things considered."

"They should have been faster," Charles said, his thin lips forming a frown. "It shouldn't have been that close."

"Maybe the emergency room was busy tonight?" Gina suggested.

"It shouldn't have even happened," Meaty said. "They should have caught and contained him down here to begin with."

"No, they should have—" Charles began, in a vehement tone. I waved my hand in among all of them to cut off further debate.

"So—what happens now? I'm not worried about the baby, but Shawn, and the charge nurse—what about them?" Had the Shadows touched them like I'd been touched? They didn't seem changed when I'd left—but how could any change in reality manage to be so complete?

"The Shadows took care of it," Meaty said, with a half shrug.

That wasn't really an answer and I thought Meaty knew it. "Like they took care of me?" I looked down at my badge. What would I have done if Shawn's grandfather's crazy-ass ghost hadn't been around? I'd have died, that's what. And it wouldn't have mattered, and no one would have cared. The adrenaline I'd been running on ebbed and I leaned back exhaustedly against the bathroom door. Meaty clapped my shoulder with one mighty hand.

"You're tired. Get some rest. Charge nurse orders."

Gina nodded. "We'll see you when you come back on."

"All right." I gulped and nodded and opened the bathroom door. I closed it behind me and stood in front of the mirror as I heard them leave the hall, still chatting among themselves. Then I heard one polite knock.

"I'm in here!" I said and went for the lock. Stupid day shift—

"I'm not coming in." I heard Charles's voice from the outside. "I just wanted to tell you they were wrong."

I looked at myself in the mirror—my hair was sticking out of my ponytail at improbable angles and I had sallow circles beneath both my eyes. I looked like I'd seen my own ghost, because maybe I had. Somewhere inside of me, a small part of myself had been deflated. And like a helium balloon that'd lost too much air, I couldn't kick it aloft again.

"They're wrong, Edie. Whatever the Shadows showed you or told you—they're not even human besides. They're liars. They lie. Okay?"

I nodded at myself in the mirror.

"Okay?" Charles asked again from outside.

"Yeah. Of course," I said. And then I ran the water loudly, so he couldn't question me anymore.

* * *

I sat in my parking lot after driving home, knowing that I'd been cursed with a day wind—the activities of the previous evening had wound me past exhaustion and back into wakefulness again. So I decided to pre-spend my next paycheck by going to the pawn shop and retrieving my dining room set.

I went to the place nearest my house, doubting that Jake'd bother to go much farther. I was drawn to a small chest of "fine" jewelry, before noticing a large rack of guns. Between the weapons and the smell, I decided it wasn't the kind of place you wanted to sneak up on anyone in. "Hello?"

A man lumbered out. He'd been making a deposit on his scotch belly, judging by his breath. "What're you selling?" he asked.

"I'm looking for a dining room set. A guy brought it by last week. He said I could still buy it back?"

The proprietor stared up at the ceiling for a moment, ignoring me. I followed his gaze, expecting to see a security camera, but found a diligent spider instead. "Fucking exterminator—"

"My table? And four chairs? Wood, metal, and glass?" I gestured to indicate the space they might have taken up, were they still in my possession. "Carved legs?"

"Yeah—sorry. They were nice. Sold fast," he answered, squinting at the spider like his eyes could shoot lasers.

"But—they were mine!"

"Sorry."

"But—they—" I stuttered.

"Talk to the police, file a report. I'll tell them what he looked like." The man shrugged, making his wife beater dance over his heavily furred chest.

I inhaled to protest and then sighed in defeat. *Fucking Jake* was what I wanted to say, but "Damn" came out instead. I looked around—nothing else here came near what I'd had before, either in quality or size. I'd purchased that set back in the real nursing days, before the minuscule pay-checks of Y4 began. I turned to leave, and then—my eyes spotted something familiar on the lower shelf of a grimy glass case. A CD player. Almost exactly like Shawn's. "How much is that?"

He bent with a grunt to unlock the case and fish out the plastic clamshell. "Five dollars."

I glared at him. "You sold my dining room set."

"Two fifty."

"Does it even work?"

He rolled his eyes. "Of course."

"Prove it."

"Prove it yourself," he said, shoving it across to me.

I held up empty hands. "I don't have a CD. And you *sold* my things."

"Fine, whatever." He lifted his hands and made a shov-ing motion toward me. "Take it. Go."

I drove my preternaturally awake self back to the hospi-tal, slung my badge back on, and went back up to the pedi floor. I walked through the day shift nurses without ques-tion, back to beds sixty-two and sixty-three, their rooms strangely quiet without any German.

"Hey, Shawn!" I said from the doorway. His eyes flick-ered in my direction. The day shift nurse was nowhere to be seen, but there was a professionally dressed woman sit-ting by Shawn's side of the bed.

"And you are?" she asked, her tone as sensible as her heels.

"I was his night shift nurse. His CD player got broken—I came to replace it." I lifted the dusty one out of my bag. "Who're you?" I asked, as she fished a CD out of his nightstand.

"His mother." She gave me a glare. "Don't you people ever read the chart?"

Don't you people ever wear visitor badges? I wanted to

say—and then I remembered that Shawn'd said his mother was dead. I gave him an accusing look and he forced a grin.

"You are trouble!" I told him.

"Come here—" he whispered.

I leaned over, one hand pressing my collar to my chest.

"Closer."

I got so close my ear almost touched his lip.

"What was it?" he hissed around his uncuffed trach. "Last night. What was it?"

I rocked back a bit. He wasn't *supposed* to remember anything. The Shadows were *supposed* to take care of things. Of everything. I looked down at him. "It was just a bad dream. That's all. It's taken care of, honest." His eyes were wide and earnest, and I could tell he didn't believe me. Luckily for me, no one would ever believe him.

"Well," his mother said, breaking up our moment. "I appreciate your sentiment, Nurse—" Her eyes found my badge. "Nurse Spence. But this CD player seems to be non-operational." She popped her CD out and then handed me the player.

"Oh." I took it and shook it some. "Maybe you should—" I offered it back.

"I'm getting him an MP3 player," she said, then looked away, much as the pawnshop man had. I inhaled to say more, but I knew from her expression that I'd already been dismissed.

I glanced down at Shawn, first trapped in the bed, and now trapped with his memories. "Sorry, buddy." I saluted him with the CD player in one hand, and walked out the door.

As soon as I sat down in my car, fatigue fell on me like a cloak. I put the CD player in the passenger seat beside me. For a second, I thought I saw its power button flicker on. I stared at it, entranced in my exhaustion. Hoping that it would come on was the only thing stopping me from crying.

Behind me, a car that had stalked me to my parking spot gave up on being polite and honked. I started, looked at the man gesticulating wildly behind me in my rearview, and found my ignition with my keys.

Before I could turn the engine over he honked again. And when my cold engine didn't take, he honked a third time.

"Look, guy, unless your wife is in your backseat giving birth—just give me a break, will you?" I said. I sniffled in a huge breath to hold so I wouldn't start bawling. Who could I call to get me at this time of day? Everyone I knew was busy working, or busy sleeping, I couldn't afford a tow truck, and I sure as hell didn't have Triple A. "Come on." A twist, a cough, then silence. Then, honking. "Please. Please," I implored my car, the asshole behind me, and the universe at large, turning the key one more time.

Grandfather spoke up beside me, and my engine sputtered to life. I sagged forward in relief, pressing my head onto my steering wheel. The guy behind me honked again. *"Schädel in Bechern!"* Grandfather exclaimed.

"I hope you're cursing him out in German, Grandfather." Grandfather kept talking as I reversed out of my spot. The incoming visitor zipped past me with only an inch to spare. I flipped him off and then I wound through the rest of the parking lot. When I hit the highway, I picked up the CD player and held it to my chest as it talked, letting it comfort me like a purring cat.

I scheduled myself for an STD exam when I got up that afternoon, for eight A.M. the next morning. It was embarrassing to call in to the County's own employee health clinic for that, under my real name no less, but I consoled myself with the fact that at least it was free.

I still had one night off. Instead of picking up an extra shift, I opted to go back to the club.

It wasn't the scientifically sound idea, but I had some questions that needed answers. Namely, if I'd accidentally slept with a syphilitic were-dragon. I found myself envying normal people more and more.

So I went downtown, looking plain and feeling wrung out, to make a round of the club. It was Friday and the place was packed, everyone ready to get their groove on but me. I looked everywhere but the men's restroom and was about to give up. It'd been a stupid idea to begin with. I wove for the door around the edge of the dance floor, envious of the people dancing upon it like they had no cares.

"Well, hello there," said an achingly familiar British voice from behind me. I turned.

It was him! I'd almost physically run into him. It'd have been cosmically laughable if I'd seen it on TV. As it was, I exhaled in deep relief.

"You're not a dragon!" Sure, I might have other STDs— bad Edie, impulsive Edie—but at least I could scratch were-syphilis off the list.

"Not last I checked, no." His eyebrows rose. I looked past him at the glamorous woman standing behind him. I couldn't tell if she'd come in with him or was just making time, but she seemed distinctly peeved.

"Um, anyhow, nice to see you again," I said, waving from the hip. I tried to walk backward, but found myself trapped by the crowd.

"Hey—" He reached out and caught my hand again, and again seemed surprised by the skin-on-skin contact. I could almost see the emotions flicker over his face as he tried to figure out what to say next. "I still owe you."

"What?" I pulled my hand back a little, but not much.

He took a step nearer to me, taller, the scent of vetiver

strong between us, even here. He bent his head down to put his lips by my ear. "I owe you," he enunciated, with his lovely accent, his breath warm against my skin.

"I don't know what you mean," I told him. The woman behind him, blond, lean, high-breasted—the look on her face said she was going to owe me an eye-gouging in a second, if I didn't get the hell away.

He pulled his head away from my ear, and addressed me directly. "The other night. I owe you. And I don't like having debts."

"Oh? Oh!" Light finally dawned, and I flushed red, from my head to my toes, glad for the camouflage of the club's surreal light show all around me. I'd never had a man try to cash in on an orgasm debt before.

"So, may I repay you?" he asked, a light smile playing on his lips. It became a wolfish leer that was not at all unattractive.

"Thanks, but—" I glanced over his shoulder.

He turned toward the woman. I didn't hear what he said, or see what expression he'd said it with, but almost instantly she bowed her head and melted away into the crowd. The brief noninstant part was occupied with staring daggers at me.

"I'm Edie," I said, putting out my other hand when he returned his attention to me. He released my hand and shook the other.

"I'm Asher."

"Nice to meet you, Asher." I smiled and gave a goofy curtsy. With his accent, it seemed appropriate, after all.

Asher returned with a slight bow and offered me his hand. "Dearest Edie," he said with exaggerated formality, "it will be lovely to take you home."

CHAPTER SEVENTEEN

I made sure I got *some* sleep before getting up for my employee health clinic appointment the next morning, sitting with others in the drab waiting room on a hard plastic chair. I was the only employee I recognized, and I hoped it stayed that way.

Obviously Asher hadn't been the were-dragon, and obviously a lot of things that I might have gotten from him wouldn't be testable yet, but I felt compelled to keep the appointment anyhow. It was always good to know your baseline. We'd used condoms the night before and Asher hadn't questioned me about the change.

He'd also made sure I'd been repaid. With interest. Which was nice. But really, it was one thing to go home with a girl like me on a Wednesday, and something entirely other to choose me over that woman on a Friday night. It didn't feel right. I hadn't expressed this to him, as I did have some pride that even my occasionally scrupulous honesty could not cure me of, but I'd made it clear to him that I didn't believe in an orgasm credit plan. Asher had foisted his phone number onto me regardless. The responsible nurse in me had felt compelled to take it, just in case anything came back positive today.

Trapped in the waiting room, I could see his number in my mind's eye, pinned to my fridge with a magnet. I tried

to imagine having a good reason to call, one that didn't
involve reporting test results to him, one that somehow resolved into us going on an actual date.

The door to the back office opened, and thankfully a
nurse I didn't know leaned out. "Edie Spence?" she read
from a folder in front of her.

"That's me." I stood, straightened my shirt, and followed her in.

I spent the rest of the day in bed, trying to sleep up ahead
of my night. As I hadn't gotten much sleep the night before, it should have been easy, but anytime I slept I had
nightmares about oceans, either real ones or ones made
of tarry black. And when I was awake in between dreams
I kept thinking about Asher's number, and when and/or if
I ought to call. Minnie wasn't helping—her paws seemed
to have organ-seeking powers and she paced across me
at least once an hour. Like so many afternoons/evenings
before, right after I began to feel like I was getting real
sleep at last, my alarm went off, and it was time to go in.

"You're extra help tonight," Meaty said as I walked in
the door.

"Really?" I said, surprised. "I mean—sure thing!"

Meaty grinned at me. "The action's in room four. Hold
down the fort out here, and we'll call you when we need
you."

I stood a bit taller behind the nursing station. This was
an amazing turn of events. I was being trusted with the
entire floor. You didn't get to be extra help nurse without
actually being known as helpful. Meaty was in room four
with Charles doing something—most likely talking to all
the visitors that I could see in the room from here—and
Gina was around the corner with her patients. It was just
me and the charge desk. I sat down and felt downright official.

"I'm in charge, I'm in charge," I sang to myself. "Meaty's

goooone, so I'm in charrrrge." I heard a snicker from the were-corrals. "I'm in charge of Gina tooooo," I continued, and there was an outright laugh.

There were labs to be ordered, and carts to be refilled—I tried to do whatever I remembered seeing Meaty do, industriously. This took about thirty minutes. "Need any help, Gina?" I called out, when all the carts were full.

"Not yet. Thanks!" she called back.

"Well, then." I straightened my lanyard like a tie. And then my badge began to glow.

Oh, no. I looked around.

There was a kid in the doorway of room four, staring at me like a creepy kid from any number of Japanese horror films. He had a dark suit on, cut perfectly for his four-foot-nothing form, shined shoes, and a bow tie. I waved. "Did you need something?" I asked, hopefully. He continued to stare.

A Persian woman poked her head out, luscious dark hair bound up high atop her head. She looked at the boy, then me, and then smiled.

"Gaius, she is protected, she cannot hear you." The boy stared up at her and she patted his shoulder. "Go on, tell her what you want."

He—Gaius—opened up his mouth to speak, with no sound. How long had it been since he'd had to talk? "I—I would like a glass of water," he stammered.

I grinned at him, and rose. "Ice, or no ice?"

"Ice. Please."

"No problem." I went to go get ice water, and when I came back I peeked into room four.

Room four was one of the bigger rooms, by about a ten-by-ten area—our ward was curved, and it was on the bend. There was a crowd in the room, milling quietly between several gleaming IV poles. All of them were dressed upscale casual, like they'd just stepped away from business lunches that might have taken place at a luxury golf course. All of them were also completely ignoring me. I'd have said something, about them or to them—visitors were supposed to be only two at a time—but I could hear the whoosh-click, whoosh-click of all the IV pumps strapped onto their poles running at full blast.

Overhead—dear God. We did tons of transfusions here, our patients being who they were. But I'd never seen a transfusion of such magnitude. There were twenty blood bags hanging from sky hooks on the ceiling, the pumps shuttling their contents at full speed into the patient on the bed. I couldn't see the recipient yet through the crowd but it looked serious. I knocked on the door for attention— "Should I call the doctor?"

The visitors nearest me started visibly. Meaty looked over to me from the patient's shoulder where he was starting a fresh line. "Gown up, and start more peripherals." I hopped out of the room to do as I was told, then rushed back in and pushed my way through all the people wearing Armani.

The man was already a maze of IV tubing—like a plastic spider had descended from the ceiling and started to wrap him up. Hands, forearms, elbows, jugulars, feet—I couldn't see a single place to start a line that didn't already have one going. For needing this much blood, he had to have an internal bleed, a huge one—but his stomach beneath the gown was soft to touch.

"Where?" I asked, finally giving up.

One of the men behind me started talking in a language I'd never heard before. Charles gestured to me from the head of the bed, after setting another IV pump to high flow. He made a zippering gesture across his lips, and pushed his hands out at me. I took a corresponding step back.

The patient seized. I hadn't noticed the restraints before. He was in four point, but not tethered too tightly. His hands thrashed against cuffs and his tied legs kicked in the bed, before his entire back spasmed, bowing him up before dropping back down.

The visitor who'd begun speaking continued. I looked around the room—their clothing matched one another, but not much else did. They were attractive, one and all, and some appeared Latino, or other variants of non-European. One was black, three were elderly, and the woman who'd spoken to me earlier kept a hand tight on Gaius's—the only child present—shoulder.

The man speaking had dark hair going gray at both temples and a medium complexion. His thin lips curled around each rough syllable, and the other people in the room repeated him at intervals. They all knew the routine—it felt like a call and response. Since this wasn't a political rally, I figured they must be at prayer. Who would a vampire pray to, though?

Meaty and Charles now stood by the head of the bed. The patient began writhing like he was demon-possessed. His eyes rolled back, flashing white under his lids, and he started frothing pink. Either he'd bit his own tongue while seizing, or he was having some sort of sudden left-sided heart failure. I looked over to Charles for guidance, who firmly shook his head.

The prayers rose to a fevered pitch as the blood drained in. I'd never seen blood given so fast—usually you had to watch for reactions, rejection, clotting issues. He definitely *was* reacting, his whole body thrashing, threatening to tip the whole bed frame over, but I had no clue what it meant. The bags emptied one by one, their pumps hissing to a stop before beeping complaints as the prayers rose in volume and were almost shouted, then—

Silence. Complete. Eerie. The only sound was the ragged breathing of the man on the bed. He spasmed again, sending the bed frame skittering sideways on the floor, locked wheels and all, before coming to a rest. Then the prayer leader drew a knife out from his breast pocket.

"What the—" I gasped and took a step forward. Charles shook his head violently, from side to side. *But*—I mouthed over to him, wordlessly. His head continued to shake.

The prayer leader walked forward and made a fast slice down the patient's right arm, cutting through wrist and restraint alike. He walked over to the left side of the bed, and cut it too in the exact same way. Then Charles and Meaty kicked tan plastic tubs we used for bed baths out from under the bed. Blood spattered down from the wounds into these, sounding like an old man's sputtering stream.

Was this vampire dying? A sacrifice? A ritual? It didn't matter what Charles said, or what Meaty allowed—this was insane. The blue line on the monitor for oxygen saturation went to zero. I'd already taken a step forward when I saw the patient smile.

The vampires surrounding the bed, who'd been so wordy before, were now quiet, one and all. I would say they sighed with relief, but that'd be showing too much emotion for them. They seemed . . . content. The wrist wounds began to heal themselves up, like they were going back in time—I halfway expected the restraints to float up and reseal around him. As the exiting blood began to ebb, their leader picked up the nearest basin and held it to his mouth. It was awkward, the tubs weren't meant to drink from—blood sloshed on either side of his mouth and made a double trail down his chin onto his collar, leaving dark stains down his shirt. When he was done he passed it along to the next vampire in line, who also drank with casual disregard. I stood still, stunned—and then Meaty and Charles rushed forward and put new restraints on the man.

"Edie—there's two pints left in the fridge. Go get them, will you?" Meaty asked, and began to unwrap a feeding tube. Charles was putting a second set of cuffs on the patient, on all limbs. "Edie?"

"On it!" I ran outside in my gown, unlocked the fridge, and yanked out two bags of blood. By the time I got back, the patient was seizing again. Meaty was shoving the feeding tube into the patient's nose as fast as possible, from an arm's length away. Charles took the blood from me and strung it up, then connected it to the end of the feeding tube's line.

Teeth erupted out of the patient's mouth, and he shrieked aloud, a sound like a locomotive in heat. I stepped back. "Jesus—" The visitors nearest me turned to glare. The level of blood in the hung bag visibly lowered, as the power of gravity and an ethereal hunger drew it into the patient's stomach. His teeth retracted, and he lay back again, quiescent.

The leader of the visiting group nodded at this. "The ceremony has been performed to our satisfaction." He turned toward Meaty. "As always, the Rose Throne appreciates your cooperation."

Meaty took a step away from the patient. "Thanks. We'll bill you later."

The leader snorted lightly. "We will retrieve him in three nights."

Meaty nodded, and the gore-stained country club exited the room, one by one. I waved at Gaius through the window. He tilted his head at me, my badge glowed again, and then he waved stiffly back.

Charles stood beside the bed, arms crossed, second pint at the ready.

"So what the hell was that?"

He grinned, but he didn't take his eyes off the draining original bag. "Your first vampire baby shower."

I felt my eyebrows reach an improbable height on my forehead. "Could you define that? The baby or the shower part?"

"It's like an angel earning its wings, only with more blood. Someone decided he was important enough to keep around. Forever. Lord and silver willing," Charles said, making a cross over his chest. "Get the tranquilizer gun, will you? I've put it behind the door."

I nodded, and closed the door. Sure enough, it was balanced in the corner, stock down. I picked it up and put the butt against my shoulder. The safety was off—down here, the safeties were never, ever on.

"Remember: him, not me," Charles said, gingerly taking a step forward.

I took a step closer, trying to compensate for poor aim by sheer nearness. I kept the gun trained on the vampire patient's chest.

"So all of those"—I glanced up at the ghosts of packed red blood cells above us, empty plastic bags tinged pink with the dregs of blood inside—"were vampire blood? Full vampire blood?"

"Mixed with Haldol, yeah." Charles laced up the next pint of blood. The resting patient snarled when Charles came near, but didn't otherwise react. "This guy's been a loyal daytimer for the Rose Throne for who knows how long. Somehow, doing something, he earned a full blood transfusion. We presedated, perisedated, and are postsedating him, but—" He pointed at me and indicated the gun.

"Sure." Who had a job that required mandatory time practicing at a gun range? I did. At least the County paid for ammo. I'd only been to the range twice so far. I moved to have a better view of the patient's chest. At point-blank range like this, I hoped I couldn't miss. The darts here were packed full of suxamethonium chloride and propofol—"sux" and Diprivan—two of the most powerful, fast-acting sedatives known to man. And also, apparently, vampires. I frowned. "You sure meds still work on him?"

"For now they will. By the time they don't, he'll be

fully transformed back home in a coffin at the vampire ranch."

I resisted the urge to roll my eyes. "So he's not a full vampire yet?"

"No. But he will be, once everything assimilates. It's half genetics, half brute strength. In some ways, vampirism is like a progressive disease, and in doing this, we force its hand. On his own, it could have taken decades to drink as much elder blood as we gave him, assuming there were that many willing local old ones. We bank blood for them now, for just these sorts of occasions. It's why they come here. The Shadows protect the communal supply, for the Thrones that choose to participate, and those Thrones create the demand."

"Who decides which and when?"

"The Thrones write up requisitions, they give them to our social workers, and then our doctors write orders and give them to us."

"So why this?" I asked, gesturing to the blood going into the feeding tube with the end of the gun. Holding this stance, my arms were starting to get tired.

"They wake up hungry and strong." Charles circled around the perimeter of the room. "Assuming they survive. They don't always. Sometimes we get this far, and they just can't make the jump. That's the genetic part."

"And if they don't?"

"Then they go into shock and the vampires put them down."

My lips parted, in either fascination or disgust, I wasn't sure. "How?"

Charles made a *V* with two fingers and pointed at his own mouth, where he was missing fangs. "Waste not, want not."

"Well. Wow." I was glad I hadn't seen that. I wondered what my reaction would have been if I'd walked into a room where Charles and Meaty were watching vampire guests feast on a restrained patient. I shuddered. Blood in chilled bags and capped vials was one thing—seeing it spilled out was another, and seeing other people drink it was yet a third. I remembered Anna sucking on my hand, and hoped I'd never see anything like that again. I wondered if that's why I'd seen her in my dreams, on a boat. Metaphorically, she was like a shark that'd bitten me. No wonder my subconscious was afraid of her.

"Anyhow, the rest of tonight should be easy," Charles said, pulling a full syringe out of his pocket to show me. "I've got orders on Ativan like you wouldn't believe."

I laughed, and handed him the stock of the gun. "Happy hunting."

CHAPTER EIGHTEEN

When I emerged onto the floor, Meaty was looking around the nursing station. All the shift's paperwork had been done and filed, courtesy of me, Extra Help Edie.

"Good job, Spence," Meaty said. "Go on break."

I saluted, pleased with myself, and set off.

I badged myself into our locker room/bathroom combo area. I didn't have to go to the bathroom, but anyone who didn't wash their hands before eating in a hospital was a fool. I turned on the faucet to wash my hands and face.

The sound of the water—I knew that sound. I saw it running in front of me, hot steam wafting up, but in my mind my vision of the bathroom blurred, and I saw freezing snow melt trickling down cement. I was cold, and there was no way I could get warm. Stagnation surrounded me, other things that'd washed into the gutter, rotting in the dark.

I wanted to throw up. My stomach lurched and broke the spell. I slammed the faucet off and clutched the edge of the sink. I had that sense of lostness, looking out at the ocean again, trapped by the endless nothing around me, immobilized by a fear . . . that I didn't feel was quite my own.

"Anna?" I whispered. My right hand found my left and traced along its scar. "That's silly. You know it is. You're okay," I told myself.

You don't just get to be a nurse and see sad and strange all the time and not have it affect you. I knew stress came out in different ways. I'd give any patient I ever had more leeway than I'd given my recent self. I'd been attacked and bitten less than a week ago. And I'd just seen us pour two gallons of blood, easily, into a man, and then seen ten or so vampires drink it back out. Things like that just don't come normal to people. It's okay to have some problems afterward. Nightmares, even.

I stood there wondering who exactly I was convincing with this line of thought until the strange feeling passed. When it did, I turned away. I hadn't washed my hands yet, but that's what hand sanitizer was for.

CHAPTER NINETEEN

It seemed like there was a lot more air in the locker room hallway. I stood and breathed, went for the next door, and was surprised to find visitors waiting outside.

I could only see three male faces—the fourth entity was shrouded in a robe and hood. All of them were vampires. I knew because even though we were all in the same hallway together, I felt completely alone. None of the companionship of shared humanity radiated off them, no warmth, no joy, no love—no hate or disgust or indignity either. Being near them was like being near a black hole—even without taking blood, they were lapping at the edges of the life I possessed, spinning it away.

"Um—the visitor bathroom is upstairs," I said, pointing to the elevator as the locker room door snicked shut behind me.

"We are here for Edith Spence," the one nearest to me said. He was classically beautiful, with long dark brown hair, narrow chin, and long nose. Eyes as green as grass.

No one had called me Edith since my grandma had died. "And you are?" I asked.

"Dren." He took a step closer. He was wearing a black duster cut in an old-fashioned way, narrow-waisted, calf-length. He wasn't threatening yet, but I felt he could be. The others behind him clearly were—two of them were dragging the fourth one forward by leashes made of dual silver chains. On its lanyard around my neck, my badge began to glow, stronger than I had ever see it glow before.

"Edith Spence, I presume?" he asked again, and I nodded. "You have been summoned to a tribunal. We are taking you into custody now." He watched me, waiting for a reaction. I firmed my resolve not to give him any.

"Why?" I asked, crossing my arms.

"Apparently you managed to kill a vampire," he responded, looking me up and down. "I have to admit I'm curious how you did it." There was a glint of emotion in his eyes. He looked long used to disappointment, but just then, I saw a spark of hope. Why?

The doors to Y4 thunked open. "Hey, Edie—I need help—holy shit," I heard Gina say in a rush behind me. Then she yelled, "Meaty!"

The doors didn't even have a chance to close before Meaty burst through them. "It's past visiting hours. Get out," Meaty said at once.

I wasn't sure what scared me more—the fact that the ones in the rear were jerking on the bound person's chains, or the fact that they ignored Meaty.

"She's been summoned. We're taking her into custody until the darkest night." Dren pushed his coat aside, hooking his thumb into a leather belt that held a gold sicklelike weapon, bound against his hip. His action seemed meaningful, like a cop putting a hand on a holstered gun. "If you're her friend, you will procure her legal representation immediately."

"But—" I began.

"Edie, be quiet," Meaty said, moving to stand between them and me.

Some internal meter for patience in the rear guard ran down. They were stepping forward now, making the silver chains dance like wind-ripped spiderwebs, yanking the bound one along. I decided that it wasn't a person, as it hobbled forward awkwardly, lurching from side to side, its brown robes dragging on the tile.

"As you may or may not be aware," Dren continued, for Meaty's benefit, "she's recently killed a vampire. A tribunal has been summoned on the darkest night to determine her fate."

I hadn't really thought about the vampire since I'd killed him. Or rather, any time I had thought about him, I'd done my best to try not to. I could still remember the look in his eyes . . . as they'd turned into dust and poured out of his head. My stomach churned again.

"I'm sorry," I blurted out.

Dren's eyebrows rose. "So you admit your guilt?"

"She admits nothing," Meaty said, giving me a glare. "She's a registered noncombatant."

Dren gave a soft laugh. "She lost that status when she killed a vampire." He tilted his head toward me in a genteel fashion. "Unfortunately for Miss Spence, a mere apology won't be good enough."

The other vampires were crowding closer now, and I still couldn't see the hooded thing's eyes. Fear pushed the stomach acid higher in my throat, and I tried to fight it down.

"I released a captive girl," I said, taking a step nearer to Meaty's back for strength.

"There was no captive girl," Dren said.

"Yes, there—"

"We know nothing of her," he said, cutting me off. "And if there was, how do we know you didn't kill her as well? There is only your word, which, at the moment, is not good for much."

"You cannot take a nurse," Meaty said, arms thrown wide.

"But we are." Dren stroked his sickle openly. The rear two reached out and unfurled the final one's cloak away, like splitting a cocoon.

Underneath was a creature no one should ever have to see. It had two arms and two legs, but they were misshapen—the legs nearly skeletal, leading down into feet with birdlike claws. The arms were shriveled, contracted in toward one another, meeting in front of its torso, which had the bloated shape of someone with end-stage liver cancer, distended skin stretched tight. Its head was long, like a pony's or large dog's, and at the end of its nose nostrils flared eagerly. Its skin was dark and rough—I wanted it to be reptilian, but it wasn't. Neither were the eyes set wide and high at the bridge of its nose. They were light-colored and recognizably human. It was like a creature out of a surrealistic painting, a Bosch come to life.

"What is that?" I whispered to Meaty.

"That's a Hound, and Dren's a Husker," Meaty whispered back.

Then I wanted to ask, "What's a Husker?" but the answer was obvious. One who husked things. Probably with that sickle.

The silver leashes wrapped around the creature's neck caused it pain—I could see the deep groove of scar tissue left by their passage. Its head strained forward, sniffing the air over Dren's left shoulder, and its lips pulled back to reveal rows of sharp yellow teeth. The look in the two vampire handlers' eyes begged me to run, so that this monstrous thing might chase me down.

I closed my eyes and huddled against Meaty's back. Custody sounded like something I wanted no part of. Maybe Anna'd been in "custody" too.

"If you take her, our staffing will be noncompliant, which is illegal according to the terms of our contracts with the Consortium."

Hidden behind Meaty, I blinked.

"Find another nurse," Dren said, in a voice that brooked no argument.

"We run a tight ship here, you know that. And you're

not the only supernatural group that we have legally binding contracts with. Just because the vampires are mad at Edie doesn't mean we can underserve the were or shapeshifter populations. Patient abandonment is a punishable offense—the Consortium takes it very seriously. If we lose our accreditation . . ." Meaty said without finishing the sentence.

There was a long silence, during which I could only hear the Hound's talons clacking against the tile floor as it waddled in place, trying to escape each silver band in turn. "Then we will take her when her shift is over," Dren said.

"She's scheduled solid through the end of next week," Meaty said. "It isn't like she can escape your summons. With the Hound, you've seen to that." Meaty reached back and took my hand, bringing me forward.

I couldn't meet Dren's eyes—but I could see his hand clenched tight on the hilt of his sickle. Vampires weren't used to being thwarted, especially not by anything as lowly as mandatory staffing ratios and insurance companies. I stared at his shadow instead, cast back behind him on the floor like a bloodstain, hoping that Shadows might rise out of it and save me.

"Then," he began, and there was the tension of strict control in his voice, "we will expect you on the darkest night, Miss Spence. We will summon you again and you will not refuse."

I could do nothing but nod.

"Now, get out," Meaty said, walking forward.

"You have until the darkest night," Dren repeated. The vampires behind him were yanking the Hound backward on its chains.

"Perhaps you didn't hear me. Get out, assholes." Meaty pointed toward the elevator shaft behind them. The elevator's doors opened. Dren made a mockery of a bow, and then as one, they turned and left the floor.

"Why do we even have security?" Gina said aloud as soon as we were back in Y4.

"Security can't stop them. Security probably didn't even see them," Meaty said.

"And the Shadows?" Gina asked. I was embarrassed now that I'd hoped they might save me, when it'd been so obvious in Pediatrics that they only held me in contempt.

Meaty opened up thick hands, facing their palms to the ceiling. "Not their business, really."

I stood there. I could breathe now, but my heart would not stop racing and my whole throat burned. "What do I do? What will they do to me? What the hell was that thing?"

Gina looked away. Charles's face was grim.

"You stay till Paul gets in this morning," Meaty said. "He's the social worker. He can give you some contacts—"

The rest of my brief life flashed before my eyes. "Am I running away?"

Meaty snorted. "Running from a Hound? No. You're going to court."

CHAPTER TWENTY

I tried to be helpful for the rest of the night. I really did. But the vampire parade had robbed me of some of my enthusiasm. It was hard not to be worried about the future when it seemed I had so little of it left.

I stayed strong until shift change. I couldn't leave the floor just yet—I needed to wait for the social worker, who didn't get in till eight. Plus the locker room would be full of incoming day shifters. I'd be safest if I just hid in an empty room until seven-thirty. I ducked into room five.

The blinds were drawn, and the room was black, except for the dim light of a monitor in standby mode. I walked across the room, reaching for the shelf I knew would be there, and managed to brace myself against it before I sobbed. I inhaled and exhaled deeply, breathing in the pungent mix of floor wax and something else, trying to keep from completely breaking down.

"I think I hear a ghost."

I whirled around. There was a patient in the bed. I could only see his outline now that my eyes had adjusted. "I'm sorry, I—I thought this room was empty."

"Only in a manner of speaking. I take it you're not my nurse today?"

I shook my head, wondering if he could see me. "No. I'm not—I should be going—"

"You can stay if you'd like."

If he was a daytimer, he'd have had an isolation cart outside. I wasn't in any immediate danger. "Thanks." I ran the back of my hand over my face, mopping up my tears.

"The hospital's a stressful place," he continued.

"No kidding," I muttered. But—foisting my problems on a patient wasn't appropriate. It wasn't good for them, and it definitely wasn't good for me. I took a deep breath to compose myself. "Sorry to wake you up," I said, and I made for the door.

"It's quite all right," he said, as the door closed behind me.

I changed back into my civilian clothes, brewing with anger and fear. There was a series of small rooms at the end of our floor: our break room, a broom closet, our manager's office, and the social worker's office. I paced outside his door.

Paul was my height, and cute despite nerd-thick glasses. They managed to give him a hopeful look, a useful trait in a social worker. Today he was overburdened with charts and flustered-looking. He had winter gloves on—he'd always had gloves on, all the times I'd ever seen him before. "Hello," he said, looking at me at my station in front of his door.

"Do you have a minute?"

"Only one. It's a rounds day—" He set his bags down to find the key to his door.

"I was summoned," I explained.

"Jury duty?"

"By the vampires. For a tribunal. On the darkest night."

One of his eyebrows peeked up above his glasses frame. "Oh, no." He unlocked his door, and opened it for me. "Please, come in."

I sat down in the only extra chair in the narrow room. Colored papers were stacked on every surface, making it look like a third-grade classroom, until you started reading what was printed on them—petitions for nonemergency care, DNRs, lists of were-safe house addresses. Maybe anything I ever wanted to know about Y4 was in here, if I could find it. It was a short office but at the back it took a right-hand turn and I couldn't see what lay beyond.

He sat behind his desk and hit a few desktop keys. As his computer came to life, he took his winter gloves off and replaced them with latex hospital gloves from a box beside his keyboard. He noticed me watching him. "Germs," he explained. Indeed. I nodded. "So how can I help you?" he went on.

"I was hoping you'd know. I guess I'm looking for representation." I crossed my hands in my lap and tried to look innocent and worth helping, instead of angry and exhausted. "They want to see me for a tribunal on the darkest night. I don't even know when that is."

He pointed to a calendar on the wall behind his computer. In addition to the dates, it had all the phases of the moon. "It's the first night with no moon in the sky. Vampire powers wax and wane against the cycle of the moon, the exact opposite of weres, so it's when vampires are at their strongest. Conversely, weres are fully mortal then, and easily injured, so that night they tend to hide."

That sounded familiar from the training class. At the time, everything had seemed so unreal—the flyers on being safe around vampires that I'd gotten to read, take a test on, and then hand in with the test—in retrospect it'd been a lot like going to the DMV, and not much like nursing on Y4 at all. Who could believe any of it until you'd seen it for real, anyhow?

Paul pointed at the calendar. "Technically, it's seven nights from now." He leaned forward, and touched my knee. I started at the contact. "Edie, right?"

I nodded.

"How in trouble are you?" He didn't take his hand

away. I was tempted to reach out and squeeze it even if he was a germaphobe.

"Very."

"Mind if I ask what you did to annoy them?"

"Mind if I ask if you're off the record?" I asked, because I thought I had to.

Paul took his hand back and I found that I missed the simple human contact. He crossed his arms and nodded. "Tell me things hypothetically."

"I might have killed a vampire to save a little girl. Technically there's a chance I might have been under a compulsion at the time . . . but I don't think they care about that so much." I didn't either. What was it I'd told Meaty? That I'd have done it again? Knowing this, would I have? Now?

"Well, that's clear-cut—you're allowed to kill vampires in self-defense. He shouldn't have been fighting you, you're a clear noncombatant."

"It wasn't exactly self-defense. I sort of—hypothetically—went to his home—lair? Lair." I reached and thumbed through a pile of pamphlets that turned out to be "Surviving Congestive Heart Failure" in three languages, one of which I'd never seen before. "She was there. I killed him," I said, without looking in his eyes.

"Hypothetically," he corrected.

"Hypothetically," I agreed.

"She was in danger, yes?"

"Being held against her will, and worse."

Paul shook his head. "You're still safe, then. The safety of the human outweighs the concerns of the vampires, according to the terms of the Consortium policy, at least inside County lines. You were still inside the County, weren't you?"

It beat the hell out of me. "Maybe. But she, uh . . . wasn't human."

Paul exhaled through pursed lips. "I see. Do you know where she is? Can she testify for you?"

"I have no idea. She ran off. She was in danger, I'm sure of it." I could go back to Mr. November's house as soon as I finished here. But I was sure if I knew where he lived, so did they—I couldn't expect to find any evidence supporting my side of things, and so what if I did? Dren said himself that I'd probably killed her—it was awfully hard to prove that I hadn't, without her in the flesh, undead as it may be.

"It could have been entrapment. Someone else wanted him dead, compelled you, and then things went from there," Paul suggested.

"I don't think so." I sank my head into my hands. "I think I just made another big mistake. It's got that feeling about it, you know?" Bitterness surged across my tongue and my heart was crawling up my throat. I knew what it felt like to make mistakes. I'd made tons of them before.

"Well, you still need representation, whatever the actual events."

"Can you do it?"

Paul snorted and shook his head. "I'm not qualified. But here—" He stood and walked to the back of his office and took the turn. I heard rummaging and the hum of a Xerox before he returned to me and handed me a slip of warm paper. "Call these names. Explain the situation but be circumspect till one of them swears to take the case. Make them swear explicitly—vampires love a loophole."

The paper had three names and phone numbers. All the vampire lawyers lived in better area codes than I did.

"And if none of them swear to?" I asked, folding the paper in half and putting it carefully into my pocket.

Paul smiled and shook his head again. "I've learned in my line of work that it's best to cross bridges once you come to them."

CHAPTER TWENTY-ONE

I drove home as fast as I could. I got in the door, and forced myself to clean the cat box, change my clothes, and wash my face, before sitting down with my phone.

The first number was a wrong one—the people on the other end of the line didn't seem to understand what I was asking, and when I tried to "hypothetically" explain they threatened to actually call the police.

The second had a pleasant-sounding secretary answer. "I'm sorry, Mr. Henrich's docket is full," she said, before hanging up.

I looked at the last one. "Please work." Minnie came up and rammed her head against my thigh. I dialed the last number and prayed.

It rang and rang. My stomach sank.

And then someone answered. The line went live, but with no sounds.

"Hello?" I asked.

"Do you know what time it is?" came the response.

I knew that voice. I *was* that voice. I was an idiot. Of course vampires slept during the day. "I'm sorry. I'll call back—"

"I'm already up. What do you want?" the voice said, in an unhappy tone.

"I need a lawyer. A vampire lawyer. I've been summoned to the next tribunal."

There was a pregnant pause. "The case against you is?"

"Murder."

"And you are?"

"Edie Spence."

"And the reason you've been summoned?"

"Swear to take my case, please," I said, all in one rush.

The vampire at the other end chuckled to himself. "I swear to offer you no-obligation legal advice and that everything you say to me during the course of this phone call falls under client-attorney privilege, seeing as I have not so far declined your case."

"What's that mean?"

"Let us say that for now you are my client and thus protected. I cannot promise that you will remain my client after this phone call, but the protection will remain."

"First off—if I'm up for murder, what happens if I'm convicted?"

"Your death. Perhaps worse."

I swallowed. He didn't sound like he even knew how to joke.

"Tell me everything," he continued.

I told him my story as quickly as I could—and also Paul's theory about entrapment.

"Doubtful. Still—the solution is easy. Find the girl, and have her speak on your behalf."

"I have no idea where she went." The last time I'd really seen her, she was leaping away over a dead vampire's flaming corpse. "How do you find a vampire who doesn't want to be found?"

"With difficulty."

There was a long pause, during which I was unsure what to say. "So you'll take my case?" I prompted.

"You don't have a case, unless you find the girl."

"But if I find her?"

"Then I'll represent you, yes."

"And if I don't?"

"Then it will all be rather one-sided, won't it?" He cleared his throat. "This is my personal line. Don't call it again until you know where she is."

And the phone went dead.

I turned off my cell phone, crawled into bed, and stared at the ceiling. Minnie tugged at the sheets with a paw until I let her underneath the comforter. What would become of her if I was convicted? The image of Mr. November's refrigerator was still fresh in my mind, as was the knowledge that Jake could not be trusted with her care. He'd sell her on Craigslist for weed. I sighed and she purred. What had I gotten myself into?

I tossed and turned, until Minnie gave up on sleeping next to me. This was exactly the sort of situation it would be nice to have someone around for. Not that I wanted anyone else to share my problems—and who could I tell about things, really?—but someone would be nice. I thought about Asher's phone number stuck to my fridge, got out of bed, and brought it into the bedroom with me. I toyed with the idea of calling it, before reminding myself that it was daytime. People like Asher had a normal life and a daytime job. I set it down on my nightstand and gave myself permission to call him in a day or two, maybe once I had a plan. I didn't want to need him—I didn't want to need anyone, *ever*—but I didn't really want to keep always being alone. Not when being alone was always so goddamned lonely.

I gave up and took an Ambien, God's gift to night shift workers. A thousand different things I woulda-coulda-shoulda occupied my mind for the three minutes it took to kick in, but after that, quality pharmaceuticals saved the day.

*   *   *

When I woke up it was dark. I panicked and grabbed my phone. Eight forty-two P.M. I wasn't late to work—yet. Or on trial. Stupid winter. Stupid vampires. Stupid depression making me sleep too long. I sat on my bed and stared out my window while I woke up. There was a light covering of fresh snow dusting the tops of all the cars outside, making them look like a row of worn-down teeth. I found the shape of my Chevy underneath the snow. I could put everything I owned in my car, even Minnie, and drive away now. But then there was Jake. What would happen to him if I broke my contract with County and Y4 and there was nothing keeping him a junkie-superman anymore?

I pulled up my blinds and pressed my forehead against the window, so that the chill outside could cool my fevered thoughts. I saw small footprints chasing down the side of the complex from the street, up to the front of my place and away again. I could see an instep in the prints, and a clear separation of toes. My breath fogged the glass, and I swiped it clean to stare again, as a wind struck up outside.

Could they—what was it Jake had said, about my neighbor's creepy kid? Only my neighbors didn't have a kid. Unit nine had a baby boy—but unless they were feeding him mutant growth hormones, there was no way he'd made that trail, without shoes, no less.

My phone's loudest and longest alarm went off, the absolute last "you need to get your ass out the door, now, to clock in on time" alarm. I turned it off, and ran for the bathroom to brush my teeth.

I trotted outside, coat and bag in tow, to stare at the footprints outside my door. There was a small patch of earth outside my window where dandelions grew in the summer. The wind had drifted snow into the shallow footprints, enough to make me pause and question myself. I felt sure

I'd seen them clearly. I was almost sure I had, I thought, as they completely disappeared.

"Edie?" someone said, and I whirled. I took a step backward, wishing I hadn't already locked my door. Asher was there, getting out of a warm car. He had flowers. Bright expensive tropical ones. I stood there for a moment, stunned.

"Hey there," I said, when I remembered how. He couldn't see, but I was smiling from ear to ear.

"I thought we could maybe go on a date." He held the arrangement out to me.

"I'd like that." I stepped forward into the parking lot's lights. "But I have to work tonight."

He got one good look at me, in green scrubs, my hair in a ponytail, and his flower-holding hand faltered. "I should have known," he said. The birds of paradise sank down to the level of his perfect thigh.

"Known what?" I asked. My guard, which sometime between last night and today I'd let drop, due to either sentimentality or exhaustion, rushed back to me. My smile evaporated and serious nurse Edie took over.

"What are you?" he asked.

"I'm a nurse," I said. And then I put it all together. The accent, the money, the car—the attitude. "Oh, God. You're a doctor, aren't you?" There was no one I wanted to date less in the world than a doctor. They could fake seeming human at first—medicine doctors more so than surgeons—but it never lasted. Whatever pleasant shyness they'd begun their careers with when they were your resident and needed your help was gone by the time they returned as an attending, knowing everything. I'd met a ton of older male doctors. The years of being right on most things, compounded by an interest in hearing their own voice be loudest, were like layers of nacre over a center of shit. They might look like pearls on the outside to people who'd never have to call them at three A.M. begging for an important test—but when you were a nurse you began to feel like most of them were swine.

I'd never known a doctor-nurse relationship to survive—unless one of them was a shrink, or a dentist.

"Where do you work?" he asked, as I got my keys out and edged around him.

"Look, it's okay. You don't date nurses, I don't date doctors. I get it. We're even." I opened up my Chevy's door, and threw my bags inside. "I'm going to be late, I've got to go—"

"Where do you work?" he repeated as I sat down. He caught the door before I could close it, flowers shaking in his opposite hand.

"What, County nurses not good enough for you?" I gave my door a solid yank. He fought me for a second, and then let go. I turned over my engine and I sat there for ten seconds as my car warmed up. He glared at me, then walked over to his own car, but not before I watched him throw his very expensive flowers in the snow.

CHAPTER TWENTY-TWO

I had the whole drive into work to think about ways I could have handled things better. Maybe if I'd just stopped things after that first night. Dammit. I knew better than to ride the same ride twice.

I tromped into the hospital and took the elevator down to Y4. At least being angry at Asher had stopped me from thinking about my upcoming vampire trial. Or about small childlike footprints in the snow that may, or may not, have been created by a small childlike vampire.

Only one way to know. I had to get some blood.

Most drugs are clear, their amounts so small as to have been completely diluted in the saline we give them in. Putting them into a person—you know it helps, but there's no visual. It's not satisfying.

But blood transfusions look dramatic. It's the stuff of life running in, and there's this ritual with another nurse before you hang it—unless you're running it into a vampire during a ceremony, whereupon transfusion reactions mean lunch buffet—when you recite batch numbers and blood types like a short scientific mass. Someone can die if you get it wrong. Always a thrill. Even before my time on Y4, I'd loved the process.

That night, it was my turn to hang blood. Gina did

the paperwork with me, her normal enthusiasm some-what restrained.

"You sure you're okay?" she asked, for the fourth time.

"Okay for now." I took the identifying paper off the packed red blood cells and handed it to her. "What would I be doing at home?" I knew what I'd be doing at home. Walking around my parking lot shouting, "Anna? Annnnnna!" like I was calling a lost cat. "I'm being far more useful here."

"If you say so," she said, signing out my transfusion sheet. I stuck it into the chart, with both our signatures.

I watched the blood go in as my patient watched TV and ate Jell-O. When there were just a few cc's left, I stopped the transfusion and took down the bag. Normally you ran blood in till it went almost dry, and you flushed the end in with saline, so the patient got down to the last drop. But right now I needed it slightly more than this guy did. I taped the bag shut, and when I went on break, I hid it in my bag.

I drove home that morning with the blood bag in my coat pocket. It'd been chilled since whenever it'd left its origi-nal donor—but right now, knowing I had it made it feel hot against my thigh. I'd been busy ever since I'd saved Anna, practically—I'd either been at work, as a patient or working, or been distracted with some guy. Maybe if I hadn't been so keen on getting laid, I'd have already solved my own mystery. Then again, who knew I would be called to vampire court? You couldn't *not* get laid, especially by a man like Asher, worrying about every bizarre possibility.

I'd wait up for Anna tomorrow. I put the blood bag in my refrigerator, beside my expired milk and prepackaged turkey slices.

Who was I to ever criticize Mr. November now?

CHAPTER TWENTY-THREE

That night, the hard part was sitting in the dark. Well— the hardest part had been getting to sleep that morning. After I'd woken up and the sun had fallen, I'd thrown the bag of blood outside. Its clotted contents looked like a buried autumn leaf against the tire-treaded snow.

And now I waited. I was used to staying up all night, but I usually had things to do, and bright lights to do them under. Minnie was asleep, and the sound of her soft breathing taunted me.

I didn't know if Anna would want fresh blood, if the plastic would somehow ruin the taste, if she wasn't into biohazards. I just knew that I'd stay up all night and hope for the best.

Snow drifted down like endless static on an old TV screen. I'd been lost in the chaos of it all, my body in a hibernatory trance, staring out the window. Any sign of the blood bag was long gone, as were the outlines of the cars across the lot. And then near dawn, just as I'd begun doubting my sanity, thinking that I was in some sort of perpetual waking dream, I saw her.

She moved through the snow quickly, still wearing the grimy shift I'd last seen her in. Her hydration was better now—she was still thin, but no longer hollow. Her frizzy blond hair was so light it was hard to see against the snow.

She made her way across the quiet lot, dug the bag out, and smelled it. Then she fastened her fingers at its edges and pulled it apart to lap at the frozen blood inside. She looked like a raccoon munching on a wrapper stolen from a Taco Bell Dumpster. Then she turned toward me, as I was watching her from the darkness of my room. She shoved the bag into her mouth and bolted away.

Overhead, I knew the moon I couldn't see through the clouds anymore was barely half full.

The next night, I was finally assigned the gentleman in room five. I got the report and then looked at the chart myself.

He was a zombie . . . firefighter? That was a bit odd. We'd only had two zombies on the floor while I'd been here—Mr. Smith was the second of them, and I'd never been assigned the first.

But I had a mission tonight, above and beyond mere nursing. I needed to get more blood. I walked into the darkened room, tubes in hand. If I got his blood now, I could toss it in my purse on break. The monitor was still in standby, casting a faint glow over him where he lay on the bed. I knew what smelled different about this room now; it was the scent of warm earth.

"Hello, Mr. Smith."

He smiled in the dim light. "Hello again, ghost nurse."

I snorted. "Well, neurologically, you're intact. Mind if I turn on the light?"

"Feel free."

My hand found the switch and I got my first look at a real live—dead?—zombie.

Mr. Smith was tall, stretching almost the entire length of the bed, with wide shoulders. The parts I could see of him outside of the sheets and his hospital gown—his arms, his neck, and his face—were all covered by almost-healed smooth rippling scars. Between the dark color of his skin as it was and the slightly lighter color of his skin as it healed, he looked like a dark pond on a windy day.

"I remember you," he said. His eyes were a light golden brown, and the skin around them crinkled when he smiled.

"I remember you too." I smiled back. "Thanks again—and sorry for waking you up."

"I don't really sleep." He sat up straighter in his bed.

As I walked into the room I formed my plan. I would do the blood draw last, so I could hurry away and hide. I hadn't heard about any IV sites, but I had a butterfly needle for the draw. I didn't really like poking someone unnecessarily, but it wasn't like he could get an infection and die from a needle stick now, was it? I reached for the blood pressure cuff, to start my set of vitals, and held it aloft. "Which arm?" I asked. A lot of patients with heavy scarring had a side they preferred, one which the cuff's squeezing hurt less.

Faint eyebrows rose. "I believe the previous nurse was having you on."

"How so?" I un-Velcroed the cuff.

"I don't have blood pressure." The corners of his lips quirked into a smile. "I have blood, but to the best of my knowledge, it doesn't really *go* anywhere."

"Oh." The lab tubes in my pocket felt heavy, and I felt my face flush. "Damn."

"You were . . . looking for some?" he asked, tilting his head forward.

"Actually, yes. Sorry." I frowned at myself. How was I going to get Anna to come closer tomorrow night when I was off shift again?

"I could . . . give you a finger?" He held up his right pinkie. "I don't need all of them. One won't hurt much." I blanched, and he laughed out loud. "I'm teasing. It would grow back—but I'm teasing."

I forced a grin. "Heh. Sorry."

"You apologize too much."

"Sorry—" I began instinctively.

"See?"

I rolled my eyes. He was right, but what did he know about me, and the things I had to apologize for? *He* wasn't Igor-ing around, stealing blood.

I looked around the room. He'd been here for long enough to have photos on the walls—rows of uniformed men stood in front of large red trucks. A cafeteria tray sat on the shelf on the far side of the room. I walked over and picked it up. A rime of brown-gray sauce and a gnawed portion of a bone remained. "What was dinner?"

"Long pig?" he guessed. I looked askance at him and he waved his arms in a negating fashion. "I'm not sure. I eat what they send me."

For a moment, I imagined him lumbering after me, slow-shuffling horror-movie style. He was far wittier than a movie zombie, but he was still technically undead. I lifted the tray—it had a good weight. I could hit someone over the head with it if I needed to. I turned around and kept the tray between us.

"How is it that you're a firefighter, if you want to eat people?"

"I don't want to eat everyone. I really only need flesh to regenerate. Which is why I'm here, so I can eat under qualified medical supervision."

"So this?" I asked, dipping the tray.

"I have a don't ask, don't tell, policy."

I supposed that, given the number of surgeries being performed in the hospital at any one time, and the number of people dying here—some of whose identities were unknown and some few of those who likely had no next of kin—it was possible that we did have enough extra flesh to go around, as disgusting as the thought might be.

"But why be a firefighter?"

"I'm almost indestructible. What else should I do?" He shrugged. "I get to have a well-paying job and save a few lives. I get burned a few times, heal up a few times, and then move on to a new town."

"You're the Bruce Banner of zombie firefighters?"

His lips broke into an easy grin. "A comic book fan?"

"My brother used to read them a lot." I shrugged with the tray. I didn't mention how fast he'd sold them when he'd found other pursuits.

"I only saw the movies." He jerked his chin at me. "What's the last movie you saw?

"It's, uh, been a while." Was he flirting with me? I'd only ever had patients who were detoxing flirt with me before, and they'd never been very subtle. More of a "Hey, nurse, can we fuck?" between periods of trying to run naked down the hall.

"That's too bad," he said. He was grinning even wider.

"Well!" I said, walking again toward the door. "I guess there's not much that I can do for you tonight, Mr. Smith."

"Call me Ti."

"Ti," I said, then managed to balance the tray on one hand and open the door behind me with the other. "So—just hit the call light if you need anything," I said, all in one breath. "I'll be right outside."

"All right . . ." He squinted, his eyes searching my chest for my badge. "Miss Spence."

"Call me Edie," I blurted out, and made my escape.

CHAPTER TWENTY-FOUR

"So, Gina—what's Mr. Smith's story?" I tried to sidle around to the were-corrals without anyone noticing. It wouldn't do for Charles or Meaty to hear the tone of my voice.

"Just read the chart. Wait—why are you not reading the chart?" She stopped her own charting and clicked her pen. "Ohhhhhhhhhhhh," she said, her inflection a wave. I sighed. It would be nice to someday live in a world where what I was thinking wasn't always written on my face.

Gina grinned and rocked back in her chair, suddenly all business. Girl business.

"Frequent flyer. This is the third time he's been here. He's a nice guy, I've helped out with him sometimes. He just needs a place where human is on the menu to hide out while he heals," she said and shrugged.

My stomach wanted to turn. But in comparison to everything else I'd seen or done in my nursing career so far—like, say, that I'd had stolen blood sitting in my fridge the previous night—I didn't think I could throw any culinary stones. "Anything else?" I pressed.

"Nope. Keeps to himself. I don't even know his first name." She shrugged. "Mr. Smith is one of those made-up protective names—" she said.

"At least it's not a month." A fake name meant he had a name, at least. Was Ti his real name? I hoped so.

"Anyhow," she continued, "not much else I can do for you. Half his chart's made-up data, anyhow. Meaty's going easy on you. You're going to have a slow night."

A slow night of sitting outside his room with far too long to think. My choices were obsess over a mostly unknown patient, obsess over my upcoming tribunal, or obsess over how I was going to get Anna to finally come talk to me at my house. None of those choices felt very appealing.

"Do you need any help?" I asked.

"I've got a blood draw I could use an extra hand on."

The corners of my lips drew up into almost a vampiric grin. "Then I'm your girl."

I used one wrong tube on purpose, in addition to the right tubes, and pocketed it instead of putting it into the room's biohazard bin. Gina's patient had been a nice elderly gentleman. I had a strange feeling that, once transformed, he'd make a very charming wolf.

I waited up that morning after getting home. The vial was in the parking lot between my car and my apartment. It'd still be dark for an hour, it was worth a shot. What else could I do to gain Anna's trust? Maybe I should have asked Gina for some tips on taming feral things . . .

Dawn neared. As I thought about getting my blood samples to reuse at dusk, a white figure emerged. Anna again. I sat very, very still.

She was beautiful in a wild way, like a caged cat at the zoo. Now that she was nearer, I knew she was something I only wanted to appreciate with a moat and a safety fence between us.

She found the plastic vial in the snow, cracked its lid off with her teeth, and poured its contents out onto her tongue like a rare elixir. Then she spat in the snow with her lips curled high.

"Were-blood!"

"So you can talk—" I said quietly, knowing that at this distance her vampire ears would hear me just fine.

She turned and threw the vial at my window. I flinched as it came through the metal burglar bars and bounced off the window screen into the snow.

"I'm sorry. I was trying to help."

"By poisoning me?" she asked. She had an accent—Russian for sure. She licked her tongue across the back of one arm, as if to clean it. Then she swiveled her head to stare at me, more animal than child. I blinked, and one second later, she was at my bars, her hands curling around them, peering in.

My heart pounded. The vampires and daytimers at Y4 had a thin veneer of humanity—the worst of it, yes, but some. Anna was entirely other and frightening.

"You can't come in unless I invite you," I said.

"Blood is like an invitation," she said with her accent. She pressed her forehead against the bars, and reached forward to scratch a fingernail against the flimsy screen. The sound resonated through my room.

"I need your help," I said.

"Really?" Her eyes lit up, and she laughed aloud. "Why should I help you?"

"You came here even before the blood," I said, playing my biggest—perhaps only—card. "I saw your footprints in the snow. I know you want something from me—we can trade."

Her eyes narrowed in cunning I knew no true nine-year-old possessed.

"Invite me in, then we will talk."

I tried to remember exactly what Paul'd told me about vampires and their promises. "Swear not to hurt me or my cat in any way, shape, or form. And don't compel me either."

Half of her upper lip curled in amused disgust. "I swear not to hurt you or your cat."

I nodded. "Meet you at the door," I said, and she practically disappeared.

I got up to close my bedroom window first and noticed that my wrought-iron burglar bars now had ripples in them where her hands had held them. I shivered, tried to tell myself it was just because of the cold, and turned my thermostat up as I went down the hall.

CHAPTER TWENTY-FIVE

She was so short I couldn't see her through the peephole. Steeling myself, I opened the door.

"Invite me," she said. With her dingy shift still on, she looked like something the wind had blown into my alcove, a sun-bleached trash bag, or a flurry of dirty snow. She had a faintly sour scent, like barely off milk.

"Please come in."

She tilted her head graciously. "Thank you." She stepped over my threshold with physical effort, like there was a trip wire she had to be careful not to set off. And then she was in my front hall, looking at my family pictures on the wall—which now I wished I'd had the foresight to remove—and she moved past me into my dining/living area as I followed. I had a couch, a wireless modem for my ancient laptop, a TV that only got three stations, and an end table with Grandfather's CD player on it. It hadn't talked again since I had brought it home but I couldn't bear to throw it away.

"You don't have many things."

I shrugged, even though she was looking elsewhere.

"Most humans have many things," she continued.

"Most humans don't talk to vampires."

"And live," she added, with a tone that sent a jolt down my spine.

"Remember your promise, Anna," I said.

And she turned around and looked at me curiously again. "Why do you call me that?"

I opened my mouth to respond—and then I realized that might be the only reason she was here now. "Is that what you want to know?"

"Perhaps." She licked her lips. "Tell me what you want, first."

"The vampires think I killed another vampire for no good reason—I need you to testify for me at a tribunal, to tell them your side."

She stared at me for a moment, and then laughed out loud.

"Hey—it's not funny—" I said. It was my life—my crappy and endlessly difficult life, such as it was, but still my *life!*—on the line.

"The vampires?" she said, with a mocking intonation made more cruel by her Russian accent—it sounded like I was being interrogated by a double agent in a Cold War flick. "Which ones?"

I tried to summon up more information about them, but all I could remember was Dren's name and the Hound. "They had long black coats," I offered up. I knew it was lame as I said it. "And a Hound."

"Huskers and Hounds." She rolled her eyes at me and then made her way to my couch. The cushions didn't even dent beneath her weight. "Anyone can purchase their services. There's all sorts of factions—all the Thrones, those cuckoo chick daytimers in training, pledged donors to both, ancient family allegiances." I could tell by the set of her lips that she viewed my request as absurd, and me as an idiot for asking. It was time for a different tack.

"Look, I saved your life—"

"You did not *save* my life. I was in no danger of dying."

My hands curled into fists of frustration. "You didn't

really seem in any danger of being freed, though, now, did you?"

And faster than I could see, she lunged at me, standing toe to toe, staring defiantly upward. I gulped. How foolish I'd been to think that a mere promise would hold a creature like this, but I pressed on. "Will you help me or not? Because if you won't, I need to start opening new credit cards and figuring out where to spend the few remaining days of my life on vacation."

She inhaled and exhaled deeply. From so near I could smell her sweet-sour scent again, and the soporific chemicals that comprised her breath. "How do you know my name?" she asked.

"An older man at the hospital. He told me to save you," I said, taking a step backward, finding myself against the wall. "He wrote down your name."

"Who?"

The name Mr. November would mean nothing to her, of course. My hands clenched into distracted fists, until I remembered the photo that'd sent me on my quest. "I think I have something you'll recognize. Wait here."

I went back into my bedroom and into my closet. I'd kept the pocket watch and the sepia photo it held—making my next student loan payment in a timely fashion ranked under "live through the next week" on my current to-do list.

What was I going to tell her when I gave it to her? "Hi, I'm sorry I killed your friend and/or relative?" Promise or no promise, there was no way she was going to help me after that, and then where would I be? Dead or worse. I sat on the ground beside my bed, and Minnie peeked out. "Stay under there. There's no way this can go well," I told her. Then I heard German begin in the living room.

"What kind of parlor trick is this?" she said, waving the CD player as I came out. Its light was warning yellow.

"That's Grandfather," I said, as she mashed the buttons on the player. She flung it across the room and it hit the far wall. "Don't do that!" I said, running after it.

"I didn't promise to not hurt your things. A pity you have so few." She sat on my couch again.

German continued to rise from the now red-lit player, despite the fact that the cover was clearly askew.

"He killed a dragon once." I picked it up and held it. It silenced in my hands as I forced the broken lid closed. "Do you want to know or not?"

Anna crossed her arms. I dropped the watch and photo into her lap.

She stared at the photo while she rubbed the pocket watch with her thumb.

If I hadn't had Grandfather to hold, the silence would have been intolerable. It was obvious that she was deep in thought, and if we'd been on Y4, I would have excused myself out of her room. Trapped in my own living room, though, I kept my hands busy by stroking the CD player's plastic case and consciously making an effort not to speak.

"We came to the New World together. My brother, my uncle, and I. And then I was separated," she began, just when I thought my resolve would break. She set the watch in the lap of her skirt, and began doing something to the small photograph with her short nails that I could hear but I couldn't see.

"By boat?" I asked, remembering my dream.

"How else?" She curled a lip at me, then returned to her task. "I was young then."

As she concentrated, I glimpsed her looking a real nine, damaged and frail. She stared into the middle distance, hands working at the photo, stirring memories inside her mind.

"He was trying to find you, you know," I said, because it seemed right to say.

"He told you that?" she asked. Her hands stopped.

"In a manner of speaking." I rocked down to sit cross-legged in front of her, holding the CD player in my lap. Its yellow light illuminated us both. "Would you like to hear the story?"

She nodded very slowly. So I began.

CHAPTER TWENTY-SIX

People who can't tell stories well don't make very good nurses. There's a causality between what happened yesterday to patients and what needs to happen tomorrow that people who aren't storytellers don't understand. I hadn't decided exactly what to say yet, but I knew enough to start at the beginning that she needed to hear.

"He was very old and very sick. He was found collapsed in the street, with two vials of holy water in his pockets. We took care of him as best we could, but he wanted out to find you. He wrote your name to me on a board I gave him, so I could finish the job."

She nodded, her gaze studious.

"And then he pulled his breathing tube out." The moment of truth. "It happened . . . while I wasn't paying attention. The breathing machine was the only thing keeping him alive." I braced.

Anna stared at me, her eyes narrowing to slits. "You killed him."

"Yes." Adding anything else would sound like I was making excuses, when really, there were none. There were mitigating factors surrounding the second vampire's death—Anna being one—but as far as Mr. November's death was concerned, his blood was clearly on my hands.

Her lips drew into a thin line, and a silence passed between us. Perhaps she was regretting her promise to not injure me. "Mere writing cannot compel," she eventually said. "And he was a servant, not a Zver."

"I don't know what a Zver is."

"Pray you never learn."

I waited for her to explain. When she didn't, I continued. "I don't think I was compelled. I just wanted to give his watch back to someone who knew him. To tell them I was sorry for what I'd done. When I went back to his address here," I said, reaching forward to turn the photograph over in her hand without touching her, "I saw your file. I knew what I had to do."

"Saw my—file?"

"Pictures," I said, and left it at that.

She recoiled, then regained composure so quickly I thought maybe it had been a trick of the light. "He knew?" she asked. "Of course he knew. My uncle was always faithful. He must have tried." She stroked the photo again. "I wonder if his impotency ate away at him, as they ate away at me." Her tongue played across her lips as she thought. "I always meant to kill them myself," she said, and I believed her.

"Why didn't you?"

"They starved me." She looked down at herself, at the photo she held. "Things have changed much since they captured me. Since I last saw the sky. I never knew where we were. We were moved from place to place—from pit to pit. Feeding the Tyeni with our sorrows. Even if I had escaped—perhaps even if he had saved me—there was no way they wouldn't come after me. I am not just a vampire. I am—" she began, then looked at me like she'd said too much. She shook her head. "You wouldn't understand. I'm not meant to be merely nine, with the body of a child." Small ripping sounds began again.

I thought I saw in her activity the industriousness of distraction, trying to hide from some part of her past.

"You're not the one to blame, Anna." I reached out and put my hand on her leg. She started like a disturbed cat, and I pulled my hand away.

"You are a strange human. Brave and stupid at once." She looked at me curiously, wrinkling her nose.

"Thanks, I guess."

She finished what she was doing, and stared at the photo anew, stroking it with her forefinger, before flicking something else off her palm. Then she addressed me. "Dawn comes. I need to sleep. But when it is night again—take me to where he lived. I want to see it."

I nodded. I should have bargained with her for her help at the tribunal—to seal the deal, as they say. But I'd just found out she'd been abused since she really was nine, at some point in the distant past. Pushing her didn't feel conscionable. "Let me get you something to sleep in."

I gave her old scrubs of mine, repurposed into pajamas a long time ago, and gave her an extra comforter. She wandered around my house like a bold burglar, inspecting closets, opening the oven door.

"How light-tight does it need to be?" I asked.

"Very," she said, with a frown.

"Where've you been up until now?"

Her eyes narrowed, and she didn't answer. If it had to be that dark, and from the smell of her now that she was near, my guess was underground. A sewer. "Hey—"

"Yes?" she asked archly.

Somehow, telling her I thought I'd seen her in a dream didn't sound like a good idea. Surely everything would be better in the morning, and by morning I meant after six in the afternoon.

"Never mind." I opened up my bedroom closet. "In the back there is probably safe. I can tape up the doors once you're in."

Before settling herself in, she shoved out all of my

shoes. I waited till she was done, closed the door, and ran a seal of duct tape around its edge. Then I tossed an extra sheet over my bedroom blinds for good measure and sat on my bed, exhausted.

Minnie reappeared, crawling out from under my bed. "Meow," she said, sitting on her rump, staring at me cross-eyed. "Meeeeeeow." It was clear she disapproved. Grandfather chimed in from the living room with a few German exclamations. I went out to retrieve him.

"I know." I picked him up, and sat down on my couch. "But what else could I do?"

Grandfather had a lot of vehement suggestions, it sounded like. But I didn't have a translator on speed dial here, and really, it'd felt like I'd done the right thing. Then again, how many times had that led me into disappointment? I sat there for a bit, thinking on this, when a tan dot resolved out of the rest of my slightly more tan carpet. I reached for it and almost lost it in my carpet's low pile before pulling it out.

If I hadn't seen it before, I wouldn't have been able to recognize it; I would have placed it as a forgotten shred of newspaper or a flattened crumb of bread. But it was a tiny sepia face, the face of the brother—well, I didn't know that for sure—but definitely the face of the boy who'd been sitting by Anna in her photo. Carefully torn out and discarded, by Anna herself.

I felt slightly less good about things than I had before and I took Grandfather back into the bedroom with me.

CHAPTER TWENTY-SEVEN

I woke with a start to the sound of ripping. The room was dark and there was a monster in my closet.

I jumped out of bed as she emerged. The closet doors were flung open, wheels rattling in their sliding tracks. Clean clothing hadn't done much to dissipate her smell. How do you tell a vampire to take a bath?

Once free of my closet, she turned and kicked its door, leaving a hole in the cheap particle board.

"Hey!" I reached for the rattling door. "That wasn't necessary."

She turned on me. "Take me to his home. Now."

I needed a shower. And she really needed a shower. But the sooner I got her to Mr. November's place, the sooner she'd help me, the sooner she'd be out of my life—which she seemed set on destroying, one article of furniture at a time.

I waved my hands placatingly in the air. "Let me get dressed."

"Hurry," she said, and turned around.

As I rummaged for jeans behind her, I realized I hadn't thought to steal blood ahead of time for the future, nor was I keen on offering up mine or my cat's. "Hey, how have you been feeding?" I asked.

"On the homeless." Anna sighed. "They taste like booze—it helps to mask their other flaws."

I pulled my shirt over my head. "Ugh."

She chuckled. "Don't worry. I haven't killed any of them yet."

"Are you going to need blood tonight?"

"I can go longer than most vampires. I am used to dealing with less."

Phew. It was one thing to go off on a crazy goose chase, and another to aid and abet an attack on somebody else. I nodded and reached into my closet to find my old coat, the one she'd helped me to ruin, what with all the blood.

"You might remember this article of clothing," I said, handing it over for her to wear. Her affect was flat, the way certain schizophrenic people's were. No life, just a dead stare, the kind I thought the phrase "thousand-yard stare" referred to in books. Only the people who wore it at the hospital weren't survivors from back in 'Nam—they were surviving whatever personal story was playing out all the time inside their own minds.

"I don't feel the weather as you do, human."

I shook the coat. "We're taking public transportation. I can't take you in what you're wearing. You'll make a scene."

She grabbed it from me, and sniffed the collar. "It smells."

You're one to talk, I thought as she put it on. "Sorry." I reached over and flipped the hood up over her head. The clock on my bedstand said six-thirty. "Is it night now?"

She nodded, though the hood itself did not move. "I am awake," she said, as if that was answer enough.

I imagined her, my only witness, catching on fire or turning to stone or whatever else it was that full vampires did underneath the glare of sun. And then I shrugged that off and helped her put on three pairs of my socks so my old rain boots would fit. Last but not least came gloves. By the time I was done stuffing and layering she looked like a very unhappy Michelin man.

"Are you done yet?" she asked, as I zipped myself up in my remaining winter clothes.

All the ways this was a bad idea were like an echoing Greek chorus in my mind. *I'll die, she'll die, we'll all die*— I shook my head to clear it. "Let's go."

The main commuter rush home had finished, but there were still people waiting for the southbound train at the station. When it arrived and the doors opened, I walked in and Anna followed hesitantly—did the rules of invitations apply to public transportation?—and when she was done we sat together on a bench.

She stared around at the train itself, from the gum stains on the floor to the maps with multicolored tangles near the ceilings. Her gaze lingered on a poster featuring a nearly naked woman selling watches, with one hand cast out protectively, and her entire other arm covered in watches across her chest. Anna touched this image like she expected the hair to be hair, the skin to be skin, and the schnozberries to be schnozberries. I watched her, while everyone else studiously ignored her in the way only other commuters can, before she came to sit beside me again.

"Was Mr. November your uncle?" I asked. She glanced up at me, her eyes still shaded by the hood.

"His name was Yuri." She went back to looking resolutely at the seat ahead of us.

I fully expected that to be the end of our conversation, but then she continued in her lisping accent. "We were a family of Dnevnoi, the loyal ones. As is our custom, the first child, when it was time, was pledged to our Throne. They would drink the blood, and become one of the Zverskiye. The second child was sacrificed to the Tyeni." She closed her eyes. "I was the first child. Koschei was the second."

Silence passed between us as the train stopped and people milled about. When it left the station, she continued.

"My parents wanted differently for us. When the revolution began, they thought we were both saved—factions in the Zverskiye were fighting as brutally as the Socialists and the Marxists were for control. In the confusion, they sent us off with Uncle Yuri to the New World to escape our respective fates." She crossed her arms over her chest, as though she was fighting off a chill.

"When we arrived it did not take long for them to find us. In America, there were no factions, only Zver. And for them to let any Dnevnoi escape, well. . . ." Her voice drifted off.

We were two stops from where we needed to get off, and I wanted to know the ending. "Then what?"

"Then we were captured, separated, and I was fed to the Tyeni regardless."

"But—" I'd seen most of her while helping her change. She had all her limbs, fingers, toes. Unless they'd taken a lung or a kidney, I wasn't sure what she'd lost.

"Not all feeding requires teeth. And not all bites leave scars," she said cryptically.

"What does that even mean?" I asked her.

"I would prefer not to talk about it."

The train shuddered to a stop and a man got onto the train and walked down the aisle to purposefully sit across from us. He looked both of us over and leered. Anna hissed at him, under her breath, and he suddenly decided that seats nearer the other exit were better for him instead.

"How did you do that?" I asked her.

"Easily," she said, and no more.

The train released us into the station and we walked up to face the cold evening outside.

We waddled down the street together toward the complex where Mr. November had lived. "What was his full name?" I asked. It might help when talking to the land-lady again, assuming he'd used it.

"Yuri Arsov," she said, trundling along beside me. The clothing had muted her feline grace, but she was still scanning back and forth across the street inside the confines of her hood.

Slow giant flakes fell from the sky. Some other time, some other place, the girl who walked beside me might have played outside of czarist mansions, throwing snow-balls at daytimer children beneath the safety of the night.

We reached the complex and I rang the bell. Explaining our reasoning to the landlady this time around would be a treat, unless Anna could do that hissy thing at her.

I rang again. There was no response.

"She's very old," I apologized. I tried the door and it was open. It dawned on me— "Anna, I don't think this is safe."

"Where was he?" she asked, looking up at me. Her eyes were like burning coals inside the shadow of the hood. "Which floor? Which room?"

For a second she stared at me harder—through me, almost—and then she was gone, bolting up the stairs, faster than I could possibly follow.

I chased up after her. "Anna? Anna—wait!" Had she read my mind? Idiotically, I'd left my badge, with whatever protective qualities it possessed, at home.

When I reached the topmost floor, Mr. November's door was open, and Anna already inside.

"I knew I'd remember his smell."

I shut his door behind me. She was in his hall closet, standing on his sleeping bag, her face buried in his shirts. Then she began yanking them down one by one, before handing them to me. "Take these."

"What the—" I began. She stalked down the hall into the bedroom without me. "Anna, no—"

In Mr. November's bedroom, the girls were still waiting for us.

CHAPTER TWENTY-EIGHT

I'd given up on asking a lot of questions since my time as a nurse on Y4: Where do vampires come from? What happens to a werewolf's clothing? Why are some zombies seemingly Haitian, and others typical movie-style ghouls?

But certain things I'd never give up on wondering about. They were the things that I knew if I stopped thinking on them it'd mean I was finally dead inside, that working with patients on Y4 had, one way or another, finally drained me dry.

The depths of man's inhumanity to other men—or women, or children, or yes, even vampires to other vampires—was one of these topics. It was illustrated on the walls here, to a horrifying extent. If I ever saw things like these and managed to be quiet inside—it would mean County had won.

Anna stalked around the room, barely glancing at the walls. She kicked over the files, spilling out sheaves of photographs upon the floor, walking across them without looking down. Finally, she returned to me.

"Leave so I may burn this place."

I shook my head. "No."

"Burn it!" she said.

"You can't—there are other people living in this building."

"Burn it all down to the ground!" she shouted. "Let their blood be a sacrifice to Yuri's memory!"

I'd only sworn her to my personal safety—I realized now I should have expanded her promise to cover all of the inhabitants inside County lines. What exactly was she? In freeing her, what had I inadvertently set loose?

"Anna, please—" I reached for her shoulder before she could do anything stupid. She whirled beneath me and held me in place with those emberlike eyes. Flames leaped inside my mind, hot and high. "Stop it, Anna."

She didn't. The heat increased. And instead of it making me want to run away, like a deer from a forest fire, she wanted me to turn toward it, to go closer. Where was gasoline? Where were matches? This place would be so much better if it were cauterized entirely, ablated like a cancerous spot. Surely this place above all places needed to be excised—and I was a nurse, I knew all about excisions. The flames glittered in my mind like an oncoming migraine, as her will sledgehammered through my brain.

"Stop it!" I clutched my hands to my head, dropping the shirts in a pile. "Stop it right now! You promised!"

The urge to burn things subsided, but didn't quiet entirely. "Look—we'll tell the police about things. And then they'll handle it. There's good evidence here—they can make other arrests."

She kicked a stack of photos, sending them fluttering through the air. "They can arrest the servants? And full vampires? What good can your human courts do, when they did not even save me?" she sputtered. She was breathing hard. I didn't think vampires needed to breathe. But if her huffing and puffing could have blown all the girls down, it would have. She whirled around, with her arms held up, addressing the room at large.

"Why—why did he save them, and not me?" she howled, pointing at the walls. And then she fell to all fours in the middle of the room, creasing the photos there with her knees and fisted hands. All the other lost little girls stared down at her, at the last little girl found.

I knelt beside her. "He was trying to, Anna. You were on his mind—he said your name with his dying breath."

She grabbed one of the shirts I held and savagely rubbed her eyes with the sleeve. "It should have been him to find me! Not you—him!"

"I know." I reached out a hand—if she'd been any other human in the world, I would have hugged her just then, but I was scared to. But then she sobbed, a gut-wrenching sound. I'd made noises like that before; I knew what they felt like, what they meant, from the bottom of my heart. I dropped the shirts and wrapped my arms around her before I could talk myself out of it.

She went stiff and quiet, and just when I thought I'd horribly overstepped myself and ruined everything—she collapsed against me and cried, deep and hard, squeezing me tight. I was glad for each and every layer I'd put on under my coat and I prayed for my ribs to hold. I hugged her back until she released me, rocking back and turning away from me to blot at her eyes again with Yuri's sleeves.

"You are a foolish human. A greater fool than any I have met before. Yuri would have approved of you." She unzipped her jacket and stuffed several of Yuri's shirts into it. Then she wiped her nose with the back of one hand, and picked up the final shirt, the one she'd cried upon, and held it out to me. "I will help you."

I took the shirt as though I was shaking her hand. "Thank you."

"You are welcome," she said solemnly, and left the room. I shoved the shirt in my coat pocket and followed.

We walked down the stairs together. It was quiet except for the echoing sound of our steps. It wasn't usual for places like this to be so quiet. Surely someone here slept with the TV on—and surely these walls were so poorly insulated that we ought to be able to hear it.

"Do you hear that?" Anna asked, just as I'd been making sure I'd heard nothing at all. She fell to a crouch and shot down the stairs.

"Wait!" I shouted, and ran down after her.

A group of ten men met us in the street, their black stockbroker-style suits casting stark outlines against the snow. They didn't need snow gear—they wouldn't feel the cold, nor would they care if anyone saw them. They were all alike, vampires or daytimers.

"Help!" I shouted. "Someone—help!" I knew this wasn't the kind of neighborhood that worked in. No one knew us, it was none of their business, and I was sure one of the vampires here would be able to bend human attention away like so many of them could. Still— "Call 911!"

One of the men advanced.

"I'm a noncombatant! She's under my protection!" I addressed him, putting myself in front of Anna. I didn't have my badge on me, but—

She raced around me, up the street, peeling off layers of clothing. She ran three steps at a time up a stoop and then launched herself horizontally at a suited man who clearly wasn't ready.

Maybe they were so used to thinking of her as weak that they were unprepared. Or maybe she'd gotten better faster than they could have imagined. She flew by the outlier, one hand out, and snatched half his neck from him as she passed. His head lolled to one side, clearly showing the stub of his spine before dust started pouring out of the hole she'd left.

The next one was even faster—guts strewn for an instant, and then many soft popping sounds, as he turned into a suit full of dust.

There were so many of them, and she was awesomely

fast—I wondered again what she was. I'd never seen a vampire in action—maybe they were all like this? As she dispatched one after another, I realized I was seeing what she was doing now. She was slowing down. Whatever superstrength homeless blood, a half-empty blood bag, and a century's worth of rage had given her was waning. Eventually one of them fought back and tossed her on her rear into the snow. I ran forward to where she'd fallen, but she wasn't there anymore—he'd kicked her like a soccer ball up into the streetlight on the curb. She'd dented its base and recovered, but then five of them were on her.

"Please help! Someone help!" I shouted, and I ran forward, trying to pull the last of them off. He swatted me aside. I fell on my ass in the snow.

He could have killed me—any of them could have. But I didn't matter to them—why should I, when without her at the tribunal, I was already dead without consequence, and for whatever purposes they wanted me?

A car arrived and their tide shifted course, drawing her toward its opening door. I saw into the backseat—and a face I recognized looked out at me. Stone-gray eyes and, when he saw me, a mocking grin. The vampire who'd first held Anna captive was there for half a second before he pulled back into the darkness of the car like a trap-door spider. The remaining suits shoved Anna in. The car drove away and those who lived dispersed, running to the ends of the earth like so many ninjas on a late-night cartoon.

I stood up, knocked the ice off my rear, and looked around. Not a single window had opened on the street, not a single blind or curtain was raised, and there were no sirens in the distance. No one had noticed our altercation at all.

The dented street lamp looked like any other street lamp that'd met a buzzed driver. The vampire dust looked like soot in the snow. Yuri's shirts were dark where they'd absorbed the melting snow, watermarks spreading out like blood. And I was alone, again. I shoved the last shirt, the one Anna had given me, deeper into my pocket, and walked as fast as I could back to the train station.

CHAPTER TWENTY-NINE

What would I do now? Where would I go? Where had they taken her? I was sore, I was cold, and I was royally pissed off. The clouds hid the moon from me, but I didn't need to see it to know my time was winding down. I sat on a different train with the same watch advertisement, only this time someone'd drawn a cock by her mouth. The graffiti matched my sentiment. I'd been dicked over. Worse yet, Anna'd been dicked over. God, to get free after a hundred years, only to be trapped again? How horrible was that? I shuddered inside my jacket, even as I began to sweat. I stared at the advertisement, and felt like if I looked at the watch faces closely enough, I could see the remaining time in my life tick away.

A group of young men loaded on. It was technically late at night. I pretended to ignore them while paying attention out of the corner of my eye. They were busy discussing something exciting among themselves, and I tried to be charitable and think they were high-spirited instead of dangerous.

One of them spotted me, and broke from their pack. He came over, and I stiffened.

"Miss?" I didn't respond. My mouth was dry. "Yo, miss?" he said, waving a hand in front of my face.

I glared up at him. "What do you want?" I said, in a voice that encouraged no further interaction.

"You're bleeding," he said, pointing at my lap. "Are you okay?"

I looked down, and saw Yuri's shirt, with blood on the cuff where Anna had wiped her eyes. And his hand shifted, to point at my coat shoulder, where there was even more blood—from when we'd hugged, I guessed. I stared at my shoulder in disbelief for a moment, before looking up at the man whom I'd erroneously judged. Someone's mother, somewhere, had raised them right.

"It's all right. It's not mine."

His eyebrows rose, but he nodded and sidestepped back to his friends. I got off at the next stop.

I trudged the rest of the way home, with Anna's bloodlike tears, or tearlike blood, on my shoulder and on Yuri's cuff. What was happening to Anna now? What were they doing to her? I couldn't leave her like that. I just couldn't.

I went inside my house and found the lawyer's number. He'd said not to call back if I hadn't found her—but I had, then I'd lost her again, and someone had to help.

The phone rang four times. I expected voice mail soon—maybe vampires had caller ID. It was night at least, just before two A.M. I paced around inside my kitchen as it rang again. Who else could I call afterward?

"Hello," said the voice I remembered. It sounded like it was going to go into a voice mail message after all, the tone was so formal and low—but there was a pause. "Hello?"

"You're awake!" I exclaimed in relief.

"Of course."

"It's Edie Spence. We spoke the other day, about the murder and the girl."

There was a pause. "Go on."

"I found her." Then I stopped and thought about what

next to say. How could I sum up the events of the night and not sound insane?

"But?" the anonymous voice on the other end of the line asked archly.

"She was kidnapped."

"Really." His inflection on the word rose and fell in ironic disbelief.

"Really. She swore she'd help me before that . . . but . . ." I stood in front of my refrigerator, staring at its ivory-colored door, as blank as my mind of good sense.

"You tell the most interesting tales, Miss Spence."

"It's not a story." I leaned forward and rested my forehead on the door. The cheap metal dimpled inward, with a thunk. "She needs our help, they took her away—you don't understand."

"She promised you she'd be there?"

"She did."

"Well, then." I heard papers shuffling in the background. "My appointment book is already full until dawn tonight. But I may have time to see you early tomorrow, before sunrise."

"You—you're taking my case?"

"If she swore she'd be there she'll try."

"You . . . believe me?" I stood up straight, and my fridge door popped back into place.

"I'm your lawyer. It doesn't matter what I believe. What matters is that she wouldn't have sworn it if she hadn't intended to help you. Unlike humans, vampires are creatures of their word."

I rolled my eyes. "I get off at seven-thirty tomorrow morning—"

"Eight A.M., then." He started spouting off an address, which I wrote quickly down. "Be on time."

"You'll help me save her, right?"

The voice on the other end of the line paused. "You

should worry about your own fate first, Miss Spence. Eight tomorrow," he said, and the line went dead.

I leaned back against my cheap fridge again, and again felt it buckle behind me. Worry about my own fate first—but how could I live with myself while knowing about Anna's?

The address the lawyer'd given me was off the public transport routes, so I drove to work that night. It was unfair that I had to keep going to work with all my personal drama. But I didn't have much time off saved, and every time I called in, I was worried I'd be fired without cause—it wasn't like Y4 nurses had a union to protect us. With my luck, I'd be fired just as Jake was shooting up the eight ball to end all eight balls, and then what would happen to him? He'd find out he wasn't superman and that he could still get high five seconds before his happy heart stopped cold.

Besides, what would I be doing at home, anyhow? Doing my depressed-oversleeping thing? Or eating everything I had in my fridge because it was there? Worrying about resaving Anna? Pacing around, listening to Merle Haggard, like Dad always did?

I pulled my Chevy into the empty visitor's lot and pulled on the parking brake. No, being at work would be better than all of those. I hoped.

I had both of Maganda's patients. I always felt good about following her—she was tiny, Filipino, and full of energy. If there'd been anything pressing that needed to be done, she would have done it already. She reminded me of the nurses at my last job.

"Mr. Smith, you know him?" she asked.

"Had him the other night."

She nodded, making her gold earrings jingle. "No change!" She passed the chart over to me to co-sign.

"And him?" I asked about room four, as I finished my nearly illegible "Spence, RN."

"Not so good. Out of the woods now, but this afternoon? Full of trees." She laughed at her idiom, and I grinned along with her.

"So, room four came up this morning with massive blood loss. At first, they thought he was just hypothermic, or hyper-ETOH, you know? But his hematocrit came back very low. Turns out he had no blood—and bite marks. He came down here, and we've been transfusing him all afternoon. Three units of packed red blood cells so far, and then I sent off a crit. Waiting on the results right now."

I nodded. I could wait for test results. And I could hang more blood if his crit came back low again. Easy-peasy. "How'd he get like that, though?"

"Don't know." She handed over the chart, and I signed it.

"Was he a donor before?" I asked, looking past her into the room, where the dregs of a blood bag were running into the patient's antecubital IV line.

She took the chart back and closed it. "Doesn't matter—he is one now."

I nodded and waited for her to walk away before flipping through the charts. As curious as I was to see Ti again—and I wasn't sure why, I just was—I knew the fresh donor needed my attention first.

His initial ED report included this gem: "status/post rabid cat attack." *Really?* That was the best cover we could use? I wrote down all the meds he needed, tucked my paper in my pocket, suited up on principle, and entered the room.

"Hello there, Mr. Galeman," I said, smiling by the foot of the bed. Mr. Galeman's chart said he was only forty, but a lifetime of sun had made his skin creased and tan, and he looked nearer to sixty to me. Not the kind of man you'd think a vampire'd have much cause to run into. But his neck had a pressure dressing taped thickly on it all the same.

"Howdy," he responded, and then reached up to thump the yellow IV "banana bag" hanging over the head of his bed. "I don't suppose this is beer?"

"Vitamins, not Thunderbird. Sorry, Mr. Galeman." I took the stethoscope off its hanger. "I'm going to listen to your lungs now—"

"Please." He flipped the sheets off his bed, revealing a barrel torso with scrawny legs beneath. I saw a plastic comb tucked into his sock, and bit my lip. He'd either been in prison or homeless. Maybe both. Only time spent without notable possessions or reliable pockets led to sock-carrying items. But he was too tan to have done time recently anywhere in our frigid state.

"Where do you live, Mr. Galeman?"

"Everyone calls me Gale," he said, closing his eyes and leaning back into his bed as I pressed the stethoscope to his chest. I listened to him breathe, raspy and wet, the sound of years of smoking mixed with inclement weather.

"Where do they call you that?" I asked when I was through.

"At the Armory."

I knew about the Armory. It was Jake's home away from home. "Did someone tell you what happened to you?"

"Yeah. A rabid cat got me." He shook his head in disbelief.

I feigned astonishment. "Really? Did you see it?"

"Well, it looked like a little girl. A cold little girl."

I bit my lip to keep from showing any expression, and he continued, his voice slightly slurred. "But I drink a lot, sometimes. I hit Wally over the head one night, I thought he was a demon, and when I woke up, he weren't one. So it must have been a cat that looked like a little girl." He shrugged, as if this sort of thing happened often. Even without the Shadows interfering, as I was sure they'd do if we released him, he'd eventually think it was a cat. It would be just another example of the enormously bad luck (though it'd have nothing to do with the booze, of course not, not that, just like for Jake his fall never had anything, ever, to do with his heroin) he'd had his entire life that'd brought him to this state.

He'd never believe it was a nearly hundred-year-old, but nine-year-old-looking, vampire.

I finished my assessment with polite detachment, feeling for pulses, inspecting IV sites for signs of infiltration. Sweat beaded on his forehead and he wiped it away with one hand before shivering.

"Want some warm blankets?" I asked, not wanting to get into the classic signs of alcohol withdrawal with him. He was already getting sixty milligrams of Valium every six hours. Nothing else I could do.

"Sounds good," he said, and nodded.

I retrieved a stack of warm blankets and returned. "You ain't got nothing to drink here?" he asked as I unfurled them. "Nothing at all?"

I shook my head. If they'd given him a choice between death due to blood loss on the street versus being here with no booze . . . I could guess which one he'd have actually picked. Or at least which choice he'd be picking two days from now. "Not a drop, Mr. Galeman, not a drop."

"Hmph." His left and IV-less hand found the pressure dressing at his neck. "Sure was a pretty cat, though."

I kept a compassionate smile pasted firmly on my face. "I'm sure it was."

I backed out of the room and waved at Meaty. "Bathroom break!"

Meaty nodded, and I made my escape from the floor to the locker room, hauling my phone out from my purse and dialing Jake as soon as the locker door closed behind me.

"Pick up, pick up, pick up . . ." Sure, Y4 could protect

my brother from the ravages of heroin. But what if he was bleeding out in a gutter somewhere?

The dial tone stuttered, and I expected a disconnect—cell phone signals wherever Y4 was was spotty—then heard "Yahlo?" from a sleep-filled voice.

"Jake?" I blurted. "You okay?"

"Sissy? Sissy—Jesus, Sissy, yes, I'm fine."

"Really?" I asked. What else could I ask him? Check yourself for puncture marks, you sure no one's bitten you lately? Seen any rabid cats?

"Sissy—what time is it?—of course I'm fine." I could hear him waking up as he spoke, and his voice dropped to a whisper. "Everyone else's turned in for the night. You know they close the doors at eight P.M."

I knew he'd be one of the many men in a cot-lined room. Had Mr. Galeman been in the Armory when he'd been bitten? Or outside of it, only to come in later and collapse from the cold?

What did it matter, anyhow, now that Anna'd been kidnapped?

"I just wanted to make sure you were safe, Jake, was all. It's going to be cold tonight."

"It's always cold at night in the winter," he retorted. "Lemme guess, you're treating some junkie right now, nearly OD'd, and you've got a case of the conscience?"

"Something like that."

"Well, I'm fine, Sissy. I appreciate you checking up on me, but it's not necessary, really." His voice dropped even lower. "I'm still superman."

I sat down on the changing bench in Y4's small locker room. "Yeah."

"K. I gotta sleep some. Eight A.M. comes up fast, you know?"

"Yeah." I'd be in front of a vampire lawyer by eight A.M. It did seem to be coming on quickly. "Love you, Jake."

"You too, Sissy," he said, and hung up.

* * *

I went into the bathroom and flushed the toilet once for
pretense, and then I looked at the sink with its faucet. I
turned both hot and cold on.

Where are you, Anna? I thought. I concentrated on the
water, the sound of it, watching it swirl down, trying to do
whatever it was I'd done before that'd mesmerized myself
last time. *Come on, Anna, come on.*

Someone tried the locked door behind me, and I heard
a muffled, "Sorry!"

Dammit. "It's okay," I said, even though it wasn't. I
dried my hands off and went back to the floor.

CHAPTER THIRTY

"So what'll they do for Mr. Galeman?" I asked Meaty when I returned.

"Paul will get him to sign some paperwork in the morning. He'll make some calls—we have to report the bite to the Thrones, after all. Either they've got someone in from out of town who doesn't know the rules, or they've got someone on their team who isn't playing by them."

I'd figured those parts out already. "But what'll *really* happen to him?"

"He'll be a registered donor, once we find out who to register him to. Or we'll keep him here till he heals up, and the Shadows'll fix him before he leaves." Meaty indicated this fixing by rubbing fingers and thumbs together industriously, then squinted at me. "He's not in thrall to the vampire, if that's what you mean."

"No, I was just curious. Thanks." I didn't envy anyone a Shadow "fixing." I looked down at the floor, at the narrow shadow cast by the nursing station's ledge, and thought that I could see them there, dark and swirling, just waiting for a chance to be set free. I shivered, much as Mr. Galeman had, then I gathered myself and my thoughts. I still had one patient left.

I remembered to knock before opening Ti's door for once.

"Come in," Ti said. He was out of bed, wearing normal clothing, wandering around the room with a patient-belongings bag in his hand. He wore jeans and a T-shirt—Y4 was temperature controlled—and I couldn't help noticing how snugly his shirt fit against his muscular arms. I shook my head at myself—patients should never be out of gowns. It made it hard to remember what team they were on.

"Packing?"

"I'm getting out tomorrow."

I turned from side to side to look at the confines of his small room. He'd already taken the pictures of his firefighting crew off the wall. "Getting out? What, this is prison?"

He paused and grinned at me. "After a month? It feels a little similar."

"The County-approved term is 'being discharged,'" I said, making air quotes around the word.

"Then I'm 'being discharged' tomorrow, oh 'difficult nurse,'" he said, making my gesture twice back at me. "You're in a good mood. Someone feed you?" he asked, glancing at me out of the corner of one eye.

Well, that was a random question. "Um. I had a turkey sandwich on my way in, and I've got another for late dinner—"

He stopped picking things up entirely and stared at me for a second. And then he laughed out loud, a melodious sound.

"What's so funny?" I asked, putting my hands on my hips.

"I—I thought you were a vampire the other night. I just assumed. You didn't act like one really, but maybe you were new—"

"Heh!" My current life might be easier if I were, but Mr. Galeman didn't look that edible to me. "No, I'm human. Totally, fallibly human."

"I thought so at first. Then I thought my teller wasn't

telling so good," he said, tapping his healing forehead. "So who was the vial of blood for, then?"

I considered telling him. It'd be nice to get everything off my chest. But—it wasn't my place to share, or his place to have to listen. I inhaled and shook my head before exhaling. "You're a patient. I try to make a practice of not sharing personal stuff with patients."

Ti looked pointedly at the clock above the door. "I'm only a patient for a few more hours." He walked around me, pulled out his visitor chair, and then went back to sit on his bed. "I've got some time to kill. And I'm already dead."

I snorted at his bad joke, and then looked at him. He was serious. Maybe if I said it all at once, it'd sound less crazy. I looked over my shoulder to the open door behind me, and reached one hand back to shut it closed.

"It was for a friend. Who is a vampire," I began. I looked past him, into the shadows his monitor cast on the wall, and wondered if the Shadows were listening in—though it wasn't like they'd help me or Anna if they were.

"And your friend—is he in trouble?"

"She's in trouble," I corrected. "And I can't find her."

"Want to tell me the story?"

"Nurse-patient privilege. I can't."

His amber eyes scanned over me. "Miss Spence, if a vampire wants to find you, they will. It's a talent they have."

"Not if they've been kidnapped." I looked up at him and found him staring straight at me. His golden eyes were thoughtful, set against his rippling dark-pool skin. I quickly looked down again, and then thought, *What if he thinks I'm not looking at him because of the scars?*— when I knew that wasn't true. I tried to bring my gaze up, but he was still looking at me, and even though I knew it had nothing to do with the scars, and everything to do with the awkwardness of feeling someone else's focused attention, I tried not to look away. I inhaled and pressed on. "I have to find her."

"Why?"

I grimaced. *Because if I don't, I'll be dead?* I ignored his question and tried a different tack.

"Is being a zombie better than being dead?"

Ti pondered this and then answered, "I doubt it."

"Ah, well," I said, then I stood up. "Anyhow—you've got things to pack—"

He leaned forward to stand, I thought to see me out. But instead he seemed to come to a decision, like a light switch flicked on inside of him. "I know someone who might be able to help find your friend. Do you have something that smells like her?"

I nodded. I hadn't even begun to think about how I was going to get her tears off my good coat. And I still had Yuri's shirt, the one she'd cried on. "Who—and how?"

"Firefighter-friend privilege," he said with a grin. "How can I get in touch with you?"

"Why would you want to get involved?"

"It's what I do. I'm Bruce Banner, remember?"

"No one's just good for goodness' sake. I don't believe in Santa and neither do you." I crossed my arms.

Ti grinned. "Maybe because I'd like to take you to a movie sometime. It'd be harder to do if you were dead. Not impossible, but probably less fun."

I stared at him. I'd never had a sober patient ask me out before. Much less someone whose name and health history I already knew. Mind you, he was a scarred-up zombie . . . but at least he wasn't a doctor.

"You promise not to throw flowers at my car?" I asked.

"I swear," he said, solemnly crossing his chest without asking why. He looked serious. He seemed serious. And I always had a pen in my breast pocket at work. I wrote my phone number on a piece of paper and handed it over to him.

"All right. Help me out and it's a deal."

* * *

I ignored Ti's room for the rest of the night—anything else I could say would seem anticlimactic. But Mr. Gale-man kept me busy—his crit wasn't low anymore, but all his other electrolytes were out of whack, booze not being the most nutritious diet. I replaced his potassium and phosphates all night long.

Gina rolled by while I was drawing up a syringe of magnesium, and ribbed me some about "Mr. Smith," but I ignored it.

"Everything all right, Spence?" Meaty asked when I came back to the main station at the end of the night to finish up my notes.

I was deeply tired of Meaty asking me that. But as I looked up to glare, I realized that Meaty really meant it. Our charge nurse didn't have many social graces, and asking "Everything all right, Spence?" was a way of saying "Hi, how are you?" or "What's going on today?" and not meant to be overbearing or always checking in. At least not all of the time.

"I'm meeting with my lawyer when this shift ends, in an exceedingly nice area of town." My little Chevy would definitely be out of place there.

"And what's his plan?"

"Don't know yet. I'll know more tomorrow night, though."

"You need some time off?"

I thought of Jake and shook my head. "Not yet."

Meaty's heavy eyelids lowered in disbelief. "All right. But let me know if that changes, okay?"

"Will do." I dove back into my charts and wrote exceptionally thorough notes until Meaty turned away.

I thought about stepping into Ti's room to say good-bye before I left, then thought better of it. If he'd call, he'd call.

If not, I was better off not embarrassing myself. In the locker room I switched into clean scrubs, said good-bye to Gina and Charles, then stepped into the elevator alone.

I hate our elevator. It's not just that it always smells like pee. It "takes off" and "lands" like an elevator should, but it doesn't feel like it's moving at all in between. I've timed it before; it takes forty seconds once the doors have closed for them to open again. That's a long time for an elevator—especially when there are no numbers for any intervening floors. It feels like a prop from *The Twilight Zone*, which, considering where it's taking me from and to, might not be far off.

This morning I stepped into it, the doors closed, and—time passed. A lot of time. Longer than forty seconds, by the time I started counting again, and longer than twenty seconds after that. The lights went off, and my badge began to glow. *Not this again.* Anxiety rose in me like a startled bird and I dropped my coat. My heart sped up, so loud in my chest I could feel it in my throat, and I couldn't count seconds anymore, only heartbeats, faster and faster. I put a hand out and felt where the metal puckered at the seam of the doors and I wasn't sure if I wanted them to burst open and free me, or stay closed and keep me protected from whatever was—

The elevator dinged. I jumped backward and crouched in one corner. The interior lights came on, blinding me, casting whatever was outside the doors in black.

"Come out, human," said a voice. "We will not harm you."

The voice was fractured and disjointed, like an approximation of human voices, gathered up piece by piece and rudely taped together for a TV serial killer's type of prank.

"Who's we?" I shouted from inside.

"You know who we are," it said.

I was afraid they were right.

CHAPTER THIRTY-ONE

I leaned forward and hit the "door close" button repeatedly.

"Come out," the voice repeated more sternly.

I cast one arm up over my eyes to let them adjust. Outside looked like a cave, with an arched ceiling, and a velvety black floor. When I stepped out, the elevator's doors began to shut behind me. I whirled, and shoved my hand between them, where the motion sensor ought to be, but they were determined to close. I yanked back just in time. The elevator sat there, out of place at the bottom of a shaft of rock.

"Where are you?" I called out and took a step forward. The carpet beneath my feet rippled and deformed. Oh, God, it was water. Or worse. "Shadows?" I yelled, my voice rising.

As my eyes got used to the dimmer light, illumination blossomed up from the ground, faint and delicate, crazy jagged lines and solitary winking lights. They came into resolution in the same way that sometimes you can't see the stars till you're out of the city, and then you wonder how you missed so many of them before. Farther out, in what I guessed was the middle of the cavern, was a solid mass of glowing light, a little flat sun. It pulsed.

"You brought me here—why?" I asked aloud.

"This is our home," the voice said. I heard the sound of

liquid pouring next to me and I turned to my right. Twenty feet away stood a creature made of the dark liquid, still streaked with luminescent stars. It looked like the Blob, and it extended a pseudopod toward me.

I stepped backward, holding out my glowing badge. "Send me back to the lobby, now." The memory of them crawling over me, touching me, made my skin shiver. I didn't want to go back to wherever they'd sent me inside myself. Helpless, lost, unwhole.

I didn't want a Shadow touching me. Not ever, ever again.

"I will not touch you here, human. Not yet."

"Keep out of my head." I kept my badge out, for whatever good it was doing. "Why've you brought me here?"

"Because we have need of you."

"What, you want to tell me how worthless I am again?" I let my badge drop against my chest. "I remember what it felt like last time, don't need a repeat performance, thanks."

The creature rippled and deformed, snaking in and out of itself, shimmering lights playing across it.

"If we wanted to destroy you, we would have already. So believe us that you still have some use."

I crossed my arms, suddenly aware that it was freezing down here, wherever this was, and my coat was still in the elevator. "You're going to have to explain more than that if you want me to agree."

"We could crawl inside your head and make you but a shell of yourself, a puppet of meat, for which we keep the only strings." It paused to let the impact of this settle in. "Please stop trying to be brave, and become the pathetic creature we both know you to be."

My short nails bit against my arms. "Fuck you."

The Shadow-thing laughed with other people's voices, loud and long, before continuing. "This hospital is built on a place for gathering powers. Before it was a hospital, it was a church. Before it was a church, it was a burial ground. And before that, perhaps even passing dinosaurs walking above dipped their heads in sorrow."

I nodded like I understood—but really I just wanted it to stop talking with that broken voice. "So?" I asked, when the last reverberation had gone away.

"There are lines beneath the County, Nurse Spence. They channel what we use as food into us, here. For us, they are like the circulatory system you know so well."

"You don't send out oxygen or nutrients or unicorns or rainbows. You're a bottom-feeder, and you only send out shit."

The Shadow let loose another mocking laugh. "Then think of us as a sponge, or a parasite, or even a baleen whale. Whatever you require in order to understand."

Halfway through its speech I put my fingers in my ears. It only let me better hear the pounding of my own heart and didn't block the Shadow-voice out at all. I gave up. "What's this have to do with me?" I prompted.

It extruded an arm and gestured to the floor. "This is a map of all available energies."

All I could see were stars and whorls and bright excited jumping lines. They looked like words written in an ever-changing language that I would never learn to read.

"A man dies near Broadway, shot by his ex-wife." A lit spot on the floor, no wider than a pencil, rippled and raised. "A political rally, where people hope and hate in equal measure." A thicker piece of light pulled up from the floor, maybe the width of my fist. "And lastly, here. County Hospital. Two thousand people—not so very many—but they are always in perfect agony, hoping not to die, and dying regardless." The flat sun I'd seen before rose up like a tombstone. It beat like a glowing heart.

I stepped backward and the floor rippled. Like a heavy stone dropped into a still pond, those ripples carried out and over to the short pillar of light, coursing up its length on one side and down on the other, in blissful ignorance of physics.

But not everyone at County died. Surely not— "You don't change patient outcomes, do you?"

"We don't need to. This is the County's hospital. The people who come here cannot go anywhere else. They wait too long for medical attention, and when they receive it, even should they live, they often wish to die along the way." The creature made its way out, warping the field of lights along the floor—lights that I now understood represented combined pinpricks of human suffering and pain. "It is not a thick conduit—not like a war might bring, or the weight of crushing tyranny—but it is steady. It has lasted so far. It will continue."

"So why do you need me?"

"We would like you to transport us."

I took another step back and looked at the elevator behind me. "You're not getting inside my head again."

The creature chuckled. "There are other ways."

"Why should I help you?"

"We will be able to find the vampire girl you seek. Surely she is currently experiencing a certain amount of pain."

I nodded. Of course, when she'd been biting Mr. Galeman, she'd been causing him a certain amount of pain too. Realization dawned on me. If what they were saying was true, the Shadows had everyone coming *and* going.

"When? Now?" The sooner I could save Anna, the better. Truth be told, I didn't know how I'd protect her from another attack, or how I'd keep her fed. But wherever she was now . . . the images from Mr. November's walls were burned into my brain. No one should be left there, wherever there happened to be.

"It will take some time. One person's pain is not very distinct from another's. We think you might understand."

I nodded. Everyone at the hospital wanted to think that

their case was special, and if you were a good nurse, you helped them keep that illusion alive. Knowing that someone down the hall had it worse than you never stopped your own paper cut from hurting, at least not until they came in and bludgeoned you senseless with their amputated leg.

"We are not typically surface creatures, and we cannot come out in bright light," the Shadow continued. Five dark columns rose out of the fluid on the floor. It moved its bulk across the floor toward these columns as it went on. "Thus our ability to interact with the outside world is limited, and there have been recent inconsistencies in our map."

"So?"

"Certain areas have gone dark to us. Someone is siphoning away our rightful pain." The Shadow gestured toward the few thin plateaus of black. "We cannot point to a simple area and say this represents a certain region above without aid. And even then, when many things are happening, triangulation can become difficult."

"Is it possible that everyone in those places are just happy?" I couldn't think of any place in the County where that would actually happen, but who knew?

"It is highly unlikely. We feed off happiness too—it just never lasts as long as pain."

"Great." I pursed my lips. "So you currently have a lack of information? From somewhere above?" I asked, gesturing grandly up toward the rock ceiling.

"Yes. Which, given our rights to all free energies within this County's lines, should be impossible."

In its creepy multivoice, I could hear a thousand different kinds of frustration.

"So everyone inside these five areas is either dead or—"

"Blocked from us, in breach of our contract with the Consortium. And we do not know where the perpetrators physically are. We cannot sense the absence of something."

The Shadow multivoice narrowed down to one distinct voice that was somehow worse than all the rest. "We have an ancient contract. We cannot be denied," it hissed.

I did not ever want to meet that voice in a dark alley. "But what can I do? I'm only me."

"Rest assured we have other pieces of meat performing surveillance," the Shadow's other voices returned. "We have learned, however, that having minions capable of independent thought is sometimes useful too."

I snorted.

"Do you have something that you can keep on you at all times?" the Shadow continued, beginning to swirl near.

I looked down at myself. I took everything off for work—no earrings or necklaces, and I'd never worn any rings. "This is it," I said, holding up my badge, which still held a faint orange glow of its own.

"Give it here."

I unlooped the lanyard from around my neck and handed it over carefully, so as not to touch the Shadow. My badge already had some qualities imbued by Y4's mysterious nursing office, prior to being assigned to me. My employee number was only on the back with label tape, and my name was just written on the front. It didn't even have my photo on it.

The creature took my badge and enveloped it entirely into its black, lanyard and all. Then it extruded my badge again through the other side, and passed it back toward me. I grabbed it as carefully as I'd handed it over.

"If you wear this, we will see through your eyes," the Shadow said, as I looped the lanyard around my neck again. "Skin contact is best."

"I bet." I left the badge on the outside of my scrubs. Behind me, the elevator doors made their opening ding.

"Never take it off," the Shadow continued.

"Fine." The elevator's light outlined the Shadow like

an eclipse. It melted into the ground, making a minature tsunami on the floor.

I couldn't wait to leave—and I also remembered my lawyer appointment that I was now becoming late for. Surviving just today wasn't enough, not when there was the tribunal in three days. "How will you let me know when you've found her?"

"When we know, you will know as well."

The Shadow was gone, so I addressed the ground. "And when do I start looking for you?"

"Now." Its voice was a faint echo, the rind of a distant, aged fear.

I shook my head. "That's not what I—" I began, but I closed my mouth. Whatever. I began shuffling my way back toward the elevator, watching the patterns on the floor ripple as I did so. Did I have any control over the pains of the outside world from here? I hoped not. I took three big steps and made it into the elevator, never so happy to smell were piss in my entire life. As the doors began to close, I thought of one more question I had to ask.

"Hey!" I shouted, cupping my hand against one door to keep it open. This time it held. "Why didn't you erase Shawn's memory all the way? That night in pediatrics, with the dragon?"

"And miss a chance to feed on all of his delicious subsequent fear?" asked the Shadows' voice, in return.

I couldn't see the creature out there anymore—but I could hear its refracted and reflected mirth, resonating up from whatever fragments of humanity it currently had hold of. I stepped back, revolted, and let the doors slide shut in front of me.

CHAPTER THIRTY-TWO

The elevator rose the requisite forty seconds and then re-leased me into the hallway that it joined. I walked quickly, down the hall and up the stairs, until I reached a room with windows. Dawn, even murky cloud-covered dawn, had never looked so good. But sunlight—shit. I glanced at my watch and sprinted for my car.

Traffic was light driving uptown. People from uptown drove downtown to work, or took trains, or had drivers drop them off. People from downtown didn't go up so much, unless they were washing other people's dishes, or mowing lawns—but there wasn't so much mowing now, in winter.

I stopped at the address the lawyer had given me, a small business park where all the building's windows were covered in heavily tinted glass. I parked in a spot near a double-parked Jag and gave serious thought to keying his car on principle, before going up to the set of equally tinted glass doors.

I double-checked the address I'd written down, noted that I was thirty minutes late, and tried the door.

It was locked.

"Hello?" I pushed and pulled the simple loop of steel, not so much as rattling the door in its daylight-proof frame. I beat it with the palm of my hand. "Hello?"

Nothing. I looked at my reflection—a little blurry from where my hand had left a smudge print. My ponytail was spiky, there were circles beneath both eyes, and I still had more than just a whiff of were piss about me. Not that I could see that in my reflection, but I could maybe understand why a place like this was also not a place for me.

But on the phone he'd said he'd help. "Come on!" I kicked the bottom of the door with the toe of my shoe.

As this felt particularly satisfying, I was preparing to do it again, when—the door opened inward, slowly. I quickly made to stand on my own two feet and look innocent of any crimes.

"We feared you were not coming, Miss Spence," said a sensuous female voice.

"I got held up at work. I'm sorry," I told the darkness in front of me.

As the door's gap widened, I took a step inside. I could see who was holding the door now, and she was beautiful.

I didn't excel at being a girl. I could fake it for a night out—I could buy the right clothes, strap up the right shoes, and put on a good game. But it'd always be just that—a game, one that I was fully aware of playing. A façade that was fun to wear, but which would eventually flake. If a guy spent long enough with me, by which I meant maybe forty-eight hours, he'd eventually see frayed jeans, sweatshirts, ratty tennis shoes, and probably one of Minnie's hairballs dried and forgotten behind the couch. Not even my cat could be counted upon to help create my allure.

But this woman in front of me—she didn't have to pretend. She'd go to sleep wearing makeup and wake up with it precisely, sexily smudged the next day. Skirts that would be too tight or short on me would fit her perfectly, pertly, and if they were snatched up off the floor after a night out, they would possess wrinkles that were totally in or ahead of style. Her hair would look beautiful in all of its stages, from shower-clean to four-day bedhead, locks merely growing more defined and exotically chunky as time passed, making people on the train—should she ever deign to ride it—bold enough to ask her what styling products she preferred.

Her lips were crimson, naturally so, and her waist-length hair was the color of deep, dark, arterial blood, a blue-red entirely unnatural and entirely unfair.

And as I took all of her in, feeling ashamed for the state in which I'd presented myself, I realized with a start that I'd seen her before. On the *train*, no less. All of her, except for the part she'd been hiding with watches.

"You're the girl from the watch ad," I blurted.

A faint smile set her lips aflame and made her glorious cheekbones rise. "You're familiar with my work?"

"I've seen it before. Them before. The watches." I pointed to my own empty wrist. I didn't tell her that the last train I'd ridden in had had a huge cock painted near her face. Maybe not being a fashion model did have *some* advantages.

Her smile tightened in a way that said she was used to people acting dumb around her, myself included. "Please come in."

She led me down a short corridor, and I was still staring. I supposed it was rude of me, but it's not every day you have someone semifamous opening a door for you. I knew some vampires had a look-away power that they used around humans—maybe this was the reverse of that, where my eyes were glued. I glanced at my badge to see if it would show me anything. She paused and opened up a door.

"Please go sit down," she said.

This new room had no windows, all of the glass outside obviously just for show. The majority of it was decorated in blacks and grays that I could barely differentiate in the low lighting. Now that my eyes had adjusted I could see an elegant-looking man with gray hair and long side-burns. He'd been changed when he was old, elderly, even, looking frail inside a suit the same color as his chair's upholstery, sitting across an expansive dark wood desk. "We do prefer the night, Miss Spence," he said, and gestured to a chair across from him.

I walked over and sat down. "I'm sorry. Work."

"This time, I'll forgive you. But it does not do to keep those who do you favors waiting."

I nodded, and glanced over to my left. The model woman sat behind him on a plush leather couch, legs crossed, a lip of skirt pulled tight across her perfect knee. "Are you the man I spoke with?" I asked.

"The same. Not a man, though. But you should know that." His thin lips pulled into an amused smile, and he stared at me. Through me. My badge glimmered in the room's eerie twilight.

I put my hand around my badge. His look—it was like Gaius, the vampire boy-child I'd seen, on that other patient's transfusion night. "Please stop."

The man shrugged, and my badge went dim. "I just wanted to see what protections your badge afforded you."

"Apparently not hearing you in my head, or vice versa, is one of them." I let my badge drop, and kept my best game face on.

"Again, we are the ones doing you favors here, Miss Spence," he said, regarding me casually with half-lidded eyes.

"Vampires never do anything for free."

"And yet you saved one, not long ago. Risked your life for her, you told me, on the phone."

"Yes. But that hasn't worked out well for me so far." I scooted to the edge of the chair. Its plush seat and high armrests threatened to envelop me. "So how can I help you help me?"

He laughed, and behind him, the glorious woman smiled. "All right, Miss Spence. I'm sure you are tired, and your occupation requires a certain forthrightness."

He stood. "My name is Geoffrey Weatherton, Esquire. Before I became a vampire, I was a lawyer, and I am still one now. It runs in my blood, you could say." His lips pulled wide at his joke, revealing the fanged teeth that would, once revealed outside of this room and on any day but Halloween, give him away.

"You said that you spoke with her, yes? The girl?" he continued.

"Anna."

"Before she was kidnapped—and she promised to come to your trial?"

"Yes, she did."

"Then I'll take your case." He opened up a folder in front of him—I hadn't noticed it before, black leather against the mahogany wood. "I just need your signature is all."

I leaned forward and took the papers he was offering me. "Want to explain this while I read?"

"I'm offering to take your case in exchange for your bloodright. Which would indebt you and any of your children into perpetuity to me and my Throne. Your bloodline would be our donors under permanent retainer."

I was relieved to find that the pages I held were computer printouts, not handwritten calligraphy on vellum. It made it feel slightly less like a devil's deal.

"Which Throne do you belong to?" I asked, looking at the papers in my hands.

"The Rose Throne. We have a vested interest in humanity."

"I bet you do. And who is prosecuting me?"

He smiled. "The Zverskiye."

I tried not to start. They were Anna's relatives, the ones that I was sure had Anna now. "And they are?"

"The Beastly Ones, roughly translated."

I looked from him to my papers and back again. "And how exactly are you all different?"

Geoffrey leaned back in thought. His eyes closed, and I wondered how much longer he could fight the rising sun. "It's a question of resources and stewardship." He brought his head forward again, and stared at me, slouching over on one side. "The Rose Throne believes that humanity needs to be cultivated."

I leaned forward, putting the papers on the desk. I'd never heard anything like that before. "Like educated? Or enlightened?"

Geoffrey's face took on a bemused expression, and then he laughed. "Like mushrooms. Chickens. Cows. Managed, herded, looked out for."

I felt stupid for having been rooked. "For your own best interests, of course."

Geoffrey crossed his bony hands atop the desk, and gently smiled at me. "Well, we are vampires, Miss Spence. The Zver prefer to think of you—of all humans—as free-range meat. Perhaps given that circumstance, you'd rather be a herded cow. Or a stalk of celery."

I grunted without giving an answer, and turned to the pages in my hand. Page after page of legalese. So this was what lawyer vampires did while they were up at night. It was tough going, but I had faith in myself. I'd translated badly written doctor's notes involving medication names that sounded like porn stars involved in Nigerian e-mail scams. I could manage this. I read through to the very end, and when I reached it, he was asleep, his chin bowed to touch his chest, as though he was a run-down toy. I shook the pages lightly for his attention and he started back awake. "How will you help me, though?" I asked. "Right now, you're counting on her to keep her word—if she doesn't, I die. If she does, I'm indebted to you. What do I get from you out of all this?"

"I, and my assistant, will make inquiries after your friend through vampire channels." He waved two fingers in the air, and the woman nodded, sending a long lock of red hair spilling into her lap. "Sike speaks for me during the day."

I looked from him to her and back again. "So I'm supposed to trust that you'll be doing . . . something? Asking . . . questions?" I folded the papers together in my lap. "Really? That's your plan? I'm signing my life away for this?"

His eyes narrowed. "I do have connections, Miss Spence. Connections that you lack. It is possible that I will find her."

"Possible," I repeated. The sheaf of papers that I held felt suddenly very heavy, like the low pan of a weighing scale. Which was worse? Being indebted to a vampire for eternity, or death by execution?

"You're worth slightly more alive to me as a legal blood cow than you are dead," he followed up. "Worth making an effort for."

I didn't trust him further than I could throw the polished marble paperweight at the end of his desk. But what was losing some blood? I'd make more. I liked living. I wasn't very good at it so far, but that didn't mean I wanted to stop any time soon.

I slammed the papers on top of his desk, and signed them with my charting pen before I could change my mind.

"A woman of action. I can appreciate that." Geoffrey Weatherton, Esquire, waited patiently for me to finish the triplicate forms, then took them politely away. He scanned over them, nodding to himself, before looking again at me. "Now, Miss Spence, we are legally bonded." He rocked back into his chair. "Tell me everything, again."

It already appeared as though Geoffrey's attentions were periodically fading, drowsing only for him to shake himself awake again. But I inhaled and retold the story from the beginning, from my first moments meeting and caring for Mr. November—Yuri, Yuri—and what had then followed.

"It does sound dire for you," Geoffrey said when I'd finished my sad tale. He was braced against his elbows on the desk, his hands sympathetically interwoven out in front of him.

I'd included the parts of my story up until Anna's kidnapping. "Where did they take her? And why?"

"The Zverskiye's motivations are ever unknown to us. One of the reasons they and we disagree so often." He leaned back thoughtfully in his chair. "An ancient blood feud? A well-organized pornography ring? You said you saw the vampire who witnessed the murder there again—"

My mind blanked a bit at this. Murder? I was . . . a murderer? It was hard to hear it phrased like that, when the deathee in question had exploded into dust and flame. But—I looked down at my hands, and remembered Lady Macbeth. Sure I'd washed my hands a hundred times with hand sanitizer since that night, but the facts remained the same.

"What happens if I give myself up?"

"Then you'll be drawn and blooded. And when they're done with your flesh, they'll continue to keep your soul. At that time, according to the papers you just signed, I will merely inherit your couch."

"My soul?" I blinked. I'd gone to church plenty of times in my youth, under parental duress, but I'd never gone willingly on my own. "You're kidding, right?"

"They did send a Husker after you, did they not? What did you think he was there for?" Geoffrey eyed me sorrowfully, and his gaze looked old. I felt distant, like not only was I looking across his desk at him, but across a gulf of time between us too.

"But . . . really? My soul?"

"Energy is currency, Miss Spence, and entropy rules the

day. It's called psychophagy, and it is, quite literally, a fate worse than death."

Soul . . . *eating*? No way. "Why?"

"Souls are even more potent than blood, Miss Spence."

"Then why aren't they out killing people all the time for them?" I asked.

"You can get blood from killing people, yes. But souls? Souls have to be earned." Geoffrey hunched forward, as if pulling the strength to stay awake from somewhere deep inside himself. "A soul has power only in its transition states, much like you might remember from electrons in chemistry. A good soul that stays good, or a bad soul that stays bad—those maintain their levels, dead or alive. They are predestined, if you will, and neither change the balance.

"But for a good soul to become bad—such a change lets off a quick release of energy." He snapped his fingers. "Like a photon in motion releases light. There are many eager to harvest these rare events. How often does a human manage to kill a vampire, and thus legally indebt their energy that way? Much less a human who was good to begin with? Not very often at all, Miss Spence. If you weren't up to die," he said, smiling at me grimly, "you should be very proud of yourself."

Small consolation. "So my soul is really what is up for trial?"

"Yes." Geoffrey's eyes closed for a long second, then fluttered open again. "I imagine you've made some plans to do a little investigating of your own? You don't seem like the type to wait patiently at home."

I flushed. "I did make some plans. I have a friend who'll help."

"Well, I must advise you to be careful—technically you're already on trial, and vampire courts don't believe in innocent until proven guilty. Dying now could leave you in a difficult state." His lips pursed in disapproval. "You shouldn't be dragging other mortals into this."

"He's a zombie."

In response, I watched the ropy tendons of Geoffrey's hands knot and bunch. His face gave nothing away, but it took a moment for his hands to still. "Miss Spence, I tell you this as your legal representative. I am a wolf who is a wolf. Not a wolf who wears sheep's clothing. Trust that he has his own reasons for helping you."

My shoulders sank two inches. "I have to do something," I protested. I wanted to think that Ti had only my best interests at heart. If zombies even had hearts.

"I understand." He reached into his breast pocket and pulled out a business card. "Call if you find out anything before I do. Sike will answer if I cannot."

"And if you don't call me?" I asked.

"Then I will see you at the trial." He nodded curtly, stood, and walked to the gloom at the back of his office. Momentarily, I heard a closing door.

Sike stood. She walked around a file cabinet, and I heard pouring water before she reemerged with a paper cup in hand. "Water?"

I took it from her. "You're his daytimer?"

"I prefer dayspeaker, but yes."

"You don't look like a daytimer." Her top showed her neck, and I couldn't see even one scar.

Her eyes narrowed at my purposeful use of the wrong name. "I do have my career to think of."

"Won't it be hard to score that *Sports Illustrated* cover once you're a vampire?" I asked.

"I'll just have to earn it before then, I suppose." She smiled pleasantly at me, but it was all lip—her cheeks didn't move, and her eyes didn't twinkle. Because we both knew the truth. She'd never get to go to Europe or New York to make it big—unless for some reason that was what the Rose Throne wanted her to do.

Just like I'd never get to leave Y4. I set my water down without touching it. "I'm sorry—I've gotta get some sleep."

"Keep in touch," she said, with a tone of voice that let me know she wished for nothing less.

I drove straight home and didn't check my messages till I was crawling into bed.

"Hey, Edie—my friend'll help. Meet me at the Westpark Shopping Center, off of the 85, near the north entrance, at three. Bring that shirt, okay? Sleep tight."

I saved Ti's number on my phone, then set it on my nightstand. Asher's phone number had migrated to be beside it. I crumpled his number up and threw it across the room for Minnie to use as a cat toy. The outpatient clinic hadn't called back with the results of my tests yet; things were *probably* fine. Everything was probably fine. Anna was probably fine wherever she was being tortured now. Mr. Galeman was probably fine, post multiple blood transfusions. Sike was probably fine with my pathetic attempts to piss her off out of jealousy, and Geoffrey was probably fine with the fact that I had a zombie on my side, who was himself probably fine as long as eventually we went on a date, where I would again probably be fine as long as he didn't want to eat my brains.

It's a good thing I was exhausted, or I never would have gotten to sleep with so much uncertainty.

CHAPTER THIRTY-THREE

I hardly ever saw anyone from inside the hospital outside of it, not even in the parking lot. I wanted to be on time for this meeting at least, and since no Shadows had risen up to delay me when I'd gone through the tunnel, apparently I'd beaten everyone else there. I sat in my parked car, feeling naked and exposed, my Chevy idling to keep the heater running, just us chickens sitting around in the middle of the gray asphalt and dirty snow. My badge was still on, like I'd promised the Shadows it would be, underneath all my clothes, its plastic edges poking against my breasts.

I'd had the night—well, morning really—to think on what Geoffrey had said. And on what Ti had said too. Before he even knew that I needed help—about just being the helpful type. I suppose you didn't get to be a firefighter without some of the same predispositions that got you into nursing. A misguided sense of purpose, for one. Thinking that you needed to save other people around you, that too.

A knock at my fogged window startled the hell out of me. I yelped and swiped at the glass. Ti was waiting outside.

"Did I scare you?" he asked, concerned, as I opened the door.

"Only a little." I grinned at him. He was in a bulky

coat with a black hood, but the healing scars covering his face were easily seen. Seeing him would have scared most people. I imagined he had to do his grocery shopping late at night, so that mothers didn't yank stunned children out of his path. But I was made of sterner stuff. Plus, I was scheduled to die in T minus three days. I could cut a man some slack.

"So what's the plan?" I bounced up and down to stay warm.

"I checked—I don't think you were followed."

"Followed?" I quickly scanned over my shoulders, back at the desolate parking lot. Not many people wanted to buy SEWING NOTIONS! or CASH CHECKS HERE! during the middle of a workday. Except for the sad green tinsel shaped into Christmas trees and hung on every light pole, we might as well have been on the moon. There was only my car and Ti's car, an El Camino in bright cranberry red.

"I assume whoever has your friend wants to keep her, right? Better safe than sorry."

"Oh." I wanted to hit myself. If I'd been thinking like that, maybe Anna wouldn't have gotten kidnapped again.

Ti swayed back and forth to stay warm in the cold. *Is he really cold, or just pretending to blend in?* I tried to shush Geoffrey's voice away. "Did you bring the shirt?" he asked.

I nodded, and reached for my door handle. I'd brought the shirt that she'd cried on. I pulled it out, burping the last of my car's heat into the cold. "Can't we just sit inside where it's warm?"

"Nah. Madge'll be here any minute."

Madge seemed like an odd name for, well, anyone really, and I almost said so, when—a truck pulled into the parking lot and headed straight for us. My instinct was to dive aside, but Ti didn't move. So I took a step closer to him instead, realizing as I did so that Ti didn't have to fear trucks barreling out of nowhere—he was already dead.

The truck threw on its emergency brake and skidded artfully to a sideways stop ten feet from the far side of my car. Several dogs in the bed of the truck stood up and started barking, tails wagging madly at the sight of Ti.

"Madge," Ti said to me, by way of explanation. "And company."

"Ti!" A rough-cut man wrapped in flannels and corduroy swung out of the truck's cab.

"Hello, Madigan. This is Edie." He stepped aside so that I could be seen. "She's the one I was telling you about."

"It's a pleasure to meet you, Edie," he said, and he seemed like the type who meant it. I smiled back, and shook his offered hand.

"Thanks—I appreciate you wanting to help."

"Well, I've got to let the gang out every now and then." He tilted his head toward the dogs peering out at us from the truck bed. One of them made a short bark at the attention.

"So," Ti continued. "About today—"

"Let's load up here, and then drive down. You got an address?" Madigan asked me, and I nodded. I gave him Mr. November's place. "Good. We'll start there and then crisscross a few blocks around for leads."

"Does that sound good to you, Edie?" Ti asked.

"Sure." I hopped into the truck cab between Madigan and Ti. The truck smelled deeply of dog, and there were all sorts of multicolored strands of fur almost woven into the upholstery by time.

I held the tearstained shirt to my chest. I wasn't sure what exactly we were going to do, but it was doing something, which was better than doing nothing at all.

I couldn't help but peek in the rearview mirror at the dogs in the truck bed. Driving the way Madigan was on the lightly iced roads seemed like a bad idea—I expected them to be sliding around, hurting themselves, as we rounded corners at almost impossible speeds. The dogs in the back appeared unconcerned, bracing themselves against the ruts in the truck bed as Madigan made rolling stop-turn after rolling stop-turn.

"So you . . . track things often?" I asked. I wasn't sure how Ti had explained things to Madigan, and didn't want to give too much away just in case.

"As often as I can. It's great fun."

"In the city, even?"

Madigan took his eyes off the road to look askance at me. "Where else would we go?" he said, staring far too long before looking back at the road and finding a slowing car ahead of us. He signaled and maneuvered around it. He reminded me of Jake playing that way old arcade game Dragonslayer, signal, merge, signal, weave. Except that my life was still worth more than a quarter, at least to me. Ti patted my leg, and I switched from making panicked fists to holding on to his hand with both of my own. It was a natural enough transition, especially since every veering left-hand turn threatened to send me into his lap.

"What do you normally track for?" I asked instead.

"You know. Lost things." He grinned in profile, showing me quite a lot of teeth. "Here we are."

He used the emergency brake to stop us, and I let go of Ti's hand awkwardly as the car settled to a stop, bumping the curb gently with the two right-hand-side tires. Ti got out of the car and I quickly followed—I'd miss its heat, but not Madigan's driving. The dogs in the back perked up as Madigan got out on his side of the cab.

"Jimmie—guard," Madigan told the biggest dog. It was black and looked like a Labrador except for its square jaw, where it looked like a pit bull. Definitely the right choice to leave guard duty here. As if it perfectly understood its owner, it sat down on its haunches and stopped wagging its tail, slurping up its long pink tongue to appear serious about its job.

"Jenny, Jack—get down." Madigan swung the gate of the truck open, and the two other dogs jumped out to run over and smell us and lick our hands. Jenny was red, with a thick retriever's belly coat, and Jack was all mutt, splotchy with black and brown and white, multicolored even down to his one blue and one green eye. "So—your shirt, Edie?"

I handed over the shirt that Anna had cried on with the bloodstained mark from her tears, without saying where it came from. Any normal person would ask about that sort of thing, it being blood and all—but I had a feeling that Madigan wasn't very normal.

He proffered the stain to Jenny and Jack in turn, who took long whiffs of it.

"Is there anything else, now that we're here?" Ti asked me.

"This is where the fight was." I walked over and ran my glove against the dent Anna had left in the lamppost. I didn't remember the light there working before the fight. I would bet it didn't work now.

Madigan kept hold of Mr. N—Yuri's—shirt. Jenny and Jack were circling outward, but how could they smell anything under the snow? Their tails were wagging and I got the impression that they were enjoying themselves, but I wasn't sure how useful they could really be. All this was really some sort of wild-goose chase, and possibly a huge waste of time. I heaved a sigh.

"Hey, don't give up." Ti moved to stand in front of me. I looked up at him. He'd taken off his hood and his dark skin was clearly outlined against the gray afternoon sky. His features had just a touch of asymmetry that made you look twice. He had a strong jaw and a wide nose, and his hair was beginning to grow back in a short layer across his scalp and he almost needed to shave his chin. Burn victims usually didn't have hair regrow; their scars precluded it. But maybe he was transitioning back to the body he'd had before, because he was a zombie. I resisted the urge to reach up and touch the new growth to see.

"I'm not the giving-up sort. I am the easily frustrated sort, though." A wind kicked up between us. I held my own arms and shivered.

"I don't put out much body heat. But I function as an adequate windblock." He grinned and moved to stand beside me. Somewhere, underneath layer after layer of cotton and nylon on both sides, our elbows touched.

Madigan whistled to his dogs and started walking up the street with them.

"Should we follow?"

"He'll whistle when they're onto something." He was watching his friend and the dogs walk down the street, and I was watching him.

"Mind telling me what all this is about?" he asked me.

He had just jumped through every hoop I'd held out and then some. But— "What's your stake in helping me?"

Scar tissue around his eyes crinkled in thought. "I have to have a stake? I can't just be a helpful kind of guy?"

"No one is just a helpful kind of guy. I'm a nurse, but I only became a nurse because they freaking pay me." I stared straight out at the red stone of Mr. November's town house. From the second floor, the old lady I remembered peered out from between her curtains, and then yanked her head back. At least she was still alive.

"All right." He rocked back and forth on the balls of his feet. "I'll admit I have some scores to settle. But none of them matter right now. I really am helping you of my own accord."

"How'd you become a zombie?" I asked.

"I didn't get a choice." He looked down at me and smiled softly. "Your turn. What's behind you that's got you running so scared?"

I hadn't thought of it like that before. Maybe he did deserve an explanation. I inhaled to tell him all of it when

Madigan whistled from down the street. Jimmie leaned out of the truck bed to butt the back of my head with his nose.

Ti laughed. "You can tell me later, okay?" he said, and began walking away.

CHAPTER THIRTY-FOUR

Madigan stood at the entrance to an alleyway. Jack and Jenny were barking quietly to one another as they paced down it, like they were having a conversation.

"Did something happen here?" Madigan asked and gestured to include the surrounding area.

"This is near where my friend got jumped."

"Well, this alley smells like vampires. Not like the one that your shirt smells like, but vampires. They must have been waiting for you."

It was the first time Madigan had said the V-word. I guessed he was in on the County's little joke after all.

"How can you tell?" I asked.

He held out a palm full of cigarette butts. "Damn things always smoke." Jenny bounded ahead, then dug in the snow, unearthing a fresh pile, right beneath a fire escape. She barked.

"Hand-rolled. Apple-flavored tobacco," Madigan reported.

I put a hand to my stomach. That part was familiar at least—I could remember the stench of rotting apples coming off the vampire that got away.

"They drove off in a car, though—" I looked up the fire escape, snaking a path up the back of a short red town house. Mr. November's building. The bottom of it was off the ground, but the top easily reached Mr. November's back window. "How hard would it have been for them to climb up there?"

"Not very." Ti walked over, bent down, and then launched himself up to catch the edge. He pulled it down along with a light snowfall of rust as it descended. Jenny and Jack ran up it as it hit the ground, paws clattering along. They reached the top landing and barked.

"After you," I told Ti, and we followed, much more slowly, after them.

The metal landing outside of Mr. November's room was littered with cigarette butts. I peeked in through the window. The room was now completely trashed. All the photos from the walls were shredded, looking like kindling left in several small piles.

"We didn't even hear them outside—" I said.

"They could have been there for days. Stalking the place, waiting for you and your friend to show up," Madigan said. "Cold doesn't bother them much either."

"But what about the daylight?"

"Daytimers. Besides, your vampire friend, the one they were waiting for—they knew she couldn't come here herself during the day."

"We were attacked by ten of them, though. Ten wouldn't have fit up here."

Ti paced in the small area. "Then one called the rest."

"Yeah." They had had enough time, what with Anna and I arguing, loudly, inside. I couldn't imagine one of them managing to be quiet outside on the escape—which felt like it was threatening to disconnect from the wall and collapse with each movement we made—but she'd been so emotional. Which was strange, when you considered the fact that she was a vampire.

A baying sound began from below. Jenny and Jack raced back down the escape, closely followed by Madigan. Ti and I followed, the rickety structure feeling less certain every step. I suddenly remembered that I'm not so fond of heights, especially not at high speed—and maybe three days' worth of work and worry caught up with me at once. Something small and black flashed in the corner of one eye, and I stopped quickly on the stairs.

"Are you okay?" Ti caught my arm as I threatened to tumble forward.

"I'm fine." I stood for a second and blinked a lot. It must have been a flake of rust—or vampire ash. I rubbed at my eye, but kept slowly going down, Ti at my side.

We exited the alley, with Ti's hand on my elbow, supporting me. I kept blinking, but the speck of gray wouldn't disappear. Madigan stood near his truck with his three dogs beside him, holding on to the shoulder of a pissed-off teen. He was dressed like the thugs hovering in the background on Nyjara's album covers, puffy black leather coat, black pants, white leather shoes, only he didn't look angry enough to pull off the look. Given time, though—

"I just wanted to pet your dog, mister!" the teenager said, yanking his arm out of Madigan's grasp.

"And not steal my rims?"

The teenager cursed under his breath. "You think you got anything worth stealing? Please."

I was still muddling with my eye; the black speck hadn't gone anywhere. I hadn't had a stroke, had I? I held my arms out, and could see them both, even and unwavering, in front of me.

"Edie?" Ti asked.

"My face—it's all the same, right? None of it is drooping?" I stuck out my tongue, wondering if it was still even. Then I held one hand up in front of my face.

I covered my bad eye first and saw Ti watching me, with my good eye. He was clearly worried. I covered my good eye up, and looked at him with my bad eye . . . and saw a glow. Like the afterimage you'd get from rubbing any eye too hard, lights and blurs. Only I wasn't rubbing it now, and the lights wouldn't stop. Had I somehow managed to get instantaneous glaucoma?

"Look, you don't just pet another man's dog. You're lucky that he didn't bite you," Madigan went on.

"He was wagging his tail. He seemed friendly enough," the teen protested. I heard Jimmie's tail thump from inside the truck's bed—his guard dog duty had been a clever sham, and this kid'd walked by, and—I looked over at the kid and winked.

"Edie?" Ti asked again.

There was a faint outline now—of . . . of Jimmie's head. Only it didn't stay the same; it faded in and out between the square-jawed partial pit bull I guessed Madigan's dog to be, and the cherubic face of a young boy. Maybe as young as six. And the teen—with this othersight, he still appeared as sullen as he sounded, but his right hand glowed.

I'd seen that glow before. My badge glowed like that, when I was around Y4-style danger. I pressed my other hand to my chest, and felt my badge's edges sharp against my skin. So this was the Shadow's self-serving gift to me.

"Hey, kid—" I stopped winking and looked at him through my normal eyes. Both his hands were empty. "Did you see someone here? A few nights ago? Dark suits, sunglasses in the dark?"

He crossed his arms. "There's lots of dealers around here."

"You talked to one of them, though. Gave him something. Touched him—"

"What're you, psychic?" he said, backing up roughly against the truck. Jimmie growled.

"Sure." I pointed. "I read palms. That hand right there, you touched one of them. Where'd they come from? Where'd they go? What'd you sell them?"

The kid looked at his own hand like it might have still

had a spot on it. Ti and Madigan were looking back and forth between us, and the dogs all had their heads tilted in a listening fashion.

"He wanted to know where to go to get girls." The kid rubbed his hand up and down on his pants, like he was wiping off a stain. "He paid me a twenty. I didn't sell him any drugs."

"Where'd you tell him?"

"Everyone knows where you can get girls around here. The only reason I made him pay me was because he looked like he could afford it." He looked Madigan and me up and down. I went for my wallet in my pocket—

"I got it." Ti pulled out a twenty instead, and held it up, right in front of his own face. The kid slowly looked up at Ti, snatched the money fast, then looked away.

"What happened to you, man?" he asked, trying to look anywhere but at him.

"Fire. The ones who did this to me are gonna pay." Ti took a step forward. His coat made his shoulders appear even wider than they really were, and his chest even thicker. "Which girls?" he asked, pulling out a hundred-dollar bill, holding it squarely in front of the teen's face.

"All the girls are on Seventeenth and F Street. After dark, that is." The kid swatted for the cash, missed, and Ti let the bill flutter to the ground. The teen did a shimmy while standing in place, torn between ducking down to get the bill and being in kicking range of Ti's legs, I felt.

"Here." I knelt, picked it up, and handed it over, without looking at Ti. I ran through my pockets and found a pen and a piece of paper. "Here's my number. If you ever see any of them again, call me." I gave the kid a sheepish look, knowing that Ti was probably glowering behind me.

"Whatever." He snatched the paper away.

The dogs that were blocking the teen's path ducked away at an unseen command. The kid turned around and stalked off, waiting till he was halfway down the block to yell "Freak!" behind him, at the top of his lungs, before running down an alleyway.

"Load up," Madigan said, opening the gate of his truck. Jack and Jenny leaped up, and Jimmie whuffled them. My vision in my left eye was still blurry, but as Madigan rounded the truck, I turned toward Ti.

"What was that about? I thought you got burned in a firefighting accident?"

"I did. But sometimes it's good to play into stereotype." He gave me a wicked grin, and opened up Madigan's door. A sheep in wolf's clothing, indeed. I sighed, and hopped up inside.

"So how about dinner tonight? Before you go to work?" Madigan asked as we neared the parking lot. "We eat late, and my wife is making stew—"

I looked at the clock on his dashboard. I'd only slept for maybe four hours that morning after my meeting with Geoffrey, before meeting Ti. I'd been counting on a long nap between now and work. Then again—as far as I knew I only had to show up to work. Meaty'd give me an easy "poor-girl-who-is-going-to-die-soon" assignment. And—Ti squeezed my knee. "Sure," I answered.

"Sounds good," Ti said. "Assuming the invitation was for both of us, that is."

"It wouldn't be much of an invitation if it wasn't," Madigan said with a grin, and made another fierce left-hand turn.

Madigan left us in the parking lot. Ti walked me to my car. I opened up the door the old-fashioned way, with the key, and tossed Yuri's shirt onto the passenger seat. Then I gave him my address, watched him walk over to his red car—who the hell drove an El Camino anymore?—and made my way home, with my cell phone on speaker.

I dialed Sike's number into my phone while I was driving, like you're not supposed to do, and called it. She picked up right away.

"Hello?"

"Hi—um—" What was I supposed to say? *Sorry for being a jerk earlier, have you made any progress on saving my life?*

Sike snorted. "We haven't found anything out yet," she said, then hung up on me.

Great.

I tried Jake as I parked my car, and waited to leave a message. "Jake—it's me. Call me back," I said, then hung up. I'd initiated all of our conversations for weeks, but that was just how we were. I called him again, and it went straight to voice mail. "Seriously, call me back. It's really important."

What if I did die? I didn't want to spend time thinking about it—but if I did, I owed him an explanation. I called him back again. "Also—I love you."

He called back as I was crawling into bed for what I realized with sadness would only be a short nap.

"Sissy?" He sounded as tired as I felt.

"Bro! Hey—are you busy tomorrow? Or the day after?"

"Depends on when." I heard him yawn.

"Whenever is good for you. Just let me know and I'll be there. I need to talk to you."

"Obviously." I could almost hear him waking up. "I'll call you—the day after tomorrow."

"You won't forget?"

"I'm putting it in my dayplanner. Right now. Love you," he said, and hung up. I wondered briefly what the chances of him actually remembering were, then I went to sleep.

CHAPTER THIRTY-FIVE

I woke up when Ti rang my doorbell. I could see him standing on my stoop when I peeked through the blinds. I clearly remembered setting my alarm—and apparently I'd slept right through it. That wasn't like me.

"Coming!" I yelled out, while still lying in bed. I played with my vision some more, one hand on, one hand off. The glow didn't stick around when I was looking through both eyes, but as soon as I covered one and just looked through the other—either one now—it returned.

I felt bad about leaving him outside while I brushed my teeth and otherwise made myself presentable—but then again, since he was undead, I doubted he'd mind. I pulled on some fresh-from-the-dryer tight jeans, a loose-fitting long-sleeved shirt, tugged on boots, and ran down my hallway to meet him.

"Hi." I opened the door, grinning. He grinned back. I realized it'd been a long time since I'd had a guy here whose name I out-and-out knew.

"Well, hello there." He stepped graciously away from my door, and allowed me space outside. I yanked on my coat as we walked to his El Camino. I was happy to see that he'd seen fit to run the heater in his own car.

It felt odd to be in a car with him—it felt odd to be out with him, period. It wasn't his fault really, just the general awkwardness that I, with my tomcatlike mating habits, usually got to avoid.

"So Madigan's a werewolf, right?" I blurted out.

"Yep," Ti said, as if I hadn't had to ask. "He called me this afternoon to ask that you don't tell his wife where we were this morning."

"Okay." I didn't like lying, but I could live with it for the next two and a half days of my life. "Some weather, huh?" I said, purposely making light of the silence between us.

"I've seen worse." He angled his rearview mirror to look at me in it. "Want to tell me about things yet?"

"Heh." I sank back into the bucket seat. "I guess."

I told him the story from when I'd met Anna, through the tribunal coming up.

"Wait—what?" We were already on residential streets, and he pulled over to look at me. "You're going to a trial where you might die in two days and you're going out to dinner with me?"

"A girl's gotta eat," I said with a fake laugh.

"That's not funny, Edie."

"I know." I stared out the passenger window. "The truth is, I don't know what else to do."

"We can start by going to find out what happened to those girls, tonight, after dinner. Once all the vamps are out."

I sighed and turned back toward him. "I can't. I've got to go back to work."

"You're kidding me."

"No, I'm not." We were in a nice neighborhood here, with nice trees and houses, where people never had to worry what went bump in the night—or their kids tying off and shooting up. "I've got to go in."

"Edie—if we don't find that vampire—"

"Her name's Anna," I said as Ti continued to stare at me. "And my lawyer's looking too," I continued, trying to sound more hopeful about that than I actually felt.

"Your vampire lawyer?"

"Yeah."

Ti closed his eyes at my foolishness. But as long as Jake was on the junk, or trying to be, I couldn't quit working, cold turkey. If his immunity to drugs were to vanish, I knew my brother would go on the bender to end all benders and wind up in the morgue. So I was trapped. "I'm sorry, Ti. I can't take time off. I just can't."

"Edie, they don't own you." He put his hand on my knee. "I know it feels like that—"

"I have my reasons, okay?" I put my gloved hand on top of his.

"Well, I'll still go out and check on things." His voice was stern. I inhaled to protest, and then realized, how much trouble could a zombie really get into?

I squeezed his hand. "I appreciate it."

He took his hand back, restarted the car, and we went on our way.

Mrs. Madigan's name was Rita. I looked her up and down with my wonky left eye while she stirred at the stove, but I didn't get any strange glowing nimbus from her. And I met Jenny—a twelve-year-old girl with two glorious red pigtails; Jimmie—a six-year-old who had black hair and a cheerful disposition; and Jack—a prepubescent fourteen-year-old whose voice had a tendency to crack. They all were introduced to me very solemnly by their father, and I pretended not to know any of them from any time before.

Rita was an excellent conversationalist, and entertained us by talking about her time in the customer service mines of the DMV where she'd once worked as a teller. Apparently Madigan had been late with a registration payment once, made her laugh, and the rest was history. Madigan and Ti told stories about their time on the firefighting brigades—that was how they'd known one another, from back in the day, and the children were endlessly polite when they weren't blurting out "Dad, tell that story about the cat on the roof that was on fire again!" for my benefit.

It was strange being there, eating dinner with them. They knew that I knew, and I knew that they knew, and there we all were, a zombie, an assortment of werewolves and/or weredogs, and me, a nurse who was getting used to dealing with vampires. I was struck by how completely normal it felt to be with them, for all of our differences. And seeing Ti interact with Madigan made some strange and unused part of my heart start to swell. I blinked one eye and looked down at myself just in case.

"All right, kids—clear the table. Edie's got to get to work," Rita said to general complaints.

"Can't you stay?" Jenny asked. I'd braided her pigtails after yellow cake and chocolate ice cream, while she'd sat in my lap.

"I wish I could, but I can't. If we don't leave soon, I'll be late for work."

"Plates now, kids," Rita said.

Jenny slid off my lap and made a face, but took her dishes into the kitchen. I dutifully grabbed my plate and went in line to follow her. "When will you visit us next, Uncle Ti?" I heard Jimmie ask behind me.

"Thanks again," I told Rita in the kitchen, as I dropped off my dinner plate at the sink.

"He leaves town a lot," Rita murmured under her breath. "Make him stick around, okay? Don't blow it."

I nodded. I didn't intend to blow anything. At least, perhaps, not like that.

No one wanted to go to work that night less than I did. Each of the children gave me hugs before letting me go out of the door. Feeling sorry for myself consumed half my thoughts as I walked to Ti's car. Not knowing what to say occupied the other half. He opened my door for me, and I sat down.

"So, how long have you been alive?" I asked, as soon as he was belted in next to me.

He chuckled as the car started. "I'm older than you."

"That's not saying much." I was twenty-five. High school, then the local college's accelerated nursing program, courtesy of a deep desire to get the hell out of Dodge and a willingness to incur student loans. "How much older?"

"I'm not entirely sure," he said, pulling us out of Madigan's drive.

"You forgot?"

"I'm missing half my soul. It makes me a little forgetful now and then."

Silence reigned for half a block. Some conversationalist I was. "Are all zombies like you?"

"Like me, how?"

"Difficult conversationalists and ruggedly handsome."

He turned to look at me at the next stop. "Most people don't get past the scars."

"Don't they ever go away?"

He shrugged. "They would if I ever gave them long enough to heal."

"Well, I like them," I said.

"Why?" he surprised me by asking.

I inhaled to buy myself time to think. "Most people look normal on the outside, but they're messed up on the inside. Maybe you're messed up on the outside, but on the inside, you're good."

A supremely awkward, at least for me, silence passed between us. "Sooo, I like them," I said, winding up. "Don't get me wrong, I don't have a kinky fascination with them or anything." Wow. *Pull up, Edie, pull up!* "It's just not a big deal, you know?" I finished, resolving not to talk again for as long as I could help it.

Ti nodded and kept looking out at the road. "Yeah, I do."

We turned onto the highway and his attention to his driving saved me from myself.

"So what are you going to do after you drop me off?" I asked as we took the exit that would lead to County. I thought about the city as I'd seen it with the Shadows, like a map of a circulatory system sketched out, with the County Hospital as its living, beating heart.

"I'm going to go to Seventeenth and ask about the girls those vampires were interested in. If they picked them up, or took them to another location." He shook his head behind the wheel, at me or the situation, I didn't know. "Someone has to help you."

"I'm not some sort of princess trapped in a castle. If that's what you think, then I don't want your help." I didn't mind help but I sure as hell didn't want pity.

I saw his hands tighten slightly around the steering wheel, and his eyes met mine in the rearview mirror.

"I choose to disagree with you," he said, after a long pause. His reflection looked at me again. "On all points."

Suddenly my badge under my shirt felt sharper than it had, and the seat belt felt too tight, and the car, which'd been just fine before, felt ten degrees too warm. I fidgeted in my seat and sighed. "It just feels weird, okay? To have people care. I'm not used to that."

Ti pulled the car into the County's emergency room drop-off roundabout. "I'm not sure what kind of feral child upbringing you had, Edie. But I want to help you. It doesn't make me a bad person for wanting to help, or you a bad person for needing help. All right?"

I gathered my belongings off the El Camino's floor. "All right." I opened the door and rose up out of the passenger side, then quickly sank back down, with my purse and bag still in my lap, and shut myself in again. "So—was that a date?"

His eyebrows, or the places they would be when they grew in, rose. "Did it feel like a date?"

"I'm not sure."

"Did you want it to be a date?"

Two could play that game. "Definitely maybe."

He laughed, and reached his hand out behind my head, and pulled me gently toward him. It was awkward until our lips touched, and then it felt just fine. I swooned a little bit, falling forward some, almost into him. He caught me, his hand chaste upon my shoulder, and we parted. I reached for the door handle and let myself out quickly.

"So you'll call me tomorrow morning and let me know what you found out, okay?" I asked, after I was safely outside.

"Yeah." He shook his head again at me. "Take care of yourself, Edie."

"I'll try!" I said with a wave, then tried my hardest not to grin like a grinning fool until I'd turned to run inside.

CHAPTER THIRTY-SIX

I shoved my clothes into my locker and changed into my scrubs in record time, swiping my badge in just before the warning beep that meant they'd dock me a tenth of an hour of pay. Even running late and being dog—weredog!—tired, there was a spring in my step now, I'd admit. It was kinda nice to be kissed by someone, and not be sure about what would happen next.

"You're far too chipper for someone who the vampires want to see in two nights," Charles said, coming to stand near my desk by my patients' rooms. I'd just gotten the world's most random report from Floater Nick. He mostly worked the rest of the hospital, and only sometimes Y4, and I think the Shadows had mucked with his brain to remove sensitive information one too many times. He didn't know where either of my patients' IV lines were, but he'd made sure to tell me about a satisfying conversation one of them had had with his cousin on the phone, and the exact firmness of the other's bowel movements.

"Thanks for bringing me down, Charles," I said, checking over my patients' medication lists for the night. It really didn't matter what he said. If getting a scattershot report from Nick and knowing that some grumpy day shift person would come on shift in the morning couldn't blow my mood, then nothing could.

"Earth to Edie," Charles said, snapping his fingers.

"Sorry. You were saying?"

Apparently, "I was reminding you you were about to die" didn't feel appropriate for Charles to repeat. "Nothing," he said, and shrugged.

After assessments, Gina came over. "Too bad Ti's gone, eh?"

"Oh? Yeah," I agreed. My life was my life. Mostly. "Who's in the corrals tonight?"

"A shapeshifter."

"Into?" I prompted. She looked blank for a moment.

"Oh! No one. At the moment. It's a weird case." She glanced over her shoulder down to her side of the hall. The room that the weredragon had been in had supposedly been overhauled and strengthened. Still paid to be wary, though. Or were-y, as the case may be. "Weres only have one additional form. Any animal, really, only they just get one particular one. Werebats, werewolves, werewhatevers. A shapeshifter can only be other humans, and only replicas of ones that they've touched once before. To be honest, I think being a shapeshifter is more traumatic. Changing into fur is nothing compared to changing into other people. For example—this one's lost his mind. For real." She twirled her finger beside her ear.

I curled my lip. I felt bad for patients with psych issues, but they were draining to deal with. "I wish we had a psych ward for them."

"We do. But he's got a feeding tube in. He'd go over there with it, and the other patients might think they were helping him, by yanking the plastic worm out of his nose."

I tried for a moment to imagine the Y4 version of a psych ward and utterly failed. And I thought we had it bad *here*. "So what's he in with?"

"His technical diagnosis is schizophrenia, but I think he really falls under shapeshifteritis. Sometimes it's a her. He changes back and forth a bit. He's lost control."

"How so?"

"It's like having multiple personality disorder, with a different body for each personality. It takes a really emotionally and psychically healthy person to keep mentally stable—and they're better off if they don't touch too many other people, ever. It contaminates their DNA or something. He's in restraints and isolation now, but it's a little late." Her lips pressed together in sympathetic pain. "He plucked out his own eyes. Said he didn't want to see himself anymore."

"Ugh." I shuddered in revulsion. "Can't he just shift them back?"

"Nope. It's a conservation of mass thing. They can't shrink down to become children again, for instance, or enlarge to become obese. But weres can go from human-sized to bear-sized, go figure."

And I thought I'd had tough patients. Then again, it wasn't like the shapeshifter patient could see Gina being disgusted, as long as she could keep her tone of voice straight. "That's gotta be difficult."

"You're telling me. I have to do a dressing change on his mangled eye sockets every six hours. It's fucking grim."

"Well, let me know if you need help." Night shift bore the brunt of things that were every six hours, hitting both midnight *and* six A.M. Nothing like having to do a dressing change right after and right before report.

"Will do." She took two steps away from me, and then came those two steps back. "You know, you could pull his information up in the computer."

"What? Whose?"

"Mr. Smith's. I'm just saying."

"You mean Ti?" I asked and grinned at her, maybe a little too widely. "That's creepy and stalkery, and completely unethical—not to mention a violation of patient privacy laws."

Gina rolled her eyes, then looked at me more closely again. "You—you already went on a date!"

"Who, me? No." I shook my head in an exaggerated fashion and laughed.

Gina clapped her hands together. "Charles owes me twenty dollars."

"You were taking bets?" I forced another laugh as my stomach clenched. Maybe Ti dated a different nurse every time he came through? "On what?"

"How fast you two would go out. Charles thought you'd spend more time being depressed and withdrawn. What with the . . ." and Gina gestured over her head, indicating perhaps the bad-news cloud that must follow me around. "But I figured you for a fast mover."

I snorted. "Um, thanks. I guess."

"Not like that." She paused for a moment, choosing the right sentiment. "I think you'd rather live your life than wish you'd lived it, you know?"

Not entirely inaccurate. "Yeah, I do. Thanks," I said, and smiled.

My patients were easy. One eight-year-old kid—he of the bowel movements—whose parents were on guard at his bedside. He had a high fever, had gotten dehydrated, and was here for antibiotics and supervision. He was asleep in his bed, but both of his parents were up, watching the late-night infomercials. I did a quick blinking thing, and realized that while both parents glowed, the child did not. As far as I could tell—and I wasn't well-versed on my new superpower just yet; *thanks for not giving me an instruction manual, Shadows*—they were daytimers, but their son was entirely human. Either he'd have to be given transfusions of vampire blood to jumpstart the gene that would set him on his vampiric path—*gee, you should be meaner to other kids on the playground, here's some steak tartare?*—or else he would be made a donor for the rest of his life. Like I would, assuming that I lived.

I wondered if they wanted differently for him, like Anna's parents had wanted differently for her, but it wasn't exactly a subject I could broach. Telling them to give the kid more fiber to eat was one thing—asking them if they wanted out of the system would be another. I stayed there staring for a moment too long, wondering if there was some sort of vampire and vampire-related-humans underground railroad that could help either them or me. When the mother glanced over, I pretended to be watching the same juicing infomercial they were before making my escape.

The second patient had recently been ICU level, but was now on the mend. Three stab wounds to the chest and a shattered kneecap that probably didn't get busted on its own. But his daytimer body was taking care of business, with the help of a few small vamp blood transfusions, just a cc or two at a time. He wouldn't get off the phone, too busy making deals with his bookie, so I took his temperature in his armpit instead of his mouth. Maybe that's what'd gotten him into this mess. I wasn't in the mood to fight him on it, regardless.

I was finishing up all my charting, taking enough time to keep my handwriting legible, when I heard "Edie— come into the break room now!" in Meaty's nursing voice.

I jumped up and looked around. Everyone else on the floor was gone. *Oh, shit.*

I ran into the break room and saw Gina, Charles, and Meaty standing there, around . . . a commemorative cake. It was shaped like a coffin, frosted by hand, and my name was scrawled across the top in blue icing.

Perhaps in any other setting it would have been morbid or tacky—no, it was still morbid *and* tacky—but I could tell from the expectant looks on their faces that it was morbid and tacky with love. Tears welled up. I looked from one to the other of them. "Thanks, guys. Really. You're too sweet."

"Well, you know—" Meaty said, and shrugged.

"Gina did all the hard work. I just tasted this part back here, for quality control," Charles said, pointing to a discreet finger swipe in the icing on the cake's far side.

Gina stuck her tongue out at Charles. "Hey—have I told you you owe me twenty bucks?"

"What flavor is it?" I asked quickly, hoping to deflect attention.

"Twenty bucks, eh?" Charles asked, looking askance at me. I started blushing furiously.

"How did you spend twenty bucks on cake mix?" Meaty wondered aloud. "You'll have to spot me. I've only got a five."

Charles and Gina went back to the floor soon after, and Meaty followed them, leaving me to eat alone. The cake was a delicious chocolate with blackberry filling, and I realized it was the second time I'd had cake that night. Usually I'd feel guilty, but hey, if this particular cake was accurate, I might as well eat up. My patients were fine, anyhow. I wondered who Ti was out there scaring by being a frighteningly scarred-up and pissed-off zombie, and if Sike and Mr. Weatherton, Esquire, were doing anything at all yet on my behalf.

Leaving half of my piece of cake behind, I trotted back to where my phone was in the locker room and made a phone call. This time Sike recognized my number.

"Nothing yet," she said, and hung up.

"But—" I stared at the "call ended" symbol on my phone. No way. I was beginning to wonder if Mr. Weatherton's services weren't some sort of time-wasting ruse. I redialed Sike to tell her so.

"I told you—"

"Look, I just want to know—"

"We're working on it," she interrupted me. We were both silent on the line, and then she took a deep inhale. "If you hadn't killed Yuri, you wouldn't be in this mess."

I couldn't refute that. She hung up on me again, more slowly this time, and I didn't wonder until afterwards how she'd known Mr. November's real name.

I went back to my half-eaten piece of cake, and shoved most of it around my plate. If the day had come that Edie Spence was too depressed to eat an entire piece of chocolate cake with chocolate frosting— Meaty opened the break-room door, interrupting my personal pity party.

"I have something for you," Meaty said, distracting me from my thoughts. Meaty produced a small glass vial from a breast pocket and I took it. The fluid inside was clear, and the sterile cap was gone, but the rubber stopper was still in place. There wasn't a label, but I could feel the ridge of tackiness that indicated where there had once been one. It was about the same size as the bottles for intravenous Protonix.

"What is it?"

Meaty looked directly at me while answering. "It's pope water. Don't ask where I got it."

I'd inhaled to ask exactly that, but stopped.

"What's it do?"

"It's a hundred times more potent than normal holy water. You apply it topically. On them, not you."

I held up the little vial and looked at Meaty through it. Even distorted by the fluid, Meaty's pale face was serious. "Save it for a rainy day, okay? Go put it in your locker."

I nodded and turned to do as I was told. But I refused to believe that we had a pope in a decantable jar somewhere downstairs. "Meaty—" Telling a nurse not to ask something should be considered an act of cruelty and be covered by a convention of war.

"Don't ask," Meaty repeated.

"All right, all right." I put the med in my locker, then returned to finish my cake.

When I got back to the ward, someone was shouting. Their voice was muffled through the doorway, but I could see Gina watching her monitors closely.

I walked over and followed her gaze.

"I've got it under control, Edie," Gina said, glancing at me. "This one doesn't breathe flame."

I peered up at the monitor with her. The cameras inside the room were focused on the patient. He was androgynous from where I sat, with close-cropped hair that wasn't parted. The dressing to his eyes covered up most of his face. He wore the County-issued blue-scramble puke-stain-minimizing gown that everyone had. He continued to yell—now that I was close enough, I could hear what he was saying.

"Who am I? Tell me who I am!"

His yells were plaintive and frightening at the same time, like they'd taken a page from the Shadows. "What kind of meds can you give?" I asked.

She gestured to her chart. "Haldol. In intramuscular injections, mostly. Hard to keep an IV line in an unwilling shapeshifter."

The shapeshifter was writhing in his restraints, his body changing shapes. The monitors and cameras weren't HD, and so I watched his fingers appear to pixilate and then resolve again, as he tried on all sorts of different forms. They went black-skinned for a moment, and I gasped in surprise.

"Pretty cool, eh? Like a human kaleidoscope."

I nodded and kept watching as Gina went to the medication machine and then came back with a small bottle and a big syringe. "It's time for another shot of Vitamin H," she said, holding up the bottle. "And I don't mean biotin."

"How can I help?"

"You can cover me." She opened up the drawer of the isolation cart that had the tranquilizer gun in it. "After the Haldol kicks in, we'll do the dressing change."

"We?" I asked. "I meant for all my helping business to be out here. In the vicinity of your chart."

She snorted and handed me the gun.

CHAPTER THIRTY-SEVEN

The shapeshifter quieted his existential howling as soon as Gina opened the door.

"Hey there, Mr. Huang. It's me, your nurse for the night, Gina." Gina had briefly explained the importance of not touching he/she/it, nor letting them touch you before going in. "I'm just coming in with a shot for your pain."

"Don't touch me!" the patient said. "Don't touch me anymore!"

"You're in a hospital now. I'm gonna give you something for your pain," Gina continued, while walking toward him, syringe out. I couldn't imagine being her, but if she'd snuck up on weres before, in their angry animal forms, she'd had practice. "It should help you calm down. We have a psychiatrist who'll be seeing you tomorrow. I've got gloves on. I won't touch you, I promise."

"Get away from me!" the shapeshifter howled, but he stilled and became a she, then went quiet. Gina looked to me and nodded. I put the trank gun's butt against my shoulder.

"I'll be injecting you on your shoulder, sir," Gina said. She flipped up the gown sleeve and swiped only once with an alcohol swab before pushing the needle in.

"Stop!" he howled, skin tone going from Asian to Anglo as Gina pushed the syringe's plunger down. "No!"

The hands that strained beneath the buckled leather restraints had fingers that metamorphosed between a man's with calluses, to a woman's dainty ones complete with perfect long nails, to an elderly person's skeletal fingers, denuded of subcutaneous fat. The characteristics and coloration of the hands and face I could see around the dressings no longer matched. The shapeshifter appeared to be going calico.

"Gina—" I warned.

"You'll be fine soon, sir," Gina said, disposing of the syringe in the sharps container, without turning her back on him. The patient sighed aloud, relaxing into his mattress, and his face and hands, which had been the most energetic parts of him, went anonymous, slack and pink.

"Don't point that thing at me, okay?" Gina said.

"I'm not." I held my aim at her patient's torso.

"Like I was saying before," she continued, as she moved around to the head of the bed, "if they touch too many other people, they end up acquiring too much . . . I don't want to say DNA, though it could be DNA. Data, maybe?"

"What's that they say about the nature versus nurture argument, then?" I asked from the doorway. Gina was unwinding the Kerlix roll from around the patient's head, so she could get at the dressings that stuffed his eyes.

"Do I look like a philosopher?" she asked, looking over at me, grinning. I grinned back, lowering the barrel of the gun.

It happened faster than I could have imagined. Gina was reaching forward, to pull out the wads of gauze that occupied the space where the shapeshifter's eyes used to be, and then there was a spindly clawlike hand at her throat. The other hand was bloated and huge—maybe conservation of mass didn't matter, if you could slide enough of it around.

"No!" I shouted. The shapeshifter hauled Gina between us, blocking any possible shot I might have made. "Meaty!"

The shapeshifter pooled mass, staying the same even hundred and fifty pounds, just rolling pieces of it around till each of its limbs were free, making each of them twig thin, while the others were trunk thick, in turn. "Make it stop! We all want it to stop! Don't touch us!"

"Take it, Edie!" Gina hissed, being garroted by the shapeshifter's right hand. She kicked him but he didn't seem to register any pain. "Any shot! Take it! Hit me! Hurry!"

"Put her down!" I yelled, running into the room. He kept flicking Gina around like a rag doll as I tried to find a portion of him that was wide enough for a shot. Everything I'd practiced on at the range didn't fucking move! I circled around the room. Gina stopped fighting and hung limp. Red circles were blooming around her eyes. The shapeshifter ripped her badge off her and threw it to the ground.

"Never again!" the shapeshifter continued. He made himself look like her, mocking her shape in his blue hospital gown.

"Meaty!" I shrieked again. He was turning toward me, and soon his back would be to the open door—

My charge nurse came around the corner like a rhino, holding an even longer gun than my own. "Net gun!"

I ducked, not knowing what else to do, and heard a zipping hiss of string. There was a thump as it made contact, and the shapeshifter and Gina tumbled down together in front of me, tangled in a pile of netting. A hand reached out—whose? Gina's, or his?—and grabbed my ankle, yanking me forward. I swung the gun around and tried to find a shot—anything covered in blue was fair game—but then he looked up at me, looking exactly like Gina, except for the gauze inside his eyes soaking up blood. "Don't touch me!" he pleaded with her voice.

I paused, and he slammed his hand forward into the

barrel, making the butt of the gun jump up my shoulder and ram into my face. My lip cut against my teeth, and I scrabbled to regain the gun as my mouth filled with blood. Charles ran into the room and grabbed the tranquilizer gun from me.

"What the fuck, you crazy loon," Charles said, holding the trank gun up like a club. He flipped his hold on it at the last moment, to point the tranquilizer end at the shape-shifter and fire, point-blank, into his thigh.

"About fucking time!" Gina coughed out, lying beside the patient that still wore her shape.

"Jesus." I started pulling the net corners up as soon as the shapeshifter sagged. "Are you okay?"

"Me, or the Lord?" Gina asked, her voice raspy. She grabbed hold of my shoulder and I pulled her out from underneath the net.

"You." Her eyes were circled in red and there was a handprint on her throat. "That—that was awful."

"You think?" Gina said, her anger palpable. I looked past her at the mess of netting and patient on the floor. It looked like an alternate-universe Gina. He'd peed him-self, I could smell it.

"From here on out, shapeshifters get chemically se-dated," Meaty announced. "Sux or propofol for the lot of them, I don't care what Turnas thinks."

Gina took a few deep breaths as we both stood. My lip was throbbing, and I could still taste fresh blood. "You'd better wash that out," Meaty said, pulling a packet of gauze out of a pocket to press into my hand.

I nodded and took it, and went to the sink in the corner of the room. There was no mirror, but I could see my blurry reflection in the paper-towel dispenser. I covertly looked around the room with one eye, and then the other. The shifter glowed, yeah, but nothing else in the room did.

Then I looked down. Beneath my scrubs, I had a subtle

nimbus. And the splotch of blood on the gauze that I held was glowing bright. "Shit," I said.

"You can say that again," Charles said, standing over the shapeshifter, tranquilizer gun at his shoulder, like an infantry guard.

CHAPTER THIRTY-EIGHT

I gave the report to the day shift nurse. For once, it wasn't upsetting. In one more day, what would anything I say or charted matter, anyhow? My encounter with the shape-shifter had made me morose, seeing Gina there upon the floor, sprawled out and sodden. It could have been me. It might still *be* me.

After my fast report, I was the first in the locker room. I toyed with the idea of cleaning out my locker. Better to do it now, while I had the time, instead of tomorrow, all rushed. I could donate my stethoscope to the future un-willing nurses of Y4. I looked at my extra coat and boxes of oatmeal—taking them home somehow seemed like defeat. I knew if I didn't get a chance to reclaim them, they'd donate the coat to a shelter. While I was consider-ing the fate of the oatmeal, I saw the vial of "pope water" Meaty'd given me earlier on my locker's small shelf. I hefted it, imagining myself holding it out at other people—vampires—like a badge, or throwing it at them like a gre-nade. I tossed it in my purse.

Gina knocked on the door before coming in. There were still red bands around her throat.

"Gina—I'm so sorry."

She didn't look at me as she walked to her locker and opened it. I stood there, trapped because her locker was closer to the door than mine, hoping for some sort of acknowledgment.

"You should have shot him when it started," she said, her voice still rough.

"I didn't have a shot then. Honest. I swear."

There was a long pause until her locker closed. Her lips pursed, and she still wasn't looking at me. "If you had a shot, any shot, that wasn't okay."

"I didn't." My mind raced through the moments where she'd been trapped. I'd tried, I'd searched, I'd failed. I couldn't even save a friend. How was I supposed to save myself? "I didn't until the end, and then I blew it. I'm sorry."

"Yeah. I know."

I opened and closed my mouth a few times, like a fish out of water. I wanted to make excuses and I wanted her to forgive me. But if she was going to, she had to do it in her own good time. It was just that potentially I didn't have much time left, and I needed all the absolution I could find.

"Thanks," I wound up saying, zipping my purse closed. I walked carefully around her to the door. It was halfway closed already when I heard her say, "Don't forget your extra cake."

I went into the break room, where Meaty was giving his report to the day shift charge. I tiptoed around the table and opened the fridge. It'd be hard to find half a cake in the sea of tinfoil and leftovers.

"Just a second," Meaty said to the other charge nurse. "Spence!"

"Yeah?" I asked.

"Take tomorrow night off."

I almost hit my head inside the fridge in surprise. "Really?"

"Really. We're low on patients. We'll call you if we need to. Tie up some loose ends. Take a vacation."

Cake retrieved, I carefully stood up. "Gina needs the vacation more than I do, Meaty."

"Don't worry, she'll get hers."

I inhaled to protest. I wasn't exactly being fired, though. And I did have a lot of things to do, assuming Anna didn't turn up. "Thanks."

Meaty gave me a knowing nod. "You're welcome."

I called Sike again on the way to the train station. It went to her voice mail. Of course. I stared at my phone, frowning for a second as I listened for the beep.

"Look—this is Edie—are you all doing anything? Anything at all? I need an update. Have you found her yet? I want to know what's going on."

The message cut off anything else I was going to say. I fought the urge to redial and just leave a message of me cussing. I shoved my phone into my purse and walked to the train station as quickly as I could.

Morning commuters at the station glanced at me, then quickly looked away. With a fattening lip, I was an object of curiosity, but no one wanted to add my problems to their own. I found a seat on the train when it arrived, watching the shadows underneath the seats in front of me. Were the Shadows in there, watching me back? Had they found out anything about Anna yet? My hand found my badge—I wished I had a way to ask them. Me wanting to talk to Shadows, that was a change indeed.

My train finished its downtown loop and the other commuters went away. It was just me staring at my shoes in the train when the doors across from me opened, and let in someone I didn't really want to see.

Asher. This time without flowers. He was wearing a suit that was tailored precisely for him, sharp-shouldered and swank. He was as startled to see me as I was to see him; I could see it in his eyes for half a second before they narrowed.

"No one else should get to hit you," he informed me with his British accent. With the apparent implication that it was still okay, sometimes, for him. Spanking was fun and all, but to the best of my knowledge it hardly ever caused fat lips.

"Not now," I said, looking in my bag for a book to read and ignore him with. I saw the pope water sitting there, thought of Meaty, and remembered the "loose ends" comment. Well, here was one, sitting right across from me. I looked up and he had a bemused expression on his face.

"Look," I began, inhaling deeply. I sucked at difficult conversations. And who could I have a conversation with that went "I probably won't see you again, because I'm going to be going on trial with some vampires"? Just people at work—and Ti. That thought brightened me. "Look, I've met someone," I said aloud. "They get me. They really get me. I've got a lot of problems, things you wouldn't even begin to understand. It's all very complicated, really."

An eyebrow crept higher on his head, pulling a lopsided smile behind. I kept going in spite of myself. "It was fun, don't get me wrong, and we had chemistry, sure, but—"

I stared at him and lost my train of thought. There was a gravitational pull between us, yes. But if I were the Earth, then he was a cool and distant moon. Light, but not heat—and I liked to be warm. "You're a doctor, I'm a nurse, it's just not a good idea."

The train shuddered to a halt.

"I believe this is your stop," he said. He stood and made no move toward the door.

"It is. See you." I stood and walked out into the station and made it halfway up the stairs.

"I'm not really a doctor, you know," said Asher's accented voice. I turned and saw his suit, incongruous with

the station's milky white walls. I quickly blinked an eye
and found him glowing, bright.

I inhaled. "Then . . . what are you?" I asked, slowly.

"I can be a doctor. I can be a lot of things. I prefer, however, to be myself." He crossed the short distance between
us. "Look at me, Edie."

I did. It was daylight outside, just six stairs away. He
couldn't be a vampire. I reached between my breasts and
pressed my badge hard against my skin.

Asher's face slowly became the face of someone I didn't
recognize. His dark eyes were pierced with blue, until
the blue overtook all the brown, like the sky after a
heavy storm. His skin tone lightened from olive to become
Nordic white, and the set of his jaw tilted, from angled
high to low and square.

"I think I met your cousin last night," I said.

"Now will you tell me where you work?" he asked.

"Y4."

"It figures," he said. He shifted back to the Asher I
knew in the blink of an eye.

"Does that mean that when you feel like it, you can be
me now?" I asked. I thought of Gina, on the floor with
gauzed eyes full of blood.

"No, actually. I did try, though, at the club, and several times thereafter. When I found out I couldn't, I was
shocked, then intrigued. Then when I learned you were
merely being protected by the proximity of your badge . . ."

"So you weren't really into me for me is what you're
saying?"

"You were a novelty."

And isn't that what every girl wants to hear? "Fan-
fucking-tastic. Good night, Asher, or good morning, or
whatever the fuck it is for you now. I'm too tired for this."
I started walking the final stairs away from him.

"That's not what I meant, Edie," he called after me. "You
have to imagine my surprise that night. I thought you were

a rare beast, something that for shapeshifters is like a unicorn—someone whose spirit can't be tamed. When I realized you worked at a hospital, and probably *the* hospital, and that was the reason I couldn't shift into you, well . . . you can only imagine my disappointment."

I whirled on him. "How about you imagine my disappointment? When some guy like you is interested in me, we have great sex, and then all of a sudden I'm not good enough anymore?"

He looked up at me like a baffled dog, and he clearly did not understand. And I didn't want to explain it to him, how girls like me never got guys like him, how I was a Wednesday-night girl, but not a Friday-night girl. I decided it wasn't worth the energy. I'm not sure what played on my face right then, but at least he seemed thoughtful.

"You've got a really confused relative at Y4 right now. You should go check him out."

Asher held up his hands. "Edie, I'm sorry."

I inhaled to tell him to shove it, and then shrugged instead. "Yeah. I know." I hitched up my purse, and walked straight ahead.

CHAPTER THIRTY-NINE

I slung my purse across my chest for the short walk home from the station. I had set out across the commuter parking lot when I heard a car honk its horn. I ignored it, and it honked again. I turned, to make sure I wasn't about to be run over, and saw my own car, with Jake sitting inside. I changed my course, picking up steam as I crossed the lot.

"How did you—" I sputtered, then realized I should be glad he wasn't on the way to trade it in.

"I went by your place last night. I saw the car out front, and knocked and knocked, then I realized you weren't home. So I let myself in with my spare, and decided I'd come pick you up this morning for breakfast."

I inhaled to be angry at him—I hadn't told him he could make a spare key for my place, but him having one was the least of my concerns. "Well—thanks."

"Well, you're welcome." He pulled us out of the lot. He looked clean, physically and bloodstreamily. Maybe he'd taken a shower at my place. His hands on the wheel were solid, competent. "What happened to you?" he asked, glancing over at me. I used the rearview mirror to check out my lip. It was as swollen as it felt.

"Last night was long." I tilted the mirror back toward him.

"Uh-huh. When'd you start taking German?"

"What?"

"That broken CD player. I tried to get the disc out, but it wouldn't open for me."

"Heh."

"I figured you'd learn Spanish for work. Or French— you've always been a mushy romantic. But German? Odd choice."

I crossed my arms, unaccustomed to being a passenger in my own car. He was lucky Grandfather hadn't exploded, or shot out laser beams, or done anything else that angry German ghosts tended to do. "It was the right price at the store. Where are we going?"

"Molly's."

"Nice." I knew the place; it was close to my house. They made a mean chicken-fried steak and eggs. "How've you been?"

"Pretty good."

"Where've you been?" I pressed.

"Around." He glanced over at me, briefly, then continued to drive. Did I even really want to know the honest answers to those questions? Probably not. We sank into the easy silence of people who love one another—or at least one person who loved the other, and the junkie who loved her back as long as it was expedient—and who really have nothing left to talk about anymore.

Our silence lasted until after we ordered breakfast. He had coffee, I stuck to iced tea, keeping the ice cubes against my lip with my tongue, and we pretended to catch up on things.

"So really, Jake—how've you been?" I wanted to reach over and roll up his sleeves to see for myself. Then again, right now, he looked so clean-cut—at least clean-shaven— that I was ill-inclined to break the illusion. I was the one who looked beaten down—hell, I had the busted lip to prove it. If everything was going to go to shit in my life, I could at least pretend that my brother was back together in his. But the nurse in me wouldn't let me *not* ask. "Are you still . . . experimenting?"

He stared off into the distance, through the plate-glass window, frosted with a mural of fake Christmastime snow. It was a thousand-yard stare, but at least his pupils constricted. "I did for a while." He inhaled and exhaled. "But I'm broke now."

He seemed so sad and forlorn. "Do I have a couch left at home?" I asked in an overly teasing tone, to break the mood.

"Not broke as in out of money—well, yeah, that too." He looked ruefully at me. "I mean I'm broken on the inside."

"How so?"

"I dunno. The synapses in my head. Edie, I can't even get all the way drunk anymore. How sad is that?" he asked me, in all seriousness.

"Not very." Pretty soon he'd have to get a job to lose himself in, maybe a girlfriend. Soon he'd be normal. If only the spell would last.

The waitress brought our food. Molly's chicken-fried steak and eggs slathered with gravy was as good as I remembered. "Can I tell you something? And you not think I'm crazy?" he asked.

What could be as crazy as death by vampire trial? "Sure, Jake," I said around a mouthful.

"I think," he said, looking around, then leaning over. "I think I'm part of some test."

I almost choked on my eggs. I forced the bolus down, and took a long swig of tea. "Really?"

He studied my face. "You think I'm crazy."

I wasn't sure what to say. I opted to cover my tracks. "Well, you have done a lot of drugs, Jakey."

"Seriously, Sissy—you and I both know that this is

weird, right? I mean, not even booze." He sighed, staring into his unadulterated coffee. "Not even booze."

"Maybe it's a chance for you to start over?" I suggested. "I mean, now that you're clean, you can get a fresh start."

"I'm twenty-eight, Sissy."

"So? It's never too late to start over." I tried to sound like I meant it.

"Have you been reading church signs lately or what?"

If I had, they would have all been of an apocalyptic bent. They were right—the end was fucking nigh. I swirled a piece of steak in the gravy on my plate to buy myself time to think. "I just want to see you happy, Jake."

"On the drugs, I was happy. I never had a bad minute while I was up on heroin. Some people see things, crazy shit, and talk to God. On heroin I *was* God. That's hard to beat."

"Heh." I studied his face, around the downturned eyes, and the full yet frowning lips. Handsome, but deeply sad. For a moment I was mad—I'd bought him this second chance, maybe at the cost of my very soul, and for what?— but I could never be mad at Jake for long. He was my brother.

"Who do you think would be experimenting on you?" I asked him, as neutrally as I could.

"What do you care?" he said, and shrugged. I waited for the waitress to refill his mug before I tsked at him.

"I'm your sister. Of course I care."

He stared into his cup before answering. "I don't know who. But I think I know where. The Armory."

It was the name of a large homeless shelter downtown, where you could catch a warm bed and a hot meal, if you stood in line long enough and kept your head down. It was where Mr. Galeman'd been staying, before he'd met Anna. Jake continued, "They've had a change of ownership, or guardianship, or whoever the hell runs the place. It used to be casual, now it's almost militarized."

I knew the recent economic downturn in the county's affairs had had an effect on the number of homeless people in the city; I'd heard Emergency Department nurses complain. "How would they do that?"

"I don't know. The food there? Maybe. And they've got a needle exchange program—they could fill them up with some sort of Narcan ahead of time—"

"Jake, don't be an idiot." I set my fork down with a clatter on my plate. "For God's sake, if you need clean needles, I'll fucking get them for you," I heard myself say. Jake looked as surprised as I felt by my vehemence. But even as I offered now—what would happen in just two short days? I reached over, grabbed his mug, and took a gulp of his coffee. It burned the top of my mouth and scalded all the way down.

"Sissy—"

In that moment I wanted to tell him everything. Everything from the beginning. From our parents' divorce to the first time my mom kicked him out. I could forgive him the pot, the acid, and the E—teenagers did those all the time and were fine. But from the very moment, the very first moment, when I'd seen a track mark on his arm, I'd been trapped, trying to save him from himself. Now was just one more fucking time.

I stood up, eyes hot. "I'll be right back."

I almost ran into the bathroom. I made fists for strength. I should tell him everything. All of it.

But then what? Things don't work out, I die in two days, and then he's left knowing that? Forever?

I'd done it to myself. It wasn't my fault entirely, for damn sure, but I'd done it to myself. I could have ignored him. I could have gone in for tough love. I washed my face before looking at myself in the mirror.

"You did this to yourself, Edie," I told my reflection. "You cannot lay that on him."

He did deserve to know that his enforced sobriety might

come to a screeching halt in two days. But that was it. Not how or why. But when? Yes.

I stalked back out to my half-eaten breakfast to find the table empty.

"I'll get it next time," Jake had written in his neat handwriting on the bill, right under the waitress's "Thanks!" with a smiley face. My car keys were left in a tangle on top of my purse.

"Dammit, Jake," I muttered under my breath and looked around. Our waitress appeared anxious, like she'd feared a dine and dash, and flashed a nervous smile at me for noticing. I pulled out cash from my wallet and left her a hefty tip.

Couldn't take it with me, anyway.

CHAPTER FORTY

I drove my car home and parked in my spot. I sat there for a second, wondering if I could leave an official letter for Jake and avoid a confrontation entirely. "Edie Spence's last will and testament—to her brother, she leaves her couch and her small collection of CDs." I rolled my eyes at myself, found my house key on my chain, and walked to my door.

As soon as I entered, the CD player started chattering at me in German. It was as bad as Minnie.

"I'm sorry. He's my brother," I tried to explain. "I know, he pisses me off too." Its light went from red to green, and then it clicked off, in angry silence or exhaustion.

I had barely kicked off my shoes and hung up my coat when I heard a knock at the door. "Jake! I'm still mad at you!" I announced, walking down my short hall. I peeked out the peephole and saw Ti there, his scars magnified a hundredfold, like the ripples in an unmade bed.

"One second," I called and undid all the latches. "Hey. Come in." I pressed myself to the side of the wall so that he could pass. He did so, managing to avoid touching me completely, which was pretty amazing, given his shoulder width.

"What happened to your face?" He turned toward me in the small hallway.

I waved my hand dismissively in the air. "A patient last night. I don't want to talk about it."

He shrugged, and I followed him out to my couch—the only furniture left in my living room—and he waited till I sat down, and then sat down an inordinately long distance away from me. I looked at him, then at the vast expanse of couch between us. "What'd I do wrong now?"

He blinked. "You're direct."

"I've got two days to live."

Ti looked down at his knees for a moment. "I went down to Seventeenth—" he began, and I had visions of sultry hookers dancing in my head. "And when I came back here, I saw a man entering your place." He looked up at me, and there was definitely hurt in his golden eyes.

"Really?" I crossed my arms. "I'm not sure which you should be more embarrassed about—being slightly stalkery or assuming that I'm dating my brother."

"Ohhhh—" His shoulders untensed, and he shook his head at himself.

"Seriously, just ask me things." I scooted over on the couch. "Even if I weren't running out of time, I don't play games. Never have, never will." Unless you were my junkie brother, I mentally amended. "How long were you out there?"

He exhaled. "Since four A.M."

"Silly zombie." I lightly slapped him on his forearm.

"I do feel foolish," he began.

"Good." It was sort of more cute than stalkery, for now. He did appear embarrassed. "Just don't make a habit of it, okay?"

"Fine." His face softened into a grin, and so did mine.

"So—about the girls?"

"I didn't get to actually talk to any of them."

And perhaps it was my turn to be relieved, just a little. "Oh? Why not?"

"They weren't around."

"You . . . didn't get there in time?" I imagined him trying to talk to one of them, a normal girl except for her occupation, and her running away from him in fear, like he was Frankenstein's monster and she was short a mob.

"In a manner of speaking," Ti said, and his voice was grave.

Suddenly I realized what he meant. "Oh, no. What happened?"

"They're all gone. Dead, I assume." He looked down at his clasped hands.

"How do you know they're dead?"

"Hookers aren't known for their financial solvency—they usually can't get away from their pimps or their dealers long enough. So unless there's a Greyhound full of them all on the way to Florida, I feel safe assuming the worst," he said.

"But—won't the police find out?"

"Find what? And when?" Ti held his empty hands out. "The city's big. It could take a while. And if they only find one at a time, they could be declared NHIs."

"What's that?" I asked.

Ti's hands curled into fists against his denim. "It means No Humans Involved. It's a way to dump cases that no one wants to look into or solve. When the cops think someone's done them a favor, by taking out the trash."

"No humans involved," I muttered. "Well, they got that right." I imagined those girls looking at the expensive suits that all the vampires seemed to wear, ignoring their foul breath, their odd mannerisms, the way their eyes kept looking through them—maybe, sadly, they were used to that—and hoping that for one night they'd be warm and well paid.

Ti's head was bowed in frustration. I reached out and put my hand on his. "So what now?"

"I'm not sure. When the bodies turn up, we can look for ideas. And I spread enough money around last night—if

anything comes up, people will call. I left an impression."
His strong hands flexed again.

A wave of exhaustion hit me. I'd been going almost full
throttle for days now—a week, really. If there was nothing
we could do, I knew what I wanted to do at least. Sleep.

But I didn't want to be alone. I looked over to him, and
out around at my living room. This couch was a life raft,
holding us up against the ocean of drab carpeting and the
rough world outside, one person probably dying, one already dead.

And as tempting as it sounded, sleep would be giving
in. It would be admitting the beginning of the end, the
wind down into the final, darkest night. Gina was right—
you had to keep moving, or you'd start crying. I leaned
forward and did the only thing I could think of to do to
stop myself from sinking. I kissed him. Even though with
my busted lip it hurt.

He braced himself, first surprised, then leaned into me,
reaching his arms up to hold my head and tilt it slightly so
I fit him better. He was slow kissing me back, tentative, as
if his spirit for these things was as fragile as the skin that
held him.

I didn't care. I pressed harder for a moment, ignoring
my bottom lip's sharp pain, and then swung around so that
I was straddling his lap, bending over to kiss his face, all of
his face, as my hair hung down and shielded us from anything outside. I took his hands and put them at my waist,
urging him to go further. And then I thought about what
the hell I was doing.

I pulled my head back and sat up, and squirmed backward on his lap. "I'm sorry."

"For what?" he asked, letting me go.

I wanted to explain, but I wasn't sure I could explain.
Him, here, now, this? But I did owe him an explanation. I
didn't want to seem like some emotionally damaged freak.
I had to try.

"I actually like you," I said, and then started backpedaling. "I mean, I could actually like you, if we got to know each other better and all."

He tilted his head forward. "You say that like it's a bad thing."

"Do you know how long it's been since I've been with someone I actually liked?" I looked wildly around the room, as if ghosts of conquests past would arise and vouch for me.

"It's okay," he said. His tone brought my gaze firmly back to him. He was quiet beneath me—okay, so he was a zombie, so that was easy—but nothing about him was threatening, or rushing. Rushing me, or rushing out the door. He didn't seem angry or mad, or scared, or anything else I'd been afraid he'd be right now. "Whatever you want. It's okay," he repeated. He smiled, not too hard, not too wide. Just a gentle smile. A safe smile. A soft smile. Damn.

"I also don't want to die in two days and not have had sex with you," I admitted.

He laughed, and reached up to cup my face in his hands and bring it back down toward him.

"Then don't," he said, half a second before he kissed me.

CHAPTER FORTY-ONE

Zombies are good with their lips.

Ti held my head in place, like I was wild or fragile, and kissed me gently. His lips brushed mine again, then pressed more firmly. I gasped a little bit; my busted lip still stung.

"Sorry, my cut—"

"Stop apologizing," he whispered. Holding my head, he pressed kisses on my forehead, kissed on top of my closed eyes, kissed down my right cheek. He tilted my head up, stroking along the line of my chin with his thumb, and kissed me underneath my jaw, where my pulse was pounding, I knew it, kissed down the path of my carotid until he reached the collar of my sweater, and pulled this down, until my collarbone was exposed. His hands found the bottom of my sweater and pulled it up slowly, and I was dying to help him take it off me, but I worried about breaking things, somehow ruining this trance. I sat still, his lips working across the vee of my throat, my breath coming in short gasps, biting down on the moans I wanted to make.

Ti crept my sweater ever higher, until I had to raise my arms to free it, and I was sitting there exposed on his lap, in only my jeans, lanyard, and bra. I reached up and pushed my lanyard back so that my badge would hang behind me.

And I realized I'd rocked down into his lap without meaning to. I was pressed against him, near, but not near enough yet.

He dropped my sweater on my floor, and his hands found the clasp of my bra, after swatting my badge aside. It was undone in an instant, and he slid the straps off my shoulders, pulling it down. My apartment was cold. Ti tilted his head down and found my breasts. And then I had to moan.

Zombies are good with their teeth.

He bit my nipple, halfway hard, rolling his tongue across my flesh on the inside of his mouth. The gentleness of his kisses was gone now, replaced with a need to know me. To taste me. He bit me till it almost hurt, in the full-ness of my cleavage, in the roundness of my breast against my ribs, one breast, then the other, his teeth against one pert nipple at a time, leaving teeth marks on me for an instant before they faded, with nothing but my memory of my burning need to prove them there.

And I could feel Ti, trapped inside his jeans, hard. I rocked forward into him as his bristles scraped against my skin, switching from one breast to the next. I rode against him, still too clothed.

His hands found one another at the top of my jeans. They undid the button, unzipped the fly. He looked up at me with his golden eyes. And then he reached up to hold me, pick me up, and lay me down on my living room floor. He grabbed hold of my jeans and underwear and tugged, bringing them sliding down to my knees. I reached up for him, expecting him to pull off his jeans and join me—I knew he wanted to, I could clearly see the out-line of his cock. But Ti grabbed for my jeans again and pulled them off me, one leg at a time, and then beheld me, naked there before him, himself between my legs.

He reached forward, pulling his hands down my stomach, and pushed my thighs wide.

Zombies are very, very, very good with their tongues.

I curled up against Ti on the open expanse of my floor. He was still wearing all of his clothing, petting me like I was some exotic beast. Perhaps, compared to him, I was.

"I think I know your name, Edie," Ti said, running his hands up against the badge's plastic, it and its lanyard the only shred of clothing I had on. It lay against my chest now, up between my breasts.

"Just humor me, okay?" I said. Were the Shadows watching this? Feeling this? Voyeuristic bastards. I snuggled nearer, because his flannel was warm. "You have too much clothing on."

He made a negating noise.

"No, really. I refuse to be the only naked person here." I reached up and cupped his chin. I ran my hand higher, and his scars made my fingers play in unexpected ways up the plane of his cheek.

"I just didn't want to scare you."

I sat up and pushed him down onto my floor with both hands. "Scare me, Edie Spence, dragon-killer? Girl who is at least nearby when the dragon gets killed? As if such a thing were possible," I scoffed.

"You never told me about a dragon," he said, as I reached for the top button on his collar.

"I have unexpected depths."

I didn't meet his eyes. Instead I watched what I was doing, unfastening one button at a time, leaving the flannel in a straight double row till it was tucked into his jeans. Then I reached up and in between it, pushing his shirtfront aside, like I was opening a present.

Ti's skin was mottled, a calico of humanity, possessing every color, from the raw pink of newer scars down to the rich flat black that I suspected eventually his healed skin would become. There were ridges, waves, where new met old, and older, all across his wide strong chest, down his flat stomach, to where I couldn't reach yet in his jeans.

"How many times have you been hurt?" I asked him, marveling over each intersection where his stories were written on him, tracing each fold. When I looked up, his eyes were watching my face.

"A lot. I don't remember them all."

"That's good, I suppose." I followed line upon line down his body, making a game of it, gathering the courage to go further—

"You're not scared?"

I flushed, but when I looked up at him I realized my secret was still safe. "Not of scars, no."

His face turned away from me, to look at my wall. "I also can't feel much."

"So you can't feel me? Or feel this?" I asked, leaning in to kiss his chest. He reached up and caught the back of my head, holding me to him. I kissed him again.

"I—I remember the memory of touch. Sometimes I think that's what it is that I feel instead. Memories of times I've been touched before."

"That's poetic. But also very sad." I grabbed a fistful of my hair and played it down his stomach, left a trail of warm breath at the edge of his jeans. "Nothing?"

"Not much," he said, his voice heavy with sorrow.

I reached a hand down and pulled clawed fingertips up the inside of his thigh. "Nothing?" I asked again, from the vicinity of his waistband. I raked my hand up the inside of his other thigh, and then seated it between his legs, rubbing what I found there.

"Some places were burned less than others," Ti admitted, arching his back slightly.

"Ooooohhh," I said. "I love a challenge."

My doorbell rang, twice in quick succession. I thumped

my head down onto the still-closed button of Ti's jeans. "You are kidding me." I shook my head, and began unfastening the buttons as the door rang again.

"You're not going to get that?" Ti asked, sitting up, pushing me back.

"No."

"It might be important."

"This is important," I said, making an expansive gesture.

"This," Ti said, making my gesture back at me with a rueful grin, "isn't going anywhere. So go get your door."

I got my legs underneath myself. "Fine. But if it's my brother, I reserve the right to kill him." The doorbell rang again. "Just a minute!" I yelled, then looked back at Ti. "You, stay here. I will be right back. Stay put."

He grinned. "I wouldn't want to end up like the dragon."

"Precisely." I made a face at him and ran into my bathroom to pull on my robe. Then I went back out to my entryway and looked out through the peephole. Maybe I was lucky and it was a misdelivered pizza.

Just outside, pacing in a circle, I saw Asher.

"We don't want any," I said, through my closed door.

"Edie, open up," Asher commanded.

"Why?"

"We need to talk." He rapped once on the door, in frustration. "Open up already."

"Dammit to hell." I opened up the door, and he immediately shoved his foot in so I couldn't close it. "I was sleeping, Asher. I work night shift. What's this—"

"I went to Y4 this morning, and saw my relative there."

"So?" I said, trying to close my door, regardless of his foot.

"Stop that," he said, putting an arm out against the door.

I gave up on closing him out and let the door swing wide. "You could have texted me, or written a letter, or, I don't know, *sent flowers,* or something."

"I talked to the social worker about our patient. And he

told me about your situation," Asher said, his British accent clipped by anger. "Everything."

"Hypothetically, right?" I sardonically joked. My eyes met his for a moment and saw his features there burble and switch. It could have been my imagination, or a shadow, or who knows, indigestion—but I recognized the final face and the emotion it portrayed was earnest.

"Edie, the shapeshifter you saw was my friend. He was spying on the Zver, passing for one of their daytimers. When they caught him they passed him around like a toy until they broke his mind. They'll do even worse to you." He stepped back and held out his hand. "I can save you if you come with me, Edie. But you have to come now."

I was barefoot and my robe offered no protection against the cold. It'd been freezing and then some last night, and the sun wasn't winning any fights this afternoon.

"I can't—"

"We have safe houses all over the country. Only a few such facilities like Y4 exist—in rural areas, we take care of our own. I can transport you away from here, set things in motion. After that, you never even have to see me again, if you don't want to." His empty hand traveled up to cup my cheek. "Though I'll admit that that thought makes me the slightest bit sad."

"Edie?" Ti said from behind me. Asher's hand dropped like a stone.

I tried to think. Could I work for shapeshifters? Going from place to place, on the lam? I didn't ever want to be a psych nurse—hell no—but I could do it if I had to. But there was Jake. And now Ti—

"Edie?" Ti asked again, nearer now. He crowded the doorway behind me, and reached a hand through for Asher to shake. "I'm Ti."

"No, thank you," Asher said, regarding Ti's hand with disgust. And then anger lit. "Are you the one that hit her?"

he asked, taking a step forward. Ti came another step forward from behind me at this affront.

"No!" I answered for him. "Both of you—no—just let me think, okay?"

I twisted away, unwilling to go far on bare feet, but I needed some space. I looked down the shared wall of the apartment complex, past the parking lot, to the cars driving by in the street. If only I could hitch a thumb out there and leave everything behind. But—leaving was only an option that I'd have considered taking a few days ago. Now, with Jake on the cusp of being normal, and Ti helping me—I stared out, ignoring how the cold made my feet burn, trying to imagine a future where everything might be okay. I'd almost managed it when I saw them there, outside my window. Footprints in the snow. Not mine, not Anna's, but huge talon-tipped birdlike prints, edges frozen, sharp. The Hound's. It'd found me. How old were those tracks? One night, two? I swallowed.

Who was I kidding, thinking I could escape? No running or hiding would save me. There would be no safe place. Ever.

"I can't." I turned back toward Asher. "There's no way I can leave. I have too many obligations."

Asher leaned in to look me directly in the eyes. "Edie, they're going to kill you. Vampire trials are always a sham."

"We have a plan—" Ti began.

"What, zombie, did they promise you her corpse?" Asher sniped. Ti took another step forward.

"Asher!" I raised my hands up. "I've made up my mind."

"But I can promise you safety!" Asher protested. I bit my lip, and my tongue found the cut that a shapeshifter had caused.

"No." Ti pulled back, and I stepped into my apartment again.

Asher shook his head. "Edie, the next time you see me, it will be as if we do not know one another."

"I'm sorry, Asher. Thank you, but no."

He stared at me one last time, as if trying to think of something else to say, then walked off.

Ti waited for me in my apartment's short hallway. I reached for him and his arms encircled me, holding me tight. He was warmer than I was, and that was saying something. We were silent for a long while together, my face nestled against his chest.

"You put your shirt back on," I complained.

"Not everyone is as understanding as you about scars."

I nodded into him. Had I done the right thing? It felt right, but—Ti squeezed me. "A life running away is no life at all."

"You're not telepathic, are you?" I pulled back to look up at him.

"No." He reached up and caught my chin, and I fully expected another kiss.

"You're bleeding," he said instead.

I ran my tongue against the inside of my lip. "Yeah. Again."

Ti ran his thumb along my lower lip, and then tasted his thumb, before picking me up and carrying me to my bed.

CHAPTER FORTY-TWO

Round two was more like making love.

I don't think I'd ever really made love before. It was awkward and sweet, with an awful lot of eye contact, and everything felt much more meaningful than it ought to have. I wondered if this was the clarity that some people get in the hospital when they know they're about to die, when the spirit world and the real world overlap. They got visitors from the past and information about their upcoming strange new future. For those people, sunrises were symbols, sunsets were symbols, the leaves falling outside, the mist rising up at dawn. It could get cloying being in their rooms, listening to them and their relatives make the meaningless into magic.

But maybe now I understood—because every single stroke of Ti into or out of me felt like a drum strike or a heartbeat, resonating far further than it had any right to do: pushing in—we still live; pulling out—we soon die . . . until things went faster and faster and life and death were mixed up in the friction of our passion and he cried out, ramming hard into me, life life life, and made me spasm around him, drawing him deeper in, farther in, taking all he had to give inside. He lay atop me, panting, and I bit his shoulder lightly just because I could.

When he'd moved off me, I walked out of the bedroom,

turned the thermostat on full blast, and returned with an extra comforter to snuggle up against his side. "Tell me everything."

"What do you mean?"

"About you. Everything everything."

He propped himself up. "Why?"

"Because. I don't want to die alone." I separated myself and looked at him. If I blinked right, and fast, I could see him there, looking like a soft yellow haze beside me. "My whole life I haven't been good at making connections. There was me and my brother, yeah, but other than that? No one else really. And most days he doesn't even count. I do all right at work, but no one really gets me. School was lonely, except for the times that I was taking care of patients, because they were happy to see me, you know? I either talk too much, or tell too much, and it scares people off, and I'm not sure what to do about that." I looked up at him, and saw his expression momentarily cloud. "Like now."

Ti nodded. I decided to lay everything on the line. "And I don't want to die alone. I want to die with someone that I know, that knows me. It's not too much to ask. At least I hope it's not."

"You're not going to die, Edie—"

I shook my head back and forth. "Answers. Everything. Now."

"You might not like hearing some of it, you know. If I start talking, I'm not going to sugarcoat things, or lie."

"I can take it."

One of his eyebrows rose. "For starters, I'm married."

My stomach lurched, but I kept my game face on. "Go on."

"She was perfect. Completely perfect." He sat up, perhaps so as not to make eye contact with me, and stared up at my ceiling.

"Was?" I asked. "You didn't—" I imagined him rising up from the grave, hungry for the brains of his loved ones.

"No. She's been dead for almost two hundred years. So have I. I was killed after what's now called the Battle of Saltville, in October of 1864."

I did some math. "In the Civil War?"

"Union Cavalry."

This was more like it. I placed my hand on his back and scooted closer. "Tell me."

"I was injured in the battle. Some Confederate asshole came through the hospital tent and knifed all of us." His voice was distant. I waited without saying a word. "Then, for a long while, I don't remember. I had a master. I don't remember much else. I did what I was told." He shrugged. "Around 1950, I woke up. I assume my master truly died, and some portion of my soul he kept in thrall was finally returned to me."

"Woke up—straight from 1864?"

He nodded. "I could barely understand the language. There were states I hadn't heard of. Cars. Planes."

I waited patiently for him to continue.

"I only barely knew what I was. And when I figured it out, I spent a long time working at cemeteries, digging graves. One time to put bodies in, and another time to pull them out." He turned to look at me over his shoulder as he said this, and I steeled myself not to cringe. "Eventually I became a funeral home manager so that no one would ask questions." He sat cross-legged, and I moved to be behind him, holding him, my breasts and silly badge pressed against his back. "There was nothing like Y4 back then. Or maybe there was—I don't know, the vampires are good at looking out for themselves, but maybe zombies weren't included. But for me, there was nothing."

"How did you survive?" I didn't mean the day-to-day business of survival, he'd made do, that was clear. I meant the endlessness of marching time, the loneliness of utter solitude. How could anyone face that and stay sane with even half a soul?

"I had a wife and a boy. They died while . . . while I was otherwise occupied. I looked them up, as best I could. The Internet's made it easier now, even though a lot of old records were lost. But I am sure they are in heaven. And if I do enough good here on earth, I'll get to someday join them. Whenever it is that I manage to cleanly die."

I blinked. "You believe in heaven? For real?"

"It exists. It has to. And I'm going to get into it." He put a hand to his own chest. "When I do the right thing, I think sometimes I can feel my soul start to grow."

Stating things you desired to be true did not make them be so. An old quote about wishes, fishes, and nets that I'd read once burbled up from my subconscious. Ti took my silence for the negation that it was, and turned to look over his shoulder at me again. "Your own soul's on the line, and you don't believe?"

I pushed away from his back. "If I believe that I have a soul—which even at this late stage in the game, maybe I don't—that might make sense. There's a spirit that people have when they're alive that they don't when they're dead. I've watched people die before. I know." Ti nodded. I knew Ti had watched people die before. Maybe even killed them himself, when he was someone else's servant. Who was I to judge—I'd killed someone too. "But if you believe in a heaven," I went on, pushing myself even farther away from him, "then you have to believe that someone's keeping score. And if someone's keeping score, if what we do really matters, then life ought to be fair. And I'm sorry, it isn't. Shitty things happen to good people all the time, and bad people never get what's coming to them. Don't tell me that there's a heaven as some sort of perverse reward for being good. That is bullshit of the highest caliber, bullshit through and though."

"Then why do you try? Why do you care?"

I inhaled and exhaled a few times, with the effort of trying to put how I felt into words. "Because someone has to. Someone who really exists." I crossed my arms on top of my breasts. "And also they pay me."

Ti laughed. He reached out to grab me, and I let him. He pulled me near and held me close. "Not enough," he said softly, after a time.

"No," I said, shaking my head. "Definitely not enough."

We lay there, thoughtful and quiet, the outside world forgotten, for a full thirty seconds. And then his phone rang. Neither of us moved for a second, because the sound felt so foreign and unfamiliar—it had no meaning in the new space we'd created. Then he sat up beside me and reached for his cast-off jeans.

"Hello? Yes. The address. Yes. Yes. I'll bring cash." He flipped the phone closed.

"Does that mean what I think it means?"

Ti looked at me, at all of me, naked atop the comforter on my bed, his expression bittersweet. "Get dressed."

CHAPTER FORTY-THREE

As an afterthought, I grabbed Grandfather on my way out of the house, and shoved him inside my coat. Ti drove us to a bank first. I asked why we couldn't use the ATM, but ATMs had limits, and the amount of cash Ti was drawing out required a teller. I was going to fight him on this, but he pointed out he'd saved a lot of money because he didn't need to eat.

And then we drove. Fear and adrenaline and the magic of good sex could only last so long. I found myself drowsing against the door of his car. We were going to buy information, and then we'd see what came next. I hoped that some plan eventually included me sleeping in it, or me getting a prescription for modafinil.

We parked in a warehouse district that didn't look so bad. There was no trash on the sidewalks, and the streets had been recently swept clean of snow. He reached under the passenger seat between my legs and pulled out a thin case. Opening this revealed a Glock 23 with a clip of .40 S&W rounds—I'd shot both of them before at the range.

"You didn't say there'd be guns."

Ti gave me a half smile. "I'm undead, not stupid." He leaned forward and tucked it into the rear waistband of his pants, then hid it with his coat. I reached for the door.

"You're not coming, Edie." He clicked the button on his door, locking mine. "Just stay here."

"You think it's a trap?" I peered out of my window and scanned the surrounding area with one eye. What distance was my crazy vision good for? All I could see glowing nearby was my own hand, and when I looked normally, just my breath fogging the glass.

"It could be. But I'm a zombie, remember?" He leaned over and kissed me on my lips. I remembered the heat we'd just had, and parts of me flared again, hungry. He unlocked his own door before I could protest, got out, and then clicked the door lock button again behind himself, trapping me in. Grandfather muttered something I was sure was unkind.

"Shush, you," I said, putting one hand over my eye and watching Ti go into the front of the building. The side of it looked like a garage. His nimbus went through the glass door and faded—there was an aftervision of it, a ghost in my eyeball, perhaps—but not even odd shadow-vision could help me see through distant walls.

"Be safe," I whispered. I concentrated harder and harder. Time passed—long enough for any true arrangement to have been made. I heard the sharp report of a gun—and then two more shots.

"Shit." I tried for the door, and found it locked. This was a nineteen-seventies El Camino, for crying out loud—but when I looked closer, none of it was actually stock. The door-lock tabs were receded completely into the door—all the better to eat you with, my dear. Ti's door wouldn't open either.

Creepy-ass serial-killer-style fucking car. I pulled Grandfather out of my coat. "Can you—" I said, waving him at the door. More gunshots, and Grandfather growled something I couldn't understand. Dropping the CD player, I scooted back to sit in the middle of the car and kicked the passenger side window with both my feet as hard as

I could. No good—I only hurt both my heels. I cussed at myself and the door before opening up his glove box. Under years of registration papers, I found paydirt. A black metal flashlight.

I didn't know what adrenaline I had left to dredge up at that point, or if my feelings for Ti had blossomed into a manic kind of love. But I scrunched my eyes closed and hit the window as hard as I could, and it shattered on my third try. I ran the flashlight against the window's rim, knocking any loose pieces down, before carefully shimmying myself out. Then, clutching Grandfather, as he was the closest thing to a weapon that I had, I ran to the front door in the open, me and my winter coat bright against the snow, not thinking a second thought about how stupid I was being until I was nearly inside.

"Ti!" I shouted as I went in. There was a reception area here, with cheap desks and thinly upholstered chairs. "Ti!"

"Edie, stay back!" I heard from the inside. My heart soared. He was still alive.

"Ducken!" Grandfather commanded, and finally I knew what he meant. I dropped to my knees as gunshots from the other room whizzed over my head. Of course Ti was still alive—I needed to concentrate on keeping me that way too. I crawled toward a desk and heard a sound I recognized from the range, but more clearly knew from horror movies and violent video games—a shotgun, being primed.

I pushed the nearest desk over and cowered inside of it. But to my left, if I winked just right, I found I could spot a nearby brightness, with a farther one nearing quickly. I could see through walls after all. They just had to be close ones.

"Ti, to your left!"

"Mädchen! Lauf weg!" Grandfather commanded.

Too late. There was a spattering volley of pellet shots

from the next room. But Ti's gun answered, or at least I thought it did, and the second aura dropped and faded.

"Ti?" I asked. I peered as best I could. I didn't get an answer, but the level of visible brightness didn't change. Another glow came into focus, on the far right-hand side.

"Ti, to your right! Far back corner!" I had no idea what the room he was in was like—but the second aura paused, and Ti's gun went off once more. The other aura stumbled and then fell.

I wanted to crawl around the edge of the desk I was hiding behind. It was only particle board, almost worthless for protection. But the walls were even cheaper drywall; they wouldn't be any better. "Ti?" He would answer, if he could. Reasons that he couldn't, I tried not to think on.

I patted my coat down and found my phone. I flipped into my history and redialed Sike. It rang two times, three times—maybe I'd blown all my chances at getting her to answer—then she picked up, and I didn't give her a chance to say hello. "Remember how you told me to call if you said I needed you? I need you!" I shouted over gunshots from the other room.

"Where are you?"

"Mädchen, raus aus diesem Zimmer! Ram!"

I gave her the address over Grandfather's rising orders, and she hung up. How far away was she? Would she really come? I added to my desk fort by putting the chair and Grandfather's CD player between the particle board and myself, then checked to make sure I could still see any action.

A swarm of dim clouds, converging on my brighter near one. How much ammunition did Ti have? I thought about running out for more—but how would I get it to him? Shots rang through the small room, leaving holes behind, and dear God, it was only a matter of time till one of them hit me and put me out of my misery. I curled into a tighter ball, no longer able to tell the difference between Ti's light and those of the oncoming people, the room beyond him becoming a growing, glowing blur.

Then the door behind me burst open, literally. Shards of glass rained down, skittering off the desk I hid behind.

"Edie?" a voice I recognized asked aloud. Sike—and she sounded pissed.

"Help Ti! Please!" I rose up just far enough to see her run into the other room, her red hair streaking behind her like arterial spray.

With my other sight I could see the other lights pull back. I heard the sounds of fighting—but her light matched theirs, and so as long as the fighting continued, I couldn't tell who was winning what. There was great speed—I assumed it was hers, and the sound of impact after impact. I imagined daytimer flesh hitting walls, tables, floors. The crunching of bone, an endless whirlwind of violence—but no guns. I crept forward, pushing Grandfather ahead of me.

Suddenly there were two smells that I could recognize. Vampire dust and rot.

I crawled faster, tucking Grandfather inside my coat. Ti was slumped in a corner down the hallway, missing his left arm. I could see the ragged stump where it had been, white bone jutting out from gobbets of pink flesh. His face was hidden in shadow.

"Oh, no," I said, coming nearer. Looking over my shoulder I could see Sike wiping the factory floor with the last of the daytimers. Literally. She spun one around, his black coat fluttering in the brief moment before his head cracked open on a vise-gripped car frame. His skull cracked and dust poured out like piñata candy.

"Ti?" I came nearer, reaching for him. "Ti, are you all right?"

He turned his head farther away from me.

"Stop that, let me see."

Ti pushed me back with his remaining good hand. And then he slowly bent forward, into the light.

I'd taken a few shifts at the burn ward, back at my prior job. I'd been given low-acuity patients; it was all I could be trusted with, without specialized training. But that didn't mean you couldn't walk by a burn victim's room and look in, or see a burn victim's family, crying by the nursing station. I'd kept the straightest of straight faces there, under any adversity. Under sheets of skin sloughing off, under charred clothing and hair, under people who smelled like homelessness and bacon. I tried to act like that again now.

I couldn't.

His face was destroyed. I knew that it would grow back, but the knowledge of that did me no good—I recoiled at the sight of him, missing half his face, white-pink jawbone exposed, a hole blown through one cheek and out the other side. I knew now why he couldn't call back to me—because he'd had no lips to do it with.

I braced myself with both hands on the cold floor and tried to swallow air, to push my bile and horror back down.

"The majority of him is whole," Sike said. There was a literal cloud of dust around her, like she'd just been shot out of a cannon. "It isn't like he'll exsangiunate."

"I know that," I muttered. But hours ago I'd been kissing those lips—getting kisses from those lips, and more. And now? I wept, and Ti made a motion to come near me, then held himself back. "It's okay. It'll be okay," I said, telling myself that as much as I was telling him. I closed my eyes and leaned into his waiting whole arm. "It'll be fine."

He squeezed me to him with his crushing strength, and then maybe remembered I was made of less stern stuff. I kept my head down, against his chest, ignoring the wet things I felt there, willing myself to be strong.

"Come on." Sike reached her hand down to me, but I

got up on my own. As I stood, Ti rising behind me, Sike went feral again—the whites of her eyes went wide. She raced off, spike heels clattering across the cement floor.

"Are we supposed to follow her?" I asked. Ti shrugged and handed me his gun. He pulled out another clip of ammunition from his waistband and handed this over as well. I loaded it in for him before handing him the gun back.

CHAPTER FORTY-FOUR

We crossed the garage. Clouds of dust floated in midair, descending to fill in ancient oil stains like so much cat litter, leaving sheets of ash on half-fixed cars. How had Sike become so powerful in such a short time? I'd have to ask her, when I stopped being afraid of her.

She'd gone down a hallway, in the direction of an office—I could see the puddle from a water cooler that the previous violence had tipped on its side.

"Wait." I pulled at Ti's shirt with one hand, and covered one eye with the other. I scanned around the garage, through the flimsy office walls—and saw two yellow forms behind the office's door. One of them was twenty times brighter than the other, so bright it burned.

"She's not alone."

Ti looked down at me, his golden eyes still the same—if only I could stare up at them and not see anything else. He jerked his head to the side, and pointed the gun to gesture me behind him.

I shook my head. "No." I turned and went forward. If there was something awful there, Sike could protect me. If there was one vampire or daytimer left alive, I wanted answers.

And maybe I was running away from him a bit, that too. I pushed the door open with one hand.

"I bring you the gift of the Rose Throne. Do you accept?"

I stopped in the doorway. Sike was talking to someone I couldn't see, someone that her frame and her coat entirely blocked. She knelt down, and I saw a face I recognized beneath the glowing light my strange sight added, rising over Sike's shoulder like a second sun.

I had only a moment to whisper "Anna," before she pulled back her lips like someone was zipping them off on both sides. Violently jagged teeth emerged, and she planted them in Sike's willingly exposed neck. Sike fell forward, with a gasping sigh.

A strangled noise came from Ti—a hissing exhalation forced over the top of his tongue. He raised his gun, but I pushed his arm up and his aim off. The bullet flew out a papered-off window, shattering it, leaving a puncture mark in the paper for sunlight to pierce through.

"It's Anna! The girl I've been looking for!" I explained. At the addition of natural light into the room Anna released Sike's neck, backing hurriedly away.

"Anna," I said, although the girl was in full vampire form. I remembered how those teeth felt, latching into me. My left hand ached in fear. Sike reached an arm straight out behind herself, not in a spasm of pain, but a firm gesture to stay away, one I was all too happy to follow. Anna slunk nearer, and set to finishing what she'd started.

I thought I had already crossed the threshold of being sick to my stomach with Ti, but watching Anna feed took my nausea to a whole new level. More blood was flowing out from Sike's neck than Anna could dispose of. I could see the dark wool of her trench coat stain even darker, and the office was heavy with the smell.

I wanted to rescue Sike, but I couldn't think of how. She was here, she'd chosen to do this, whatever it was— we'd heard the fragments of some ritual as we'd come in. She was a daytimer. It was . . . her job.

But there was just *so* much blood.

I would have turned into Ti to hide from it, only looking at him right now could only make things worse.

At last, Anna was done. Her teeth retracted, and she became the girl that I recognized. Her tongue lashed around her lips, licking up the last of it.

"Are you okay?" I asked both of them from the far side of the room. Sike sagged to her hands and knees for a moment, and it was strange to see what had been such a powerful creature powerless and winded. Like how you felt bad for the old tiger in the tiger cage, even as you knew it could still bite off your hand.

"I'll be fine." Sike moved to stand in one fluid movement, and flipped up her coat's hood so that I couldn't see the marks Anna had left on her neck.

"And—Anna?"

"Hello again, human," Anna said, sounding pleased with herself.

"Do you two know each other?" I asked, gesturing between them.

"We do and we do not. We may discuss it in the car." Sike pushed past me and started walking out the door. Anna smiled, and liberated a lighter from one of the clothed ash piles in the room. She flicked it on once or twice and grinned. Even without vampire teeth straining out, it was horrible.

Sike had a long black car parked out front, windows as tinted as its color. The doors chirped audibly as she approached, and she opened up the passenger side rear door.

"Get in."

I did so, sliding all the way across the leather. Her backseat was full of yellow legal pads and pencils.

"Look under your seat. There's a sheet there—pull it out."

I did as I was told, as Ti settled into the seat beside me. The cloth was heavy and completely dark. It unfolded as

I pulled at it and handed it up to her at the front of the car, momentarily holding it up between Ti and me. Like playing peek-a-boo with a corpse. I tried to smile reassuringly at him when he reappeared. "What about Ti's car?" I asked.

"He'll report it stolen." She looked over at him, at the mass of thrashed tissue that was my sort-of-boyfriend. "I suggest you do it for him."

I didn't know what to say to that. Ti shoved his gun into his coat, and reached for a pad of paper and a pencil with his one good hand. Sirens began in the distance—this wasn't a bad neighborhood, where people could ignore that much gunfire. It was just an empty business park on an early Saturday afternoon, and it took a while for someone to realize that that loud repeated banging sound wasn't someone with a shitty carburetor.

Anna raced out of the building with a massive piece of carpeting over her head as a sunlight shield. She dragged it behind her, galloping along, until Sike opened up the passenger door from the inside of the car and she could jump inside, to be enveloped in Sike's waiting lightproof sack.

"All done!" she said from inside the fabric.

"Thank you," Sike said, putting her car into drive. I turned to watch through the back window as we departed. Smoke poured out of the building as we pulled away.

I didn't care where we went. I didn't feel excited, I didn't feel sad—this was shock again, I knew it.

Ti scratched words onto the notepad in his lap, and then nudged my shoulder with his own to get my attention.

"I was afraid of this," he'd written in neat capitalized print.

"Of which part?" There was a lot to be afraid of.

He drew out a smiley face, then wrote, "All of it?"

"Heh." It was hard to look at him. It took all my nursely

powers not to throw up, right there, on Sike's expensive black leather seats.

"Of you having to see me like this. Ever," he continued on the page.

"I've seen worse," I said bravely, when it wasn't true. The worse that I'd seen—well, they'd already been dead. Or on the way. Not trapped in some freakish limbo. But that was the only thing freakish about Ti—he'd been injured while *helping* me. I couldn't turn my back on him now.

"Where are we taking the stinking zombie?" Sike asked, angling her mirror so that she could see me in the backseat.

I looked over at Ti. We couldn't go to the hospital—there was no way we could walk in during the daylight and try to explain this. I wasn't sure how big an envelope of safety the Shadow's abilities provided. If even one person in the parking lot saw him like this . . . damn. Besides, Ti didn't actually need any hospital's care; he wasn't crashing. He just needed someone to watch out for him, till nightfall at least. "Madigan's?" I asked aloud.

Ti nodded. I tried to remember the address—then Ti wrote it down. I gave it over to Sike, who programmed it into her car's GPS while steering with one knee.

Anna leaned back, the fabric looped high up over her head, to look at me. "Why are you with a zombie?" She definitely, self-righteously disapproved, the way only children, vampires or not, can. She didn't seem at all fazed by the rime of drying red around her mouth.

"I don't have to explain myself to you," I said, and turned to Ti. "Was that a trap?"

He shook his head, and began writing. "Tip was good. But the informant was dead when I got there."

"Oh. Well. Saved you some money, then, I suppose." I went back to staring straight ahead. I heard more scratching on the legal pad and glanced down.

"I'm sorry, Edie. I never meant to hurt you."

"I know," I whispered. "And you're not. It just takes some getting used to, is all."

"I just wanted to help," he continued writing. "All this will heal in time."

"I know that too." I took the pencil from him. "How long?" I wrote down, and nodded to the front seat, where the vampires couldn't hear us.

He took the pencil away and wrote back. "Depends."

I wanted to ask on what, but I was afraid I knew. Y4, at least for him, was for show. A place where he could heal incrementally, in the time frame it might take a normal human to heal, so that when he went back to his job, nothing out of the ordinary would be noticed. I found another pencil on the floorboard.

"Don't do anything stupid for my sake." I underlined the word "anything."

"Too late," he wrote. And another smiley face.

"Dammit, Ti—" I forced myself to look up at him, to try and see past the mess he now was, to rewind the time back to this afternoon. I reached up to push an errant lock of hair back up over his ear. Then I discovered it wasn't hair, but a piece of scalp. I inhaled to scream, or at least squeak really loudly—but what came out was a snicker, then "Ewwww!"

I laughed at myself, and I carefully cleaned my finger on his shoulder. "You know, I've had men tell me I've fucked their brains out before. I just never thought they meant literally."

Ti drew another quick smiley face. "We're okay?" he wrote down, right afterward.

"As okay as people like us ever get. Messed up in the head, yeah—but okay." I smiled up at him. He was disgusting and smelly and falling apart and he looked like half of death warmed over—but he was here, now, with me. I took his good hand and squeezed it.

"Thanks, Edie," he wrote when I was done. He paused, then continued. He finished an "I" before I snatched the pencil up from him, and put it behind my ear. Any statement beginning with "I" was bound to be bad. I didn't want to hear "I am sorry" ever again in my life or, God forbid, "I love you." Loving someone had never gotten me anything good. Silence, right now, was better. I closed my eyes, leaned over and aimed high, to kiss him near his temple on his unmarked cheek.

CHAPTER FORTY-FIVE

I made Ti wait in the car while I went up to Madigan's door. Rita answered the knock, though I heard dogs barking farther back in the house.

"Ti needs a favor, Rita," I said.

She took me in, and then one eye squinted in disapproval. "You look a mess, and smell worse than that. Come in!"

I shook my head. "I can't. You should send the little ones away. There's been a fight, and Ti needs someplace to hole up for a while."

Jimmie's black wide-jawed face made it up to the screen door. Too late. I made a shooing hand gesture and he yawned, then sat down.

"What's this?" Madigan asked, coming in from the back.

"There was a vampire fight. Ti was injured—it's gross, and I'm telling you that as a nurse." I glanced over my shoulder back at the car, glad the windows were tinted black. "We found the girl I was looking for, and I've got until tonight to finalize things."

"So everything's okay?" he asked.

Was it? It didn't feel okay. Then again, how often did anyone see their boyfriend blown to bits in front of them, and manage to survive? "I think so. I hope so. But really—your kids don't want to see this."

Jimmie pressed his nose up against the screen door and whined. He might not be able to see Ti, but he could smell me.

"All right." He leaned down and swatted Jimmie's rear. "Go to your room. All of you," he said to the other dogs I hadn't had the chance to see. I heard nails on tile through the mudroom until they hit carpet again.

"Do you have a sheet you don't mind losing? So that no one else can see?" I asked. Rita nodded and ducked away, quickly returning with a blue cotton sheet. "Thanks," I said to her, and louder, so that anyone who could hear—as I imagined werewolves and weredogs had pretty good hearing—could hear what I said. "Thanks, really. I mean it."

Rita nodded, and crossed her arms up over her chest.

I ran back out to Sike's car and opened the back door. Ti was waiting there. His eyes appeared dark with concern, and I tried not to look at the rest of him.

"They'll take you in for now."

He nodded. I handed him the sheet and he unfolded it one-handedly, draping it around himself to look like a spectacularly creepy ghost.

It was his turn to reach up and put hair behind my ear—no, to retrieve the pencil I'd tucked there. He wrote down, "Don't trust anyone" on the pad, before he stood up and saw himself out. I didn't have to ask who it was that he meant.

"My car's going to smell like zombie for weeks. You can't detail out that stench," Sike complained from the driver's seat as we pulled away from Madigan and Rita's home. "Where to now?"

Where to, indeed? "My place, I guess." I gave her the address.

"They don't pay you much, do they?" she stated.

"No."

Anna tented the lightproof sheet over her head. She and Sike were sharing a low conversation in a language I didn't understand but that I thought was Russian. I wondered if they had vampire business to discuss, or vampire gossip. I fiddled with my cell phone, feeling lost and forgotten in the expansive back seat.

Jake's number was first on my speed dial. I sank lower in my chair. I was still mad at him for ditching me the other day. He'd keep going on his self-destructive path, but at least he'd be alive. Finding Anna had saved me that conversation. In the front seat, their conversation ended, and Anna slumped over in the passenger seat, lightproof fabric crumpled around her. Sleeping, perhaps.

I stared out the window and watched the gray of snow and gray of asphalt go by, all tinted to the same monotone moon-surface shade by the car's windows. I fell asleep too.

"We're here, human." Sike pulled into a parking spot near my apartment. I got out my keys. Heat billowed out—my house was roasting inside, this month's electric bill would be insane. And now I might actually be alive to pay it. I held the door open.

Sike had to walk around to Anna's side of the car and prompt her awake. The smaller vampire seemed dizzy, stumbling out, and for a second I wondered what would happen if a corner of the lightproof fabric flipped back, and I watched my only hope crisp and burn in the meek afternoon sun.

Sike herded Anna toward me. She stepped up and into my house, but Sike was halted at the threshold.

"I thought you were just a daytimer?" I asked her. From the look on her face, so did she.

"I have had a lot of my Throne's blood recently." She stood at the edge of my doorway, looking both beautiful and perplexed. I watched her reach a hand back, into the sunlight, and it seemed no different than any other extraordinarily pale human hand I'd seen before.

Sike looked up at me. "So let me in," she said.

I tried to remember the wording I'd used with Anna earlier, when I'd thought I was being clever. My exhausted brain wouldn't come up with anything. "Never hurt me or my cat," I said, instead of a more solemn vow. Sike snorted.

"I swear to never physically hurt you or your cat."

"Good enough. Come in," I said, and went inside. I took off my coat and set Grandfather down on my kitchen bar, where he started talking again. "Ugh," Anna complained, on her way to my bedroom.

"Be nice." Everyone in my house was bilingual but me. I peeked into my bedroom and saw Anna leaning against my closed closet door, the blackout fabric she had looped loosely over her head making her look like a shriveled beggar.

"I'm exhausted. Hide me," she said, without looking up.

I walked past her and opened the other door. She knelt down and this time she shoved all of my shoes over to one side of my closet, kicking at them weakly. I tossed my extra comforter in after her.

"This house smells like zombie and worse," Anna said, curling into a ball on my closet floor.

"Don't worry, you're not moving in." I grabbed her lightproof cloth and quickly closed the closet door before slinging the black fabric up over my window to block out all the remaining light. In my kitchen, Grandfather was silent. I had collapsed onto my bed when I remembered Sike.

Home stretch, I told myself, like I told my patients when I was doing anything painful to them. *Almost over. Everything's almost over.* I lurched back upright. She was standing by my thermostat in the hallway, setting it down to a more moderate setting. Should I offer her water, tea, blood? I didn't know what I ought to be doing—all I knew was that I needed to sleep almost as badly as Anna did.

"Do you need me for anything?" I asked her.

"I presume you have a couch?" she asked.

"In the living room. You can't miss it." I pointed behind her, and she followed my direction. "Do I need to do anything special for the trial?" I called after her.

"Just show up."

Worked for me, now that I might actually survive it. I sprawled atop my bed and let myself feel hopeful for the first time in what felt like forever, and then I fell asleep.

CHAPTER FORTY-SIX

I had another strange ocean dream. I was standing on the shore of a black ocean at night, and the sand beneath my feet kept shifting, no matter how hard I tried to stay still. I had to walk along it, faster and faster, until I was running, and it still kept sucking away. The tide went out and I ran down past the waterline, hoping the water-packed sand would be less treacherous, but then the stars were obscured by a huge wave of black and a roaring sound began—

My nightmare was interrupted by a familiar weight at the end of my bed. I moved my feet so that Minnie could come near.

But the weight increased. It rolled alongside me, and I wondered if it was part of my dream, or one of those dreams—even worse than the one I'd been having—where you wake up and none of your limbs work, the kind that inspired alien-abduction stories, as if aliens were the worst things there were. The weight crept higher, to be beside me, taking up more space than Minnie ever had. It fit against me, hip to hip, back to chest, the curve of legs to legs. Frizzy hair tickled underneath my chin.

I don't think I could have been so still if I hadn't been so exhausted. But I didn't blink my eyes open, or scream, or shift around in bed. I thought one thing, *What if she bites me?* but I wasn't alarmed by this, only deeply tired at the thought of having to be afraid again.

And then she turned to pick up my arm from where it'd been folded up against my chest to wrap it around herself, and tuck my hand against her cheek. I thought I could feel the beating of her heart, but then realized that was silly, that it just must be my own. Exhausted, I inhaled the sweet-sour scent of Anna's still unwashed hair, sighed, and went back to sleep.

When I woke up I was stiff and my room was pitch-black. I checked my face for a blindfold, and then remembered the blackout sheet I'd put up over my own dark curtains. I went through my pockets and found my cell phone.

Seven fifty-five. Dark outside now, for sure, and I wasn't any less tired. I sat up in my bed and turned on my lamp, registering that thanks to my prior exhaustion, not only was I still filthy, but all of my bedsheets were as well. I turned toward my closet, and saw its door was open.

"Ladies?" I asked, then, "Minnie?"

No response from the living room, but I heard a frightened meow from beneath my bed. I knelt down on the floor and reached out to Minnie with my hand.

"I promise you, Minnie, when I'm done with this, you're never going to have to hide again."

Minnie licked my extended finger as if she was sealing a pact, and I rose to walk to the living room.

Halfway down my short hallway, I realized my living room smelled. Not like fresh dirt or old sex, but like blood and bodily fluids. I ran the last few steps to turn and see Sike sprawled out on my couch like a homicide victim, and Anna nowhere to be found.

"Sike?" I dropped to my knees beside her. My instinct was to put fingers to her throat, to feel for a pulse, but—to do so would have been to stick my fingers into one of several open gashes. "Dear God, Sike—" I put my hand in front of her nose instead, and watched for her chest to rise.

"Mr. Weatherton?" she asked.

"No. It's Edie. Stay here," I said, though she wasn't in danger of going anywhere. I ran to the bathroom for the plastic bin where I kept everything I'd ever "stolen" from the hospital. Maybe a hundred alcohol swipes were littered over a dense core of gauze, half-finished rolls of tape, and other stray hospital things. I grabbed a towel on my way out.

"We should wash all this out, Sike." Sike didn't look drained so much as she looked gnawed upon. There were multiple puncture wounds, so many that they merged together—like Anna had bitten her and then shaken her like a merciless dog. Any career Sike might have had in modeling was now at an end.

"She needed it," Sike said. "I told her it was okay."

I tried to parse the little girl that'd snuggled beside me, asleep, with the thing that'd left these marks, and failed. "Don't make excuses for her. She's mostly immortal. You're not. Can you sit up?"

She tried to nod, hissed in pain, then tilted forward ever so slightly. I shoved the towel beneath her, for all the good it'd do now—my poor couch was ruined. I got a washcloth, soaked it in saline—an intentional hospital steal, after I'd once gotten a really bad cut on my knee—and patted her neck a few times with it, wishing the washcloth were sterile too.

"It'll heal. Mr. Weatherton will help."

"Help how? More blood?" I opened up every piece of gauze I had and moistened them with saline. We hadn't broached the topic of Anna yet. I couldn't leave her like this.

Sike smiled weakly. "I am feeling human again."

I snorted. I folded up the wet pieces of gauze and wedged them into the flayed pieces of her neck. Then I found a roll of pressure tape and pulled off strips long enough to keep them there.

I did a serviceable job. By the time I was done, she looked all right. Even paler than usual, which was pretty damn pale, but instead of a victim she looked like an accident survivor.

"You could have woken me up, you know," I said when I was through. When had this happened? Before Anna'd curled up against me, or after?

"I was a bit occupied, you know," she said with my tone back at me.

"What, with all the bleeding?"

Sike pursed her lips, then reached up to the back of the couch and pulled herself upright. The towel tried to follow her until I yanked it off.

"Well," I said, looking around my room. "She's not in my oven, is she?"

"What?"

"Never mind." If I had had my old dining room set, this was where I would have sat down, on one of the extra chairs it would have provided. I sat down, cross-legged, on the floor. "So where is she?"

"She went out."

"Out . . . where?"

"You don't know what it was like. You can't possibly understand," Sike began. "She has not been truly free for a century—"

"What?" I put my hands to my head. It felt like the wind was punched out of me. "Are you kidding? She left? Why?"

"It's not for one such as I to question—"

"What. The. Hell." I pointed at her neck. "Are you really going to feed me the party line?"

"You don't understand—" She tried to look away, then gasped in pain at the movement.

"What's there to understand? She almost killed you!"

Sike grimaced. Unfortunately for her, I liked my nursing license too much to steal narcotics.

"What happened at that garage today?"

"I saved you and your zombie boyfriend."

"Don't pretend that was altruism," I said, and she snorted. "Why'd you even come to save me, if you were going to let her go?"

"Because—" Sike began, and her voice faltered.

"Because," I began, to prompt her, but then I realized the truth. "Because it was never about me, was it."

Sike closed her eyes. "I was sent to save her, to feed her the blood of the Rose Throne forefathers, so that she would feel indebted to us, as much as one such as she can."

I could feel my brows furrow on my forehead. They'd sent Sike in like a human blood bag. I was revolted anew.

"But I chose to come," she continued, and after a long pause she added, "Because I knew what it was like."

"Tell me. I want to know."

Sike finally opened her eyes, and stared me down. "Do you really think Sike's my original name? And how old do you think I am?"

The pictures on Mr. November's floor. The other girls he'd written "saved." "You knew his name was Yuri," I answered her.

Sike swallowed and nodded. The motion made her wince in pain. "Once upon a time, I had another name. Another life. I had a family, and a home. The Zver ruined that for me, kept me alive with the dregs of vampire blood long enough to break everything I knew inside. Yuri—the man you killed"—and here her stare hardened at me, and I realized why she'd hated me, from the beginning, when we'd first met—"Yuri saved me from them. It was accidental—he was looking for her. But when he found me, he rescued me, and others like me, and took us to the Rose Throne."

I tensed. "Did they treat you well?"

"Well enough. He bartered for our safety. Said that if he ever found Anna, he'd give her to them."

"So if the Rose Throne knew that the Zverskiye were . . ." I paused, unsure what to call what Anna and Sike had gone through—

"They would never act on their own. Yuri could be their tool, and they would sometimes give him blood, but they could never announce their interest in Anna until she was actually found. If they knew the Rose Thone was interested, they would have sent her even farther away."

I couldn't not ask any longer. "Why were they torturing you?"

"Why did they torture any of us?" She gave me a haunted smile. "To feed the things that protect them. The Tyeni."

My mouth went dry. The Shadows had the hospital to feed on. Was that what the Zverskiye were feeding with the sorrows of little girls?

"Their ways are the old ways, some of the oldest among us. Their daytimers are bound through strict tradition. Each eldest child from a family will go on to become a full-blooded Zverskiye—they have so many violent internal skirmishes, they need to continually replenish their supply of soldiers," she said with a snort. Was Anna's trip to America with Yuri and her brother intended to avoid that?

Sike went on. "The second oldest is drowned in the Tyeni. Metaphorically. It didn't feel like drowning at the time."

I couldn't meet her eyes. "Then what . . . were the pictures for?"

"To create more despair. Even distant pain caused by the Zver was theirs to claim. Imagine pain trickling like water down a cave wall, until it joins other threads of itself, finally dripping into the river flowing underneath."

"And I thought bookies and drug running was bad," I murmured to myself.

"Oh, no. That's just to get money. Power's an entirely

different thing." She closed her eyes again, and seemed to be steeling herself to attempt to stand.

"Sike—why couldn't you just get her to stay?"

Sike stopped in her progression and looked at me. "You mean you don't know?"

The list of everything I currently did not know would fill a fucking library. Sike saw the look on my face, and took pity on my ignorance.

"The Zver call them *nochnaya*. She is a vampire child from two daytimer parents, an actual child of the night. She's the reason they keep us daytimers tame, in the hopes that someday, one of us, one of our children, will be like her." Sike inhaled and exhaled deeply. "Right now, she is still a little girl. A hungry, angry little girl. But she can grow, and change. Because unlike all the rest of them, she is actually alive. Hadn't you noticed it?"

I pursed my lips, remembering imagining her heart beat the night before. Maybe I hadn't known it—but I'd felt it.

"She'll live forever until she chooses not to," Sike continued. "And then when she dies, and rises again after three days . . . To vampires, she will be like unto a god." She looked at me, her eyes daring me to challenge her. "One doesn't tell a god when to stay, or when to go. She wanted to be free, and so she left."

I didn't think Sike would have stopped Anna, even if the Rose Throne had directly told her to. There was too much similar between them. She touched her bandaged wounds with curious fingers.

"She's been so hungry, for so long. I am lucky that she let me live."

And the thought that I might have come into my living room and found Sike's corpse lying on my couch was the last straw. I almost shouted at her, "You would have let her kill you?"

"I would have died for her, and welcomed it."

I shook my head. "You can't mean that, Sike—"

A slow, true smile spread across her face. "I'll never be powerful enough to exact vengeance for all that was done. But someday? She will be."

She pondered this for a cheerful moment more, before lurching up into a stand. I jumped up after her, ready to catch her if she fell.

"I have to go now to get ready for your trial," she said, folding the tatters of her shirt over her shoulder before picking up her coat.

I shook my head. "Stay here."

"I'm fine."

"Yeah, right." And maybe her car was so fancy it'd drive itself. "Sike, you've lost a lot of blood. They'll understand."

She shouldered her coat on, with a hiss of pain, and straightened its collar before speaking again. "Mr. Weatherton signed a contract. That is all that matters now." She stalked toward my front door.

"Will she show up?" I called after her.

Her hand was on my door handle. "I would shrug, but it would hurt," she said, and let herself out.

And then I was alone with my bloodstained couch. If Anna didn't show up tonight, I wasn't so sure Mr. Weatherton would still want the case.

CHAPTER FORTY-SEVEN

I sat in the middle of my very empty living room for a moment, gathering my thoughts. First off—I needed a shower. Badly. I was ten different kinds of gross.

Secondly, I should have written a letter to Jake and given it to Sike before she'd left. It wasn't too late, though. I got paper from my nightstand and rummaged in my purse for a pen. Then I remembered about the pope water. I swirled my hand around inside my half-closed purse, searching, and found nothing.

I unzipped my purse all the way and dumped all of its contents out on the floor. I still had my wallet and keys, but the pope water was gone.

I tried to remember the last time I'd seen it. Meaty'd given it to me, and right after that I'd tucked it away. Ti wouldn't have stolen it, and Sike surely wouldn't have. Who else had I seen, between then and now?

Jake. Dammit to hell.

When I'd been in the bathroom at Molly's. He'd been looking for money, no doubt. When he found an unlabeled but obviously medically related bottle in my bag, the temptation had been too great. It could have been a bottle of spit for all he knew . . . but of course he hoped that it wasn't. He'd hoped that his nurse kid sister was bringing something illicit home, something that he could shoot up.

I was so tired, so worn out, so exhausted—and yet—
fuck. Fuckity fuck fuck.

I called Jake a thousand different names under my
breath as I drove to the Armory. At least I knew where he
was staying—that was a change. I parked a block away,
and trusted my ancient car, my current appearance, and
my crappy mood to protect me as I walked the block in.

"We've already closed for the night," the lady at the
front informed me.

"I'm looking for my brother. I have to talk to him. It's
a medical emergency."

She frowned at me. "Who?"

"Jake Spence." I held my hand up to indicate his relative height. "Dark hair, healthy looking?" *Asshole, thief,*
my mind continued.

"We really don't allow visitors—"

I fished my badge up and out of my shirt. The County
logo gleamed clearly under the cheap lighting, a tree reaching up from three hills. "I'll just be a minute. It's an emergency, I swear."

She frowned but relented. "Fourth floor, a few cots in.
If he leaves, he can't come back in tonight."

I nodded curtly. "Thanks."

I raced up the stairs, fueled by anger and fear. I had to
stop myself at the landing and breathe a few times, not
to catch my breath, but to calm down. I wanted to slam
the door open and go in yelling, but the other people here
didn't deserve that—just Jake. I went in.

The room had a five-by-five grid of cots. There were
signs on the walls posting the rules of the Armory, reminding people to take showers, cajoling them to come to
church on Sunday.

Three heads bobbed up at my entrance. Each of their
faces had the exhausted look of hypervigilance, wiped
out by PTSD from some previous personal war. I waved

my hands negatingly at them and made my way to where I saw Jake, asleep.

"Jake, wake up." I kneed his cot. He continued to snore. Just because he couldn't kill himself with drugs didn't mean he couldn't keep trying. My brother was never a quitter. As I knelt down to whisper louder, I smelled beer on his breath. This time, I shook him hard.

His eyes fluttered open and slowly focused on me. "You look like hell, Sissy," he said.

"I feel like hell. Where is it?" I shook his shoulder again.

"Where's what?"

I inhaled and exhaled very slowly, and then addressed him like I would a patient I was about to throw down with. "Jake, I don't have time to play games." I watched realization dawn on his face—perhaps he saw the look in my eyes now that he most frequently saw in the mirror. *Want.*

"But it's just water, Edie. It didn't do anything."

"Where is it?"

"Why? What is it?" he asked, sitting up.

"Jake—I shouldn't have to explain myself to you! You can't just take things from me. You can't take anything from me anymore!"

"Fine. Hang on." He yawned, then reached over to rummage in his bag, retrieving the bottle. Turning back toward me, he finally took all of me in, the shirt covered in zombie scrapings, the splashes of almost-vampire blood. "Edie, are you in some sort of trouble?"

I snatched the bottle from his hands and held it up in front of my eyes. Empty. Dry. I slammed it down onto my thigh.

"If you wanted to care—it's too late." I didn't want these words to be the last ones out of my mouth at him, but I'd been holding so much in for so long. "You never cared about anyone but yourself, Jake. You always came first for you. I gave up so much to help you out, and you never even said so much as thanks." I inhaled deeply and blinked back tears. "This is good-bye, Jake. I love you, I'll always love you, but this is good-bye."

He reeled backward, stunned. I stood up and stalked down the stairway, past the disapproving shelter manager, straight out to my car. I unlocked my door, sat down inside, put my forehead against the steering wheel, and sobbed.

When I could drive again, I got home quickly. Exhaustion helped. I was too wrung out to care. Everything felt dry— the bloodstains on my shirt, the cardboard taste on my tongue—and the events of the past few days felt distant and blurry, like I'd watched them happen to someone else.

Anna was gone. I'd rescued her twice, and she'd abandoned me. Ti cared, but he was gravely injured. The lawyers didn't care if I lived or died, and Meaty, Charles, and Gina thought I was dead already.

Tonight Dren would come to take me away and there'd be nothing I could do.

Worst of all, I hadn't even saved Jake, goddammit. It was all for nothing. All of it.

I went into my house and picked up all my medical things, shoving them back in the box, and took that box with me into the bathroom. Heaven forbid my landlord should find alcohol swabs littering the floor—he might think I was a junkie! I set the box down and kicked it as hard as I could, sending it skidding into the far tile wall.

Then I pulled the bottle of pope water out of my pocket, fully expecting to throw it in the trash. But the heat from my body or the angle I'd carried it had made two infinitesimally small drops coalesce on its glass wall. I flicked it with my fingernail, sending them to the bottom of the vial.

What, if any, good would that be? I couldn't even get them out. Unless—

"No way," I whispered. Then I ran to my box of supplies and hauled it out of the bathroom and dug through everything until I found an insulin syringe. Diabetic medicines were given in minute quantities, units so small you felt stupid double-checking them with another nurse. I popped it out of the package and pulled its orange cap off with my teeth—and really quickly remembered to hit the cap of the bottle with an alcohol swab, as Lord only knew what needle Jake had shoved in there before me.

I pierced the cap, and slowly drew the pope water out. Three units worth—0.03 milliliters, written down. Barely anything. It was so clear it was hard to convince myself that there was anything in the syringe but air.

What to do with it now? I held the tiny syringe upright. I could drop it onto my tongue. Or—I could do what this syringe was designed to do. I tore open a new swab, lifted my shirt, made a circle on my stomach near my belly button, and then shoved the needle in before I could talk myself out of it. I'd given a hundred-million subcutaneous injections on other people before, but this was the first one I'd ever done on myself. I pushed down on the plunger, barely feeling it move, pulled the needle out, and waited for some response.

Pain? Heat? Bruising? Swelling? I watched the tiny pinprick, hoping for some reaction, and got nothing instead. I only knew where I'd been injected because I'd been the one to do it—I couldn't have pointed out the spot to anyone else. What if to make pope water work, you had to believe in the pope? I laughed, and even to my own ears, it sounded a bit hysterical.

I pushed the syringe's safety cap out to shield the needle, and tossed it into my trash. Littering biohazards was becoming a hobby of mine. I caught sight of myself in my bathroom mirror, across the hall.

Damn, did I need a shower. Of course what I really needed I wouldn't get—a break.

CHAPTER FORTY-EIGHT

I stripped, leaving everything on the floor where it landed, before getting into the shower with just my lanyard around my neck.

My water and its heating was the only utility bill I personally was not responsible for. The purpose of this shower would be to ensure that I got my last month rent of money's worth. I scrubbed myself and my funky lanyard double-clean. Then I stood there, head bowed, and let the water rush over me. It beat against my face and torso, until I was numb to the sensation and inured to the heat. I opened my mouth to inhale and the sheet of water parted for me— and more water instead of air rushed in, bitter and vile. I gagged and opened my eyes and my shower walls were gone. My lungs spasmed, the water I'd inhaled making me want to cough, and if I coughed—I looked up and couldn't see any light. Endless ocean all around. No boat, no shore, just salt water. The cold buffeted me, moving with the wake of something I knew I did not want to see. My eyes stung, my throat knotted, and I drifted, suspended in the viscous dark.

With no other choice, I took a breath. I could feel the cold grabbing at my cheeks, forcing its way inside me, crawling into my mouth and down my throat. It flowed in me and through me, against my struggles and gagging, until all the water around me flowed inside me and disappeared, like I was inhaling it against my will and couldn't stop, and I plummeted down, back into my shower, falling into a fetal position curled around the drain.

When I could move, I crawled out of my shower and puked dark salt water onto my bathroom floor.

CHAPTER FORTY-NINE

My first cogent thought was that I wanted to brush my teeth and I was afraid to turn on the sink.

I clambered up my towel rack, shivering, grabbing a towel to dry myself off. My badge was lying on the ground in my shower, its lanyard halfway down the drain. I retrieved it, and slammed the shower door shut afterward. I threw a second towel down on the mess I made and ran out of the room.

I sat on my bed, knees to my chest, with my hands clutched over my mouth. My trial was forgotten . . . or maybe this was it somehow, already begun.

German began from the other room and my phone rang. I got it off my nightstand.

I looked at the number. Ti. Last time I'd seen him, he'd been missing half his face—but . . .

"Ti—you wouldn't guess what just—"

A different voice cut me off. "Edie? It's Rita. Madigan's wife."

That made more sense. "I remember. How is Ti?"

"About that—look—Edie," she began. "My family, we pass for normal. We're good people, Edie. You met us, you know that, right?"

I nodded into the emptiness of my bedroom, wondering what her speech had to do with me. "Of course. Rita, what—"

"And there's no moon tonight, Edie. That meant that Madigan couldn't stop him. We're all normal, all human, tonight. There's nothing we could have done."

I crept to the edge of my bed. Grandfather's German went up another notch in volume. "Rita, what are you talking about?"

My doorbell rang.

"I've got to get the door now—" I stood.

"Edie, don't answer it," Rita said.

"What?" I pulled on my robe and ran down the hall to look through the peephole. A man with broad shoulders, a hat, and a high scarf was there.

"Madigan didn't want me to call. But—we're the same, Edie. I thought you'd want to know. He's done horrible things and you don't want any part of what he's done."

Outside, the man knocked.

"Edie," said a slurred voice that I thought I recognized. "Edie, let me in."

The man outside looked up at me. I recognized his eyes. "Gotta go," I told Rita and hung up.

CHAPTER FIFTY

"Edie, please. Open up."

I looked out the peephole at him, looking in. He *was* talking to me. And one hand was flexing in apparent frustration, while the other—the other that should not be there—sat quietly inside a leather glove.

"How is it that you can talk?" I closed my eyes and pressed my forehead to the door. What was it the wolf pretending to be the grandmother had told Little Red Riding Hood about his teeth?

"Edie—" Ti said from outside, his voice still slurred. "Edie, come on."

"Not until you tell me how it is that you can talk." I could still taste salt on my tongue.

There was a slam against the far side of the door. It rattled in its hinges and I jumped back. "Edie, they're going to kill you. We've got to leave here, now."

I reached out for the doorknob and opened the door with the safety chain on, for all the good it'd do me. "What about the trial?"

"It's a sham, Edie. Go pack some things. We're leaving now. We've got to hurry."

I stared at what I could see of him, underneath his hat, and above the scarf, the eyes I knew, and wondered what I couldn't see. Those eyes—I remembered them. Staring down at me as he'd covered me with his body, intense and earnest. "Please, Edie—we've got to go."

I unlocked the door, and ran back into the safety of my bedroom. I pulled on clothing as fast as I could, and hauled out my biggest bag. I threw things into it quickly, stupid things, things you could buy at a drugstore, a fistful of underwear, an old hairbrush, a half-empty bottle of Diet Coke. Grandfather's voice became commanding. I chunked him into the bag too.

"Hurry!" Ti urged from the hallway.

I upended a bag of cat food in the kitchen, and set the faucet onto low. Grandfather's commentary was muffled by my undergarments.

Ti was waiting for me, motioning me down the hall like an air traffic controller with his good hand, scarf still protectively high. I stopped at the sight of him. "You have to show me."

"Damn it, Edie!" He twisted his face away from me and pointed out the open door. "Go get in the goddamned car!"

"Not until you show me!" I yelled back at him.

"I'm trying to save your life—" he said, his voice sibilant like a stroke victim's. I stalked over and reached up for the scarf. His golden eyes stared down, but he didn't move to stop me. I yanked it down.

His skin was his, until just under his nose. And then a lightning bolt of scar began, zigzagging up his cheek and down his chin where whole white flesh seamed against his original black. I took a step back. Lips I'd never seen before, never *kissed* before, spoke again. "It's still me," they said. "And we need to go. Now. They're going to kill you and drown her."

"Drown her?" I paused.

"Anna. In some ritual. They're going to drown her like a witch," he said.

"Oh, no." My experience in the shower, and everything

Sike had told me—I kept trying to add it up, but I couldn't quite make it match.

"Edie, we've got to go. We don't have much time," Ti pleaded.

"I'll say!" said a cheerful voice from behind Ti, outside. "Is there another vampire tribunal I don't know about? I'd hate to miss anything." Dren the Husker leaned forward and rapped on my doorjamb. He spotted me behind Ti and waved. "I don't suppose you'd care to invite me in, eh?"

I crossed my arms. "Not in the least."

"Ah. Well." He folded himself up against the wall behind him, putting his boot heel up so that his bent knee blocked the door. "Say, you weren't thinking about running, were you?" He unholstered his sickle with nonchalance and reached up to play its tip along the brick face of the wall behind him. The sound of metal on stone echoed through the small alcove.

"Actually, no." I dropped my bag.

"Edie," Ti said, his voice low. He was gesturing to me, and I knew what he wanted. He'd tackle Dren, I'd run out the door, and somehow we'd make it out into the night, and leave everything I knew behind.

But I couldn't. If my time in the shower had been anything like what Anna was going through—I couldn't let her be abandoned to that awful dark.

"Edie, she's a monster."

"I know." I'd seen what she'd done to Sike, twice over. But she was also one hell of a damaged little girl, with no one else left to look out for her. The Rose Throne wanted to use her, the Zver wanted to kill her, and I—I wanted a clean conscience. I couldn't just run away. I turned toward Dren.

Ti caught me with his good hand. "Edie, they're going to kill you. And I'm going to try to stop them, but I don't know if I can."

Dren pushed himself off my alcove wall. "You can't, zombie. But you might as well come along. The Zverskiye have invited everyone. I'm as fond of carnage as the next person. Only, you stop me from doing my job before we get there, and I'll husk her without a second thought." He made a gesture with his sickle in midair.

Ti pointed at him. "If you touch her, I'll pull you in two."

"Not before I husk out what's left of your soul, and leave the rest of you to rot."

He and Ti stood there, at an impasse. I pulled out Grandfather and set him in the hallway. "Watch Minnie, okay? If I'm not back soon, get someone's attention, so she won't starve." He made what I took to be a noise of assent. Then I stood and straightened out my shirt, looking between Dren and Ti. "We've got to go."

Dren twirled his sickle up into a saluting motion, then reholstered it, and waved me forward with his hand. "Of course, my dear. It doesn't do to make vampires wait."

Together, we all went outside into the darkest night.

CHAPTER FIFTY-ONE

"I'd have never told you about Anna if I'd thought it'd inspire this," Ti muttered, walking beside me in the open night. The Hound shuffled along behind me, waddling its bulk, nostrils flaring, breathing me in.

"I'm sorry."

"Stop apologizing."

We walked side by side in the cold, and I wanted to hold Ti's hand. His scarf was pulled high again. My gloved hand reached for his, and too late I remembered I was on his left side, and the hand that I held was most likely not his either.

For most of a mile, silence ruled. Some few people were out on the streets. Whenever they saw Dren, they seemed to veer away, sometimes at right angles to their current path. They never made eye contact with the Hound, as if the Hound were too horrible to exist at all. I could hear it behind us, nails clicking on the sidewalk, preventing any escape.

That entire time I held Ti's hand I tried not to think about where it'd come from. I felt like I was the star of some cheap horror film, where the call was coming from inside the house—only in my case, it was coming from inside my boyfriend.

At the train station we took the stairs down, and the

Hound followed us awkwardly, leaping past us to land on the platform below. We took the next train, even though there were people in it. At Dren's entrance, all of those sitting stood, and all of them now standing turned to look away, showing us only their backs. The doors closed, and the train rattled along.

It was then that I turned to face Ti. I opened my mouth to ask how. But then I realized the better question was: "Who?" I shook the hand that I held, so he'd know what I was talking about, and wondered how loudly I'd scream if it up and fell off.

"I have a friend who is a cop. I help him take care of problems, sometimes," Ti said, deliberately slow, his *S* sounds sibilant. He, or what remained of him, looked down at his still left hand that I held. "Nerves take the longest to regrow."

"You . . . just killed someone. Today. For me?"

"I didn't kill him. I just took his face and broke off his arm."

I blinked. "Is that supposed to make me feel better?"

"He was alive when I left." Ti shrugged, then continued, "It'll be hard for him to make meth anymore, missing an arm."

And he thought Anna was atrocious! He gets to rip off someone's face, just because they run a meth lab? "You're the monster."

Ti's bearing stiffened at this, and he turned away to look resolutely out a nearby window.

What else was there to say? Nothing. I couldn't go back in time and undo what he'd done, or change what I'd done to set him in motion before that. I thought about all the things I should have done differently, when I'd had the chance—but I realized that this conversation here, now, had been deliberate. I'd known things were wrong for almost a mile. But I'd waited to have this conversation until we were stuck in the train together, when he couldn't leave me, even if I wanted him to. Because deep down, I didn't want him to go.

"Is s-s-someone having a lovers-s-s' s-spat?" Dren asked. I glared at him, and saw his lips curve into a vicious grin. The lights in the tunnel passing outside glinted off his fangs and his hand stroked the holster of his sickle in a suggestive manner. I could see the Hound out of the corner of my eye, its clawlike hands fluttering together over its bloated torso. I swallowed, and looked back to Ti, who was still staring away from me, chin high.

"I have a thing for monsters, remember?" I said quietly. He turned to look down at me again. I pulled his scarf down and leaned up. I kissed him full on his strange new lips, which parted as he drew me near. His tongue was cool like I remembered, and I tasted metal. I pressed into him before we parted. "You're my monster, all right?"

He nodded into my hair. "All right."

Because the monster you knew was always better than all the ones you didn't.

CHAPTER FIFTY-TWO

The train made three stops, during none of which any passengers got onto or off the train. I knew it had to be someone's stop, but they were all frozen by Dren's look-away/stay-away. I held on to Ti's good hand, wrapped around me, and stayed quiet.

Four stops past that, Dren snapped his fingers, and the Hound began bringing up the rear.

"Uptown?" I asked.

"It's unsettling how well you know the trains of this, your own fine city," Dren said, rolling his eyes. He made a gesture toward the open doors for both of us to pass. "Shamble on, sir," he said as Ti walked by. Ti growled in response.

This platform was empty. The train behind us closed its doors. I turned and watched it go with longing.

Dren moved around us and began mounting the stairs two at a time. The Hound managed them awkwardly, side-stepping itself up. We emerged into the station, and up from there onto the surface again, and Dren began leading us deeper into the night.

"Are you sure you don't want to run?" Dren asked as he walked ahead. He'd pulled his sickle out of its holster again, and was twirling it from hand to hand.

"Yes." I continued to walk along the path he'd taken.

Dren turned around. "Both of you could, you know. I would give you a head start. Cross my heart." He ran the tip of his sickle in an X over his own chest. "I'll count to a hundred. You and your zombie lover. Take off now, go."

"No."

"To a hundred and three," Dren said, matching pace with me. The Hound waddled alongside of him, gnashing its teeth. "Oh, fine, a hundred and twelve, then, will you take that?"

Ti put his hand out to stop me. "What's your angle?" he asked Dren, sounding like he had a mouth full of marbles.

"Souls are sweeter than bloodrights. You should know that, zombie. And bloodrights are all I'm getting paid for this mess." He pointed his sickle at me. "But fair's fair, I'd give you both a fighting chance. No fun in chasing after you if I didn't get to stretch my legs."

"No," I repeated, walking along. Our surroundings were getting noticeably more familiar. The lighting was improved, and the litter on the streets was lessening. We were near my old hospital, the one I'd worked at oh-so-briefly what felt like a lifetime ago.

"You want to know what the difference is between a reaper and a husker?" Dren asked. "A reaper—"

My nerves snapped. "Can you just tell us where we're going? And then after that, shut up?"

Dren squinted at me. "Someplace where you should feel right at home." He ran ahead twenty steps, then clapped his sickle against the Providence General sign behind him. "And look, we're not alone."

Ti and I turned toward the hospital. The lawn in front of Providence General looked like a triage zone, with clusters of people standing around. I covered one eye, and saw that most of them glowed.

"What the—" I began to ask, as a car turned beside us and pulled in. More vampires disembarked, chatting with one another. They were all dressed glamorously, in long velvet dresses, like they were attending a show.

"The Zverskiye sent out invitations to all the players. Of course their entourages came, and with the entourages, the merely curious. Vampires hate to be left out."

Ti made another growling noise from beside me.

"Invitations to what, precisely?" I asked.

"If you don't know, then how should I?" Dren looked back at me, eyes glittering. "But it's all very exciting, isn't it?" He trotted down the hillside, and more reluctantly, Ti and I followed.

The automatic doors of Providence's well-appointed lobby opened up for us, and it looked like a freak circus had been set up inside. Regal-looking ladies sat across the backs of sturdy leashed men, hobbled into kneeling positions with chains, occupying open spaces where the lobby had run out of seats. Vampires who looked like British mods lounged on the coffee cart in tight leather pants, sifting their hands through open bags of beans. Others fit right into their surroundings, wearing normal clothing, leafing through the available magazines and looking like bored soccer moms detoured by skinned knees on their way home from the park.

Among all these, health care workers wandered through on nightly duties, studiously ignoring any of their activities, oblivious even to the sound of coffee beans plinking onto the floor.

"I had no idea there were so many vampires in the city," I whispered. Ti took my hand and rubbed it against his coat. I could feel the heel of something metal in his pocket. I nodded to him, as if to myself.

"You don't often see them all in one place. This is big." Dren directed us through the emergency medical service's doors.

Providence was a private hospital now. It was older, but with privatization had come the funds to refurbish their facilities, one overpriced MRI at a time. I knew from prior personal experience that there wasn't too much action here. Any real traumas they sent off to trauma centers—especially any real traumas without adequate health insurance. But you wouldn't have known how boring it was from watching the vampires. The first cubicle had a businessman with a GI bleed set to suction—I could tell by the tube going into his nose, and the coffee-colored residue that'd been sucked into the suction canister on the wall. Vampires sat on the countertops and empty beds in the room, watching him like bored cats eyeing an errant bird.

The next cubicle had a shrieking child, holding both his ears. His mother was trying to console him, and the doctor there was writing a prescription for antibiotics as fast as he could. Only one vampire sat in this room, watching the child over steepled fingers.

"Why're they so bold?" I asked Dren. Was it always like this? Had I just never noticed before?

"The Zverskiye have been making promises of change. We shall see. You, it seems, will have first-row seats."

I didn't look into the rest of the trauma bays as we passed. I pressed against Ti's side, and felt what I hoped was Ti's gun against my ribs, until Dren showed us to the back stairway, which had clear plastic taped up over the door and WARNING—CONSTRUCTION signs posted. A black-robed vampire with a waist-length beard stood in front of this, his hands hidden in his sleeves. He was metering in guests like a doorman. Two stockbroker-looking vampires were let in with a small nod. Behind us—behind the Hound, really—a woman with an ornate headdress and a corseted waist was waiting her turn.

"We're on the guest list. Look under *D* for dinner. Or *Dren*. One of those two," Dren said to the man.

"Who's he?" the vampire asked, with a thick Old World accent.

"He's her protector. He's going to try to kill you all," Dren said.

The vampire looked Ti up and down. "Your hat, scarf, coat, all of it, now."

Ti unwound his scarf first. I could see the muscles of his jaw tense and release underneath the darker portion of his skin. He took off his hat then, and coat, revealing his new arm, connected just below the elbow. It was oddly larger than his own—it made him look like a mutant creature from a video game. His gloves came off last.

The vampire patted down Ti's jacket and found the gun. He put it inside his robe. "Anything else?" he asked Ti, eyeing his tight shirt and fitted jeans. Ti shook his head, and the vampire stood aside.

We walked inside single file down the stairs. It looked like we were nearing the old operating rooms, but I couldn't see past Ti's shoulders. The Hound was behind me, talons clattering on the sea-foam-green tile, its hot breath foul.

"This is their home turf, you see. They don't find you terribly threatening," Dren explained. "Neither do I."

"That's too bad. By the time this night is through, I might need another arm," Ti said ahead of me. We reached the lower level, where vampires were standing from wall to wall.

Dren laughed. "I suspect you will end up needing more than that. But now my deed is done." He stepped aside and turned around. "It's a pity you couldn't be bothered to run, girl, but I've earned my keep. I might as well stick around to watch you die." He dipped into one of the crowds; the Hound followed him after a final gnash in my direction, and I moved to stand beside Ti.

CHAPTER FIFTY-THREE

In a previous incarnation, my first hospital had been a teaching institution, back before private practices had bought it out and made it into a for-profit money machine. In those days, before monitors and cameras, they'd had the grand teaching amphitheaters, with steep rows of seating so that surgeons-to-be could watch. Without the teaching angle, and with the for-profit money, building new operating rooms was sexier than remodeling old ones. These rooms had been abandoned, used for storing random items or having random hookups.

That was the basement I remembered. Waist-high green tiles, all the better to hose down with bleach later, low ceilings, and broken lights, all the better to not closely look at who you were fucking after shift. Not that I had ever done that, more than once or twice.

But what was in front of us now was different—all of the operating bays had been conjoined, the walls between them ripped out, leaving disjointed seating behind. Pipes and ducts were exposed from above and below, huge metal conduits that thrummed with live wires or running water. Lights hung from copper wires on the ceiling, shooting down thready illumination that didn't penetrate much. And everywhere, vampires, sitting atop pipes, standing on the rubble between the rooms, crowded into the remaining seating. They were in separate groups, gathered into crowds that were dressed alike, or were at least alike in their bearing, and all of them were looking at me. I hid behind Ti.

"Let her pass!" shouted a voice from below. Ti started making his way down, and I followed him, balancing one hand on his back as we went down the rubble-strewn wall. I looked around behind us, and almost twisted my ankle on a loose piece of concrete. What was there to see, anyhow? More vampires? I stood briefly taller than Ti, as he jumped down a level, and saw Sike there, standing beside Mr. Weatherton at the bottom. I scanned desperately for Anna, but didn't see her light, and I wondered where they were keeping her. Ti picked me up and set me down beside him.

"This is grim," he said when I was nearest. I nodded.

The bottom was rubble and concrete, like a giant hand had scooped out the clearing, leaving uneven furrows behind. Geoffrey and Sike were on the opposite side of a massive drainpipe, as wide as I was tall, which had jagged cement edges exposed to air. We made our way toward them and when we passed the pipe I looked into it, expecting only hollow black. Instead, it was full of fluid, almost to the brim, and small waves caused by unseen sources made it ripple, revealing sulfurous yellows, curdled whites, and streaks of gray. The whole thing, from the cement pipe to its rotten core, reminded me of an abscessed tooth. I hoped that wasn't what they were going to drown her in.

Mr. Weatherton gestured us forward, the sleeves of his robes making him look like a skeletal bat. He wore a high white wig, and there was a dusting of powder on his shoulders. The elderly vampire made a face at Ti's addition to our party, but did not send him away. Sike stood beside him, in a modern suit with a high collar that hid her neck.

"My client is here! Shall we begin?" he addressed the space in front of us. His voice echoed up the hall. I hadn't realized till now how quiet the entire room was—now that I'd stopped concentrating on not falling, I could hear that there was nothing moving in this room but me.

Behind the drainpipe, there was another half-chamber and its seating area. We were facing a gallery of Zverskiye, black wool coat after black wool coat, lining the rows like crows on power lines. The only hint of color in their midst was a vampire with ornately embroidered robes, red silks patterned and lined with gold, his arms crossed and hands hidden in their opposite sleeves. He wore a crown.

"Who is that?" I whispered to Sike, and was embarrassed by how far my voice traveled.

"They call him their Czar. He's their judge-king for this region," she answered back.

"If you are not interested in conducting this trial—" Weatherton continued, addressing the vampire that appeared to be their ruler.

"Silence, spy." A vampire emerged from the darkness. He was dressed like a cross between a doctor for surgery and a janitor, with hip waders and a blue sterile gown shrouded around him, sleeves ending in elbow-high black rubber gloves. The drainpipe belched a cloud of noxious fumes as he passed it, coming toward us, and the disgusting slurry of its contents began sloshing over its edge.

"I was invited," Weatherton said in an insulted tone, lifting his robes as the first tendrils of fluid started rolling near.

"Indeed you were. But we both know that you are a spy." He flourished upward with one gloved arm. "As are most of those here tonight, whether they'd admit to it or not."

There was a stirring in the crowd around us, like the

sound of rubbing leaves. "I was told there would be a trial here? Soon?" Weatherton asked archly, sidestepping a small stream. "If there is not, perhaps you would like to call a plumber—"

The gloved vampire ignored this jibe. He looked up to the Zverskiye judge, who inclined his head slightly. "We have certain rituals that must be accommodated, before we begin."

"Do they include moving to higher ground?" Geoffrey asked.

"We require that the accused is bound while we deliberate," the gloved vampire snapped. Another vampire rolled up an empty operating table, with empty four-point leather cuffs. "Given that our normal trials involve vampires, I'm sure you understand."

"She is a mere human—"

"A human who killed a vampire. A rare human indeed." The gloved vampire gestured to the table. Ti held on to my shoulder and shook his head.

"I would know who it is that I am arguing with, before I make any accommodations," Weatherton said.

"I am Koschei the Deathless."

Weatherton's eyebrows arched high. "You seem very young to be deathless."

"You seem very old to still be alive."

Weatherton ignored this and turned to survey the surrounding vampires, before coming full circle to focus on Koschei. "I am Geoffrey Weatherton, Esquire. I have never lost a case, and I do not intend to start now." He stepped forward, and reached back for me.

"Edie—" Ti began. Weatherton's hand shook a command. If I let them tie me to that table, what were the chances that I would make it off it again? Sike had told me that my trial was incidental—all the Rose Throne wanted was Anna. But—I scanned the room again with my strange vision. She was nowhere in sight. If they didn't have her yet, then they wouldn't give up on me. I shook my head at Ti and stepped forward.

Weatherton held the table still while I sat on it and lay down. He fastened each of the leather restraints comically loose—and as he did so, my badge began to heat up, glowing even through my sweater.

The same vampire that'd brought out the table circled it again, reaching for the cuffs, tightening them one by one. At the end of this, he pointed to my badge.

"Is this a trick?" he asked gruffly.

"I'm a noncombatant," I explained.

"Not anymore." He picked up my badge through my sweater and cut it off, taking a chunk of sweater with it, leaving my empty lanyard behind. He cast it behind himself, and I watched it fall like a shooting star. Any protection it might have given me was gone.

Weatherton tsked aloud. Weariness radiated off him, not caused by his age, but by his exhaustion at the fools he was being forced to deal with here, and the revolting circumstances he was being forced to work under, what with the drainpipe still vomiting up dark fluids that coated the room's floor. Weatherton walked around the head of my table, looking at his sodden shoes before returning his gaze to Koschei, his voice both bored and irritated at once. "I heard you have a witness? If so, bring him forth."

"I make the rules here, grandfather," Koschei said.

"The rules are the rules, as they have always been. The Consortium requires propriety, and I require speed. As you have noted, it is already past my bedtime."

There were snickers from some in the audience at this. Near the edge, I could see Sike nodding her head.

Koschei frowned and produced a piece of paper to read from. "We are here to prove that the accused caused the untimely death of our brother Kristoff. We will show that she went to his place of living, lied to gain entrance, and then assaulted him with holy water, resulting in his horrific demise."

"And I heard that you had a most excellent witness to this crime? Someone who saw it himself, or herself?"

I inhaled softly. Would the Zverskiye admit that Anna had been there?

Koschei held up a small bag and continued as though he had not heard. "These are Kristoff's ashes. I will scatter them now, so that you may know him, by his scent."

He flung the bag outward and it went end over end, spewing out not all that many ashes in a thin gray stream. As I squinted to protect my eyes I could hear those vampires around me breathing in deeply, intentionally, along with their murmuring to one another afterward.

Weatherton took a step forward. "This bag of ash is all the proof you offer?" He turned widely, arms outstretched, making a show. "Where is your real proof? I was informed there would be firsthand testimony."

The surrounding crowd rustled again. I strained my eyes around their sockets to see without lifting my head. Even if they weren't going to produce Anna, where was the horrible apple-tobacco-scented vampire I'd seen that night, and later on? The one with the stone-gray eyes?

"If you cannot prove she killed him—" Weatherton continued, after a dramatic pause.

Koschei shook his head. "Then we will go on Pascha's prior testimony, which we were previously a party to."

"And I will not have the chance to cross-examine him? My client is not up for only death, but psychophagy, and she is to be convicted by hearsay?" Weatherton's voice was indignant.

"Silence, Rose Throne! This is our court, not yours."

"Obviously!" Weatherton threw his hands up into the air. It was strange to see a full vampire displaying such emotion. "How am I to prove her innocence, when you will not let me speak?"

"As we know from Pascha's prior testimony, she is guilty, and your speech is not required," Koschei said. The red-robed judge-king vampire seated behind him nodded.

Weatherton shook his head violently. "This is a travesty, and all those present know it." He began to pace back and forth at the crater's edge like a wild beast. His actions and gestures were meant to telegraph emotions to the farthest reaches of the upcurved room—he was putting on a show, and the Zverskiye vampires had front-row tickets.

I got the feeling that nothing Weatherton could do would change events; the Zver had seen to that. It was obvious that he was buying time. How long? I looked down, and saw that there was an even layer of the noxious substance from the drainpipe across the bottom of the floor now, still multicolored and revolting.

"We here know what it is like to consider eternity. To be deprived of it is a horrible thing. But consider the plight of a human, who works at a hospital, no less, and knows full well the brevity of human life!" As Weatherton's voice echoed around the cavern, I looked to Ti for strength. He was offset behind Sike, watching Koschei, while using Sike to block himself from Koschei's view. But I could still see him, working the fingers of his good hand at the seam where his new arm met his old. I imagined I could hear the wet tearing sound as the tissue gave.

"It is as hard for us to understand them and their motivations as it is in turn difficult for them to understand those of a gnat or a fly. But try to imagine what it is like to be compelled—as she was, tired from a long shift, facing daylight on her own—with the whispers of an ancient and rogue Zverskiye daytimer echoing in her mind, forcing her to go against her will and better judgment—"

As Weatherton paused at this, letting those two words in particular ring out, Ti paused in his labors too. Then he reached into the hole he'd created in his arm with one probing finger. I bit my tongue not to make a sound of disgust. Whatever he was doing, I knew I should look away. But—

"Surely you can understand that working on Y4 has its dangers," Weatherton continued, as I saw Ti begin to pull something forth. "And I would like to introduce briefs as evidence, showing how hazardous working there is for its nurses. There have been three workplace homicides there this past year alone—"

It was a gun. I could see it out of the corner of my eye. Ti'd pulled a revolver out of the meat of his arm. He slid it into his armpit to hold, with the barrel cocked open. I was trying to ignore him and pay attention to my defense when he started fishing his fingers into the space between his jaw and his lower lip.

Weatherton went on, addressing the Zverskiye judge in particular. "Her value to your society, to my society, and to the Consortium as a whole, working at Y4, is far more than any cost you can extract from her now, here."

"Are you saying she is innocent?" Koschei asked, his tone incredulous. I watched Ti extract a bullet from somewhere inside his lip and quietly place it in a chamber of the gun.

"Without a doubt. And even if she is not, she deserves leniency."

Koschei laughed. "Pascha said she is guilty."

"But where is Pascha?" Weatherton proclaimed.

"He . . . is indisposed," Koschei said slowly, tilting his head with a leer.

There was a ripple of assorted emotions through the crowd. Amusement, disgust—boredom now that Weatherton's show had stopped. I saw Sike in front of Ti rock forward to stand even taller, to look desperately around the room.

"There were two witnesses that night!" Weatherton yelled, regathering attention to himself. "There was your

Pascha, who apparently cannot be bothered to show—
and another. A female vampire, a mere child. You are
preventing her from testifying as well!"

Koschei's lips lifted, revealing a row of predatory
teeth. "I regret to inform you that she was captured killing Pascha. As such, her fate is already sealed." He looked
behind himself, and the other vampire, the one who'd cut
off my badge, pushed a sheeted someone forward on another bed, making a wave in the foul substance on the
ground before them. I could see her light beneath it, even
before Koschei took off the sheet.

Anna. Tied in four points like me, but hers were silver
chains. Weatherton's arms sank as she appeared. Her face
was angled away and up from us, and I prayed that she'd
turn to see me there trapped like her, so I could make some
gesture, to let her know that she was not alone. And then
her head twisted toward me, and I saw her black-and-blue,
bruised face and swollen-shut eyes—and where the Zverskiye had riveted a silver plate over her mouth.

"Oh, no," I murmured, before biting my own lip in
horror.

"So you see," Koschei continued, "she is already being
punished for her crimes. And now it is your turn to be punished for yours, Edith Spence. The verdict is guilty, is it
not?"

"This is a mockery of a trial—" Weatherton protested
as Koschei advanced.

"Don't worry, old one. I'm sure you'll still get paid."

"When the Consortium hears of this travesty you have
conducted, you and yours will be held accountable—"

"By then, it will be too late." Koschei didn't even turn
around to see the nod of his judge's head condemn me.
He shoved Weatherton aside, and the older vampire fell.
"We will have both her life, and her soul."

"I don't think so." Ti spit the last of his bullets into his gun, slapped the barrel closed on his thigh, and aimed over Sike's shoulder at Koschei's face. There was a click as the trigger pulled the hammer back, and then a thunderclap as the bullet shot forth.

CHAPTER FIFTY-FOUR

Koschei's head reeled back and I saw him drop. I strained at the cuffs, trying to get free—I could see innumerable vampires swamping Ti, as his gun kept ringing out. "Don't kill him!" I screamed. "Take my soul! Don't kill him!"

"Why not? He's already dead." Koschei arose from the ground, covered in the ghastly fluids that were still pouring out of the cement pipe, and braced himself on the edge of my operating table. I got to watch the wound the bullet left in his forehead heal as he looked down at Weatherton, who was still laboring to stand. "Deathless, you see?"

"Aren't we all?" Weatherton said, finally righting himself with a dismissive shake.

"Stop them!" I begged him. Even I could smell the rot in the air, even over the stench of whatever the drainpipe held. "Take it already. Just stop!"

"Zver," Koschei warned from the end of my bed, and the sounds of violence stopped. Cold drops of whatever it was—I hesitated to think of it as water when it was so repellent—spattered off him and onto me. They felt like shards of ice, and the skin they touched went instantly numb.

I—I had felt like that before.

"Ti!" I cried out, wrenching my hands against the cuffs. A groan answered me. He—part of him, enough of him—

was still intact, but much of him was scattered. I saw Sike kneel down and start to shovel things toward his open torso. Intestines.

"Ti, stay there!" I yelled. Technically he didn't need any of his organs . . . but how much of him could they remove and he still stay alive? Or whatever it was that he was? He reached the remains of a hand out toward me. He wasn't whole, but— "Just stay there!"

"Keep him down," Koschei said to his countrymen, returning to my side. From inside his gown, he brought out a canvas roll, as wet as he was from his dunking, and set it on my table. He untied the laces that wrapped it, and it rolled open with metallic clanks. Implements were held inside by straps, tools with ruined blades, like a Civil War surgeon's rusted operating set. Fluid drained from the case and ran down to me, bone-chillingly cold.

"Like the Shadows," I whispered.

"Shadows are what you all call them. We call them Tyeni," Koschei said, bringing up a curved tool. He set it between my breasts, in the space that his servant had carved out of my sweater, and yanked it down in a straight line, like an autopsy cut, grinding its tip against my sternum, slicing through my bra. I fought not to cry out. "And when we find your soul, we will feed it to our Tyeni here, and it will power them to life. And we will have our own Shadows, that answer to no one else." I felt the warmth of my own blood flow down me in a line to cup in my collarbone and then spill into my armpit. Angry nerves sang, raw and open. Koschei leaned over me to leer, angling the blade again. "It might take a while. Souls can be difficult to find." Another spray of wet dripped from his cuff, landing on my throat. I could grit my teeth through the pain so far—but the cold was like a slap and the shock of it made me gasp.

And what did Shadows do? Other than collect pain and suffering, and feed off sorrow? I remembered clutching the baby's crib after the dragon was gone, as cold then as I was now, and how everyone but me and Shawn were made to forget—

"Anna!" I lifted my head to find her. "Anna! They want you to forget!"

Koschei rammed his gloved fingers into my hair and shoved my head against the mattress. He rubbed a cold thumb on my forehead. "Of course we do." His grip on my hair tightened, and he brought his tool up again. "Sometimes, souls live in eyes."

"I'm here because I didn't forget you, Anna! Yuri didn't forget you, and I didn't either!" I wrenched my head to the side, out of Koschei's grasp, and scrunched up my entire face to close my eyes.

I heard metal hit metal, once, twice, three times—and then I heard a gasp from the surrounding crowd. I waited for a blow that didn't come. When Koschei let go of my hair, I risked opening my eyes to see Koschei staring over his own shoulder, and I lifted my head to see what it was he was staring at.

Metal hit metal again—and then the table under Anna collapsed in on itself. She brought her bound wrists together, bending the bed frame behind her back until it shattered. She undid her wrists, one at a time, and kicked her foot bindings free. And when she was done, she grabbed hold of the plate riveted over her mouth and pried it off, like she was opening the lid off a can. Draining sores studded with silver circled her mouth. She spun to address the Zverskiye at large. "Did it occur to none of you to put me on a silver bed?" She leaned over and spit blood into the ankle-deep water before turning toward Koschei with a ragged grin. "Little brother. It has been too long."

She leaped for him.

CHAPTER FIFTY-FIVE

Everything stopped. Then, Anna was on Koschei, stabbing him with the silver plate, and the blade he'd just used to cut me went flying. The operating table I was lashed to spun sideways.

Koschei's assistant ran up to my bed. "Where is it?" he asked aloud, picking through Koschei's remaining tools. He found a short triangular blade and looked down at me. "Where?"

"Where is what?" My voice cracked in fear as he raised the knife over my abdomen.

"Your soul—" he answered, slamming the knife down into my stomach.

It felt like I'd been punched. All the air rushed out of me, and I was left gasping for mercy. "Stop—please—"

He ignored me and wrenched the blade sideways, sending another wave of pain after the first. He raised the blade, sending my own blood spattering up my chest. I gritted my teeth to stop from screaming at the sight and—

Another vampire ran up and tackled him, taking him down into the mud. They wrestled, spinning my table again. I tried to lift my head up to see my stomach, but it hurt too much to move. I went stiff instead, staring at the ceiling, listening to the growing sounds of anarchy from all around me.

The lights began to fade. Gut wounds were awful, messy, tragic, and sweet Lord, I hurt more than I'd ever hurt before, but—how much time had passed? Surely not enough to bleed out. But my fevered logic couldn't refute the massive darkness descending from above like the belly of a black spider. I knew I was dying. And then I heard the sound of breaking glass as the lights winked out above. From every recess the operating basement possessed, shadows began to multiply and gel.

A pitch-black drop formed on the ceiling, the height and width of a man, then fell down. I turned my head with a gasp of pain to follow it as it dropped onto running vampires. Both of them disappeared inside of it, pinned like amber-trapped flies. Neither of them came out again.

Shadows. The Shadows. Keepers of the County, finally come to defend their rights.

"About fucking time," I whispered.

"We come to take back what is ours," said a chorus of horrific voices, directly into my mind.

Fighting sounds continued from beside me, sickening wet crunches and pops, the sucking sound of mud taking hold, then giving way. My bed was kicked, and the whole contraption rattled, wheeling around again like a rooftop in a tornado—and for a moment, I could see Anna again. Somehow seeing her made me able to concentrate on her voice, and I listened to her yell above the other chaos.

"You told them I was younger than you, Koschei. Say you lied! Say they should have chosen me instead! Say it!" She was crouching over Koschei, her hands embedded in his hair, bringing his head down onto the edge of the drainpipe again and again, as he beat at her with broken arms. "Say it!"

"They should have saved you instead!" he finally howled in defeat.

Anna stopped. "No," she said, panting above him, holding him halfway. "They should have saved everyone."

She moved to bring his head down on the pipe again, but shifted him, so that this time the pipe caught his neck. It snapped. She shoved and he screamed, until she ripped him in two. Then she held his head aloft like a Gorgon, showing it to the few Zverskiye who remained. It stared out at us, gasping apologies and blinking, until it collapsed in on itself, scattering dust. The remaining Zverskiye ran away at this, and she ran after them.

CHAPTER FIFTY-SIX

The vampire that'd tackled Koschei's assistant earlier rose up near my feet, covered in dust that stuck to the wet spots on his black robe. He came for me, reaching for the cuffs at my ankles.

"No!" I kicked as best I could and tears leaked down my cheeks from the pain.

"Edie, stop it. I'm trying to help!" He held my ankle down and undid the restraint.

"Who—"

"Who do you think?" He glared up at me. He was dressed like a Zverskiye, and he also had gloves on—the lines of his face softened for a moment, underneath the crazy beard caked with mud. Another Zverskiye ran forward to stop him. Before I could shout a warning, a wave of Shadow took the new one down.

"Asher?"

"Your friendly neighborhood shapeshifter to the rescue." He undid my wrists, and then looked down at me. "I'm not sure how we're going to manage this."

"How bad is it?" I asked.

"I don't think you can walk this off."

"Thanks. Where's Ti?"

Asher ignored me. "You need to get to a hospital."

"We're in a hospital." Were my guts going to come out

if I stood? That was such a juvenile thing to call them. Guts. Things had proper names, and I knew them—large intestine, small intestine, liver, stomach. I fought to lean up on my arms, and not look down. Things were hurting less, which was probably a bad sign. I looked at the floor where I'd last seen Ti. He wasn't there anymore. I tried a different tack.

"Where's Anna?"

"I'm not sure. But remind me to never piss her off," Asher said. He leaned forward and picked me up, one arm beneath my knees, the other behind my back. I hissed in pain.

"I thought you said it would be like you didn't know me, next time around?" I said through gritted teeth.

Asher grunted. "That's because unlike your zombie boyfriend, I'm not one for stupid heroics. I wasn't going to try to save you while there were a hundred vampires around."

"And now?"

He scanned our surroundings. "Between your crazy friend and the pissed-off Shadows, we're down to the toughest thirty or so. The odds now are significantly better."

"Put down my client," said a commanding voice from behind us.

Asher looked down at me before turning. *Do not tell her what I am,* he mouthed. I nodded.

Asher spun us, and Sike was there, covered in gore. "He's a friend, don't hurt him," I explained quickly. Sike looked unconvinced.

"This is why I don't help people," Asher muttered, with an excellent Russian accent. "It never works out."

"Where's Ti?" I asked Sike, changing the subject.

"I was helping to reassemble him." She flipped open her cell phone and made a call. The side of her face where she set the phone was covered in blood, and her hands left smears on her coat pockets when she returned her phone into one.

"Are you okay?" I thought to ask, belatedly.

"Don't worry," she said, flipping a clumped lock of hair over her shoulder. "None of it's mine."

All of what I saw on me was mine, and more by the moment. I stole a glance down, felt dizzy, then crossed my arms and held onto my elbows, scared otherwise I'd touch something I shouldn't.

A shadow fell on me, from behind Asher. "Edie."

My heart thrilled inside my chest. I should know—I could have reached in to feel it, if I'd wanted to. "Ti?"

He stepped out and was revealed. My boyfriend was a patchwork quilt of a human being, but that didn't matter in the least.

"You're alive—"

Lips that were and were not his smiled. "Not technically." He held his hands out to Asher, who released me to him.

"I demand safe passage for my services," Asher said to Sike.

"Granted," she said, and he disappeared. She pointed behind Ti and me. "I've called a car. Go upstairs, now." Ti nodded, and turned to follow her commands.

From my vantage point, crushed against Ti's chest, I could see-smell-feel where meat met meat and watch dust leaking out of each of Ti's seams. He was like the Scarecrow in *The Wizard of Oz,* losing dust instead of straw.

"Who were they?" I asked him.

"Daytimers. They won't last."

"And then?" I felt him lean forward, to climb us up the observation room's hill.

"And then we'll see."

I was quiet while he managed several large steps, navigating a path around pools of Shadows that were actively searching across the ground, with sticky tendrils waving in the air. I didn't think they'd get us, as I thought the Shadows and I had a deal, but I didn't want to put that to the test.

"Stop," a voice ordered behind us. It sounded familiar. I looked up and saw recognition on Ti's face. "Turn around."

Ti didn't move.

"Turn around, or I'll take your soul where you stand, zombie."

Ti squeezed me tighter to his chest and turned. Dren was there, pointing his sickle behind him. "Those things just ate my Hound." He took a menacing step nearer us, and Ti stepped back.

Ti answered for both of us. "It's not our fault you backed the wrong team."

"I don't expect to get paid after this mess—but your soul's still up for grabs, girl," he said with a leer. "And I need some recompense."

"Don't do this, Dren," I whispered.

"Husker," Ti began, his voice low in warning.

Ti couldn't fight back, not while holding me. And dropping me would only damage me more. We could rush Dren, but then there was still the sickle to account for—

"Dren, please—" I reached my arm out toward him. Muscles that didn't connect right in my abdomen anymore twitched and slid out of place. I screamed in pain and my arm fell.

Drops of blood I hadn't known were cradled in my hand sprinkled forward with the motion. Dren reached out with his free hand, lightning fast, and caught one in mid-air. Then while looking at us, he grinned, showing fangs, and brought his hand back toward his mouth, surely to lick from wrist to fingertip.

He stopped just as I realized I was looking at him. Not through his fingers, but through a hole that had appeared in the middle of his palm, as a portion of it crumbled into ash. His fingers teetered, and then one by one fell down, dusting like so many smoked cigarettes.

"Your blood—" he began, staring at his hand, transfixed, as the ash crept down his hand.

"Is spiked with pope water," I answered him.

He looked at me for a moment, then reversed his hold upon his sickle, and brought it whistling down—not on us, like I'd feared, but through the meat and bone of his own wrist. The remnants of his hand dusted in midair.

"Let us pass, Husker," Ti said. Dren didn't answer. He was panting in anger, staring at his mutilated arm.

"How could you husk me without getting my blood on you?" I asked. My hand that wasn't pressed against Ti found more blood to use as a weapon, just in case.

Dren put his sickle down. "Later," he answered.

I sagged against Ti's chest. Things were going gray. "Yes. It is."

CHAPTER FIFTY-SEVEN

Ti mounted the stairs two at a time when we reached them. I could see the trail of ash and gobbets of flesh behind us as we made our way back to Providence General's lobby.

Zombies don't have look-away like vampires do. And so while I could see the mass exodus of vampires pouring out of Providence General, no one else could. All they could see was Ti, holding me, as he strode through the bays of the emergency room, shedding ash and meat. People were picking up phones. I hid my face in Ti's armpit as people tried to take our picture.

"Stay back!" Ti growled, and the good employees of Providence General did so. We made it to the ambulance entrance, just as a dark-tinted car flew into the drive.

Ti opened the back door, and we sank into the car together.

"Drive," Ti commanded as he closed the door, and Sike's car raced off.

Ti cradled me to his chest. I clung to him, feeling parts of him sift away like hourglass sand. And then I started to feel like that too—drifting and lost. "Edie, wake up," he said.

"Are we there yet?" I asked without opening up my eyes.

"No. Edie—"

"Are these my guts, or yours?" I asked, nestling my head into his shoulder. Moving hurt less and less now. Hooray for me.

"Mine. Maybe. Edie—just be quiet for a second, will you?"

"No," I said, but then was quiet anyhow.

"Edie, I've got to go."

"No—"

"At the meth lab, I'm sure people saw me. But even before that—there's only so many times you can get burned and survive and your coworkers don't think it's strange. Add that to the fact that I don't age—and that that entire hospital's staff saw me there tonight, looking like a Frankenstein—"

"No one believes night shift." I curled my hand into his chest. He was warm compared to me; I felt so cold. "I'm tired, Ti. You can't leave me. Not now."

"I've got to. At least for a while. But I don't know how long that'll be."

"This—that—that's not some euphemism for dying, is it?" I looked up at him. His face was blurry, and I didn't know if it was all his new skin or my tears. "Because you—that's not fair."

"I'm not dying, Edie. Just going. We'll get you to the hospital first, though. I'm not leaving until I know that you're okay."

"Don't go." I hid my face against his chest, felt the flesh there give beneath me. Another wave of exhaustion and chill pulled me down. "We'll talk about it when I wake up, right?"

"Good—" I heard him begin, and I knew he was about to say "good night" or "good-bye" but I didn't hear enough.

CHAPTER FIFTY-EIGHT

"Human."

Things felt strange—but they smelled familiar. Too familiar.

"Human."

Something hit my face, hard. I blinked, and saw a frizzy blond halo looking down. "Human?"

"Tired," I whispered, but I wasn't sure I made a sound.

"Human, do you want my blood?"

I blinked my eyes open. There were two Y-connected IV sets over me, draining red fluid in. "Blood?"

"That's mortal blood. I am offering you more." A skinny wrist blotted out the emergency room lights. A red gash appeared on it, and then blood on this, bright red, like a seam.

I closed my lips firmly.

"I will not force you." Anna's strong fingers grabbed my chin, twisted my head, and made me focus my attention on her. "But if you die, I will be very upset."

My vision faded, and she disappeared. "Ti?" I asked. "Anna?" I looked around. County's emergency room was full; I could hear screaming children, crying mothers, the clamor of twenty different languages, all the hustle and bustle of life and death around me.

And I was just another stab wound on a Saturday night.

I flagged down a nurse by attempting to crawl out of bed. "Call Meaty. On Y4."

She looked unsure. Of course she was, I'd just given her the name of a person she'd never met, and a location she'd never been to.

"Extension six-sixty. It's important. Tell him Edie Spence is here," I pleaded.

She could have ignored me, but she didn't. I saw her go for a phone as I relaxed back into bed.

CHAPTER FIFTY-NINE

I woke to the smell of cleanser and floor wax. I knew Ti was gone. Through half-lidded eyes, I could see red nails.

"Edie Spence?" a nurse I knew was day shift said nasally. I pretended to be asleep. Apparently I'd lived, or this was a very authentic hell.

She didn't care enough to roll my eyelids back and check for pupil responses, which was good, because with her acrylics she might have taken out my cornea. Instead she poked me in the chest a few times, and I did my best to lie there like a lump of unresponsive meat. I heard her leave and knew she'd chart: Withdrawal to pain? Negative.

After that, I shifted around in bed like a sleeping person might. I was sore from stem to stern, had two peripheral IVs in my left arm, and there was an abdominal binder around my midsection. Other than that, I didn't really hurt.

Not physically at least. But now that I was awake, memories came rushing back. Ti, saying he was going away. How long had I been out for? Long enough, some part of me knew. I had to fight the impulse to curl up in bed; it'd be a dead giveaway. So I lay there limp and ragged, waiting for sleep to come again. One of the drips going into my arm was a narcotic—I could see the bright pink "Dose Check!" warning stickers on its bag.

Wait a second. I knew how IV pumps worked. I could—

"Way to get the most out of your County-sponsored health insurance policy," said a familiar voice. I started, caught with one arm reaching for the IV pole, and turned to see Gina's smiling face.

"Gina? What're you doing here?"

She grinned down at me. "I saw you move some when I walked by outside. I thought I'd come in and check."

"But why're you on day shift?" I strained to look past her shoulder. "If that day shift nurse comes back, I'm still dead, okay?"

"It's nighttime. She's working a double—covering for you. Hang on." She made a silly face at me, then ran out the door.

"Like I have a choice," I said to her departing form.

She returned with a bouquet, and arranged it on my bed table, handing me the card with an expectant smile. I took it from her, inhaled and exhaled slowly, and then opened it with shaking hands.

It read *Congratulations, from Asher* in purple ink with a heavy slant and a heart over the *i*. Tears threatened. I closed the card again and looked up at her.

"I don't suppose I had any visitors while I was asleep? The tall, dark, and zombie kind?" I tried to keep my voice light while I asked, and failed.

I had obviously not had the reaction Gina expected. She looked from the card to me and back again, then shook her head.

"Okay, then. Okay," I told myself more than her. I hugged myself, my arms tracing the binder's course across my torso. It would take more than its elastic to hold in my breaking heart. I pointed with my chin at the flowers. "Take those to someone who deserves them, down the hall." I shook my IV lines with one hand. "And if you don't mind, I'll take more of whatever's in bag number two."

CHAPTER SIXTY

Time in the hospital passes slowly.

I knew this, as a nurse, but as a patient—it's like being in jail. There's nothing to do but watch the clock and suffer through the vast wasteland that is daytime television.

I was trapped on Y4 under bowel rest from the surgery they'd performed to stop all the bleeding inside of me, allowed only sips of water and other clear fluids, until my GI tract performed to their satisfaction. I knew all the technical reasons for being here, but actually *being here* sucked.

I clicked on the evening news my first night.

"There's been no explanation for the outbreak of mass hysteria at Providence General on Saturday night," a female news anchor announced, standing outside in the snow. I closed my eyes. "It's possible that forgotten tanks of nitrous oxide in the older part of the hospital rusted through," said someone who sounded like a hospital spokesperson. "Investigations are continuing, but we can assure the public that Providence General is completely safe and open for business."

"Assuming you can pay," I muttered.

"Meanwhile," a male voice segued, "the brutal mutilations of three drug dealers have led police to suspect a gang war is ongoing. I warn you, the photos we're about to show you will be graphic. These photos are not suitable for children."

I opened up my eyes to see the man who'd originally had the rest of Ti's new face. I leaned over the top railing of the bed as my stomach heaved. Luckily you don't throw up much if you haven't had anything to eat in three days.

"You're sure you don't want to talk about it?" Meaty asked. It was really hard to tell Meaty no, but I managed. It was the end of my fifth incarcerated night shift, and the morning was edging up on dawn.

"Maybe when I get back, you know? I need to gain some perspective." The truth was, I wasn't interested in rehashing anything with anyone just yet. My scars from surgery were healing nicely, but the rest of me felt like it had a sucking chest wound that no one else could see.

Charles had his arms crossed, in an imitation of Meaty. "I suppose the important thing is that you lived."

"Exactly." I forced a smile. I was wearing four pairs of scrubs, layered for warmth under Gina's extra coat, and my work shoes, which I'd left in the locker room what felt like ages ago. "Which one of you has a bus pass for me to make it home?"

Meaty produced one. "You're sure?"

"Later. I promise." I took the ticket. "I'll be back. You'll see."

The bus ride was uneventful, even if it seemed like every pothole the driver went over was meant for me. I got off at the station, and walked down the street to my apartment, comforted that there weren't any strange footprints on my stoop in the recent snow. I tried the handle and it gave, just like I'd left it. I walked in with a sigh, and set my bag down.

The first thing I noticed was that the faucet was off.

And my apartment didn't smell like a litter box. Grandfather was still sitting by the doorway—I scooped him up.

"Minnie?"

No sound.

I walked through my apartment, holding Grandfather like you would hold a knife or a frying pan. The kitchen and living room were clear, the hallway was empty, the bathroom was empty—I went into my darkened bedroom, where the lightproof sheet was still over my blinds. I looked under my bed—no Minnie. And then I turned toward my closet, which was open just a hair. I peered inside and saw Minnie, curled up on Anna's lap.

I sat on my bed for a long minute, gathering strength and trying to figure out what I ought to do next. Then I took the sheets off my bed, walked them down to the laundry, and came back.

I took a nap once my sheets were done, but made sure to get up before nightfall. Anna emerged from my closet like a fairy-tale Sleeping Beauty, all stretches and yawns, greeting the night instead of dawn. She wore a shirt I didn't recognize, but scrub pants I was sure were my own.

"Good morning," I told her, when she was done. She nodded, and sat on the bed beside me.

What was between us now? The tenuous connection of people who'd been through tragic circumstances? I'd felt like this with patients at the hospital before, after emergencies with them, or when I was left with their surviving loved ones. I never knew what to do with myself then, and I certainly didn't know what to do with myself now.

"Thanks for taking care of my cat," I said, when I couldn't stand the silence any longer.

Anna nodded. "She's nice. I've never had a cat before."

"Her name's Minnie," I said.

"I read her tag." Anna sat still, with her hands holding

one another between her knees. "You would have healed faster if you'd swallowed my blood."

"Yeah. And I know you could have made me, but you didn't," I said. "So thanks, but no thanks."

She nodded again, while looking at her hands. I bent my head down to better see her. "What are you doing here, Anna?"

"This was the only place where they couldn't reach me."

She could probably take any daytimer. And no other vampire could come in without an invite, as long as I was alive. She had fought so hard to escape her former life, and for what? Just to hide out with me and my cat? It was so sad it made me want to cry.

"Is there a plan?"

"I need you to contact the Rose Throne for me."

"No. You can stay here. Screw them."

She gave me a sad look. "I can't live in your closet forever, human. No matter how much I like your cat."

"I can't just turn you over to them, Anna." I stood up and began pacing my small room. "Doesn't being a *nochnaya* come with a palace somewhere?"

"What does being a *nochnaya* even mean? I do not know what that makes me yet. I was raised by humans. I have not met another like me before and neither has anyone else. The Rose Throne has kept the best records. They might be able to help."

"But at what price? They'll have an angle if you go to them." I had scars now from the angle that they'd had on me.

A rueful smile slid across her face. "I believe almost everyone does. Their interest plan seems easiest, however. Please call them now."

I wasn't sure she was making the best move. But what other options were there? Not very damn many, at least not ones that wanted her alive. "All right."

My dead cell phone was in my belongings bag. I charged

it up enough to write Sike's number down and take it to the landline in my kitchen.

"Hey, it's Edie. Come over, please," I told Sike's voice mail.

I turned around and Anna was in my hallway, looking at my family photos on the wall. She spoke without turning toward me. "That night in your room, when I crawled right up beside you and listened to you breathe. I wondered what it would have been like if my life had been different, if everything had gone according to my parents' plans. A safe life with Yuri, without all the pain."

I hung up the phone. "I'm sorry I killed him, Anna."

"I am too." She turned back toward me, to look me in the eye. "But I forgive you for it. And that's what is strange in me." She put her hand to her chest. "Vampires do not grant forgiveness. I know—I asked enough of them for it. I begged them for forgiveness, for my imagined crimes."

Minnie ran out of my bedroom and twined around Anna's ankles. Anna knelt and gently knuckled her head. "Anna—" I began.

"I can forgive you, and know it. Where I could not forgive them." She ran her hand in long strokes along Minnie's back. "When I left to find Pascha and feast on him, I was strong enough to defeat them there where they found me."

"But you didn't."

"No. I went with them willingly. I fought enough so that they did not know that—but I went with them. I knew of their plot for you—but I was tired of being angry. Anger is exhausting. Maybe that is another thing different between me and other vampires—the things that are human about me can become tired, and that exhaustion makes me weak. I thought, what if I went along with them? What if I did just let them sacrifice you, your soul grant them the power to create their Tyeni, and then they make me forget? I could have been one of them, never knowing any better—and I have so many memories that I do not wish to keep.

"There was a time when I was ready to forget, I think. The betrayal of my kind, the loss of my parents, the hatred of my own brother—these are things one longs to lose, to pretend one never knew. But then you appeared, and I could not let you be killed by them."

"Because you made a promise not to hurt me or my cat?" I guessed aloud.

"Because the blossom of your outlandish hope that somehow, some way, good would rule the day—I could not take it from you, no matter how often it had been stolen from me." She stood, and she seemed taller than she had been before. I wondered if it was a trick of the light.

"I fear this is what it is like to be the *nochnaya*. Not an all-powerful creature, but one limited by emotions. Trapped by things like mercy and hope."

"I'm glad you did what you did, Anna."

She nodded to herself. "I think, so far, that I am glad too."

We were saved from any further thinking by a knock at my door. Sike tried the handle, found it open, and came in.

"Are you ready to go? Get your things." Sike brought an empty bag with her and gave it to Anna. At her appearance, Grandfather made mumblings from the bedroom. "You should get that appliance of yours checked out," Sike said, handing me a sealed envelope.

"You knew she was here?"

"All along. But it would have been presumptuous to force her to come with us."

I opened the envelope, and inside found an itemized bill. "You're kidding me."

"Our services do not come free—"

"Or cheap," I said, looking at the final amount.

"We offer easy installment plans for indigents, such as yourself."

I folded the paper up and tore it in two. "It seems to me that you lost my case. That negates any contract we once had."

"There's the small issue of a retainer—" Sike said.

I pushed the two pieces of paper back toward her, thumping them against her neck, where her injury had been. "I should bill you all for services rendered. Bite me."

She took the papers from me. "We just might."

Anna returned with her bag. I peered a little bit, to make sure she wasn't smuggling out my cat. "There will be no bill, and no biting. She is mine."

Sike looked from Anna to me, one cool eyebrow raised. "Then it will be as you say." Sike opened the door and gestured, but Anna hesitated and looked to me.

"Who are those people?"

It took me a second to realize she was asking about my family photos on the wall. "My mother and brother, mostly."

"Are they alive?"

I nodded.

"Have they ever tried to kill you?"

"Not precisely."

"Be good to them, then." She gave me an awkward hug—and it wasn't till I saw the blood on her cuff that I realized she was wearing one of Yuri's old shirts.

CHAPTER SIXTY-ONE

For a week I earned no-questions-asked disability and, through Jake's use of my car and five bucks at a time, made an extensive survey of pint-sized ice cream flavors available at my local grocery store. I pretended not to notice that he never gave me change.

And then the time came that I had to go back. I couldn't say that I was looking forward to it. But I hauled Gina's extra coat and wore my own on the train in.

I nodded at the night security guards at the front desk and they nodded back—I doubted they recognized me and I didn't have a badge to prove I belonged there, but I was dressed in green and looked like I knew where I was going. Me and my sack lunch tromped down corridors and stairways till I found myself outside of the elevator down to Y4, without any badge to open it up. I pressed the buttons beside the door, but they'd never worked without a badge before.

I stared at the closed orange doors. "Open sesame," I commanded. They stayed closed. "Winner winner chicken dinner?" I tried, without much enthusiasm. I leaned forward and beat my hand on them once. "Oh, come on!" The metal gave a satisfying thunk, and somewhere inside, gears came to life. The doors opened, the smell of were piss wafted out, and I stepped inside. I pressed the button for Y4, and started counting seconds.

Nine, ten, eleven—the elevator came to a stop.

"Hello, nurse," said echoing voices I was disheartened to recognize. My badge dropped from above to land at the floor near my feet. I looked up in spite of myself. There was a webbing of Shadows across the top of the elevator, flowing around its deep-set lights. They were stretching out into the corners, like roots seeking fresh soil.

"Are you going to pick that up?" they asked solicitously, while creeping down the wall to block the elevator's door. I looked down at my badge. The lights began to dim.

"Do I have to?" I tapped at my badge with a toe. God only knew where it'd been since I'd seen it last—assuming I believed in Him—and anything that fell on the floor anywhere in the hospital was always suspect. Somedays there wasn't enough hand sanitizer in the world to chase after a dropped pen.

"That is what we're here to discuss," the Shadows said, obliterating the elevator's entire orange door. "Because you do not have to pick up that particular badge again."

It took a second for me to process what they'd said. "Really?"

"We have been pleased with your service, human." The Shadows' multivoice took on a singsong tone. "We offer you the chance to forget."

"Why?" I asked, stunned.

"Why not? When we are finished, you would never know that you had ever worked on Y4. You would never know that vampires and weres do indeed exist. You could forget your doomed relationship with a zombie. Let us help you, as you have helped us."

They sounded frighteningly eager to assist me. I backed away from the encroaching blackness on the floor. "Then what?"

"We would take you to the fourth floor. The people there will be happy to see you, and you will be happy to see them. There, you would step off, and it would be like none of this had ever happened."

The elevator doors opened, and I could see the fourth floor out there—nurses milling, patients smiling. The easy congeniality that came with knowing that none of your patients wanted to murder you. The doors closed again.

If I were honest with myself, I'd have to admit that it looked tempting.

"And my brother?"

"He would stay clean as the day is long. All that would change is you, and your place in the world. You could be a new you. A better you. A happier you."

I waited, measuring things. Nurses on the fourth floor could probably make payments on a new car, or have a two-bedroom apartment. Those things—they would make life easier, yes. But happier?

And there was no way they didn't have a reason for offering me my freedom. What would happen if I ran into Dren on the outside and the Shadows had helped me to "forget"? Besides, nurses on the fourth floor didn't get chances to be heroes often. The Shadows could have at least offered to place me in an intensive care wing.

I reached for the door buttons with my left hand, and saw my old scars from Anna's first bite. I hit the "door close" button with my thumb.

"I already have a job that I like. That I'm good at." I pointed at the ceiling. "I remember the way you made me feel that day—you guys were wrong about me."

The Shadows were unfazed by my posturing. "We do not often offer mortals a second chance. Your feelings of heroism will fade."

"I'll keep my job now, thanks."

I had the sense of the elevator dropping again, and the darkness began to recede.

"Hey—Shadows!" I rapped on the wall. "I want a raise!"

Their laughter erupted from all around me.

"Gee, thanks." I crossed my arms and looked up at the ceiling. "Why me for all this?"

"Why not you? Anyone could have done what you did," said their echoing voice. I frowned for a moment, and then realized they were just trying to feed off me again. The elevator doors opened onto the familiar tile of Y4. Kinder coworkers/siblings or non-lethal patients would come in time—or they wouldn't. But at least I knew who I was, and that I'd done a good job, for now.

"But it was me," I said. I flipped off the ceiling, and stepped out onto my floor.

DON'T MISS WHAT HAPPENS NEXT!

Read on for a preview of
Cassie Alexander's next book

MOONSHIFTED

Coming soon from St. Martin's Paperbacks

"Who knew a Code Silver isn't when an old-timer tries to beat you with his walker?" Charles said as he double-looped his scarf around his neck.

I grinned at him as I pulled my gloves out of my pocket. "Technically, a walker's still a weapon." We'd been trapped in a cold, dark room watching safety refresher videos all morning, an exquisite torture for nurses used to staying up at night. I wound up my scarf and pulled on a cap. "Why don't we get any cool codes, Charles?"

"We do. Code Fur. Code Fang." He patted through his pockets, maybe looking for his own set of gloves.

I hadn't been in on any admissions since I'd been hired as a nurse at County a few months ago. But the vampires, weres, and other assorted casualties our floor catered to had to come in from somewhere. Not that the rest of the hospital knew that we kept vampire-exposed humans— daytimers—in our beloved County Hospital's basement, but we must get advance notice somehow, even if it was just via a phone call.

I inhaled to ask another question, and then looked up at him. I could tell behind his scarf he was cracking a smile. "Awwww, you liar."

"Nurse Edie is Code Gullible."

"Whatever, old-timer."

Charles laughed and held the building's front door open. "After you."

I braced myself and headed outside.

Winter weather was like a slap in the face—the portions of my face that it could still get to. We were two days before Christmas, and the skies were bleak. I was swaddled up in my warmest coat, my brown hair had had hat hair for what felt like weeks now, and between my own hips and the three layers of clothing I had on underneath my coat, I probably looked like a Jawa from the original *Star Wars*, only with blue eyes peering out.

Charles and I were going out for lunch, to the Rock Ronalds. It was in front of the hospital on the next cross street down, and it was where our recently released patients would take their legally prescribed methadone to trade for illegal heroin and crack. I wouldn't go there alone at night, not even the drive-through, but during the day with a male coworker I felt safe—plus I desperately needed caffeine if I was going to make it through the afternoon.

"So what really happened, anyhow?" Charles asked, as he double-tapped the signal change button on the light post.

"Um." I rocked up and down on my toes, watching the orange stop hand across the six-lane street. I knew what he was asking, but I didn't want to rehash the past, so I shrugged without meeting his gaze. "You know. I got stabbed by vampires. My zombie boyfriend ditched me on his way out of town. That sort of thing."

"Too fresh?"

"Yeah." I inhaled, and looked up. He was smiling again; it gave him crinkles around his eyes. Charles was a good nurse—and maybe even a better friend, if I'd let him be, in a wholesome father figure kind of way. He'd been working at Y4 for longer than I'd been alive. I couldn't help but smile back. "We have Advanced Life Support recertification coming up together in four months. Hit me up then."

"Gotcha."

The light changed, and we both looked both ways twice before crossing across the street.

The bell over the door of the Ronalds rang as we walked in, and a color-coded height sticker measured us as we passed through the door, just in case.

Charles ordered fries with a side of fries at the counter, and I took off my gloves to hand him money for my Diet Coke. I realized this was the first time I'd ever hung out with a co-worker outside of work. It was on lunch break from work, but still, it counted for something. I grinned at him as I returned from the soda fountain.

"Code Fang," he said, and laughed. "You totally bought it."

"Yeah, yeah, make fun of the new kid."

"We don't get enough new people for me to tease."

"Maybe if so many new hires didn't die—which no one ever told me, by the way—you'd get more chances." I followed him to the nearest table and sat across from him.

"Would you have believed us if we'd told you?"

I drank a deep gulp of my soda and considered this. "Probably not."

"For the record, I told you not to go back into that guy's room." He glanced meaningfully toward my left hand. It had a semi-circular scar across the back of it, from where I'd been bitten by a vampire. It didn't ache, except for when it was cold, which, since we were in the depths of winter, was all the damn time.

I rubbed at my scar. "If in the future you have a choice between blatantly warning me about possible death versus vaguely warning me in a smug fashion, please go with the former."

He nodded. "Duly noted."

At my last job my biggest fear was being coughed on by someone with active TB. But at County, and in particular floor Y4, where Charles and I both worked, the opportunities to screw things up and maybe also get killed were endless. Floor Y4 catered to the supernatural creatures that no one else knew about: werecreatures in their mortal phases, the daytime servants of the vampires, the sanctioned donors of the vampires, and shapeshifters that occasionally went insane. And sometimes zombies, that sometimes nurses dated, with poor outcomes. At the thought of my now twice-dead love life, my urge to make small talk chilled.

Across from me, Charles was starting in on his second cone of fries. Funny how knowing exactly what a ton of salt and fat could do to your heart didn't stop you from wanting to eat them. Like nurses who still smoked and worked in oncology. Charles watched me watching him eat, and tilted the cone toward me. I waved away his offer—it still felt too early to eat; my stomach was on night shift even if I was awake—and he shrugged.

"You sure you don't want to talk?"

"Yeah."

Charles measured me as he polished off the fry cone. "Here," Charles said. He wiped his hands on his napkins, and then opened his coat and reached for his shirt buttons.

"What are you doing?" I whispered, and glanced around to see if other restaurant patrons were looking.

"I'll show you mine if you show me yours." Three buttons down, he started pulling the fabric out and away from his neck. "Seven years ago. Were attack. Shattered my clavicle. I couldn't lift my arm over my head for six months."

I couldn't see anything—it was shadowed by the clothing he'd bunched away to show me. But I believed him that the scars were there. Even if they didn't show—they were there. I shook my head. "I'm not showing you mine. Just trust me, it looks like I got a C-section from an epileptic."

Charles released his collar and straightened his shirt. "That sucks. But on the plus side, at least you didn't wind up needing to start a college fund."

"True that." I helped myself to one of the loose fries on his tray.

"So now we're scar-buddies. Right?"

I nodded quickly, a little ashamed at how badly I wanted Charles and I to get along.

"Then listen to me, Edie. What I'm trying to say is this—I remember how it was to be you. All excited about the adventure—it's not a safe way to be. You have to protect yourself. You have to remember that to them, we're disposable."

I didn't need to ask who *them* was. *Them* was the vampires that'd tried to kill me. And also the boyfriend who'd left town. I'd felt pretty disposable then. The new scars didn't help me to not feel like that, either.

"So no heroics. Be safe. I want to keep you around."

I was genuinely glad someone unrelated to me did. "Thanks."

"You're welcome." He finished his soda and stood. "Let's get back. Only five hours of films to go."

We bundled up and pressed outside again. "What do you think the next film will be?" I should have gotten a Diet Coke for the road. Maybe then the need to pee would keep me awake through class.

"*Ignoring Ebola: One Thousand Ways to Die*," Charles suggested. "Or, *Mr. Radiation, Uncle X-ray's Spooky Friend*." He did a little cartoon dance, and I laughed.

"I liked the one where they explained how to evacuate the hospital, by taking people one at a time down the stairs." I wasn't even sure Y4 had stairs. I'd only ever taken the elevator in and out.

"God. If we did that, it'd end up being some sort of horrible Hurricane Katrina thing. Some people would get left behind, others'd make bad choices. If it ever gets that bad, I'm staying home." Charles hit the button to change the intersection's light, and I decided to press my luck.

"So tell me about the were attack?"

Charles kept his eyes on the light across the street, but I could see him squint into the past. "Ask me when we have advanced life support recertification. We can trade war stories then."

"Fair enough."

There was a man with tufts of white hair sticking out from under his snow cap six lanes across from us, looking both ways, watching for traffic from either direction. The traffic slowed as the light changed. Charles and I stepped off at the same time, just as the man did across from us. We were across half a lane when a truck that'd seemed to be slowing down for the red light sped up instead. I heard the engine shift gears, looked up, and saw the man coming toward us do the same.

It hit him.

He crumpled forward against the hood, arms out, like he was hugging it in a moment of game-show triumph. Then it launched him into the air and I stopped in the middle of the road, stunned, unable to believe that I was actually watching someone fly. He made an arc, landed, bounced, and skidded to a stop, smearing red behind himself.

Half a second for the impact to occur, another half a second for the landing, and then the sound of screeching brakes as all other rightful traffic through the intersection came to a halt—except for the truck, which kept going. It only missed the man's landing body by inches, and drove away with his blood in its tire treads.

"Jesus Christ," Charles said, and started to run for the injured man. I ran after him.

"I've already called nine-one-one!" yelled a bystander. I could hear someone retching behind me as we reached the man's still form.

"Everybody, back! We're nurses!" Charles yelled.

Fuck me fuck me fuck me. I was no paramedic. I was used to people whom the emergency department had already cleaned up and put tubes and lines in. He was so injured—where to even begin? Charles knelt down, and put his fingers on the man's neck. "He's got a pulse. He's breathing." I knelt down beside him. Dark bruises were blossoming around both of the man's eye sockets.

"Raccoon eyes," I whispered, having only seen it once before on a trauma test in nursing school.

"Brain shear, go figure." Charles spared me a dark glance.

We had no supplies. We couldn't move him and risk injuring his spine. One of the man's legs was twisted the wrong way, denim torn open, exposing meat and bone below. A moment earlier, and we'd have seen the stuffing of him, ragged edges of skin, yellow-white subcutaneous fat, red stripes of muscle tissue. But that moment had let his blood catch up with his injuries, and now it welled out from arteries and leaked from veins. It filled up his wounds, overflowed their edges, spilling like oil onto the ground, and when he ran out of it—I gritted my teeth and reached in, pushing against his broken leg's femoral artery. Blood wicked through the fabric of my glove and was hot against my hand.

"Here's an old-timer trick." Charles knelt straight into the stranger's thigh, his knee almost into the groin, only pausing for me to pull my hands out of the way. The blood leaching out of the man's leg subsided—although that could be because there wasn't much left. "It'll clamp down the artery completely."

I inhaled to complain now was not a good time for class—but I stopped when I realized teaching was what Charles did to cope. Our patient groaned, and tried to move his head. I crawled through the gravel and broken glass up to the man's head. "Sir, you can't move right now.

There's been a bad accident." I put my hands on either side of his head. His snow cap had been peeled off, along with part of his scalp, and his wispy white hair was sticky with blood. "I'm so sorry, just please stay still."

"Aren't you going to breathe for him?" someone behind me asked. I glanced back and saw a man with a cell phone jutting forward.

"What is wrong with you?" I swatted the phone out of his hand, sent it skittering into a slick of blood-stained snow by the curb. "Show some respect!"

"Hey! That's my new phone!" The bystander started pawing gloved hands through the grimy snow to get what was his. There was a shadow there, cast by the man himself, and I saw it shudder, swallowing the phone inside its blackness like a throat. I wondered if it'd been a trick of the light.

The injured man moved again, his whole torso shuddering. "No no no no no." He reached a hand up to fight me, clutching around my wrist with the strength of someone who had nothing left to lose. "Stay still, okay? It's all going to be fine," I said, knowing I was lying. "Just stay still."

He groaned and the shape of his jaw shifted, becoming narrow and more angular. His teeth pressed forward, stretching against the limits of his lips, lengthening, showing yellow enamel. His beard began to grow—just like fur. "Charles?" I asked, my voice rising in pitch. It was daytime, on a cloudy December day—but I looked over my shoulder and saw Charles's face turn dusky, like the surrounding gray sky.

"Code Fur, Edie. We need Domitor, now." He fished in his coat pocket for a phone. "I'm calling the floor." The sound of a distant ambulance began in the background. "Get back here before they do."

I stood, found my feet in the ice and blood, then I was gone.

I froggered through the rubberneckers on either side of

the highway, then hit the edge of the hospital grounds, my feet pounding against cement. We de-iced the sidewalks as a courtesy to our patient population, who frequently had to crutch, walker, or wheelchair themselves in. The frozen dead lawn was too treacherous and slick to run on.

I ran past the office complexes that kept our bureaucracy running, between twenty rows of cars in an employee parking lot, around the edge of our loading docks, and made a beeline for the main hospital doors.

Running through the hospital as a nurse in scrubs is easy—people get the hell out of your way; they assume you've got someplace important to be. Running into the lobby in civilian gear covered in blood, however—

"What's going on?" our officer guard held his hand up, and looked behind me for pursuit.

"Emer-gen-cy—" I gasped. I yanked my badge out of my back pocket and dangled it for inspection, as I brushed past him. "Gotta go—"

"Not so fast—"

"Gotta go!" I yelled, and ducked down the next hallway, running for the stairs.

I wasn't in shape at the best of times, and working at Y4 didn't pay enough for me to have a gym membership— and ever since I'd started working there, getting to the gym had been less a priority than staying alive. But I raced as fast as I could, my knees and chest screaming— because I'd left Charles out there with a werewolf, in the middle of who knew how many gathering civilians, himself a prior victim of a werewolf attack.